REAPER'S PACK

All the Queen's Men, #1

RHEA WATSON

Dedicated to all the darlings who feel a little less lonely with their soulmate(s).

And to those taking a chance on an author trying something new, I see you. I appreciate you.

Let's do this.

CONTENTS

CONTENT WARNING

Please note that *Reaper's Pack* includes content that may not be suitable for all readers. In this full-length standalone novel, you'll find a Why Choose romance, graphic violence, mentions of abuse, death, and detailed steamy, steamy steam. Please know your own limits and discontinue reading should something take you beyond your comfort zone.

REAPER'S PACK

ALL THE QUEEN'S MEN, #1
Rhea Watson

One grim reaper. Three hellhounds who refuse to bow down to her. A monster hunting them in the shadows...

Ten years ago, I was judged worthy of life after death and returned to the mortal realm as a grim reaper. Scythe in hand, I guide souls to deliverance—and it's time for a promotion.

My new territory is triple the size of any I've worked before. High death rates mean one busy reaper, and the only way to keep up is with a pack of hellhounds. Faithful. Strong. Merciless. Hellhound shifters are a reaper's right hand in the field, shepherding and guarding souls until they can be reaped.

We get our pick of the litter from the best breeders in Hell, but for some reason, I'm drawn to the pack no one wants.

An alpha who refuses to yield.

A beta who doesn't take me seriously.

A runt who flinches at every command.

I want them—even if they don't want me.

Because the hunger in their eyes tells a different story. But the fact that they can't decide whether to love me or hate me, fight me or screw me, is making our situation *way* too complicated.

Still, I refuse to give up. If this infuriatingly handsome trio can't be trained, if we don't pass the trials, they go back to a cage and a cruel demon master.

Yeah. Not happening.

Reapers and hellhounds are natural allies, and the sooner we secure our bond, the better, because as it turns out…

All our lives depend on it.

❧ 1 ❧

HAZEL

"Place your scythe on the table and register your identity in blood, please."

Please. Rather polite for a demon. My grip tightened around the handle of the weapon gifted to me ten years ago by Death. I knew it better than I knew myself, every groove of the yew staff, the glyphs carved into the shimmering curved blade forged from a star—one of the Corona Borealis constellation, unique to my scythe and mine alone. There was literally no greater weapon in the universe, a herald of doom, the deliverance of death, a reaper's right hand.

And this little *boy* wanted me to hand it over?

Ha.

I drew a breath, ready to tell him, no, in fact, I would hang on to it, when Alexander placed his scythe on the onyx table before us without a second's hesitation.

"Just a formality, Hazel," he mused, flashing me a handsome smile. My reaper mentor, the one who had been minding Lunadell for nearly a decade on his own as the human population exploded from a suburb to a bustling metropolis, had a knack for quieting my concerns with nothing more than a grin. With the looks of a sinner but the mind of a saint, he probably had human souls *swooning* over him when he showed up. None of the screaming, wailing, begging that I had dealt with for the last ten years.

Still. My scythe was a piece of me—my only true companion since I had been chosen by Death to reap. And this was the first time someone—a demon, specifically—had asked me to just hand it over. I nibbled my lower lip for a moment, indecision gnawing at me, before finally delicately placing my weapon on a surface that looked better suited as a sacrificial altar than a check-in station at one of Hell's top hellhound breeding facilities.

Beside me, Alexander flipped open an enormous tome, swiping through yellowed pages until he reached the last used. Golden fingerprints gleamed back at us, catching the light of the gaudy crystal chandeliers above. I glanced up, scanning our new locale with raised eyebrows. White marble stared back, floors, walls, ceiling, flecked with grey and gold, smooth and cold. While I had only ventured into Hell a few times since I'd gone from human soul to grim reaper, it always amazed me how similar it all looked to Heaven.

Well, sort of a black mirror reflection, actually. The architecture had its similarities, but statues of saints and angels and beautiful women down here were grotesque ghouls and screaming demon princes and gore. So, not quite the same, but Lucifer had dragged that love of white marble from paradise down into the pit. The interior of every building drowned in the stuff, while the exterior walls... Well, Hell had a knack for staining everything it touched.

"Now you," Alexander muttered, a full head and a half taller than me, wide and robust and blond, his elbow catching me just below the shoulder when he nudged me. Swallowing thickly, I pricked my finger on the tip of my scythe's blade, then pressed the bleeding digit to the book, taking the spot directly below his. Like angels and the gods of old, reapers bled gold, and when I pulled back, a perfect fingerprint glimmered in the breeder's ledger—my first step toward acquiring my very own hellhound pack.

The thought of which still terrified me.

"Alexander, do I—"

Tortured shrieks erupted from the young demon behind the table, the agonized pitch launching my heart straight into my throat. Horror bounced off the marble walls, and I whipped around to find the poor sod hurling Alexander's scythe back onto the table, his hands shredded down to the bone. The noises he made—like he was still a human soul being ripped apart in the deepest circles of this awful place, no longer the demon they had made him. Broken.

I lurched forward when he collapsed, instinct kicking in: stem the oozing black blood, wrap his bony fingers, find a way to keep them from further deterioration. Alexander caught me by the shoulder with an annoyed huff, his expression bored and utterly unmoved by the sight before us, like he had seen it a thousand times before.

"Idiot boy," he grumbled, flicking his wrist to examine his watch. "Honestly."

No one had ever been stupid enough to touch *my* scythe, but blood and screaming men were nothing new to me either, and the desire to help, fix, resuscitate was one I couldn't shake. I'd died a nurse on the Western Front in 1943; even some seventy-five years later, having died and come back, my life very different from what it once was, it was difficult to ignore the call to action inside me.

The wall opened to our immediate left, and out strode the demon in charge—Fenix. While we reapers almost always dressed in black—Alexander in a pair of tailored trousers and a collared shirt, me in a floor-length, shapeless dress— demons embraced all manner of fashions. Today, Fenix strode forth in a burgundy suit, his black hair slicked back, sinfully attractive. Most demons had an air of dark beauty about them, just as angels were blessed with unnatural loveliness; physicality truly was the best way to damn *and* save humanity.

"Sorry, sorry, sorry," Fenix boomed, crocodile-skin shoes clicking across the marble floor, his strides as long and lean as his physique. "Apprentices... what can you do? Some just aren't cut out for the work."

Before either of us could get a word in, Fenix cuffed the sniveling demon apprentice by the back of his neck, hauled him up, and tossed him in the general direction of the door from which he'd emerged. Black blood droplets stained the floor behind him as he shuffled along, this nameless boy who had lost his hands in a single moment of stupidity—who, now useless, would probably be stripped of his demon status and hurled *back* into the torture pits as a damned soul.

I watched him go, an ache in my chest as he shuffled through the door. In my periphery, Alexander and Fenix clasped hands for a stiff shake. It shouldn't matter to me what happened to the boy. He was a soul condemned to eternal torment; he didn't *deserve* my pity.

None of them did.

Yet he received it all the same. I bit the insides of my cheeks as hard as I dared, using the brief flash of pain to refocus, then faced the towering pair at my side with a thin smile.

Fenix offered his hand to me now, long fingers reaching, reaching, reaching, as if drawn to my throat. I acquiesced to the formality, his flesh hot and his grasp hard. His smile almost matched Alexander's, handsome and sultry and striking—damning, to the right eyes. Unnerving to mine. But no matter my personal feelings about him, this demon was one of the top hellhound breeders in the realm. He was the *only* one Alexander would work with and had produced champion lines of shifters for centuries.

His hounds had one purpose: to serve grim reapers charged with large territories. After all, in a population of a few million, there were countless deaths each day. A sole reaper, even two like Alexander and me in Lunadell, simply couldn't handle the numbers. We *needed* a hellhound pack to control wayward spirits, to corral them, to keep them, to catch them so that we could do our job and get them to Purgatory for judgment.

Every soul lost was a poltergeist in the making.

And the angels responsible for hunting and destroying violent spirits were a bunch of lazy assholes who preferred we reapers let as few slip through our nets as possible.

"Hazel, I presume?" Fenix arched a perfectly waxed black eyebrow at me, and I forced my smile to stretch a hint farther across my face.

"Yes." My hand ached when he released it, but a few flexes in and out of a fist behind my back soothed the pain away. Contrary to popular belief, we reapers could *feel* the same as demons, angels—any supernatural creature. Not as intensely as humans, of course, but we weren't robots.

"Right!" Fenix clapped his hands together, positively giddy as his black gaze slid between me and Alexander. "You'll be selecting your first pack today... Congratulations."

That brought a nervous smile to my face and sparked a flurry of butterflies in my belly. Acquiring my very own hellhound pack was a promotion in a job I loved, a job that garnered me respect—where I wasn't called love, sweetheart, or poppet; where I wasn't spoken down to because of my gender. Before I'd died in an air strike, Alexander and I wouldn't have been treated the same. The world just wasn't there yet. Now, we were equals, even more so after the angels in the reaping department informed me of my relocation to Lunadell.

Whether Alexander shared my perceived equality was a murkier subject. While he hadn't expressed much, he also hadn't exactly done backflips when we'd first met and he learned I had only reaped for ten years before this. The reaper next to me had harvested souls on the celestial plane for nearly seventy before he had been granted his hellhound pack.

"Thank you," I managed. Fenix *sounded* proud of my accomplishment, sure, but he was also about to make a killing in gold from my higher-ups. His packs were the most expensive in Hell, and he all but floated around the table, guiding us deeper into the stark, unfurnished marble foyer. I trailed after the two tall creatures before me, arms crossed, and cast one last glance back to my scythe. It was where I'd left it, and while I didn't bring it everywhere with me when I was off duty, being without always left me feeling hollower inside than I already did.

But as we strolled into an elevator, the doors and inside panels made of pure gold, I knew my scythe would be waiting there for me when I returned. No one else could touch it— literally. These gifts, forged of ancient trees and stardust by Death himself, were nuclear weapons, capable of killing *any* being in this realm and the next. At no point could we risk them falling into the wrong hands.

"We have some *excellent* contenders this year," Fenix remarked as the elevator started its gentle descent. "Wonderful lines, perfect sires, competent bitches... Many of the older packs are well-oiled machines at this point. They'll need little training."

"Mine hardly needed the allotted three months," Alexander noted, chin lifted, a touch arrogant. "A testament to your stock, Fenix."

My mentor had a pack of eight hellhounds, all monstrous black beasts, all devoted—mind, body, and soul—to their reaper master. I couldn't even fathom that sort of loyalty, but it would come, in time. I had three months to get mine into shape before they faced their final trials administered by an archangel, or it was back to square one.

And I had no intention of going through this process again. The pack I chose today would be *mine*, period.

The gold box around us stopped suddenly, jerking into place in a way that made my stomach loop. As soon as the doors whizzed open, my companions shouldered through, briefly barring my view, and for a few precious moments I could pretend all of Hell was gold and white marble. That was dashed once the doorway cleared, and I shuffled into the dark corridor with a scowl.

This was the Hell we all expected: black rock and ash, volcanic runoff hardened with sorrow. Barking erupted as soon as I set foot on the gravelly earth, the wide corridor ahead arched and lined with barred gates. As part of my reaper training, I had seen the deepest circles of Hell, the torturous pits full of demons and damned souls. All reapers needed to know the light and the dark; we had been plucked from Heaven, worthy souls destined to reap, to serve Death honorably, but we had no experience with Hell. And it was just that—a horrible, brutal, awful experience. The souls I marched to Purgatory, the cruel and the violent and the heartless, had no clue what awaited them.

But I did.

And it made my job *so* much easier knowing they were headed here, that as desperately as I wanted to unleash vengeance on them for their earthly crimes, torment awaited.

Fenix's hellhound kennels reminded me of the deepest circles of Hell, only the howls of hounds replaced the screams of human souls. In theory, none of the shifters *here* were tortured for eternity, but as I approached the first gate, the same emotions I'd felt in the pits clung to me like a second skin.

Maybe I was too sensitive. Alexander continued to joke and chat with Fenix like they were old friends, neither flinching when a yelp or a screech punctured the barking chorus. Maybe I just needed tougher skin.

Maybe...

No. I might have walked each step on unsteady footing today, unsure and out of my depth with the changes this promotion brought, but my gut was certain: this was a foul place.

"Just go with your gut," Alexander remarked suddenly, as if he'd read my mind, his melodic baritone cutting through the tensely chaotic air around me. He stepped aside and gestured to the nearest gate. "The right pack will call to you... just like the right house."

Shit. I still hadn't found a place to hold my pack once I got them topside. Another monumental task to do today. After all, who needed a forever home when you spent every single second alone, loitering out of sight on the celestial plane, waiting for humans to die?

Squaring my shoulders, I approached the gate with as confident a stride as I could muster; hellhounds responded to strength, and there was no way I would land a pack without it. Alexander stepped aside to give me an unfettered view of the creatures inside, and my first look at an unclaimed pack threatened to cut me off at the knees.

Twelve hellhounds sat waiting, silent and red-eyed. Huge. Muscular. Alexander had recommended studying topside dog breeds before coming here today; hellhounds traced their ancestors back to the native hounds of Hell and Earth's canine shifter population. Rumors swirled that to this day demons like Fenix still kidnapped female shifters to breed them with Hell's wild dogs—whenever they could catch a male, mind you. The hounds of Hell were savage, enormous creatures, untamable and vicious. Breeding would have been done by force; I deeply pitied the shifters involved, always had.

The pack before me looked as though they had been crossbred with a pit bull terrier. Same large head, stocky build, smooth coat. Red eyes. Twelve pairs of them trained squarely on me. They sat in formation, the largest at the helm, the rest fanning out behind him. Around their necks were gold collars, spiked—on the inside.

"Keeps them from shifting," Fenix remarked, materializing at my side, his croon making me flinch. Damn it. I glanced up at him wordlessly, and he took that as a question, to which he smirked and offered what others might consider a charming one-shouldered shrug. "The human forms have opposable thumbs... Tricky little devils, those. Can get them into all sorts of trouble. I always recommend keeping them like this, but to each their own."

"What do you think?" Alexander eased into my personal space on the other side, the pair boxing me in. "Contenders?"

"No." I didn't need to think about it. This pack made me feel... cold. And small. "No, not these."

"Moving on," Fenix said with another thunderous clap of his hands. "Many more to see..."

And my *God*, there were. Four levels of hellhound kennels awaited me, and it took the better part of an hour to work through the first two floors. None of them called to me. None of them made me *feel* anything. A few alphas had even charged the gate the moment I stopped in front of it, forcing Fenix to step in, his demonic voice echoing harshly through the corridor. That cowed some, but the last unruly pack was still on the receiving end of their master's admonishments

9

while Alexander and I loitered by the elevator doors, waiting to head down to the third level.

"It takes as long as it needs to," he insisted when I let out an exasperated huff. "Your pack is for life, Hazel, and we have very long ones."

"I know." I pinched the bridge of my nose. "It's just... a lot."

"I understand. You'll find them soon."

A part of me wondered if he enjoyed my struggle to connect; my reaper mentor had an exceptional poker face, handsome and smooth like a cherub, but the smug lift of his lips gave him away. He had never said it, but he probably thought I'd been fast-tracked into this position—and I deserved to suffer a little along the way.

I rolled my shoulders back, then stood a little taller. Let him think what he wanted. I was a damn good reaper. I loved my afterlife job and took it very seriously. And more than that, I was *ready* for this next step.

So, you know...

Suck it, Alexander.

That was what the humans said these days, right?

The elevator doors opened, swallowing Fenix's rage into the golden compartment. Alexander swept in and planted a hand on the door, shooting the breeder an irritated look, his mouth tight. Just as I started to follow him, however, something caught my eye.

A gate.

Smaller than all the rest, to the right of the elevator and off the beaten path. Shrouded in shadow, cobwebs collected on the bars and silence greeted me from inside. Logic insisted I ignore it, that I push forward and keep searching, but my feet had a mind of their own, carrying me straight to it.

Like every other kennel, the interior was domed and

dusty, crafted of rock and ash. A water trough hung from the wall, while a little shed at the back suggested a den or a toilet facility of some kind. Bones littered the foot of the gate. A lone flickering light hung from the ceiling.

And in the middle of it all, a giant pile of black fur. My eyes narrowed as I wrapped a hand around one of the metal bars, moving in for a closer look. Either that was one enormous hound, larger than any I had seen thus far, or—

A head popped up from the mass, and my heart skipped a beat.

It wasn't one hellhound, but—three?

Red eyes blazed back at me, the gold collar catching the dingy overhead light. We locked gazes for a moment, and warmth rushed over me. Pleasant, nostalgic, beautiful *heat*. I swallowed hard as the hellhound slowly rose from the pile of his companions, and as he stood, I sank to my knees, unable to tear my eyes away.

He was… stunning.

I had studied dog breeds intensely for the last few days, learning looks and characteristics, selecting those I thought I could best work with and keeping them at the back of my mind. But as the leggy, shaggy hellhound extricated himself from the heap, he challenged my knowledge and threw me for a loop.

Elegant. Graceful. Long black fur and a pronounced but narrow snout.

Small. Smaller than any of the hellhounds I'd seen today. One of his ears had a notch taken out of it.

Belgian sheepdog. That was the look.

Groenendael, specifically.

Rare on Earth. The first I had seen down here.

Beautiful. Just. So beautiful.

I hadn't the strength to rise when he padded toward me, but I managed to smile. In return, he paused—and slowly wagged his tail. Tears pricked my eyes, and I blinked them back with a shaky laugh. His tail pumped harder, and he trotted forward, ears down, head low. Decidedly not the alpha, but I didn't care about that.

My hand trembled when I threaded it through the bars of the gate, reaching out for him, for that twitching nose. The hellhound whined, low and long, and the heat rippling across my skin did a deep dive, scorching through my veins now, burning me from head to toe, on a direct path to my heart. So close. We were but a foot apart when—

"Hazel, don't put your hand in the fucking kennel," Alexander growled, hauling me back by the shoulder. The hellhound dropped to his belly, that fluffy wagging tail tucked squarely between his back legs, his red eyes wide and frightened. The flames inside me burned with rage now, and I shoved the reaper's huge hand away, glowering up at him and fumbling to my feet.

"Alexander, stop—"

"It's dangerous," he told me, wearing a look that screamed *you goddamn idiot* like a neon sign. Hands in fists, I whirled back around to find the other two in the kennel rousing at the commotion. The first that caught my eye was far easier to identify: Doberman pinscher. Long head, sleek frame, muscular and intimidating, the black fur broken up by tawny patches along his snout and front legs. Red eyes stared up at me unflinchingly, and while he gave off none of the warmth of the sheepdog-esque hellhound, the inferno continued to blaze inside of me. Looking at them, standing in their presence, was like *home*.

And it had been a very, very, *very* long time since I had felt the siren song of belonging.

The third hellhound shot to his feet in a burst of sudden movement, the largest creature I had seen in *any* kennel. Cane corso in appearance—that was an easy one too. Robust and overwhelming, with a square jaw and a thick, short coat of black fur, he soared above his companions, those mammoth paws almost the size of my head. Raw intelligence sparked in his gaze when it darted from me to the cowering shaggy hellhound a few feet away, and one gruff, deep bark had the smallest of the lot scurrying back to the pack. I bit my lower lip, hating to see the first hellhound I'd connected with shiver and slink. Alexander continued to talk at me, but I'd tuned him out completely, so focused on the three hellhounds watching me, assessing me, studying me with brilliant red gazes and terse postures.

With a deep breath, I brushed the cobwebs from their gate, then coiled a hand around one of the bars again. This was it. This was that *feeling*—I just knew it.

"Sorry about that," Fenix said, stalking into the scene completely unaware of what had happened. "Sometimes you really just need to bark them down, you know? Can we… Oh." I looked back at him when he paused, his dark brows furrowed. The demon shook his head, waving off the trio before us. "I wouldn't… This pack requires someone with more experience. They aren't a good fit for you. Not for anyone, really. No one wants them—"

"I want them," I said without missing a beat, finding my voice at last, finding that confidence that I'd struggled with all day. Gone was the unsteady quiver, the weak knees, the indecisive internal monologue that had followed me around since I'd been told I needed to choose a pack.

The cane corso hellhound—he was alpha. That much was clear. But as I faced Alexander and Fenix, stared down my nose at them despite the sprawling height difference, *alpha* pulsed through every fiber of my being.

"Hazel, there are more packs to look through below—"

"This is it," I insisted, silencing a scowling Alexander with a raised hand. "This is the one."

"A pack of three?" My reaper mentor scoffed. "That isn't enough. You need a few more—"

"Technically, we would be a pack of four." Working as one, reaping together, guiding souls to Purgatory for judgment. For the first time in days, my head, heart, and gut were on the same page. In life, I had endured warfare—the worst humanity had ever witnessed. Small units of soldiers had overtaken whole Nazi battalions on the front. This was absolutely doable. "It's quality over quantity. I want them."

"I'd hardly call them *quality*," Fenix sneered as he picked at his nails, like I wasn't worth his time now that I disagreed with his opinion. Indignation blazed in my chest, and when he met my narrowed gaze, he shrugged again. "Look, see the rest of the packs before you make a stupid decision like this."

I bit the insides of my cheeks, glaring up at the two men so hell-bent on changing my mind. When I was alive, women had no voice. Our fathers, brothers, and husbands made the decisions. But that wasn't the way of the world anymore, and it most *definitely* wouldn't be my afterlife.

"No," I said firmly. I turned my back on a sputtering Alexander, a glowering Fenix, and locked eyes with the hellhound alpha. He was mine. They were *all* mine. "This is my pack. Where do I sign for them?"

2

HAZEL

"Yep, yep, just bring them straight on through..." I propped open the double doors that led into the foyer, locking them in place as a trio of Fenix's underlings heaved in the giant wood crates on dollies that contained my pack. A gust of hot August air followed them, whipping through the empty entryway and rattling the rest of the abandoned manor.

Three days just wasn't enough time to make a house a home, but I had done my best.

Located six miles south of Lunadell and well off the beaten path, nestled in the outskirts of Selene's Forest, sat a structure long forgotten by the local humans. Three stories tall, crawling with ivy and weeds, most of the shutters hanging by a single nail, the roof in need of reshingling and several of the windows broken—our new house. For ten long years, I had wandered, so focused on doing my job, on reminding myself I *wasn't* human and didn't belong in their world anymore, that I had never needed to put down roots. But my hellhounds required stability. They deserved a place to call home, a territory to claim and protect. So, I had given it to them.

Sort of.

The territory, at least. Some furniture. A ward around the whole property, well into the trees so that they had wilderness to patrol without a human happening upon them. A basement larder full of raw meat…

But still it seemed inadequate.

Perhaps that was just the way Fenix had made me feel. Unable to pass through my ward, he and his demons had been forced to wait for me today at the property line, surrounded by old red cedars and enormous deerflies. My scythe had sliced through the shimmering protective barrier that hid my new homestead from the world, a magical shield that operated on the mortal *and* celestial plane, temporarily allowing them to pass through with my new pack. Dressed in another fine suit, gold around his neck and glittering on his fingers, Fenix wasn't exactly accustomed to Earth's rural backwoods; mud stained his viper-skin boots by the time we'd crossed the forest, and he was still out there now, stomping about and aggressively wiping the soles on the cracked front steps, snarling through his teeth.

While he hadn't said another word about my choice in pack, his disdain for them and my best attempt at a home was obvious when he finally joined us, strutting into the manor like he owned it. Hands in his pockets. Lip curled. Eyes wandering and judging.

"Could do with a coat of paint," Fenix mused with a dismissive sniff, twisting his enormous thumb ring. I hummed in agreement, too nervous about my pack's arrival to give a damn anymore that the place wasn't up to his snobbish standards. Adrenaline pounded through me, so much sharper on the mortal plane than the celestial, like fireworks pinwheeling in my marrow.

Once the demon's apprentices had the wood crates off the dollies, they slipped outside, metal wheels clanging all the way down the front stairs, and I quickly saw to the doors, closing and bolting them with shaky hands. My back pressed against the aged wood, finding it sturdy despite the creaking hinges. It propped me up when I wanted to sink to the floor, and I wrapped my arms around myself in a solo hug, both for comfort and support. The next few moments would change the rest of my afterlife, honestly. A few nerves were expected, whether Alexander agreed or not.

The wood crates seemed to dominate the front foyer, the space unfurnished and a little too stark for my liking. Across the room, twin stairwells wound up to the second floor, recently swept by my own hands, not magic, and crowned with black wrought iron railings. An enormous, dusty floor-to-ceiling window overlooked everything from the landing, the panes filthy from the outside. While I had cleared out most of the dead leaves and spider nests and debris, the house still desperately needed a top-to-bottom scrub, the third floor the worst of them. Wainscoting stamped the walls, a throwback to an era gone by, and as Fenix approached the smallest wood crate, I found myself wishing I had taken some time in the last three days to properly decorate.

A snap of the demon's fingers produced a cattle prod, the end shaped like Poseidon's trident, whitish blue bolts dancing between the prongs. I stilled, the air crackling with dark magic, a magic so similar to the one I had been blessed with once Death made me a reaper. While I couldn't craft hurricanes or wipe out a city with a thought, I had some of the most basic magic at my disposal: summoning, healing, cleaning, teleportation, and protection—like the ward I had cast around my new territory. Nothing fancy. The scythe amplified my powers to unlimited, but I'd never taken advantage of that; reapers weren't chosen because we were power-hungry.

Unlike the creature before me, with his cruel smile and dark beauty. Once a human soul himself, Fenix must have had the ideal temperament for a demon; he exemplified it now, the brutality, how he relished it. A well-aimed kick at the wood crate knocked open one side, the plank crashing thunderously to the tile floor. My heart launched into my throat, and I pushed off the door, eager to get a look at my hellhounds in the raw light of day.

Only nobody came out.

"*Move*," Fenix barked, kicking at the crate again. A heartbeat later, he thrust his cattle prod into the opening, and a horrible screech sounded from its depths, paired with the distinct jolt of electricity and the scent of singed fur. Fury snapped inside me; I raised my hand, no longer trembling, and summoned my scythe. It whipped through the first floor, zipping around walls and slamming home into my palm.

How *dare* he hurt my pack.

My fingers coiled around the yew staff just as the demon reared back, as if to strike again, and the snarl boiling in my chest dimmed to a simmer when a black mass of shaggy fur scampered out of the crate. The Belgian sheepdog. My first true connection.

Terrified.

Belly to the ground, the hellhound slunk this way and that, turning on a dime, so obviously searching for a new safe place to hide that it ripped me apart inside. My grip tightened around my scythe when Fenix scowled down at him.

"Pathetic, this one," he sneered, catching the hellhound's hind leg with the cattle prod. Another yelp echoed through the foyer, and Fenix snorted. "Good luck getting anything out of him."

"Don't touch him with that—"

A deep, chilling snarl rumbled from the largest wood crate, drowning out my own growl with something far more effective. I jumped when the crate shook—when a sound like a shotgun resonated throughout the house. The wood groaned, the whole box shifting a foot forward like the hellhound inside was throwing himself up against the panels. That had to be the alpha—no mistaking that guttural voice. Fenix approached quickly, though some of his smug confidence faltered when he kicked open this crate, retreating fast with the cattle prod raised defensively.

As I'd guessed, out came the cane corso hellhound, immense in size, teeth bared and red eyes narrowed. He charged into the foyer like a bull, and the skittering smaller hellhound beelined straight for him, hiding behind his huge frame with a whine. The alpha faced off with his demon overlord, hackles up, saliva dripping from his jowls. One wrong move from Fenix and he'd attack—I felt it in the air, the warning, the tension, the history between them. I raised my scythe's blade to roughly hellhound height, glancing warily between the pair; while Fenix probably deserved a good thrashing, I had no intention of allowing this momentous day to turn into a bloodbath.

Muted sunlight slanted in through the window over the second-floor landing, catching on my blade and drawing the alpha's gaze my way. Even without the third hound added to the mix, I felt it again—that sensation in my gut, humming over my skin and scalding through my veins, the fire and nostalgia and *home*. The comfort, the sanctuary of their presence. These three were my pack, no doubts there, but all my emotions still crashed together like a maelstrom. Focus evaded me. There was all this *good* surging about inside, filling me, warming me, recharging me after ten long years alone, and yet the violent chaos of their arrival, of Fenix's handling of my pack, collided hard with all that good, making it difficult to think.

Overwhelming me.

Making me weak when they needed me to be strong.

The demon opened the third and final crate without any great fanfare, stepping aside with the buzzing prod in hand as the Doberman hellhound sauntered out. Casual. Calm. Collected. Calculated. He crossed to his companions without so much as a snarl or a raised lip, but those red eyes oozed intelligence, drinking in every little detail of the room—every little detail of me.

Heat bloomed in my chest, and still I struggled for control. This had gotten away from me; already I was failing.

"Come here, you shits," Fenix grumbled, vanishing from sight one moment, then materializing next to my pack the next. The alpha hellhound snapped his enormous jaws at him, but Fenix had speed and finesse on his side. Deft fingers found the golden collars around their necks, and he tore them off without bothering to undo them, the inverted spikes ripping into throats and painting my dusty floors red.

"Stop!" I shouted, rushing forward, scythe at the ready as cold fear washed over me. "Don't do that to them—"

"They'll heal," Fenix told me as he backpedaled from a snarling alpha, a deathly quiet beta, a cowering runt. He hoisted the cattle prod, creating a five-foot barrier between them, the sparks at the end sizzling out a warning. Black demonic eyes slid my way, paired with a smirking mouth that would probably melt an unsuspecting human. "That's sort of the point of breeding them with shifters... They're virtually indestructible."

Bright red splattered the off-white tile, jarring in its vibrancy. Reapers were there when a human died, and oftentimes death was bloody. But I bled gold. Demons bled black. It had been a very, very long time since red had any sway over me, but my God, it did now. Unshed tears stung my eyes as I looked to my pack, searching for injuries and finding nothing but black fur tinged with blood, the flesh underneath healed over, something so superficial unlikely to scar.

Yet how many scars were on the inside? Born and bred in Hell, housed in dank kennels, reared by a hand like Fenix's—would these three ever be whole?

Probably not.

And the realization made me *ache*.

"Shift," Fenix barked. When nothing happened, the air still and hot and brimming with years of hate, the demon stalked forward and thrust the prod hard into the alpha's side. My chest tightened, and a charged energy coursed through every inch of me at the electric shock blistering against the hellhound's flesh; the alpha endured it without a sound, like he had done so a thousand times before. Still as a mountain, he stood over his cowering packmate and stared Fenix down, as if daring him to do it again.

And he did.

Only this time, the demon caught the smallest hellhound on the shoulder, stabbing hard and true, the scent of burnt fur fused inside my nostrils. I hurried forward when the alpha lunged, those huge jaws only *just* missing Fenix's arm as the demon scrambled back. In all the commotion, the smallest hellhound did as he was ordered: shifted from beast to man. A beat later, the other two followed, and by the time I situated myself between them and their tormentor, scythe at the ready, three men stared me down.

Three very naked, very tall, *very* gorgeous men.

Steam rose off their sculpted bodies in waves, the heat of the shift washing over me even at a distance. The alpha still stood out as the largest; at my best estimate, he neared seven feet, though he hunched now, still protecting his companion. That *body*—he was a wall of muscle, olive-skinned and brooding. Tattoos snaked around his forearms, lines of solid black that seemed to have no beginning and no end. Scars crisscrossed over his chest, his defined abdominals. I forced my gaze up, fire flaring in my cheeks.

So naked.

Don't stare at their cocks, Hazel. I'd never seen men so, so very naked before in a setting like this, where I wasn't reaping or nursing, and it...

Oh. It flustered me.

Another failure.

His eyes. The alpha's eyes flustered me too, dark and hooded—angry. Another scar cut through his right brow and halfway down his cheek. A black mane trundled over his broad shoulders in frizzy waves. His full mouth set in a tense line as he glared down at me, his rough beard in need of sheering.

The other two lacked facial hair, though they were certainly no less handsome. The beta had transformed into a tall, lean man with brilliant blue eyes, a head of chestnut curls, and cheekbones that could cut glass. Flawless porcelain skin shone with sweat, the shift between beast and man noticeably taxing. While he lacked his alpha's hulking muscular definition, he appeared wiry and strong, his hands crowned with long, graceful fingers and surprisingly clean, short nails.

And those *eyes*. Royal blue and mesmerizing; I could lose myself, easily, in those eyes.

The last of the bunch, my first connection, had short cropped black hair, brown skin, a heart-shaped face, and beautiful, big hazel eyes. He stood perhaps an inch shorter than the beta when he finally climbed to his feet, and it pained me to see he was just as scarred as his alpha. The marks on his perfectly carved torso reminded me of... bite marks. Like another hellhound had sunk his teeth in and refused to let go.

While they might be indestructible to some degree, my

boys could scar. With enough force, an enemy could leave a memory on their flesh—and that infuriated me.

As we sized each other up, I felt them. Even with the space between us, my skin hummed as though I had just traced every peak and valley of their magnificent figures with my fingers. The bond was immediate and unnervingly visceral, their heat fueling me, bringing me back to life after ten lonely years of death. My reaper skin was cold to the touch, my kiss rumored to bring destruction. But in that moment, somehow touching but not, I was hot-blooded—I was home.

And the alpha and beta glowered down at me with the same disdain Fenix had for the mud he'd scraped off his boot.

The demon inserted himself into the moment—*our* moment—by tossing the spiked golden collars onto the ground between me and my pack, into the blood, and wrapping an unwelcome arm around my shoulders.

"Boys," Fenix started, his words laced with cold, cruel mirth, "meet your new alpha."

The full weight of their stares, their judgment, their scrutiny, suddenly made me feel very small. I swallowed hard and gave a little wave with my scythe.

"Uh… Hi."

3

GUNNAR

New alpha.

Ha.

In all my life, I had only yielded to one alpha, and he stood next to me, his fury hammering through our pack bond. *Uh… Hi.* I tipped my head to the side, my lips itching to spread into a patronizing smile to counteract the reaper's awkward greeting, something to cut her off at the knees, put her in her place.

But my usual venom had taken a back seat—because that fucker Fenix was still *touching* her. My gaze lingered on the demon's arm around her shoulders, thoughts of their intimacy overtaking my rapid assessment of this place, of our new circumstances. Just how familiar *was* she with our former master? Did she welcome his hands on her? From her tense posture, I could assume the answer—no, no, a thousand times no—but I knew nothing about her beyond her appearance.

Hardly the look of an alpha, and I had seen my fair share over the years. Most were brutish, big; Knox certainly fit the stereotype, but he possessed an innate strength I found lacking in every other alpha who had tried and failed to rule me.

He exemplified it now with his protective stance in front of Declan, walling off the weakest among us—*caring* for his own, a perceived weakness among demons and most other hellhounds. In my opinion, there was immense strength in softness, in recognizing the varying abilities of every individual. Declan had always been small. His former packs abused him mercilessly, and he carried that with him to this day. But he was bright, eager, and diligent—should he be given the chance.

Would this reaper allow him the opportunity to shine, just as Knox had, or would she dismiss him like all the rest?

I scrutinized her silently as she shrugged Fenix off. Her fingers danced over her scythe's wood staff, as though adjusting her grip. The most powerful weapon in all the worlds stood before us, clutched in the hand of a petite, albeit curvaceous, female. Clearly she had been found worthy of handling such profound majesty, but I struggled to picture her on the battlefield, caked in blood and cutting down foes with a blade forged in the cosmos.

Yes, we all knew a reaper's scythe—what it could do to us should we be foolish enough to caress it. The stories passed from pack to pack, from demonic trainer to trainer, right up to the top of the hierarchy, who stood sneering back at us now, his own weapon still humming dangerously. The pain of its touch was amplified in human form; my body tensed instinctively, preparing for the shock I'd endured countless times before.

But it would be *nothing* compared to the scythe in her hand.

That was why none of us had attacked yet.

She might have signed her name in blood for our pack, paid for us with Heaven's gold—but she would never *own* us.

By sundown tonight, I'd have an escape mapped out. By sunrise tomorrow, we would be gone, lost in the wilderness I had scented upon our arrival.

Simple.

Almost *too* simple, perhaps, but I always welcomed a challenge—the rare time one presented itself.

"Have a blast, sweetheart," Fenix crooned, clapping her hard on the back as he sauntered toward the front doors. Wealth glittered on his fingers, around his neck. Arrogance dripped from every pore. I gritted my teeth as I watched him go, loathing that he had taken one last opportunity to *touch* her before making his grand exit. Showy fucker. Once we were free, I'd find a way to kill him—if Knox didn't get to him first.

The demon didn't even have the courtesy to shut the doors properly behind him; he let them fall closed, but the breeze kept them from locking in place. They bumped with each gust, the lone bit of sound in an otherwise hushed, tense atmosphere. The four of us continued to stare, sizing each other up, the room crackling with a strange energy, like the air before a fight. The hairs on my arms rose. My nipples pebbled. My muscles tensed. Yet I remained still, watching, waiting, wondering who would break first.

Of course it was Knox. Predictable. My alpha turned on the spot, murmuring to Declan, and ducked low to meet my packmate's gaze, no doubt asking after him, his mental state. Declan's anxiety rippled frantically through our pack bond, a grating sensation that I felt in my teeth. Two years after taking him on, however, I'd gotten used to his moods—to his fear, his stress, his lingering trauma. Knox, meanwhile, radiated a powerful calm, though today his aura had a fiery undercurrent to it, pumping us up, preparing for battle.

I rolled my shoulders back, blocking out my pack's internal strife. A rarity among our kind: the gift of *focus*. And in that moment, mine was pinned squarely on this new reaper, a reaper who seemed to have no fucking idea what to do with herself.

Although...

She was rather beautiful when the light hit her.

No other reaper had ever coaxed such a compliment from me.

Short in stature, she bore a rounded face, but none of her features were lost to the shape, her cheekbones as sharp as her chin. Wide-set eyes stared back at me, light coppery brown and unreadable. I'd expected blue with that shock of stark white hair, hair that she wore in a loose braid over her shoulder. She shared the same smooth, hauntingly pale skin as other reapers I'd seen, but hers flushed suddenly, a startling pinkish-brown that flashed all the way down her neck when her gaze flicked down and then shot back up.

My eyebrows rose, my smile incredulous.

Had she a problem with nudity?

Did it embarrass her, my cock—Knox's, Declan's?

Well. She had better get over it fast; clothes never survived a shift.

Not that any of us had been gifted so much as a scrap of fabric under Fenix's care.

"So, I don't know what they told you," she started, her voice slicing through the tension with the ease of a blade through flesh. My jaw went slack for a moment, taken aback by the melodious lilt of her words, paired with that delicious, breathy rasp...

Surely the choruses of Heaven could never sound so fucking angelic. Knox and Declan fell quiet beside me, visceral interest from all three of us echoing through our pack bond. They heard it too—the beauty, the softness, the rich inflection. Had any of us experienced something so exquisite in our lifetime?

Certainly not in Hell.

"But, uh, my name is Hazel," she continued, her cheeks flushed again—as if she too sensed the shift between us, the way we locked onto her as a predator homed in on its prey. "I'm a grim reaper. I've been reaping for ten years…"

Knox kept his back to her, still and silent, but out of the corner of my eye, I spotted Declan keenly peering around our alpha, his anxiety quieted, his interest piqued. She might have been a grim reaper, but there had to be some siren in the mix too. How else could she ensnare all three of us with but a few meaningless words?

"I died in 1943," Hazel remarked, fidgeting with her scythe now as she glanced between me and my packmates. "I was a nurse in France on the front, and I was killed during a bombing. I was born in Britain, but we're in North America now… West coast Canada, specifically. The year is 2020, and we'll be reaping a coastal metropolis called Lunadell alongside another reaper and his pack."

None of that mattered. We wouldn't be here long enough to set foot in Lunadell or to cross paths with this other pack. I digested her sentiment, sure, but for once, my racing mind fixated more on the melody than the content.

No one said a word, and Hazel cleared her throat softly in the hush that followed her little speech. Did she wonder if we could understand her? All three of us had been schooled in the English language, but I also had the Nordic dialogues at my disposal. Declan was fluent in Arabic and Hebrew, while Knox had Spanish, Portuguese, and old Aramaic and Latin under his belt—should he need to eavesdrop on angels, of course. We understood every damn word that came out of her mouth, but it was the *way* she said them that knocked us on our asses.

At least, it did for me.

And that worried me more than I cared to admit, but it was a distraction I could master, just like everything else.

"No one told me your names," the reaper said, her wide, imploring eyes falling to me, the only one who seemed to be giving her any real attention. "Just your pack ID number…"

Pathetic, her unspoken plea. As I'd suspected, she wasn't alpha quality. *Maybe* a decent beta, but I wasn't willing to give up my position anytime soon.

Still, catering to her had its benefits. I placed a hand over my heart. "Gunnar."

Her whole being seemed to lift at the introduction, and something in me bloomed right alongside her. Heat flooded my body, similar to the fire of every shift, but I swallowed it down, ignored the pleasurable tingle ghosting along my flesh. After all, it wasn't pity that made me speak to her—and it sure as fuck wasn't her beauty either. There were benefits to lowering her guard, and a polite smile and a few choice words would likely do just that.

"This is Knox," I continued with a wave toward my alpha, "and behind him is Declan."

"Okay… Okay, good. Gunnar. Knox. Declan. Hi." Her little pink tongue swept across her full, lush lips, a damnable distraction that had me weak in the knees again. She nodded and pushed her braid over her shoulder, the movement unleashing a cloud of her natural scent into the air. I clenched my jaw hard when she smiled, longing for the usual rush of smugness that hit whenever I'd bested someone, worked my way under their skin. Instead, I was off-kilter —distracted.

A moment later, she vanished, and I exhaled sharply, like that would rid her smell from my nostrils for good. The next inhale brought it all back, and when she reappeared out of nowhere, scythe in one hand, a pile of black material balanced on the other, her scent struck with the force of a fucking tempest.

Once, an old trainer had dragged me and my then pack to the Elysian Fields to practice herding human souls. The resting place of the ancient Greeks had been the one bit of brightness in an otherwise bleak, black past—the closest to paradise a hellhound would ever experience. In those fields blossomed thousands of wildflowers, aromatic, intoxicating, beautiful; they were my one and only frame of reference for sweetness, for a fragrance that wasn't blood and shit and raw flesh.

Hazel's scent reminded me of sweet alyssum. Subtle. Delicate. The little bunches of blooms grew in clusters, with soft white petals and a warm golden center. A human soul enjoying his afterlife had told me they smelled like honey.

Not that I knew what honey was, but from that moment, I craved it—lusted after it, ached to taste whatever produced that scent on my tongue.

Back then, I'd tried to whisk a few precious blossoms back to the pit with me, hidden under my collar, but my efforts had earned me a severe beating.

Today, just for a moment, I allowed myself to breathe her in, to relish the sweet alyssum, to remember in vivid detail one of my very few pleasant memories, not reacting in the slightest even when she offered me the pile of folded cloth.

"I wasn't sure of your sizes," Hazel admitted with a pointed look at the stack, willing me to take something from the top, "but I'll have a better wardrobe for you guys tomorrow now that I've, er, seen you."

Now that she'd *seen* us, eh? My smirk had color pluming back into her cheeks.

Oh, she was going to be such *fun*.

Begrudgingly, I accepted the top piece of the pile, then held my breath as she drifted by to force her offerings on the others. Like I needed that sweet, subtle scent of hers to addle my brain more than it already had. I unfurled the garment to find a pair of black trousers; it had been an age since I'd been allowed to cover myself in shifted form. Some trainers permitted it. Fenix had never approved such luxuries; he preferred Hazel's response to our nudity, wanting to throw reapers off their game, if only for a moment, with a sculpted, sometimes scarred, body.

The clothing few trainers allowed in Hell's pits was always coarse, rough—something to toughen your skin and your mind. This was... soft. Thick. Wooly on the inside, smooth and supple on the outside. Frowning, I slipped the trousers on, then winced; the crotch area climbed right up my ass, compressing everything. Even when I tugged it down, a stretchy waistband accommodating my body no matter where it sat, the legs stopped halfway up my calves. Far too small.

Behind me, Declan had already slipped into pants *and* a shirt—black, like mine, and also a touch too small. I bit back a smirk. Always eager to please, that one. Eager to prove himself more than the runt his mother had immediately abandoned, who his siblings had tried to kill within the first month. Apparently, Hazel was worthy of his efforts. Unsurprising, given her scent, her voice—young ones like Declan were easily swayed by attractive females.

I exhaled sharply when she brushed by me again, scythe over her shoulder, sweet alyssum tickling my nose and stirring my cock.

Fuck. Another quick pants adjustment took care of that; no need for her to see the effect she had on me, because it wouldn't last for long. Even if her scent snared me, we'd be long gone before it made me do something stupid.

Knox, meanwhile, stood there like a fucking mountain, holding a single black garment at his side and staring down our new reaper mistress. When she rounded on the spot, Hazel's expression faltered when she saw him, and her throat dipped delicately with a gulp. Arms crossed, I waited, grinning and glancing between the pair, eager for a predictable outcome from their standoff.

My alpha had an effect on people. He intimidated them with his size, unnerved them with his dark, hooded, scarred stare. He challenged them with his calm patience, his willingness to wait them out. Knox seldom snapped, seldom exploded in a fit of rage we hellhounds were known for—and if he did, you were *fucked*.

He'd made a reaper cry once through the bars of our kennel with his stare alone, even more menacing on four legs than he was on two. As Hazel locked eyes with him, I counted down the seconds until she cracked—I estimated twenty.

Twenty-one seconds later, Knox tugged on his own pair of pants. The smallest of the bunch, they came up to his knees and hung low on his hips, the generous fabric stretched taut over his muscular thighs. Declan's eyebrows shot up, his surprise mirroring my own. Shock skittered through the pack bond, but Knox gave no indication that he felt it. Instead, he crossed those burly arms, rose up to his full height, and waited.

Well then.

That was… interesting.

As the strain leeched out of the air between us and her, Hazel's scent seemed to sharpen, becoming even more apparent under the temporary truce and affecting the others just as it did me. Lust trembled through the cords tethering Declan, Knox, and myself together, the invisible strands that bound us as a pack. They could be severed, strengthened, and expanded to accommodate fluctuating pack dynamics, but their purpose remained: to bind us, to wordlessly express our feelings and avoid misunderstandings and in-pack fighting.

And right now, desire slaked the pack bond, hot and heavy, our heightened sense of smell our undoing with this reaper.

I rolled my shoulders back again and faced off with our new mistress alongside my alpha, my scowl pathetic next to his—but, you know, unified front and all. Because at the end of the day, it didn't *matter* what her scent did to us, or that she was undoubtedly the most striking female I'd ever laid eyes on. None of the physical mattered in the slightest.

As soon as she signed her name on our contract, Hazel had become the enemy.

And no amount of beauty, no potency of sweet alyssum, would ever make us forget that.

4

KNOX

Well.

This was better than Hell, at least.

Just how much better remained to be seen.

Because while the reaper before me was attractive, dressed in fitted black trousers and a loose black shirt, her curves an irritable distraction and her dainty feet bare, even the most vicious demons in Hell were beautiful. All of them. Even if they had been about as appealing as a boil on a warlock's testicle in life, demons were reborn exquisite, seductive, alluring. I had endured their cruelty all my life, suffered beneath their whips in the fighting arena, tortured and ripped apart before laughing, *beautiful* creatures.

She hadn't snapped a collar around my neck yet or beaten my pack. She wasn't brandishing a lash and barking orders, but she clung to a scythe, a weapon that could end our lives permanently in a second. No healing from that. No coming back. That blade would render us no more than blood and rotting flesh, shit for the insects of this world to devour until there was nothing left.

Her beauty was nothing to me. *Nothing*.

Fuck the lust racing through the pack bond. Fuck the ache in my chest, the tightness of my throat, the dry, starchy feel in my mouth. All she—*Hazel*—was to me was an obstacle, a barrier to the freedom I was determined to give my pack. I would either go around her, or through her, but one way or another, I would get what I came for.

I would free Gunnar and Declan.

And never again would we serve.

As far as I was concerned, we had been sold from one master to another. Nothing more. Nothing less.

And by first light tomorrow, she would be a thing of the past.

Something pleasant to dream about, maybe.

"So, I just thought I'd let you guys know," she started, her voice like the mournful song of a nightingale. "I've warded up the entire property."

Gunnar stiffened beside me, and I ground my teeth together. So much for a simple escape come nightfall.

"It's a trust thing," the reaper carried on with a one-shouldered shrug. "Nothing will get in to bother you, but I also can't have a hellhound pack running loose unsupervised. I just can't, and I hope you understand that."

Declan shuffled about behind me, recovered from the cruelty of Fenix's hand, his interest in *her* like a boulder catching on a thin, taut piece of twine, weighing down the pack bond and driving me up the fucking wall. He was young, inexperienced with females, with kindness, but if this carried on, we would need to have a serious talk.

"I also know that you've all had training in Hell." Hazel lifted her scythe to her other shoulder, the blade catching the muted sunlight streaming in from the window—the very same light that highlighted all the dust and loose fluff floating in the air. How would it feel to be on the receiving end of that blade's bite—better or worse than what I'd already suffered? Would it be quick, or would the pain twist and twist and *twist* until you begged for death?

The reaper shifted her weight from foot to foot, her stare burning into my forehead as she spoke.

"As a refresher, we will do all our reaping on the celestial plane. As Hell-born shifters, you can access the plane just like me and angels and demons—and human souls. You'll be invisible to everyone *not* on the celestial plane, and the roads within are what we travel to take souls down to Purgatory for judgment.

"We have three months to get on the same page. In that time, my goal is to familiarize you with modern humans and their technology. I always think it's better to understand who we reap—what motivates them, what scares them, what they want in an afterlife. After that, it's crucial to come together as a unit. At the end of the three months, we face trials administered by an angelic representative of Death. If we fail… we… well, you risk going back to Fenix, and I don't want that, because, you know, he seems like a dick."

Gunnar snorted, and a smile threatened to play across my lips when I glanced over at him. He schooled his features quickly, our opinions no doubt aligned regarding the delicious female talking at us.

Still, she had a touch of fire. That was admirable.

Admirable, but ultimately inconsequential.

"For now, I think we should just get you guys settled in." She thrust her chin toward the nearby staircase. "Your bedrooms are upstairs… I'm sorry it's a little, er, dusty. I haven't had to live anywhere since I started reaping, so this was the best I could do on short notice. I'll get it sorted as quick as I can."

"We can help," Declan offered, poking his head around

my right bicep with an impish grin—a look that made the reaper flush. "With the tidying. I can… I enjoy tidying."

"Oh." She tucked a few loose strands of white hair behind her ear, her whole aura seeming to brighten. "That's great. I'd like that."

For fuck's sake. Gunnar rolled his eyes, the sentiment carrying through our bond, and Declan wilted behind me.

"I have a bedroom for each of you upstairs…" Hazel cast us one final look, wary, as though unsure if she could turn her back on her newly acquired pack. I had no intention of charging the second she turned away; only a coward attacked his enemy from behind.

As soon as she started up the stairs, hips swaying hypnotically with each step, her pale, delicate fingers ghosting over the railing, Declan followed like a good little puppy. A slight raise of my hand stilled him at my side, and he grimaced when our eyes met, his darting to the floor in submission.

Declan had a pure soul—a rarity amongst our kind and seldom ever appreciated for its value. He could be impulsive at times, but he was a good pup. Smart. Funny. Intelligent. Honest—with the ability to shut his fucking mouth when necessary. I liked him, and in my many years, I liked very few creatures, hellhound or not, but I was also still his alpha. Not Hazel.

The reaper had climbed halfway up the large, winding staircase when she finally paused. To her credit, she didn't look back; she just waited, knowing that we had no choice but to eventually follow. Gunnar cracked his knuckles noisily at my side, his gaze fixed on her white hair, his interest in her palpable. I cast him a warning look—*keep your fucking head in the game*—before strolling up and after her. My pack trailed behind me, Declan bringing up the rear, and Hazel only moved again when I was a step below her.

As promised, she had an individual room for each of us. Packs ordinarily lived together, slept together, ate together, hunted together. The concept of personal space fell on deaf ears with my kind, and yet Declan's impulsivity had him barreling into his new quarters *without* my permission. I let it slide, allowing him a few precious moments of pleasant curiosity; he'd never had anything for himself before. It seemed cruel to deny him that.

Nearest to the stairs, his small room had two windows, cracked but sunlit, its furnishings sparse but clean—new, judging by their scent, or lack thereof. A bed. A dresser. A stool in the corner. No breeder allowed furniture in the kennels, but I'd seen it all before in the trainers' barracks.

Seen it.

Envied it.

Gunnar's room connected to Declan's through a shared toilet, and while his furnishings were similar, he also had a trio of bookshelves overladen with tomes. The wiry hellhound went straight for them, long fingers perusing the spines, his interest *finally* off Hazel. I lingered in the doorway, watching, fighting another smile; he would love those books. All his vast knowledge had been acquired either secondhand or courtesy of his own ingenuity. My beta was a brilliant creature, but this would expand his mind to the point of unbearable; a glutton for facts and information and history, Gunnar loved to lord his knowledge over others.

And, like Declan, I let him have that for a beat—let them enjoy themselves, bask in what was probably the bare minimum to Hazel but a lavish indulgence to us. The thought made my jaw clench tighter, my hands in fists as I trailed after the reaper down the shadowy corridor. It lacked decoration, our new and fleeting dwelling, with holes punched in the walls as if art had once hung there, back when this abandoned manor actually served a purpose.

Mine was the room at the end of the hall, with no door and a frame that required me to duck down and turn to the side to pass through. Larger than the other two, it offered a bed big enough for three hounds, an arched window that projected out from the exterior wall with a cozy bench at its base, along with a dusty, soot-filled brick fireplace, and a lone, albeit grand, armchair situated in front of it. Given its opulence, I assumed this room would have belonged to the master of the house, and while I refused to so much as glance back at the reaper hovering just out of sight, I appreciated that she recognized our hierarchy.

Going into this, I had assumed we would be given cages—one for each, chain-link and narrow, most likely outdoors, where we would spend all our time until the reaper needed us.

This was unexpected.

My toilet area possessed both a standing shower stall and a clawfoot tub; Fenix had always boasted about the women he had in *his* golden bathtub, the fae he tricked down there, the witches he lured in with promises of riches and prestige, perhaps even marriage. How strange that when I looked upon one now, a very naked Hazel flashed across my mind, stretched out inside, her feet hanging over the edge, her rosebud mouth smiling up at me.

A low growl caught in my throat, and I pushed away from the attached room's doorway with a scowl. Heat raged in my chest, burning up my throat and treading the thin line between lust and loathing.

"I hope this is okay," Hazel said as I crossed to the enormous window and ripped open the curtains—literally. The frayed material came apart in my hands, and I tossed the slip of useless fabric aside; it fluttered to the ground, pooled at my feet. Hazel said nothing to that, only sighed when I positioned myself in front of the window to glare at the grounds.

Greenery glared back, first the scraggly, overgrown gardens at the base of the house, then the muddy grass that stretched outward to the forest. For miles and miles, tall trees reigned, proud and thick and ancient. Thorny green leaves splayed out on thin branches. Hardly the most welcoming sight, but it was a far cry from the arid nothingness of Hell, of black rock as far as the eye could see, of jagged earth and angry plants hell-bent on eating you if you got too close.

We might have been in the middle of nowhere, the land in need of a caring hand, the property made up of a vast, endless forest—but it was safe. Child's play compared to the harsh landscape I knew better than I knew myself.

"I'm going to make something for you to eat," Hazel told me. Now that we were alone, I really *felt* each of her words, my body responding as it never had before—willing me to concede, to approach her, to touch her. A rush of interest prickled down my frame and settled in my core, but I ignored it, keeping my back to her. The floorboards creaked when she stepped into the room; did she even realize how she smelled, how her scent made her a ripe temptation for a hellhound twice her size?

"I don't... I don't have to eat," she continued, babbling hurriedly as I glowered at nothing and everything. "I mean, I *can* eat, and drink and sleep and, you know, have... Anyway. I can do it all, I just haven't for a long time, so if I forget to feed you guys, let me know."

Because it had to do with the well-being of my pack, I offered a curt grunt of acknowledgement. Her reflection snagged in the window, dwarfed by mine, those full lips demanding my attention.

"So... I'll just go do that," she said after a long beat of

silence. I forced my gaze to the forest, searching for an out and only finding the very faint rainbow shimmer of the ward caging us in. Against my will, my traitorous stare dropped down to her reflection again when she huffed, her glare somehow both lovely and terrifying—the best kind. "Okay. Cool. Well, great talk."

This time, I allowed my grin to surface, tracking her in the windowpane as she stalked out of the room in a snit. There it was: the whisper of fire I'd sensed earlier when she disparaged Fenix. While I could appreciate a passionate female, a creature with a spine, bark, *and* bite, it didn't matter. None of us would be here long enough to enjoy her spirit.

If anything, that fire would make our situation more difficult.

Because already her absence affected me—and that was a fucking problem.

Hazel took her scent with her, but it still lingered, still toyed with my heightened senses—my memories. She smelled like coastal air, like a bright morning and stormy seas. In my youth, I'd been assigned to a pack along the ridges of Hell's Sea of Lost Souls. My time there had been fleeting, as I'd refused to yield to any alpha at the facility, but sometimes the demons in charge took us outside to the rocky shores, worked us beside the sweeping tide, our paws swallowed by wet sand, our bodies battered by gale-force winds. In the savagery, there was beauty. The sea was wild but free, strong, resilient, and constant.

Staring out at the whitecaps, at water so deep and dark it was nearly black, had been a happy moment for me—a time when I'd realized there were more powerful forces in my world than the bastards who cracked the whip.

Now here was this reaper who smelled like that memory,

who could very well be as wild and free and resilient as the sea.

And I had to leave her.

Tonight.

Or *I* would never be free. My pack would never be free.

Declan's presence hovered at my doorway, and I finally abandoned the window, drifting over to the brick hearth, beckoning him inside with a casual toss of my head. He strode in slowly, hungrily drinking in the room, eyes darting about, memorizing every detail. Gunnar followed soon after, though he offered nothing more than a cursory sweep of the place before joining me at the fireplace, perching on the rounded armrest of the nearby chair with a shake of his head.

"Well? Do we have a plan?"

"I was about to ask you that very question," I mused, tracking Declan as the pup wandered over to the window, taking in the outdoors with the same vibrant curiosity as he had with everything else. "Do you know how to break a ward?"

The muscles along Gunnar's jaw rippled, as though clenching his back teeth. "No. We'd need a specialist. From what I understand, only the caster can dismantle their ward."

"And it's very unlikely we could hire outside assistance."

"Agreed."

"The trees are so big," Declan murmured, perhaps not intentionally aloud. His face flushed when Gunnar and I fell silent, and he finally joined us, taking a seat at the end of my bed. "She seems nice—"

"That doesn't matter," I told him. "She could be the nicest reaper in all the realms, but we were not born to serve, Declan. We have a right to be free."

"We can't kill her." Gunnar stood, fingers steepled as he paced back and forth in those too-short trousers. "At least, I have no knowledge of how to kill a reaper..." His deep blues slid to me, and I shook my head. We were made *for* reapers, and yet most of us knew almost nothing about them. My beta's lips thinned, brows furrowing in thought. "I figured as much. Whether she has the scythe or not, we can't... I mean, we could possibly overpower her physically if we separated her from the scythe, maybe force her to lift the ward—"

"I'm not torturing her," Declan insisted, his expression more serious than I had seen in quite some time. Her safety *mattered* to him—but if I ordered it, he would do as he was told.

Still, I had no interest in torturing her either, no desire to hear her screams echo through the empty halls of this house. We might have been born and bred in Hell, but we were better than demons. This pack of miscreants was better than *all* of them.

"We'll track her movements," I said before Gunnar could argue for brute force. "Research the modern world so we don't go into it blind. Wait for a moment of weakness, then exploit it. She'll leave at some point, and that will require her to pass through the ward. Everything has a soft spot, even magic."

"So, for now, we, what, *humor* her?" Gunnar stammered out. "I'm not playing fetch for some fucking reaper—"

"I'm not saying we have to make it easy on her," I told him, holding his glare until he calmed down. "Or pleasant. But we can use what hospitality she offers in the meantime. When was the last time any of us slept in a bed? Had running water? Clean clothes? Hmm?" I looked between Gunnar and Declan, who said nothing—not when the answer was so fucking obvious. "This is less than ideal. We didn't expect a ward, and we should have, but we'll adapt. It's what we do best."

"Agreed," Gunnar remarked stiffly, his arms crossed, that mind no doubt racing for a solution. Just as he drew a breath, his eyes sparkling with something important, Declan stood and held up a hand.

"Wait, wait," he started, padding toward the doorway, "do you smell that?"

My mouth watered—because I sure as fuck did, and it was the one thing right now that smelled even better than Hazel.

Raw, bloody meat.

⚜ 5 ⚜

HAZEL

Today could have gone better.

But, in all honesty, it could have been a whole lot worse. Fenix clearly treated his hellhounds like crap; maybe aggression was the best way to bend them to your will, but that just wasn't me. My mum had always said the way to a man's heart was through his stomach, while Dad had told me a well-fed dog was the most loyal. As the sun worked its way across the sky, white fluffy clouds stretched along the horizon, I intended to take both pearls of wisdom and put them to good use.

Good food, and lots of it, may just be the key in getting them to trust me.

Because I hadn't done enough to stop Fenix from abusing them, and the pack had years of demon rule at the back of their minds, skewing their perception of me.

So. An uphill battle, for sure.

But I was up for the challenge.

I planted my hands on my hips, surveying the mountain of raw venison piled up on the kitchen island. Cooking—yet another challenge to conquer today. In the last ten years, I had *watched* humans cook. Hidden on the celestial plane, I had explored all-you-can-eat sushi bars, steak houses, gastro pubs, and cupcake bakeries. Food now played a bigger role in the human social fabric than ever before. I'd sampled here and there, but stepping out of the celestial plane, inserting myself in a world that had gone on without me, always made my heart heavy.

With the pack, I couldn't avoid it anymore. Yesterday, an electrician had been out to the house with the wards disabled. He worked for ten hours, all by himself, electrifying the house, replacing wires, getting the building up to code. It wasn't perfect. He'd told me he needed to apply for more permits with the city, but I had gently erased his memory of the whole day after accompanying him out to his truck, parked miles away on the last bit of useable road on the property.

Accidents happened in this line of work, and the memory alteration spell had been one of the handiest in my arsenal. While I felt a bit guilty each time I toyed with the inner workings of a human mind, sometimes it was necessary; no one needed to know we were out here, inhabiting this overgrown manor. The wards hid us from the world; I couldn't allow for any witnesses in the meantime. We had electricity, and that was what mattered.

Now I just needed to learn how to use all the fancy kitchen appliances I'd swiped from department stores a few days ago, which had involved popping out of the celestial plane inside the store, grabbing the item in question—i.e. every piece of furniture in the house—and dragging it out of the mortal realm and into the ether. From there, it was just a matter of teleporting it all back into the house. Still, even for a reaper it was no small feat, especially the larger, more cumbersome kitchen pieces. Refrigerators had come a long way since the thirties, and the touchscreen dials on the stove certainly necessitated an adjustment period.

The espresso machine might as well have been a spaceship, honestly, but at least it came with an instruction manual.

I nibbled my lower lip, still surveying the bloody clump of meat. Best to stick with the basics, probably. Meat, vegetables, bread. Totally manageable. The cooking show I'd streamed this morning said I should season and sear the meat first.

Oh. Wait.

I needed to trim the fat off, right? Eyebrows furrowed, I leaned in, trying not to inhale the scent of raw deer flesh as best I could, and tracked the streaks of white through the red. Okay. First that. Then season. Then sear. Then…

"Damn it." I straightened and flicked my braid over my shoulder, toes tapping on the old checkered kitchen tile. The recipe had called for an outdoor grill—and lots of butter. The latter sat in the fridge, amongst the other basic necessities the internet had told me to acquire, all of which I'd swiped from a grocery at three this morning. But I didn't have a grill.

Rounding on the spot, I padded over to the high-tech stove, hands clasped behind my back, and scrutinized the dozens of little touch options. Could I… grill on this thing? Did a grill pop up from somewhere?

I pressed a button and something slowly climbed out of the back of the stove.

Nope. That was a backsplash. I pursed my lips. Was frying in a pan the same as grilling? Would I ruin the deer carcass if I did that?

Why was this so stupidly complicated?

Out of the corner of my eye, green and orange beckoned

me home. There sat the head of celery and the cluster of earthy carrots with their green tops, the perfect sides. Maybe I should start with them. I sifted through the carrots, separating them, fiddling with their leafy heads. Boiling vegetables certainly hadn't changed since I was alive; at least I could still do that without consulting the internet. Easy.

I'd barely gotten the stainless steel pot filled halfway when footsteps echoed out in the hallway, and seconds later in stormed the pack. I shut off the rushing water and set the pot aside, lips parted, ready to ask them how they wanted their meat cooked—rare, probably—when all three beelined straight for the kitchen island. Behind me, warm, hazy late-afternoon sunshine spilled in through the huge windows that ran the full length of the wall, each pane topped with stained glass florals. Oak cabinets lined the room, uppers and lowers, storage plentiful but seating limited. I'd planned to set up dinner in the formal dining hall through the swinging door— but the boys had other ideas.

A chorus of growls, snarls, and snorts erupted as all three snatched up whole cuts of venison and ripped into the bloody meat. My nose wrinkled.

"Uh. Oh. Okay." I held up my hands to settle them—*them*, three of the most gorgeous men I'd ever seen in this life and the last, chowing down on raw meat. The savagery excited me, the noises throbbing low in my belly, but the blood smeared around their mouths, dripping down their chests, sort of ruined the hot guy allure. "Gentlemen, if you could just…"

Wait. Two seconds.

Ugh.

"Do you want me to cook that for you?" Obviously not, but it felt worth asking. "I had a… recipe…" More snarls and heavy breathing answered, with Knox gnawing on the biggest piece. "It's a garlic, parsley, and butter recipe… for steaks."

Yeesh. Gunnar and Knox continued wolfing down their meal, not slowing even a little at my offer, but Declan stopped, lowering about a quarter of the chunk he'd initially snatched to the counter, his mouth bloody.

"Sorry, Hazel." Butterflies rustled to life in my belly at the way he said my name, as though his lightly accented voice was the dawn, rousing them from sleep. I swallowed hard, trying to both focus on him, on his velvety tenor, his bee-stung lips—that faint lilt might have been Arabic, but I couldn't be sure—and the actual words coming out of them. "We usually eat it raw."

"Right." *Gross.* "Sure." I nodded, struggling to find something nice to say about a raw meat diet—because he was clearly trying to connect with me while the others seemed content to pretend I didn't exist. So, despite the smell, I flashed a smile and nodded to the venison in his hand. "Probably makes things a lot easier, I guess."

A memory cut across my mind's eye, so visceral and real that it knocked the wind out of me. My first home-cooked meal, the one Mum had given me complete control over from start to finish: shepherd's pie. Cooked for my parents and for Royce. The smell of raw pie crust and salted mash and slow-roasted beef tickled my nose, made my mouth water. Royce's eyes, green and beautiful, kind, staring at me from across the table as he shoveled forkful after forkful into a mouth that was always laughing. His lips later that night, illuminated by moonlight as we said goodbye at the rickety gate.

"I want that pie every Sunday for the rest of our lives."

He'd kissed me while Dad poked his head through the curtains at the front window, his insistent knuckle-rapping shooing my fiancé into the night.

An air strike had taken me out in forty-three.

Royce survived to storm Berlin after the Russians.

Even though he had returned to Surrey, lived the rest of

49

his life there and married a sweet girl and had twelve grandchildren, they had allowed me to reap him when he died.

Lung cancer three years ago.

Those eyes.

That red hair.

The shepherd's pie.

I licked my lips, shirking the memory with a shake of my head and a clearing of my throat. They came and went, snippets of my human past. Not often these days. I had done a good enough job detaching from Royce's world in the last ten years, constantly reminding myself that I *wasn't* human anymore—that I had no right to walk among them, to *feel* as they felt.

But tonight, with the scent memories painfully fresh, I felt. Deeply.

Disappointment. For the first time all day, it tickled my belly, tightened my throat—disappointment that I couldn't cook for my hellhounds, that I had lost that connection already.

"Yes, but raw never changes, you know," Declan insisted, his honey-smooth words shooing away the last remnants of my past. "It always tastes the same." He wiped his mouth on his shoulder, smearing blood on the too-big T-shirt. "I would be interested in trying what you had in mind... the, uh, parsley butter. Sounds delicious, Hazel."

He liked to say my name. I suddenly felt *that* instead of the disappointment, his satisfaction warming my cheeks, even when Gunnar snorted noisily. A quick glance in his direction showed the beta hellhound picking fatty white streaks out of his venison cut, still shirtless, his bare, sculpted chest splattered with blood. Knox, meanwhile, chewed and ate and ripped flesh without breaking his focus on Declan and me, his gaze dark and hooded—unflinching, unreadable.

Unnerving.

I fidgeted with my nails, knees threatening to buckle under the weight of it all.

"Well, all right then." I rolled my shoulders back and zeroed in on Declan again. If only one of them bothered to give me the time of day, then I would take it and run. "I haven't done much cooking in a while... I might be a bit rusty."

"And I've never cooked at all," the hellhound admitted as he rounded the island and headed straight for me, the meat in his extended hand like he was offering me the most bizarre present I'd ever received. "But I would like to try, if you'll let me... If you need the help, that is."

"Of course. That would be great." Relief washed over me as I took the gnawed venison cut, needing both hands to his one to hold it. His cautious little smile made my butterflies take flight, flitting around my belly, the beat of each wing drawing something both unfamiliar and welcome out of me. The offer of *help* threatened to make me cry; already I could see why Declan had been my first connection in Hell. Not only was he outrageously attractive, but he was sweet too.

Of course, it could all be manipulation—catching more flies with honey than vinegar and whatnot.

Abruptly, a few of those butterflies nose-dived into oblivion.

In life I'd tried to see the good in people, but after ten years of reaping every sort of human, I knew better. For now, best keep my guard up. Declan *could* be as sweet as he made himself out to be, or he could be a pawn for the alpha who hadn't stopped glaring at me since he'd charged out of his crate.

Holding Declan's venison out in front of me, I looked between the other two hellhounds in the kitchen. "Do you want me to cook yours, or—"

Gunnar snarled and shook his head, then tore into the last of his meat as if I might steal it right out from under him. Knox, on the other hand, carried on eating without acknowledging me whatsoever, which was great.

Just great.

"What are these?" Meanwhile, Declan had gotten away from me, loitering in front of the stove now with a stalk of celery in one hand and a carrot in the other. "Do you eat these?" His nostrils flared, chest stuttering through a curious sniff. "Are they the parsley and butter?"

Manipulation or not, his inquisitiveness plucked at my heartstrings. "No, they're sides for the meat. Just something complementary."

I kept an ear out for the other two once I turned my back and joined Declan at the counter. He trailed his nose along the length of the unpeeled carrot, dirt hidden in its grooves, then snorted when the fuzzy green tops tickled his nostrils. I held back my smile, not wanting to make him self-conscious. Genuine curiosity was just such a beautiful thing, and if this wasn't an act, I'd hate to see him lose it.

Because Declan was my *in* with this pack—that much was clear.

Gunnar was a wild card, someone who I could probably force into a conversation with the right prompting.

Knox... I looked back as Declan tossed the carrot aside and focused on the celery stalk. His alpha remained at the head of the island, hands bloody, eyes hard and almost pure black, that enormous frame filling the room like the biggest kitchen I'd ever seen was still too small for him.

I sighed softly. Knox would be a problem.

A crisp *crunch* tore me away from the brooding alpha, and a giggle slipped out before I could stop it. Declan had chomped off half the celery stalk, bottom first, and had the same horrified look on his face that I'd had when I first saw the trio dive into the raw venison. When our eyes met, his features morphed from disgust to, well, a sad attempt at a smile.

"It's great," he mumbled through a mouthful of half-chewed celery. His mouth said one thing, but his eyes screamed the opposite. "Really just... exceptional. Delicious stuff."

"Okay, so no to the celery." I plucked the remaining half stalk from his hand and pushed the rest across the counter with my elbow, grinning. I then dumped his leftover venison hunk in the cold pan on the stove, my hands bloody. "Noted. Let me just find the recipe for the venison, and we'll try to make something that's *actually* good."

"M'okay," the hellhound forced out, clearly battling to keep that enthusiastic expression in place. The second I left the kitchen, he was spitting out that celery—hopefully not on the floor.

"Garbage is under the sink," I whispered with a wink, willing my hands clean with a flicker of magic. "Be right back."

I felt his eyes on me as I hurried toward the kitchen door, that bright, curious gaze soon joined by two others, all three palpable and somehow distinct. The hairs on the nape of my neck stood on end, and when I slipped into the hall and went for the first-floor sitting room to grab my tablet, I realized that whole encounter had happened without my scythe.

We could be civil, apparently.

The thought of which—*finally*—put a bit of pep in my step.

And a smile in my heart.

Through our combined efforts, Declan and I had proven to be, at best, mediocre cooks. The venison had been a little overdone. The seasoning could have been more aggressive. The carrots had turned to mush. But my sweetest, most interactive hellhound ate every last bit of it—even licked his plate clean—all under Knox's watchful eye.

As soon as we'd started following the recipe on my tablet, Gunnar had bailed, having finished all his raw meat, but the pack's alpha stayed through everything, not saying a word but watching my interactions with Declan like a hawk.

Not a demonic hawk, mind you. Knox's looks were darker than a demon, more primal, perhaps even ominously ethereal. As we cooked, I'd swallowed my discomfort, suffering through his relentless black gaze on me for the sake of seeing the task to the end. And now, hours later, I was glad that I did, because it had taught me a few very important things about at least one of my hellhounds.

Declan took orders well. He did whatever the recipe called for, but only after I read off the instruction or asked him to. The hellhound looked to me for *everything*, then completed the task diligently—perfectly, even. It had proven my initial read of him correct: eager, thoughtful, and thorough. All traits Alexander had told me you wanted in a hellhound.

That and staunch loyalty. This evening's cooking endeavor had given me some confidence that Declan would excel once we started our actual training, that we could work together as a team. Of course, there was still time for him to prove me wrong, to rip the rug out from under me and show his true colors. They all had that chance, and while at the end of the first day I felt gingerly optimistic about our potential, I kept my guard up all the same.

Because after cooking, the boys had gone back to the silent treatment. I had taken the trio on a tour of the house, from the basement cellar right up to the rickety attic with holes in the roof. As the sun dipped below the horizon, setting late this time of year, I'd shown them the grounds up to the tree line—the gardens, the overgrown walking paths, the ruins of an old caretakers cottage, the field where we would soon practice tracking, retrieval, and the sit-stay-come routine Alexander had drilled into my head. Neither Gunnar nor Knox had looked too thrilled about any of it, but every now and again Declan had shot me a trying smile.

So.

That was something, right?

After the tour, I'd let them be, and the pack disappeared up to their floor without so much as a backward glance. Although I could have dipped into a little magic to tidy the kitchen, I cleaned it all by hand, right down to scrubbing the countertops, all of them stained with something somehow resistant to soap and elbow grease. Standing in the doorway now, admiring my work, it was hard to see what had actually been done over the last hour; despite my efforts, a layer of grime clung to the whole house from top to bottom. I let out a defeated huff.

Gut job. Everything needed to go at some point, but unfortunately for the pack, their training took priority. But in time, I would get it up to snuff. They deserved that... Hopefully.

With my scythe resting on one shoulder, I drifted from the kitchen to the foyer, then up the stairs toward the second floor. It had been an age since exhaustion touched me, but tonight, in the settling darkness, it made every step labored, my eyes heavy, my cheeks sore from forced smiles and one-sided conversations. On the landing, my free hand went to my hair, loosening the base of my braid in front of the dusty window. The woven white locks peeled apart as my hand worked its way up, my reflection captured in a glass pane speckled with dirt. At least the muck was on the outside. Like today, it could have been worse.

In the distance, an endless sea of red cedars danced in the breeze, their pointed tops swaying to and fro. A peaceful summer night met my absentminded staring, just as quiet out there as it was in here. I glanced at the staircase branching off from the left of the landing, up to the pack's floor. Maybe it was a little... *too* quiet?

So, instead of going right, I went left—into pack territory. To give them some breathing room, I had set up my quarters in the right wing of the house. Even though I didn't *need* to sleep, I could, and I had allowed myself a room with a bed, a little table to set my antique record player on, a closet to hang my black wardrobe in. The pack had more than me, and in my mind, that was the way it should be; they needed more than me, on this mortal plane and the next.

Ruffling my hair, a mass of unruly white that spilled halfway down my back, I paused at the top of the stairs just to listen. The nightly exhale of the house responded, the foundations groaning, the walls sighing. But no hellhounds.

Declan's room was the first in the corridor; it sat dark and empty. I frowned, scanning the whole space, just as capable seeing in the dark as my pack. Nothing. With a firm grip on my scythe, I hurried down the hall to Gunnar's room, to the bookshelves I'd filled with tomes that I'd hoped at least one of the pack would appreciate.

Empty.

Fear crept up my spine. In the time I had taken to diligently scrub the kitchen, had I missed an escape attempt?

Had they played me?

With that in mind, I sprinted to the open doorless frame dead ahead, then stumbled to a halt a few feet inside Knox's room.

Because there they were.

My pack.

My boys.

Fear released me from its grasp, giving way to exhaustion once more. My whole figure sagged at the sight—at Declan sprawled out across the end of the king-sized bed, still wearing that bloodstained shirt, an arm thrown over his face as he snored softly. Up against the ornate wood headrest, Gunnar slumped, head hanging, thin lips slightly parted and brilliant blue eyes closed, an open book in his lap.

Here they were.

Even my scythe weighed on me tonight. I took it off my shoulder, holding it in both hands, letting it hang in front of me as I surveyed the dozing pair. They each had their own room, but they had ended up here.

They'd wanted to be together.

I should have realized...

Unshed tears blurred the dark bedroom, and I blinked them back with a sniffle. My presence felt like an intrusion into a deeply personal moment between the pack, and I stepped back, watching, trying not to cry, only to pause when moonlight glinted off a pair of eyes in the shadowy corner. I stilled, blood running cold.

Knox had repositioned the furniture, dragged the armchair into the corner next to the fireplace...

So he could face the door, I realized.

So he could stand guard while his pack slept.

His massive frame of pure muscle dwarfed the chair, his posture rigid, his expression masked by that wild hair, the thick beard.

But his eyes said enough. I faced him without a word,

imploring him to see that I wasn't Fenix, that I was *good*. If I had a black soul, a cruel soul, I couldn't reap. I would have been in Hell, on the list to reincarnate as a demon.

My goodness probably didn't matter though. His eyes slid to my scythe, and that highlighted the issue between us. I possessed the ultimate weapon—period. I could end all three of them in a second.

I brought my scythe back to my shoulder, keeping one hand wrapped tightly around the yew handle. No way would I walk these halls without it—not yet. A reaper wasn't dead, but we weren't alive either. We were the right hands of Death, a creature unlike any other. Knox couldn't kill me if he tried, but he could wound me. *Hurt* me. Tear my flesh, rip out my throat. Paint the walls with my golden blood, then do it all again the next day when my body regenerated.

The scythe was my safety guaranteed—my *power* guaranteed.

Hellhounds were domesticated, sure, but only in comparison to their rogue counterparts, the true hounds of Hell. Compared to Earth's shifter community, the trio before me was *wild*.

And I hated that I needed my scythe to keep them in line, but there was no way around it yet. Without trust, as much as it pained me, I'd have to remind them of my nuclear bomb every chance I could.

Silent as ever, Knox sunk deeper into the floral armchair, a menacing shadow watching over his own. Even if he never said a word to me, I understood his concerns—because I had concerns of my own.

Only there was nothing I could do to address them tonight. Probably not tomorrow either.

Maybe not even this first month.

So I left.

Halfway down the hall, the weight of the day quashing me

brick by brick, I paused and looked down at the chipped wood floor, feeling all of *it* again after a day of distraction.

The crushing loneliness.

The emptiness inside.

That's what we reapers were: empty.

And nothing in this world, the next, or the beyond, was ever going to change that.

6

DECLAN

This was paradise.

Why couldn't Knox and Gunnar see?

A clear blue sky above, unfettered sunshine warming our skin. A balmy breeze and fresh, real, honest to goodness grass at our feet. Scents galore—and not just brimstone and shit and death and blood. A house of our own. A territory that stretched to the horizon in every direction, safe and secure inside a ward. Birds in the trees, chattering. A circling hawk. Creatures with no connection to Hell, not a demonic inkling in their body.

A gorgeous reaper whose smile could set the world on fire.

A reaper who smelled like fresh dates and agarwood bakhoor, who made the three of us four—who sent my mind back to a time of endless roaming and full bellies and kind eyes. A time gone by. Fleeting. Painfully fleeting. A time my packmates no longer remembered, probably, but I still felt in my marrow, still longed for in the dead of night after the nightmares ripped me awake.

This was what I imagined Heaven to be like, smell like,

feel like. This place was everything we had always wanted, reaper or not, and it was their own stubbornness that kept my fellow hounds from realizing it.

But I would follow them wherever they went, even if it was away from here. If—more like *when*—Gunnar found a way around Hazel's ward, I'd walk with them into the great wide world, dragging my feet, a new hole in my heart. Because they were my brothers, my soulmates, my pack. The two stubborn assholes meandering about in front of me now, trailing too far behind Hazel, squinting in the afternoon sunlight, were a part of my essence.

No other pack had so openly accepted me before.

No one else had loved me.

I had the scars to prove it.

Their unwillingness to see paradise, however, was starting to get under my skin. We were only a day into our training as Hazel's hellhound pack, but already their inability to make nice had me ready to scream.

I didn't.

Because I understood.

Gunnar and Knox had suffered through the same fucked-up bullshit as I had in Hell. Knox came away wearing those tribulations on his skin, flesh that usually healed from any injury slashed and torn and scarred. Gunnar carried it all on the inside, whether he'd admit it or not—I saw the agony in both of them. I'd recognized kindred spirits from the moment we were introduced through the bars of our kennel, me on a leash with that spiked collar cutting into my throat, Knox and Gunnar on the other side, sniffing me out, more intimidating in looks than any alpha-beta pair I'd suffered before.

Their spirits were softer, however.

I owed them my life.

And if I could, I'd pay that debt by making them realize

just how fucking great we had it here—even if we *were*, technically, collared again. Hazel was our new mistress. She hadn't given us physical collars like my last reaper had, but the ward was basically one giant collar, and it would be a monumental battle to make my packmates look beyond that.

Although nearly impossible to see in the mortal realm, if you caught it at *just* the right angle, you might detect the rainbow-colored shimmer of the magical barrier. Gunnar and Knox would test its strength as soon as Hazel left us to our own devices, but I just appreciated its beauty—the security it offered.

She offered it too—security. Beauty. I'd sensed it the moment our eyes first met in Fenix's cage, and that feeling amplified here. Hazel had fed us *twice* today already, at regular intervals, my hunger properly satiated for the first time in years. Between our meals, we had learned about modern human devices; Hazel had taken us to the third-floor study, the only room on that level without a hole in the roof, where she introduced us to television, computers, and touchscreen tablets. The importance of understanding the souls we were set to reap had been stressed, and much of this month would be dedicated to studying modern-day humans.

The electronic devices were supposed to help with that, each one like a library that fit in the palm of your hand. It had been a little difficult to navigate at first, but overall the devices were fairly intuitive. Gunnar picked it up the fastest, as usual, while I preferred watching human behavior on the television.

Knox just tapped around distractedly on his tablet screen, staring Hazel down like he wanted to eat her.

Not that I could blame him, really.

Alphas were born, not made. Knox came into this world with instincts none of us could ever touch—and one of those was the intense *need* to protect his pack. Although Hazel had been nothing but good to us so far, her voice sweet, her smiles lovely but short-lived, we all struggled to shake the shackles of our pasts.

How could you trust anyone after a lifetime in Hell, raised under the boots of demons?

Hazel guided us down a gentle slope, drifting toward the forest, her scythe resting on her shoulder. She looked rather delectable in her thigh-length trousers, her flowy black shirt; when the wind hit her just right, that loose fabric stretched taut over her curves, eliciting an intense physical interest through our pack bond. When she finally stopped, her feet bare and toes wiggling in the grass, her eyes narrowed against the sunshine, so did we. Knox set the distance, while Gunnar and I stood behind him.

Without realizing it, all three of us had crossed our arms, a united front of fuck-you to the reaper before us. Frowning, I dropped mine to my sides, fidgeting with the fit of my new trousers—jeans, Hazel had called them. A gust of hot air toyed with my hair and ruffled Hazel's white waves, her scent catching and carrying toward us. A quick glance at Gunnar, then Knox told me my packmates would have preferred to be upwind from her. Their nostrils flared, same as mine, and a renewed desire twanged through our bond. Gunnar's jaw clenched briefly as he looked back toward the house.

"Today we're going to work on recognizing a soul signature on the celestial plane," Hazel told us, planting her scythe's wooden staff into the earth. When she released it, the most powerful weapon in all the realms stayed upright on its own, its hooked blade carved with ancient glyphs I'd never understand, somehow both terrifying and beautiful. Hazel caught her wild hair in both hands, smoothing it back and out of her face as she said, "A freshly departed soul will be different than the souls you've seen in Hell. It feels different.

Smells different. Behaves different. So, it's important to recognize that.

"If we pass the final trials, you will be responsible for tracking souls without me and holding them until I can reap. Lunadell is substantial. Bigger than anywhere I've ever reaped. Hundreds of humans die each day—from disease, murder, accidents, and old age. One reaper, even with their hellhounds, can't manage that. It's paramount that you can scent, track, and contain souls on your own and as a pack."

My last reaper had kind eyes too, a warm presence despite his ice-cold flesh, but I hadn't had the chance to train with him; my old pack turned on me the second we left Hell, eager to pick off the perceived weakest link before we even started. I welcomed the challenge now, the chance to prove my worth, no matter how the others felt about doing what was asked of them.

"The first step in all of this is accessing the celestial plane," Hazel remarked, snatching up her scythe and huffing her hair out of her face with a frown. "No matter what anyone has told you, *you* are celestial beings—like me, like demons, like angels, like the old gods. You can travel the celestial roads through worlds, and you can do it without me." She cleared her throat, cheeks pink—perhaps from the wind, perhaps from the way Knox and Gunnar looked at each other like she had just given them their key to freedom. "I mean, the ward works on both planes. So. You know. It's not... Never mind. Let's practice going in and out of the plane together."

For once, my packmates had no objections to her command, which didn't surprise me. Going from the mortal realm to the celestial was a valuable skill that we had never been taught by our demon trainers; this was our first taste of *power*, so of course Knox and Gunnar wanted to take advantage of it. We reaped on the celestial plane. Lost souls waited for us there—and I wanted to help them. Finding my way onto it, through it, was essential.

Not easy, mind you, but nothing in our lives ever was. Hazel insisted that, as with all magic, it was about intention. Wish it, want it, *think* it hard enough and your mind can make anything happen.

My mind was just a little too interested in a certain reaper, unfortunately, which meant I was the last to eventually access the plane. We spent the better part of an hour on the attempt, Gunnar sliding from one realm the other first, then Knox, then finally, *finally*, with the assistance of all three and Hazel standing downwind from me, I crossed over.

Like walking through a blast of cold air, stepping from the mortal realm to the celestial plane was disconcerting at first. Inside, the world was so much brighter, every element in sharper focus, yet somehow muted too. Scents lacked their potency. Twittering birds turned to whispering echoes. The wind through the piney branches no longer sang but hissed. Standing there with my pack, a little light-headed now that I'd mastered a smidgen of magic, I decided the mortal realm was just *better*. More exciting.

But the souls were here, and so was Hazel, the smell of honeyed dates and incense the only one *not* dulled—which made it all the more overwhelming. The others sensed it too; Knox and Gunnar immediately found a position upwind from her, at a distance, and I followed in their footsteps so that I could concentrate.

Scythe planted at her side, Hazel produced a brilliant white orb between her delicate hands, molding it, perfecting it, making it round and thick. Recognition rippled through the pack bond; she had created something to mimic a soul signature.

And she'd been right—it *was* different to the human souls

we had seen in Hell. Brighter, stronger, it hummed with an enthralling energy that the damned lacked. It buzzed and trembled, full of life, like the essence of humanity still clung to its depths.

"Every soul feels different, but this will give you an idea of what to expect," Hazel told us softly, her hands circling the orb almost with reverence. It possessed one other element the damned souls didn't: it smelled like... like... I stepped closer, entranced, racking my brain for a word to describe it and coming up short. Sweetly scented, it invoked relaxation and calm.

"It smells like an orchid," Hazel said, her eyes on me when I shook myself free of the orb's hold. "Humans associate the flower with death. It's sometimes used at funerals, the symbology... They don't understand *why* they associate it with us, but they do. Most souls smell like this, the sweeter fragrance of the flower, but there are some that smell like sour meat, just like some orchids smell absolutely foul. Those ones usually have a one-way ticket down, if you know what I mean."

Knox and Gunnar exchanged another silent look, and in that moment, Hazel deflated just a little. She really was trying to connect, and there was nothing worse than trying your fucking hardest only to be met with outright rejection. Been there. Done that. And it felt like shit.

"This one smells wonderful," I offered, leaving my packmates behind and closing half the distance between us. The orb cast an unearthly white glow across her already deathly pale skin, and it made her look like an angel—like the *queen* of angels, especially when she smiled.

"Doesn't it?" Hazel slowly brought her hands up, sniffing the orb as one does a wildflower, her eyes closed, expression peaceful. "I'll never tire of that smell."

Would I ever tire of making her look like that? Making her *feel* whatever she did right this second, lifting her spirits?

The connection between us should have frightened me—my desire to please her even more so. But I had bonded with Gunnar and Knox in an instant, the feeling mutual, so why couldn't I do the same with Hazel?

"Today we're going to work on a simple find and retrieve exercise," Hazel informed us, slowly rolling the orb between her hands, suddenly more like a ball than a floating celestial lookalike. "You'll practice tracking and herding, two really important skills for hellhounds. Find the orb. Bring it back. Easy." She wet her lips, her hair rustling in the muted breeze. "Losing souls isn't an option, okay? We're going to save everyone we can, because they all deserve judgment."

Gunnar chuckled coldly, watching her as if Hazel were just like all the other fuckwits we'd had to deal with day in and day out in Hell. His expression made me bristle, my irritation streaking through our pack bond like a jolt of lightning. My packmates' stares burned into the back of my head, both of them catching my slip, and I squared my shoulders, almost daring them to say something. Gunnar was being an asshole for no reason; he deserved to *feel* it.

Hazel's hand had wrapped around her scythe in the few tense beats of silence that stretched between us, no doubt sensing the friction, maybe even preparing to intervene. Scratching at the back of my neck, I forced an impish grin and nodded.

"Got it. No lost souls. We can manage that."

Knox's stare intensified; I was talking too much today, acting like I ruled the pack, like I had the right to speak for them. But no one else was saying anything, and it was getting awkward.

Besides, I loved herding. Of all the tasks I'd been trained in, *this* was my favorite.

Without a word, Hazel launched the orb into the forest, and all three of us tensed. Senses on high alert, every muscle in my body stilled as I tracked the target. It arced over the pointed treetops—cedars, Hazel had called them—and then vanished beneath the canopy. That lovely sweet scent trailed after it; if we were in the mortal realm, the elements would have swept it away like the tide, but the celestial plane seemed to offer a buffer, which made the smell of a human soul linger. It called to me, to us, interest and focus and energy pulsing through our bond, crashing together, threatening to whip us into a frenzy. Heat rose between me and the others, the shift calling us home. My tensed body shook at the effort to remain on two legs.

No one moved.

All this energy flowing under the surface, a riptide ready to drown us, and no one did a damn thing. Painful as it was, I turned my back on the forest, on my goal, and met Knox's dark gaze. Head lowered, I asked permission without uttering a word, and nothing about his stiff, looming figure suggested he had denied me.

If he didn't tell me *no* in the next ten seconds, I was doing this.

I mean, he had ordered us to humor the reaper, so neither of them could fault me.

And if Gunnar had something to say, let him. All this silent judgmental staring was so unlike him it was starting to freak me out.

I'd learned that today—*freak me out*. Thank you, human television program, for expanding my vocabulary already.

A slight, painfully subtle thrust of Knox's chin toward the forest was the permission I needed. Giddiness exploded in my chest, and I stripped down hurriedly, not wanting to ruin the clothes I'd found this morning in a neatly folded pile at the end of my bed—my *own*, personal, just for me bed. The garments were new and clean and soft, and smelled faintly like Hazel, and I just…

How could they not see this was paradise?

Seriously.

I dropped from two feet to four paws in a flash, my senses even more heightened in my hound form. A soft gasp escaped from Hazel, and I briefly zeroed in on her flushed cheeks, the graceful bob of her throat when she swallowed. Her scent threatened to take me, as powerful as the current that we three felt before a shift, but I forced myself away, refocused on the task at hand.

Somewhere in that forest was my prize. Today, it was just an orb, a snippet of magic conjured by Hazel—there were no stakes. But as I charged toward the trees, I imagined it was a wayward soul, a human spirit lost and frightened, confused to find themselves dead and alone in a world that looked just like their own, but also somehow completely different. That was the proper mindset, right?

Fear and I were old friends. It had been an unwelcome bedfellow, a constant in my life from the day I opened my eyes. Deceased humans likely felt fear when they woke up in the celestial plane, and that would drive me.

It should drive the others too, but time would give them their motivation. Nothing I said or did now would make a difference.

The grass underfoot, so lush and full and green, grew sparse as I crossed the tree line. Unfettered sunshine vanished, cutting through the canopy in scattered golden beams. The forest was thick but maneuverable, the earth beneath my paws unlike anything I had experienced before. Rocks and mud and roots touched me, welcomed me, threatened to trip me up. Birds scattered before I reached them, on a whole different plane from me yet sensing my presence anyway. We four were invisible to the mortal realm now, but the creatures of these woods seemed somehow aware that they were not alone.

I paused briefly, heart beating slow and steady, and nosed at the air. That smell couldn't evade me, even as it zigzagged around trees and punched through branches. It called to me somewhere to the left, and left I went, tuning in to the sharp buzz moments later. The landscape would take some getting used to, but that was part of the challenge, surely. A challenge I faced head-on, and within minutes, after only a few twists and turns and one backtrack, I found it.

The wayward soul.

Hovering between two saplings, shimmering, trembling.

Mine.

Once I had it in my sights, there was no shaking me. I chased that damn orb through the forest, completely in tune with it—eventually outsmarting it, cutting it off at the pass, flying between a cluster of non-cedars and tackling it to the ground.

Much to my surprise, it was hard. Not just a glowing ball of light, but a physical being too. I had never touched a soul before; this was a surprise. But I swallowed my shock, up on all fours, nudging the orb in the direction I wanted.

Which was…

Damn it. Everything looked the same in here.

Until I found her, smelled those ripe dates, sensed her warmth, and then finding my way back home was a breeze. The orb tried to lose me a few times along the way, but I guided it with a snap of my teeth. While it had no ankles for me to nip at, I improvised, and soon enough we burst out of the trees and into the open field again, where I was met by a beaming Hazel. She whooped and clapped her hands together, radiating delight in a way that made my chest rather tight, my heart unnervingly full.

"Declan, that was amazing!" she praised as the orb drifted back to her palms. "You did so good!"

No one had ever told me that—except for Knox and Gunnar. Outside of my ragtag pack, no trainer or breeder or hound had ever complimented me. I shifted back, my furless flesh coated in sweat, the heat of the shift rolling off me, and then speared a hand through my hair with a bashful smile.

"It was easy," I told her, unsure of what else to say, how to respond to such blatant praise. In fact, I wasn't even sure I had a response in me for that sort of thing, so I took a note from Gunnar and deflected instead. "Let's do it again."

Hazel and I looked to Gunnar and Knox in tandem, hers a cautious inquiry, mine a pleading stare that resonated through our bond. I wanted this for them—to experience the hunt, to relish a victory, to hear her praise.

To *feel* it in their bones as I did.

Much to my surprise, Knox broke first. He peeled off his shirt, then jerked down his still much too small trousers, and Gunnar followed suit. They shifted without acknowledging Hazel, but each greeted me with a friendly mouthing, their teeth brushing over my hands, their tails slowly flicking side to side.

I sat at the bottom of our trio; I could expect no more than teeth and growls and a dismissive greeting, but they always gave me so much more than that. Shifted back into my hound form, their affection thrummed openly between us, and I nipped at Gunnar's legs with an eager yip, then nuzzled beneath Knox's strong jaw with my ears down and my tail whipping back and forth. My alpha responded with a forceful push toward the forest, his head held high, his cropped ears up and alert.

Hazel hurled the orb underhanded this time, and it looped up, then zipped out like an arrow, straight and true, blitzing across the forest before disappearing within it.

We were off in an instant, Knox leading the way, Gunnar and I fanned out behind him, paws thundering, dirt flying, birds scattering.

And, honestly, I couldn't imagine a better way to spend the day.

7

GUNNAR

"Why do the male humans fight over the one female?" Declan asked from the other end of the couch upon which we both sat. It was one of many new pieces of furniture that had slowly but steadily filled the crumbling estate over the previous fortnight. The pack and I would retire to Knox's room shortly after sunset, snoozing the night away knowing that we wouldn't be attacked, startled awake, or beaten in our sleep, and come first light, our reaper had procured something else for us to mark up with our scent.

Most of the pieces were *for* us, filling our bedrooms, the study, the kitchen. Not that it mattered. In time, I would break her wards, and no amount of furniture or regular meals or fresh, temperature-regulated running water could change that.

I did enjoy learning about modern humans, however, and there was no better study of them than through the television. While I favored the morning talk shows and the evening news, reality television shows, usually featuring competitions for love or money, were rather telling.

And damning, honestly.

Because between the disastrous doldrums forever bleating on the news and the idiots prancing about on these competition shows, obviously the human realm was a fucking mess.

"No idea, Dec," I muttered, stretching my arm out along the back of the couch and then crossing my ankles on the little wood table before us. On the screen, two would-be alpha males, shirtless and rippling with muscle, struggled against their restraints—a group of other males attempting to prevent the fight, apparently—while a lone scantily clad female drunkenly scream-slurred their names. I chuckled when she hurled her drink at the skirmish, the glass missing by a mile and shattering somewhere off camera. Really. A fucking *mess*. Demons *had* to be pulling the strings behind these shows. Lust. Wrath. Pride. All that we watched during our morning study sessions suggested the seven deadlies were alive and well. Add a bit of booze and it was a damn parade.

"I mean"—Declan shuffled upright, on the edge of his seat, unable to pry his gaze from the ridiculous scene unfolding—"they are fighting *for* her, are they not?"

I grunted. "Seemingly, yes."

"Why don't they just share her? We've seen she enjoys both of them—"

"Because humans don't share mates."

The hairs on the back of my neck shot up when Hazel's melodious voice drifted into the room, her scent hitting shortly after. While Declan looked back, swift and eager for her attention, ever a pup smitten, I continued to stare at the large flat-screen. The fight had been broken up without an ounce of bloodshed.

Boring, but predictable. From what I'd witnessed on these

shows over the last fourteen days, it was all peacocking—males jockeying for position and production staff charging in to stop it before anything really happened.

"So, why don't humans share?" Declan asked. Our reaper seldom wore shoes around the property, but the telltale click of those tiny heels across the hardwood set every inch of me aflame. I stiffened, withdrawing my feet from the coffee table and crossing one leg over the other instead, then pointedly ignored her when she materialized in my peripheral view.

Shoes meant she was going out, as she did every morning. She'd cross the ward, temporarily opening it to pass, and seal us in behind her. Unlocking my clenched jaw, I focused on breathing through my mouth and glaring at the television screen, as if either would make her scent any less potent. White waves tumbled over her shoulders when she rested her elbows on the back of the couch, her ease in the pack's presence grating.

Her mere *presence* grated honestly, the effect she had on me, on the others, worsening with time. Physical desire throbbed through the pack bond whenever she popped into our sphere, though Declan was the only one to really act on it. In these moments, I preferred to ruffle her feathers if at all possible. Knox, meanwhile, sat across the large room on the lone high-backed armchair, enormous black headphones over his ears, eyes intent on the tablet in his lap like the rest of us didn't exist.

A part of me had started to suspect there was something more between her and us. Possibly a fated bond, given our intense, almost immediate attraction.

But that *also* didn't matter. Soon we'd be gone; I could never be a slave to my mate. *Never*.

"Humans just... don't share," she said after a long beat, the show on a commercial break, one of far too many. "These days, it's all about monogamy. Two people, one relationship. That's been the norm for a long time."

"Huh." Declan faced the screen again, fiddling with the fabric ties of his trousers. "Strange."

Hazel brushed her hair behind her ears, unleashing another wave of sweet alyssum in my direction. That hair... I ought to just shave it off, if only she ever slept deep enough to risk it.

"And why is that strange?" she asked. Sensing an opportunity, I twisted in place and caught her gaze, those eyes brown like maple syrup and flecked with gold.

"Because," I crooned back at her, fingers itching to toy with the ends of that white mane, "hellhounds almost always share their mate. There's usually only one, maybe two, females per pack, and she belongs to *us*, not just *me*."

Color flared in her pale cheeks, bright and satisfying. Declan could glower all he wanted from the far corner of the couch, but getting under her skin meant I had an iota of control in this tedious situation we found ourselves in, and I wasn't about to stop anytime soon.

"Tell me, reaper," I said, inching toward her and cocking my head to the side, "have you ever been shared?"

"*Gunnar—*"

"That's a very rude question," Hazel said coolly, cutting off Declan's outrage as she straightened and backed away from the couch. "And, frankly, it's none of your business."

"No, no, of course not," I purred at her retreating figure, grinning as she stalked over to Knox with her little hands in fists. Power reclaimed—albeit only temporarily, for the sway of her hips was just a little too pleasing to my sensibilities.

Declan's irritable huff had me rolling my eyes, big and overexaggerated, just for him, so he knew what an absolute *child* he was being about all this. Just as he opened his mouth, courage swelling along the invisible tether between us, Hazel gasped in horror.

"*Knox!*"

I scrambled for the remote and muted the television, the air crackling as it always did before a bout kicked off between our reaper and our alpha. Hazel ripped the tablet from Knox's hands, yanking out the headphone cord in the process. Moans and groans and skin slapping suddenly echoed throughout the room, and Hazel stabbed at the screen, silencing it just as swiftly.

Unfazed by her outrage, Knox tugged the earpieces down so that the large leather headphones coiled around his neck, his sea of wild black hair clamped beneath.

"Perhaps you can explain the nuances to me," he said dryly, "but are humans required to urinate on their mates?"

"Oh my *God*." Hazel tapped around the tablet with a trembling finger, shaking her head. "The internet is so vast, one of the greatest resources humankind has ever seen, but trust a *man* to go straight for the porn."

"You told us to study humanity," Knox drawled, his smirk immune to her withering look. Declan rearranged himself on the couch to peer back with me, both of us watching the scene unfold from across the room next to the cracked windows, the half-full bookcases.

"What's porn?" my packmate asked, his innocence almost endearing. Hazel's blush sharpened, and she cleared her throat.

"It's nothing—"

Knox snorted. "*That* wasn't nothing, I can assure you."

"Actually," I said, fingers flying across my own tablet—for the internet *was* a vast and invaluable resource, after all. "Porn, short for pornography, is a print or visual material containing explicit—"

"It's not relevant!" Hazel snapped. "You guys aren't here to watch *porn*."

"You see, I beg to differ," I said, lazily scrolling through an article listing the top ten free pornography websites at my disposal. "Sexuality is a prominent part of the psyche for *all* creatures."

"Except for angels," Knox added with a scoff. "Celibate bastards."

"Tell me, Hazel..." She flushed bright pink again when I said her name, for besides Declan, we said it so rarely. I rather enjoyed saying her name *because* it flustered her—and not because I savored the taste of sweet alyssum on my tongue as I enunciated every syllable. With her full attention on me, I locked and tossed my tablet aside, lifting a curious, suggestive eyebrow. "Does Death fuck?"

Her gorgeous mouth opened and closed a few times. Did she ever consider the fact that her horseman employer might have a sexual appetite? Could he even touch a lover without killing them? Certainly worth a bit of research, if only to satisfy the morbid curiosity now blustering about inside me.

"You guys are ridiculous," the reaper said at long last, her words slow and deliberate, like she was trying very hard to stay civil. "Just study like you're supposed to." She held up a hand, eyes flashing dangerously when my lips parted, about to purr something lecherous at her. "And *not* porn. Study behavior. If a soul dies during sex, it's not like they'll still be *having* sex when we reap them, okay?"

My silent smirk and Knox's cool chuckle were the nails in her coffin. Jaw clenched, the lines of her heart-shaped face sharp and annoyed, Hazel turned on the spot and stormed out, announcing that she would be back for lunch. I pushed my sleeve back to check the wristwatch I'd found on my bedroom's nightstand this morning. Lunch was always at noon, on the dot. Three hours to go. As always, she'd leave us to our own devices until then.

Where did she go in the mornings? Did she attend to work—or pleasure?

One of these days I'd root out all the gory details.

One of these days, I'd find a way around her wards.

Until then, I tracked her and her routine, from which she seldom varied. Gone in the morning, but not before feeding us breakfast, back for lunch. Training in the afternoon. Dinner. The nights in this old manor were quiet; I'd found her sitting in her quarters a few nights ago, staring at the wall, scythe across her lap, expression somehow both vacant and aching.

Like one of these electronics on sleep mode.

I hadn't shared that particular incident with the others just yet, not until I knew what to make of it.

But I much preferred her like this, animated and vibrant. At least her fire didn't make me feel... off.

"That was uncalled for," Declan remarked tersely after the little click-click-click of her shoes disappeared downstairs. "Clearly sex makes her uncomfortable... You didn't need to push her."

I snorted and unmuted the television. "Puppy love."

"Being a decent hellhound is *not* puppy love," Declan snapped, his frustration simmering through our bond. We both glanced back when Knox chuckled again, not coolly or dryly this time, but affectionately, a sound reserved for Declan and Declan alone. After all, Knox and I respected each other, loved each other, but we were brothers. Near equals. Confidants. Declan had a way to go before he reached that level in the pack dynamic.

The pup still needed to prove himself.

"Puppy love indeed," our alpha mused, and Declan threw his hands in the air with a low growl. My packmate crawled across the couch and snatched the remote from my hand, then cranked up the volume, the humans all friends again on the show and taking shots together. He then settled back in his seat with a huff, arms crossed, stewing.

I rolled my eyes and picked up the tablet, returning to the article on top porn sites, then tapped the first link.

Might as well see what all the fuss was about, right?

❧ 8 ❧

HAZEL

"What are you doing?"

Three weeks in, I knew my pack in all their forms, on two legs and four.

Declan—a shaggy silhouette with a pointed nose and tail. On two legs: a compact Adonis with full lips and cropped hair, muscular in definition but not bulk.

Gunnar—angular and sleek muscle and short fur. Leanest of the bunch, wiry and long-limbed like a dancer.

And Knox... In his human form, Knox was primordial, a god risen from the deep, hell-bent on drowning the world. He was dark and brooding, burly, tall as a mountain and twice as unyielding. As a hellhound, he took intimidating to a whole new level, his body just raw, untamed muscle, his head huge, his red eyes harsh enough to make even a reaper quake.

He radiated alpha energy, and it didn't surprise me that he fought with every other alpha hellhound he had met in his life. They probably attacked because they felt threatened, their position in jeopardy against a superior being.

But here, *I* had to be alpha, only I refused to scar him like the others had, refused to add more harsh lines to his wild beauty.

My grip tightened around my scythe as we squared off now at the edge of the property, without an audience for the first time, the ward shimmering beside us. I had no interest in scarring him, sure, but to find him *here*, sniffing along the ward, around the spot I usually came and went from, was damning—and I couldn't just let it slide. Usually the pack stayed in the house when I went out, so to find him nosing at the far reaches of his territory, deep in the cedar forest on the celestial plane, concerned me.

I'd been trying so hard to make this a home for them, to make them comfortable with me, to keep them on track so that when the trials arrived in a little over two months, we would *all* be ready.

With the ward sealed firmly behind me, the sun at its noonday peak, I planted my scythe in the ground and crossed my arms, waiting for an answer. Not that Knox or Gunnar gave me real answers yet, preferring to poke and prod, to wheedle me until I reacted, but he couldn't hide behind Declan's sweet disposition here. I'd asked a direct question, and we weren't leaving until he answered.

Slowly, the hellhound raised his snout from the base of the ward, its faint rainbow shimmer a constant reminder that he and his boys were firmly trapped in here with me, whether they liked it or not. My eyes narrowed when I spotted it: a hole in the ground, like he had been, what, trying to dig his way under? I bit the insides of my cheeks; the ward extended through all the realms. Casting it before their arrival had taken more out of me than I cared to admit, but the safety of my pack *and* the surrounding human community had been paramount. No one was getting in or out, no matter how deep they dug, no matter what they threw at the near-invisible barrier.

And it pissed me off that Knox didn't seem to get that.

We stared at each other for a painfully long time, his red gaze locked on mine, and I refused to blink first—not even when my eyeballs dried out. I'd blinked first with him too many times already. He didn't take me seriously. Neither did Gunnar, but Gunnar didn't call the shots with the pack—Knox did. And if the trio were to ever get completely onboard with me and the job they were made for, then Knox was my in.

I knew it.

He knew it.

And all that knowing had us locked in an unspoken back-and-forth, the pair of us dancing around power, control, and alpha territory for weeks now.

Stubborn bastard.

That red glare seared into my brain, even as Knox shifted from beast to man in the blink of an eye. His hellhound form was already tall, nearly as tall as me, but he shot up another few feet on two legs, naked and sweaty, an ancient god of chaos and darkness and beauty. I forced my gaze up, pointedly avoiding the chiseled body that drove me to distraction after every shift. Even at a distance of four, maybe five feet, his heat touched me, licked across my skin and pooled in my cheeks. I needn't look to see his muscles, slick with exertion and ridiculously taut, each one prominent, on display, like he had just finished an intense workout. His chest heaved briefly as he breathed through his nose, enormous hands in loose fists, that great heart of his no doubt hammering its slow, steady drumbeat.

Ugh. Stubborn, *gorgeous* bastard.

"I'm patrolling my territory," he rumbled, his voice a smoky, gravelly rasp that I felt in my low belly, both arousing and frightening. I lifted my chin, unwilling to let him see how every damn part of him affected me.

83

"No," I said, pleased that my voice didn't shake. "No, you're trying to find a way around the ward." There was no point in pretending I didn't see his attempt. I pointed to the gaping hole in the forest floor beside him. "Are you trying to dig *under* it?"

He blinked back at me, his expression, his stance, giving nothing away as he said, "I smelled something suspect."

"Bullshit."

We fell back into one of our usual stare-offs, tension simmering between us, my whole body reacting to him in ways I wished it wouldn't. Finally, I sighed and coiled a hand around my scythe.

"Knox, we need to get on the same page here—"

"My pack is not yours to purchase," he growled, his gaze like steel as it swept over me. "Just because Heaven paid Fenix's price in gold... means nothing to me."

I shook my head. "I don't... *own* you."

"Bull*shit*," he parroted back to me, mirroring my previous inflection with uncanny precision. "We're your property, your pets."

"You know, some humans love their pets more than other people." I bit the insides of my cheeks, wishing *that* hadn't just tumbled out unchecked. Knox rolled his shoulders like he was gearing up for a fight, his expression suggesting I'd slapped him. Clearing my throat, I forced a strained smile. "Sorry, I just... You're *not* my pets. I was just saying... Look, we're supposed to be a team here—"

"We'll never be a *team*," Knox snarled back at me. "We'll never be more than that scythe, just a tool at your disposal, and no number of niceties will make us forget."

I gripped my scythe harder—for support, mostly, when I realized I was shaking. "Knox, I'm doing my best."

The hellhound glowered at me briefly, mouth twisted in a sneer that I felt in my bones.

"I've no interest in your best, *reaper*." He took a half step toward me, his size more pronounced, his heat suffocating. "All that matters to me is my pack and their security, their freedom. You… are inconsequential."

Oh. Wow. *Inconsequential* hit harder than I'd expected. For his stature, Knox seemed like the type to bellow whenever anger struck, all animal fury and blinding rage and bulging muscles. But he was calm as he said it—*inconsequential*. Calm and stiff, the word a perfectly aimed dagger. The quiet, decisive strike hurt a lot more than some shouting display, and my vision blurred temporarily with unshed tears. I sniffed and blinked them back, hardening every part of me so that a single word from this hellhound could never strike so deep again.

"I'm not inconsequential." Suddenly that was my least favorite word. I kept my voice even as best I could; this was about him and *his* issues, his baggage. "And neither are you, or Declan, or Gunnar. Maybe they made you feel that way, like you're all just *dogs* that should be kicked, that should live in a filthy kennel on scraps of nothing until you're needed, but that's not how I see you."

He had trimmed his beard recently. I blinked, only just noticing the neat edges, the smooth, almost glossy sheen— like he had taken a comb to it. Strange, to fixate on such a little detail. *That* was inconsequential, not me, not him, not the others. All of this mattered, and the sooner he realized we were in this together for a greater purpose, the better.

Knox risked a full step toward me, his dark gaze sliding from my scythe to my face, my hair—briefly down to my chest. Swallowing hard, I held my ground and stiffened when he stole another few feet away from us, so close now that his earthy, musky scent struck like *he* had slapped *me* with it. Conflict ripped across his features, unreadable and beyond frustrating to anyone who didn't share that intrinsic pack bond with him.

And then it all stopped. The tension humming between us, around us, fell away when he let out a sharp breath and relaxed.

"I don't care what you think, reaper," he said, his words low and harsh. "I just don't care."

And with that, he shifted back to a great black hound, eyes red, every inch of him dismissive, then padded away into the forest. Trembling, I lilted to the side, into the thick, smooth trunk of a red cedar. That... hurt. A lot. Pain sliced through me like it never had as a reaper, disappointment coursing through my veins, a cold, cruel fist twisting in my gut.

This time, when the tears welled, I brushed them away with a scowl. I could have just let them fall—there was no one around to see.

Except there was.

Through a dense patch of foliage, I spotted an enormous black shadow and brilliant red eyes. No longer dismissive, they watched me, silent and unblinking. My head tipped against the bark, throat exposed, wordlessly asking for a damn truce already.

Knox disappeared amongst the trees a few moments later, and my knees finally gave way. I sunk to the forest floor, staring at the hole he'd dug at the base of the ward, and then closed my eyes with a long, weary sigh.

I couldn't sit in the woods and wallow about *inconsequential* forever. The pack needed lunch. Sticking to a schedule was one tactic Alexander had recommended to get everyone used to what was expected of them, and so far, I had adhered to our house schedule as rigidly as I could.

Except today.

Today I was late as I dragged myself up the stairs to a manor whose physical flaws still glared at me whether I acknowledged them or not. Over the last three weeks, I'd prioritized food, comfort, and *things* over cracked windows and cobwebs and missing roof shingles. But if the guys were just going to ignore me, hate me, then maybe I could take a few days off and fix the damn thing already.

No. That wouldn't solve anything. Running from my problems had never been my way, and I wasn't about to start now just because a certain alpha was being a difficult asshole.

Scythe over my shoulder, I pushed open the unlocked main doors, a gust of humid August wind ripping through the foyer. Dust flew up with it, then slowly trickled back down when I kicked the doors shut behind me. My feet were ready to veer left toward the kitchen, but the uneven plunking of piano keys stopped me dead in my tracks.

Someone had found that old, woefully out of tune grand piano in the glass-enclosed sunroom on the far side of the first floor. I'd played when I was human and had decided to keep the instrument that came with the house for the nostalgia. Only I hadn't plucked up the nerve to lift the hood and play anything more than the odd note or two. Whoever sat at the bench now was experimenting with pitches and pedals.

My gut told me to just go to the kitchen and make lunch.

But my feet did a one-eighty, veering right instead of left, and carried me all the way to the sunroom. Back to me, Gunnar sat at the piano, tapping at various keys, the notes painfully familiar. A little smile graced my lips when he played the F-sharp chord, probably without even realizing what the combination of keys produced. To his credit, he had swept the dust off, those black and white teeth the cleanest things in the room.

I could have backed away, allowed him this moment of sweet solitude within the warm room, sun beaming through the dirty windowpanes in all its golden glory. Instead, I slipped inside and listened for a few moments, watching him work it all out for himself, his expression serene but focused. The hellhound was so smart, maybe even *too* smart for someone like me, but it was what I most admired about him. Declan's eagerness to learn paled in comparison to Gunnar's natural ability to just *do*.

Still, for all that innate talent, it would take him ages to master the piano.

"I can teach you to play," I offered, and his long, lean fingers clunked down heavily across a plethora of keys, the tuneless, mismatched combo swelling up to the domed ceiling. He didn't jump or flinch; I hadn't surprised him, but he suddenly wore the same tension that Knox always did across his face, in his shoulders, when they all interacted with me. That insane sense of smell, ears that could detect a mouse skittering across the attic from here—Gunnar had known of my presence, probably well before I'd walked through the door.

But he hadn't acknowledged me.

And that made the cold hand in my chest clench just a little tighter, the sting of Knox's brusque dismissal flaring all over again.

Gunnar gave an inch with the slight turn of his head in my direction, the planes of his handsome face smooth, his sharp cheekbone catching the sun, and I responded by taking a full mile, marching over and planting my scythe next to the piano, then perching beside him on the bench. The hellhound scooted over so that our bodies only touched briefly, thighs aligned, arms nudging, and the separation threatened to hurt me all over again if I let it.

But I wouldn't.

I couldn't. Not if I wanted to survive all this.

"It's out of tune," I told him, scanning the keys. "It'll sound better when I fix it."

Not that I knew anything about tuning a piano, but magic was a beautiful gift—once I figured out the appropriate kind.

Gunnar tapped absently at a black key—D-flat, C-sharp. I licked my lips, hating the silence, hating the off-tune melody punctuating it like he was counting down the seconds until I left.

"My grandmother taught me how to play before she died, then Mum took over," I said, pushing through the awkward air around us. Both of my hands found familiar keys, fingers working on muscle memory as they played the first few chords of "Heart and Soul." I had a recording of Bea Wain singing it in 1939, and there was nothing more uplifting than unconditional love crooned to the tune of an old big band.

Heart and soul, I fell in love with you heart and soul…

Heart and soul, the way a fool would do, madly…

"I… I can teach you." The notes faded slowly, my hands in my lap. I shrugged. "You know, if you want."

Gunnar and I looked at each other at the same time, and his nostrils twitched like he was breathing me in—not unusual for a creature with an exceptional sense of smell, but I still fidgeted self-consciously, wondering what I, a dead thing reanimated, smelled like to him. His royal blues roved my face briefly, up to my hair, down to my hands, before he faced the piano again with a shake of his head.

"No," he remarked as he rolled his shoulders back. My heart plummeted at that one word, only to flutter softly back to life when he copied the chords I'd just played, making a few little errors along the way. Gunnar rested his fingers over the keys when he finished, glancing at me out of the corner of his eye. "No, I prefer to teach myself."

I battled back a smile. Finally—a rejection that wasn't about *me*. I could work with that. "Do you like music, then?"

"It's soothing," the hellhound murmured as he trailed a finger over the keys, not pressing hard enough for any to sing off-key. "Something you can do alone, enjoy alone, but you aren't *really* alone."

A lovely sentiment, that. Gunnar had always struck me as the hellhound with the sharpest mind, one that raced and worked, always spinning beneath the surface. Here, as I studied his defined profile, those cheekbones *begging* for my caress, I wondered if music made the waters still—just for a little while. Even if the notes were out of tune, music offered respite to a mind that was always *on*.

And that was beautiful.

He possessed even more depth than I'd thought.

"I think I have something you might like," I said after listening to him replay the same few bars I had, this time nearly perfect. "One second."

My gifted magic allowed me to teleport anywhere I imagined. It was how reapers whipped across cities to collect new souls, with Death's somber voice slithering around their skull. He gave a name, a location, a cause. We always knew what we were walking into, and as I gripped my scythe and teleported upstairs to my bedroom, I was suddenly acutely aware of how silent it had been in my head for the last few weeks. Technically I was off duty to train my hellhounds, but I missed Death's sullen, seductive rumble—because his whisper gave me purpose, set my heart on fire, made me feel *alive* in the afterlife.

Anyway. It didn't matter. I'd hear him again soon like we had never been apart, and I could already envision my pack staring at me like I was insane, listening to the voices in my head.

Voice. Singular. Perfect in every way.

But that was an issue for another day. Today, I grabbed my record player, which sat tucked away in its leather case, unused since I had moved into this house. I'd stolen the 1930s phonograph in New York and had lugged it around with me for ten years. Case tucked under my arm, I also nabbed my box of old records, records I had collected—stolen, popping out of the celestial realm in shops and human homes just long enough to take what I wanted and vanish—over the years.

Hands full, I barely managed to get ahold of my scythe, but when I did, I disappeared from my empty bedroom and materialized in the first-floor sunroom in the time it took to blink. Gunnar jumped this time, my sudden return probably more than a little jarring, and I shot him a grin as I set my scythe against the piano, then dumped the rest on its closed lid.

"I loved listening to the phonograph when I was alive," I told him, popping open the case and lifting the needle. "We didn't have the technology of today. Music wasn't a given, you know? And I know you can listen to it on the laptop or the tablet, even the TV, but I just think there's nothing like a record." With the player set up, I thumbed through the box of vinyl, then plucked one of my favorites from the bunch. "The sound is just... better."

Gunnar stood while I slid the disc out of its worn cover, his hands clasped behind his back as he strolled around to the other side of the piano, as if to keep his distance. He watched me almost warily, like he didn't trust the machine—or, more likely, *me*—but then I dropped the needle and out purred a young Bob Crosby and the Rhythm Boys, and I *had* him. The hellhound's jaw went slack as a jazzy big band tune filled the room, so rich and pure, so extravagant, its sound unlike anything the music industry had to offer today.

Wanting to let him explore, to sate his curiosity without a reaper over his shoulder, I grabbed my scythe and drifted back. As soon as I left the piano, Gunnar darted around it, his head cocked as he watched the record spin.

"I need to get started on lunch," I told him, not wanting to delay this afternoon's retrieval training because of this—bonding over music. Gunnar ignored me, utterly transfixed on the record player, and I nodded. Right. Back to silence. But at least this wasn't a purposeful silence. *He* hadn't called me inconsequential. I headed for the door, already working through the recipe for today's midday meal, when suddenly—

"Hazel."

He said my name.

I stilled. Death always set my heart on fire, sure, but that flame paled in comparison to the inferno that erupted when Gunnar said my name.

"You're right," he said, his hushed voice barely rising over the music. When I glanced over my shoulder, I found his hands pressed together and steepled fingers to his lips. Gunnar's head bobbed ever so slightly to the music, that dark blue gaze still completely trained on the record player as he added, "It really *does* sound better."

Grinning, I left without a word, *inconsequential* the furthest thing from my mind at last.

※ 9 ※
DECLAN

"Are you ready?"

"Absolutely." I'd never been so ready for anything in my whole life. Every inch of me hummed with a quivering energy that made me antsy, maybe even a little distracted. After all, it was an honor to be the first of my pack chosen for some solo training outside of the ward. Standing next to Hazel at the far reaches of the property, magic shimmering before us, moonlight slanting through the trees all around us, every damn emotion struck me—all of them fleeting, one not overpowering the other. Fear. Excitement. Anxiety. Dread. Elation.

One month ago, we had arrived in crates. The last time anyone had ever put their hands on me in anger, with malice in their eyes and cruelty in their hearts, had been thirty long days ago, and under Hazel's care, I felt like a completely different hellhound. I moved with a new confidence, never cowering, never whimpering, never hiding behind Knox as I'd done from the moment I first joined this pack. Our routine gave all of us structure, a sense of purpose. The others still refused to bow to our reaper's commands, but they went through the motions during the day with Gunnar sniffing around the ward at night, searching for an out.

Yet shortly I *would* be out. Hazel, dressed in a flowing black robe, her hair free and dancing beneath an unseen hand as we stood on the celestial plane, had chosen *me*. Before Knox. Before Gunnar. I would be the first to reap, a thought that both deeply thrilled and greatly worried me.

Because what if I came back tonight and the others despised me. They had congratulated me halfheartedly when she'd shared the news over this morning's breakfast, but what if jealousy had sunk its ugly claws in deeper and deeper as the day went on?

What if they kicked me out afterward, attacked me just like every other hellhound?

Beyond all that, what if I failed her?

What if I *couldn't* reap?

What if I lost a soul?

Her cool hand found my forearm, startling me from all those intrusive, pesky thoughts. She squeezed, smiling warmly up, and the thoughts evaporated, leaving a strange but welcome calm in their absence.

"One soul tonight," she told me, her skim luminescent under the moon's glow, her eyes more gold than brown. "We'll collect her, take her to Purgatory, and see that she walks through the gates. That's it."

"Simple," I said with a forced chuckle, my attempt to sound totally *chill*—as the humans say—a complete failure. Hazel gave my arm another squeeze, and when she released me, her touch lingered, my skin prickling where her fingers had once been, where her palm had pressed.

"You're ready for this, Declan," Hazel insisted, brows twitching up when our eyes met. "Trust me... You're going to be great."

No one had ever anticipated greatness from me before. They predicted miserable failure no matter what I tried, and as Hazel sliced a thin opening into the ward with her scythe, I struggled to accept her optimism.

"Come through," she beckoned, stepping into the opening, crossing the ward as it billowed like curtains around her—curtains made of the strongest magic, a shimmering forcefield. Given the difference in our heights, I had to duck to pass through the tear she made in the protective boundary. The forest on the other side was much the same as it was in our territory: cedar trees and uneven earth and rocks and dirt and reaching roots. Hands in my pockets, I watched her reseal the ward; her scythe could destroy, but it could also mend.

The others feared it.

I respected it.

"Okay, so, take your clothes off and shift for me," Hazel instructed, her tone—sweeter and gentler than usual—a welcome tonic for my nerves. Clearing my throat, I dragged my soft grey tee over my head and handed it off to her, trying not to focus on the fact that when she folded my clothes, her scent intermingled with mine, the combination heady, distracting. Trousers came next, leaving me naked in the early-morning shadows.

Hazel glanced down briefly, her gaze trailing across my body, then looked *very* far up, lush lips pressed together as she held out a hand expectantly for the rest of my clothing. Her cheeks colored like they always did at our nudity, and the same pleasurable thrill vibrated through me, my cock swelling somewhat with interest. The sensation would undoubtedly ripple through the pack bond, my feelings broadcasted to Knox and Gunnar no matter the distance.

Although I could have ogled her blushes for hours, I shifted as quickly as I could—for her sake, not necessarily mine. Down on four paws, I inhaled the forest, filling my lungs with cedar pine and cool, damp earth. Hazel set my clothes in a neat pile next to the ward, then crouched, not needing to bend all that much given my hellhound form stood nearly as tall as her.

"Come here, Declan," she urged, scythe in one hand, the other outstretched toward me. I padded over without hesitation, my slowly wagging tail a dead giveaway for how she made me feel, whipping even harder when we touched.

Her scent dominated all others around me, made stronger when she ruffled her hand through my fur. Given this was the first time she had been physical with my hellhound form, it was a wonder I stayed standing. But I managed, stiff and enamored, allowing her to stroke my snout, trace my ears, scratch down my back. When she finished her slow, deliberate exploration, she stooped before me, our eyes locked, and smiled.

"Now, let's collect this wayward soul, shall we?" She licked her lips, her smile blooming at my low whine of agreement. "Yeah... She deserves peace."

The reaper drifted closer, her hand finding a place on my back again—and then the world went black.

Despite the constant pressure between my shoulder blades, her hand never once abandoning its post, panic sliced through me. While the darkness came and went in a matter of seconds, it felt like an eternity, a trudge through the deepest pits of Hell—pits I'd been dragged down a few times in my life, collared and leashed, sneering demon trainers at my heels and unimpressed former packmates always a breath away from snapping at me.

As quickly as the black took hold, it vanished. The world came back into startling focus, a little too bright, a little too sharp on the celestial plane. A looming grey building replaced familiar cedar trees, a dozen new scents assaulting me at once. We stood on uncomfortably hard ground now—cement, concrete, *something*. A fountain occupied the center of the courtyard, a handful of humans loitering around it, cast in both shadow and light, cloaked in night, illuminated by the trio of white lights atop metal poles.

Trembling, I looked up, and huge green letters blazed back.

St. Bartholomew's Children's Hospital

Right. Hazel had said… She had told me…

I couldn't remember. Couldn't *think*. Sirens wailed in the distance. Human chatter and night creatures and rubber squealing over roadways and the hum of a dozen nearby lights, all varying in intensity, paired with cigarette smoke and body odor and unnatural smells—

"It's overwhelming," Hazel murmured, and once more she calmed me. Her hand massaged the thick base of my neck, and her voice washed over me with the firm constancy of a rushing river. I nosed at the unwelcoming ground, hard like the front steps of our home, and then looked back at her —for support, for guidance, for reassurance that unlike every fucking scenario I'd faced in the past, there wasn't an enemy just *waiting* to jump out of the shadows and tear into me.

She shuffled closer, scratching behind my ears. "Take a minute and calm down. The human world is… a lot. Lunadell is big, and big cities are busy. Sensory overload. I get it. We'll go when you're ready."

The only figure in my life who had ever successfully calmed my frayed nerves with a firm touch and a few softly murmured words was Knox.

And now Hazel.

Focusing on the lines of her porcelain face, somehow both soft and sharp, a dichotomy of clashing beauty, settled my thundering heart. Examining the streaks of gold in her eyes, twinkling in a sea of warm brown, stilled my racing mind. Her hand on my back, her touch gentle and constant, grounded me in the moment. Slowly, our surroundings became clearer, and the storm of noise dimmed.

Finally, I could see Lunadell for what it was—chaos, sure, even in the dead of night, but organized in its own way. Towers soared all around the hospital, the lights muted, the stars hidden. The figures smoking by the fountain appeared half-dead, staring blankly, the lone coupled pair muttering to each other in strained whispers.

"Are you ready?"

Her voice was the sweetest music, yet it possessed an edge here. Reaping was her life now—her duty. From all I'd seen and heard, she took said duty very seriously; yet another trait I admired in her. I glanced her way, then managed a gentle *woof* to let her know I was, in fact, ready for this. Her smile sent a rush of heat from my heart to my belly, threatening to drift lower the longer she touched me.

"Good." My reaper stood and pointed her scythe toward the main doors. "Let's go collect our soul, then. She's just passed on."

The differences between the celestial plane and the mortal realm were few and far between, subtle in their own ways. Besides the fact that we could walk amongst humans totally invisible while on the celestial plane, one key variant was the doors. All doors were open to us here. Walls and other structures held their integrity. We were still forced to climb stairs, but whether a door was open or closed, bolted shut with every imaginable lock, it didn't matter.

Hazel and I passed through the revolving main door of the children's hospital without the panels so much as shuttering. Inside stretched a long corridor, freshly brewed coffee in the air from a nearby vendor, the overhead lights whiter than reaper's flesh. We bypassed a desk for inquiries, the woman behind it in all pink reading a worn paperback. Shops stood empty to the left, one filled with books and plush toys, another with snacks and clothes. Not a human in sight, though I could sense them throughout the five stories of the massive, albeit drab, building.

On the celestial plane, humans had a strange vibration. *Almost* that of a soul, but much duller.

Hazel stopped just before we reached a blue metal door, upon which was plastered a sign with black stairs and a strange humanoid figure walking up them. Her thin brows furrowed, body tensing, and I stiffened when her delicate fingers coiled tighter around her scythe's staff. Another soft, inquiring *woof* had her shaking her head, and she strode back down the hall, her little heels clicking with every hasty step.

"I just… I felt something," she said distractedly, scanning the corridor with a frown. "Like a ripple in the plane. I… I've never felt it before. Did you…?" The reaper glanced back at me, her confidence noticeably shaken. "Did you feel something?"

I felt *everything* here, but probably nothing unusual for my first time out of our secluded territory. So, I shook my head, and she turned away with a curt exhale, then marched back down the corridor like she was searching for something. I padded after her—then stopped, dead still, heart in my throat, when I heard it.

The wretched wail of a newly departed soul.

Every muscle froze as the sound skittered across my body. It settled between my ears, in my heart, calling me home with a stronger pull than Hazel's training orbs ever had. A newly exposed soul vibrated with the intensity of the sun, crashing over me, dragging me into its orbit so that I *couldn't* ignore it even if I tried. It shuddered and shook, the air alive and crackling all around us, an explosion of sweetness ripening in the air. Orchids, Hazel had said. New souls smelled like orchids.

My reaper still seemed distracted with whatever had caught her attention; a new soul must have been old news for her by now anyway.

But to me…

It was brilliant and potent, crying out to me despite the fact I couldn't see it anywhere nearby.

She had done an exceptional job training us, our reaper. Over these last weeks, Hazel had produced orbs for us to hunt and track and corral. In the here and now, instinct took over. I knew what I was supposed to do: hunt, track, and corral.

But Hazel was distracted with something concerning enough that it still bothered her. I should probably follow, stay at her heels, assist in any way possible.

Only I couldn't tear myself away from the soul's cry. Both soundless and deafening, it swelled and swelled and swelled, threatening to burst inside me if I didn't *do* something.

So I did.

I charged through the blue metal door and took the stairs four at a time, my paws seldom on the tiled ground for long. A part of me hated to leave her, but she *had* stressed the importance of catching and keeping all departed souls. We couldn't lose them—not one. Not if we could help it. And while she was otherwise occupied, I *could* help it, and so I would.

The soul's song grew louder, fiercer, with every floor I climbed. Not the second level. Not the third either. I bypassed the fourth, then paused on the fifth, ears up, alert, every cell in my body on fire. No. It wasn't here. I'd gone too far. Snorting, I padded down the steep steps between levels, then sprinted through the next metal door to the fourth floor.

A sign over a nearby desk told me all I needed to know: *Intensive Care Unit*.

I'd heard that combination of words recently—from the television, in fact, from that doctor program where they seemed to fuck more than they healed.

A commotion erupted from a room to the far right: beeping, shrieking, shouting. Above it all, the soul.

I might have been the smallest hellhound of any of my packs, but I was still quite large. Intimidating, most likely, to a recently departed soul. So while I moved with purpose, I also practiced patience. I slowed my approach, padding toward the door with a group of humans crowded in front of it. A woman screamed and wailed into her mate's chest. He looked on into the room, tears streaking down his cheeks. Humans who smelled like those two, whose presence hummed on a similar frequency, clustered around them— family, perhaps. I threaded through the group and paused in the open doorway.

Pink curtains over the windows. Drawings on the walls— poorly made, most likely the work of a human child. An enormous stuffed bear on an overturned chair. Flowers in glass containers. Humans in—what were they?—*scrubs*, hurried but calm. One beating the chest of the small, frail girl in the bed, tubes coming out of her arms. The machine beside the bed had been featured on the television shows; its somber, low-pitch note, no longer beeping in a steady, constant rhythm, always told the viewers that the patient had died, the doctors had failed.

But still they tried.

Admirable, these humans.

And in the end, not my concern.

For there was her soul, this frail girl with a mane of black curls and sunken cheeks. She sat huddled in a corner in such a tight ball, like she was trying to make herself as small as possible. My heart softened immediately, for I knew that posture well.

She was frightened.

Wide eyes gobbled up the scene unfolding, the humans on the mortal plane fighting to save her, not realizing she was already gone. Slowly, that terrified gaze slipped to me and widened farther. She shrunk deeper into the corner with a wail, her little body shimmering—pale with death, but somehow still vibrant, her skin the same light brown as her mortal body, her nails stained with purple polish. She wasn't wearing the hospital dress anymore, but a beautiful yellow ball gown. She was a lovely thing, and I had but a second to react before I lost her.

Before I, a creature who had never scared *anyone*, sent her fleeing across the plane.

We locked eyes for a moment, our connection tenuous and strained, before I licked my lips and dropped low, backside in the air, tail wagging. My toes spread as I slumped forward, back bowed, the universal posture to invite another hellhound to play. Only Gunnar and Knox had ever taken me up on the offer; all the others used the invitation as an excuse to attack.

Perhaps the hounds of this realm behaved the same, because the little lost soul blinked back at me, her hands that were once so tightly clutched around her bent knees slowly lowering to the floor. My excited yip had a smile inching across her lips, hesitant, innocent, blossoming when I wagged my tail harder and whined.

She needed the distraction. I bounced forward a few paces, mouth open, tongue lolling out, then trotted to her side, all the while keeping as low to the ground as I could, not wanting to tower over her unnecessarily.

Although the little creature remained fixed to the floor, tucked snugly in the corner, at least she didn't run when I dropped to my belly and scooted to her side. She withdrew her hands, hiding them in the flourish of her yellow gown. Faintly, her old body's scent permeated the air: decay and vomit and brine. Her soul smelled sweet, like the bluish-purple weeds that dotted the overgrown gardens back at the house. Energy hummed off her, the air thick with it, with a new soul, but I focused on *her*—the human child in the yellow dress—and not the physical beckoning of her life force.

Snuffling at her dress, I nuzzled my snout against her leg, her whole being the size of my head and neck. But I made myself small, sidling closer with a low, insistent whine. When I stilled, the girl shifted in place, and suddenly there was a teeny, tiny hand in my fur. She gingerly brushed over the top of my head, and when her knees lowered ever so slightly from her chest, I seized the opportunity to shove what could fit of my head—just my snout, really—into her lap.

Her lips bore a half-smile now, her eyes glossy with tears, her cheeks slick with confusion, with fear. My tail thumped noisily against the wall beside us with every back-and-forth beat, and she exhaled a giggle when her hands found my ears.

Aren't they soft, little one? Soft and safe.

As she rubbed them, explored the tufts of black fur, I closed my eyes. I trusted her to touch me. She could trust me not to hurt her.

And in that moment, a bond was made.

The tiny creature beneath me stiffened, and I scented Hazel before I saw her. So near, so suddenly. Fear pounded through me; I had left her side—without permission—and acted impulsively on my own. I had approached a soul, my *first* soul outside of Hell, without her.

She must have been furious.

How would it feel, her rage? Would she use her hands or the blunt end of her scythe to remind me of my place?

A shuddering whimper from the girl's soul had me slowly, fearfully looking back to the door. There stood Hazel, robed in black, billowing material, cheeks a dull pink. Beautiful. To a soul destined for Hell, I imagined she was rather terrifying too—a grim reaper in the flesh.

But she wore a smile now. Slight, subtle, calm. I had tasted anger all my life; it was something every single one of my senses experienced, even at a distance. See the rage in their eyes. Feel the fury rolling off them. Hear the gnashing of teeth. Taste the blood in my mouth as I bit down on my cheeks to stifle my cries.

There was no anger here.

Only serenity.

And with an exhale, I let go, settling my snout back on the girl's lap and keeping her pinned as Hazel swept across the room. She entered my periphery like a shadow, then floated to her knees like the gentlest falling rain.

"Hello, Cleo." Scythe on the floor and just out of reach, Hazel arranged all that black fabric around her, then looked directly into those wide, terrified eyes. "My name is Hazel." She gestured to me with a slight nod of her chin. "And this is my friend Declan. We're here for you."

The floodgates opened, and little Cleo slumped into the corner, fighting against the weight of me to curl into a ball. Hazel gave her a moment to weep, then gently stroked the golden ruffles along the hem of her gown.

"Is this Belle's dress?" she asked, a question that meant nothing to me but something to Cleo, whose sobs softened slightly. Hazel smoothed the skirt out with a laugh like silk, like the flutter of the little winged birds who inhabited our forest. "Is she your favorite princess?" When Cleo nodded mutely, Hazel sat back, her pale hands threaded together on her lap. "Mine too."

"W-what's happening?" Cleo had a sweet voice, just like her scent. Quiet but confident, the odd hiccup and sniffle terribly out of place.

"Your heart stopped beating, sweetheart." Hazel picked up her scythe and planted it on the floor beside her. "It's time to go on."

Cleo's dark brows furrowed as she considered my reaper's words. Then, with a sniff, she brushed both hands over her cheeks and cleared her throat. "Did I... die?"

I studied her features intently; how wise beyond her years she appeared in just a matter of seconds. How many souls fought it—their new reality? How long did Hazel spend convincing them that they were, in fact, dead? Minutes? Hours? Days? And in that time, how many other new souls slipped into oblivion?

"Yes," Hazel remarked. "You died."

I admired her tone—neither pitying nor patronizing, she spoke with a gentle frankness that seemed to appease a weeping Cleo.

"We're here to take you to the other side," Hazel told her, "so that you don't get lost along the way. It's not scary... I promise."

Given the child's age and demeanor, the manner of her death as a withered body in a hospital bed, I had serious doubts she was bound for Hell. Instead, paradise awaited her. The thought that I—a hellhound of no importance, a runt despised by even my own mother—could help her find her way to an eternity of bliss warmed every inch of me.

"What about my mommy and daddy?" Cleo's breath hitched as her watery eyes drifted to the doorway. The human healers had stopped pounding her chest now, yet her parents remained outside, the mother's wails gut-wrenching. "They can't come, can they?"

"No, but you'll see them again," Hazel said.

"But they can't see me now, right?"

"No, not anymore."

"Can I say goodbye?"

Hazel nodded, white brows twitching up as she murmured, "Of course, sweetheart."

Gripping her scythe, Hazel rose to her feet, and I followed shortly after. Cleo sat stock-still for a moment, and then her little hand found my side. Fingers worked into my fur, and I barely felt the tug as she used me to haul herself up. Standing beside me, dwarfed by my height and the sheer volume of her princess gown, the child's soul didn't let go. She held tight to me, even as she started walking, and I followed at a dreadfully slow pace, one step for every four of hers.

We stopped in the doorway, Hazel bringing up the rear, and Cleo clung to me with one hand while the other reached out for the man holding her sobbing mother.

"Daddy?" Her hand slipped right through him, another curse of the celestial plane. Doors and humans, apparently, would never bar us again. Lips trembling, Cleo tried again, abandoning me for her parents. She stumbled through their bodies, then burst out into tears on the other side. I hurried after her, licking her tears and whining.

"Your parents love you very much, Cleo," Hazel insisted, seeming to float through the crowd of humans to join us. She crouched in front of the weeping soul, taking a moment to smooth a stray black curl away from Cleo's tearstained face. "They will miss you for the rest of their lives, but one day, they will stop crying. They'll remember the good, the sound of your laugh, the way you looked in your flower girl dress and shouted *fuck* at your aunt's wedding, in front of the whole church. They will think only of the good times, not the bad. And they will heal. It will take time, but they will. I promise you that too."

Behind us, the humans drifted into Cleo's hospital room, and it was written all over her face—she longed to follow them.

"I don't want to go," the child whispered, staring forlornly at her parents' retreating forms. Her chin quivered for a moment before she dissolved into a mess of tears again, but before I could lick them away, Hazel planted her scythe firmly to the floor, then swept the soul into a hug. From the way she cradled Cleo's head, her eyes closed, her brow furrowed, she *cared*. This wasn't just about collecting a new soul and taking it to Purgatory for Hazel; any simpleton could see that.

And it made me feel for her more than I already did.

Which, if Knox and Gunnar found out, would be a problem.

For now, I basked in it—the heady affection in my heart, the closeness we shared to soothe a broken girl.

"You're so brave, Cleo," Hazel murmured into her hair, totally focused on the soul, her gaze never once straying to me. "Braver than so many grown-ups out there. And you know who is waiting for you on the other side?" She eased away and wiped the soul's damp cheeks with her thumbs. "Grandpa's waiting, and he'll make sure you find your way too."

Cleo managed a sniffle and a nod and nothing more.

"Would you like me to carry you, sweetheart?" Hazel asked, lightly gripping her scythe. Anticipation prickled through me; I'd never seen Purgatory before, only heard the stories. Normally every new setting scared the absolute shit out of me, but from what others had said, Purgatory was just… nothingness.

Hard to be terrified of nothingness.

Cleo shook her head at Hazel's offer but still said nothing, not even as the reaper stood and adjusted her robes—robes that seemed to billow on their own accord, the air dead around us.

"Do you want to walk, then?"

Still nothing.

A knowing smile touched Hazel's lips, and she tipped her head toward me. "Would you like to ride on Declan's back?"

Cleo shot me a shy glance, and I perked up, tail wagging at the thought. *Of course, little one. Of course I'll carry you.*

Fidgeting with her enormous skirt, Cleo finally managed a slight, blink-and-you-miss-it bob of her head. Hazel scooped her up and set her just below my shoulder blades, and tiny fingers scrambled deep into my fur. She rode me with both legs to one side, neither foot dangling lower than the curve of my rib cage, light as a feather and seated like a true lady.

Hazel's touch carried more weight. Clutching her scythe, she dropped to her knees before us, gaze locked on Cleo, then pressed a hand to my side.

"Close your eyes, sweetheart," she told her. "We'll be there soon."

Teleportation came easier this time. No longer a bundle of nerves, I was so concerned about Cleo's experience with it all that when we vanished from the hospital's intensive care wing and reappeared in what I could only assume was Purgatory, I barely noticed.

Until the cold hand of nothingness crept over me. I blinked, wincing when Cleo *ripped* at my fur, her breath quickening. Grey fog shrouded the realm in perpetual shadow. Beneath my paws, a pebbled path stretched out ahead and way behind, probably to the horizon and beyond. Lampposts dotted the walkway, tall and metallic with a great white orb at their peak. The air smelled of gravel and smoke, silent as the grave until Hazel took her first step.

Her robes fluttered around her as she strolled forward, slicing through the fog, her scythe catching the lamplight and looking like the star from which it was born. Rock and dirt crunched with each of the reaper's steps, and I followed, paws quiet over the cruel earth, my pads absorbing the bite of the pebbles. Cleo wrapped her arms around my neck as best she could, hugging tight, and then buried her face in my fur. I stood straighter, walked faster, eager to get her out of here.

A short while later, great golden gates silhouetted through the mist, slowly coming into focus. They stretched up for what seemed like miles, their spired tops lost in the grey sheen. I snorted the damp earth smell out of my nose, which had Cleo looking up briefly. While the gate was intimidating for what it represented, the figure looming before it was enough to send any soul fleeing.

Or so I thought—until the fog cleared, a temporary respite inside a perfect sphere in front of the gates. As soon as we crossed into the circle, I stopped, stunned, to find myself face-to-face with an angel.

He was lovely. Tall. Olive-skinned and green-eyed, white wings that could withstand an attack from any weapon save the might of Heaven. Dressed in a white robe that mirrored Hazel's black attire, he clasped his hands together as his supple lips stretched into a warm smile.

"Hello, Cleo Avante. Welcome."

"Cleo, this is Peter." Hazel helped the soul from my back, and instead of shrinking away again, Cleo seemed instantly infatuated with the angel, her eyes wide with wonder now, her cheeks dry, her tread confident as Hazel led her to him. My reaper crouched down beside her, likely for the last time, and pushed her curls over her shoulder. "He's going to take you inside."

A part of me didn't want to let her go, but I did nothing as Hazel slipped Cleo's hand into Peter's. The angel radiated warmth, kindness, something reserved for the souls headed upward, surely. Damned souls deserved a colder reception.

The golden gate opened on its own, swiftly and soundlessly, and Cleo paused at its threshold to glance over her shoulder at us. Scythe held loosely at her side, Hazel waved. I offered a low whine and a tail wag, which made the child giggle. Peter unfurled his feathery wings to their full width, sweeping Cleo under them, and the pair disappeared into the white mist on the other side of the gate. Even if I couldn't see her anymore, I watched, squinting, *trying* my damnedest to peer into the ether—to make sure she was safe. But before I could ask, Hazel stroked a hand down my back, the world went black, and we reappeared in the moonlit forest where all this had started.

"Oh my god, *Declan*!" Hazel leapt away as I muddled through the teleportation aftershock, clarity coming for me hard and fast when I spotted her throw her hands up, scythe and all, and spin in place with a whooping cry. Somewhere nearby, birds chattered indignantly back, the morning young, the forest at rest—and interrupted, now, by a cheering reaper.

Giddiness frolicked about in my belly, and I hastily shifted from beast to man, naked and sweaty, content to watch her spin and dance forever.

Until she found her way into my arms quite unexpectedly. I caught her with a grunt, her body flush with mine, her arms around my neck, her scythe's staff pressed straight down my spine. Startled, mind abuzz with the sensory overload of *her*, I stumbled back a few paces before drawing Hazel closer, welcoming her soft curves home, my nose in the nape of her neck.

"You were *amazing*," she squealed, her head thrown back, her voice echoing through the trees. While I couldn't see, I imagined moonlight glinting in her eyes, every part of her a thousand times more exquisite than that angel. Gone was her mask of calm neutrality, replaced with a girlish glee that made me want to spin too, twirl her around so that she giggled and held tighter. Her reaper façade was so painfully obvious now; here, her voice pitched higher, lovelier, and as I clutched her, felt her hair whisper across my bare arms, I swore that she was trembling.

"I'm so proud of you," she whispered, praise that seared straight to my marrow, words I would remember for as long as I lived. "You were incredible. I knew you would be. I chose her for you, and you... you were perfect."

Tears welled, my heart full, my knees weak. I clenched my eyes shut and buried my nose deeper, breathing her in, willing her scent to tattoo across my flesh so that I would never go anywhere without her ever again.

"Thank you, Hazel," I forced out after a few beats of silence, my voice rough, my throat thick. She stiffened, as if finally remembering herself, and withdrew from our embrace with flushed cheeks and eyes that refused to meet mine. Brushing her white mane behind her ears, she positioned her scythe between us, perhaps unconsciously, perhaps on purpose, and then looked in the general direction of the house.

"You're welcome," she said almost breathlessly. She then fetched my stack of folded clothes and handed them back to me. I made no move to put them on, not wanting to miss a moment of her blushing, of her lips as they fought her brilliant smile.

"Let's go back," the reaper said with a nod to the nearby ward, "and tell the others how well you did."

I gestured for her to lead the way, and she did, walking a

few long strides ahead of me. When we passed through the ward, however, the shimmering magical wall sealed up tight behind, we fell in step together and returned to the house without a word.

Our hands occasionally brushing along the way.

10

GUNNAR

Over the last month, Hazel's daily routine had, much like ours, become clockwork.

And I made note of every minute detail of it.

Breakfast at eight o'clock. She was trying to turn us omnivorous, serving an array of cooked meats, breads, and fruits that the pack gobbled up—because why wouldn't we? Much of it tasted far better than the raw flesh we'd been raised on.

As soon as we drifted into the kitchen and settled on the stools around the island with a feast before us, she was gone. Out to the ward, which she parted with her scythe, then through the opening and into the great wide world. The reaper would return around noon for lunch; in the time between, we were expected to study human history and behavior.

Which, for the most part, we did.

Knox had actually encouraged it, and I'd always been a glutton for information; studying humanity came easy to me. The more we knew about the realm we intended to lose ourselves in, the better we would eventually assimilate.

Not that Declan seemed all that interested in assimilating anywhere *without* Hazel, his puppy love infinitely worse after their first real-world training session the other week, but, at the end of the day, he'd go with the pack. We all would.

Afternoons were for training, as individuals and as a team, the tasks asked of us steadily increasing in difficulty as the weeks went on. Then supper at six o'clock. After, the night was ours. Hazel sat in her bedroom, alone, in silence, or occasionally outside on a rickety bench to watch the sunset. Once, I'd caught her in the shadows outside the sunroom's door, slumped against the wall, listening as I played her records. Generally, come nightfall, we all retreated to our wing for a reprieve from her scent, her curves, her smile—her sweet laughter, the sound ringing in my ears even in sleep.

That was our day, every day, for the last forty. August had rolled into September, the weather taking a slight dip, the humidity cut in half and the winds fiercer when it rained. Hazel never strayed from her routine, nor did we—and that would be her undoing.

For as soon as she left us at breakfast today, a smattering of cured meats at our disposal, along with scrambled eggs and sourdough buns, I followed. Knox gave me permission with a slight nod and a flick of his gaze toward the main door, while Declan purposefully ignored the whole thing, busying himself with the new coffee maker and pretending that what I was about to do wasn't happening.

Burying his head in the sand, more like.

If we ever wanted to leave this place, to cross through the ward and get the upper hand on the tantalizing creature who haunted our—my—dreams, it *had* to be done. Her scythe was the ultimate weapon, her ward utterly impenetrable.

Except when she crossed through it. Declan had confirmed it—unwittingly, of course, his excitement about his first reap loosening his tongue. When she cut through the magical barrier, it stayed open for a set amount of time. Over the last five days, I had confirmed it for myself, following her out to the edge of the property, scrutinizing every second of her comings and goings.

Scrutinizing *her*.

But never mind that.

Sometimes, Hazel sealed the ward behind her with her scythe. Other times, if she appeared distracted, she wandered off into the forest on the other side without so much as a backward glance. When that happened, the ward sealed itself, as if on a timer.

Sixty seconds.

That was all I had. Sixty seconds to race through undetected, silent as the grave.

If I failed, the ward would slice me in half—no mercy, no quarter. It would do its duty to protect all within it.

If she saw me, heard me, *smelled* me, then the plan was fucked. Any hope of slipping free from bondage—gone.

Tracking her had been enjoyable, but that pleasure fell to the wayside this morning. There was too much riding on this moment for my usual lazy study of her actions, her expressions, the swish of her silvery-white hair with every fucking step.

The wind was in my favor this morning, just enough to rustle the cedars, but not so wild as to give my scent away. I followed her at a brisk pace, tracking her through the forest, using all her training tips against her. Even if she *hadn't* trained us in tracking, her smell was a dead giveaway, catching on spiny green branches, her black dress leaving dewdrops of sweet alyssum on the scraggly underbrush. Even with my eyes closed, I'd find her.

An unsettling thought, really, one that I pushed far out of my mind—because if I thought too deeply on her, on how easily she drew me in, how her scent and her voice and every damn part of her called to every damn part of me, then I'd lose her.

Body low to the forest floor, I followed at a safe enough distance, downwind, watching the up-and-down motion of her scythe's curved blade through the trees rather than Hazel herself. They were one and the same, a reaper and her scythe, and while she had stopped carrying it everywhere around the house, she took it with her on these daily jaunts into the mortal realm. Why, I had no clue, but I would soon find out.

When she stopped at the ward, its magic slightly warping the forest on the other side, like peering through a stained glass window, I dropped. In my shifted form, I blended with the shadows, the darkness fading fast beneath a rising morning sun. Same as always, she sliced a line clean into the ward, then stepped through. I waited, holding my breath, still as stone.

Today was a distracted day—a day she didn't turn back and close the ward herself. Sixty seconds. Enough time for *anything* to creep through, including a hellhound.

Ears up, I listened to her gentle footfalls on the other side of the ward, then blitzed for the opening when it was clear she had carried on walking. Unsuspecting, our reaper. She seemed to have developed some trust in us these last forty days; Declan had had a lot to do with that, and that worked in our favor, whether my packmate liked it or not.

I slowed as I approached the ward, fearing the cruel cut of magic slicing through my body if I made a mistake. Any hesitation, however, meant I might lose her on the other side. So I took a chance, risked it all, and hopped through the opening in the barrier.

And landed neatly on the other side. Stunned, I staggered to the shade of a young cedar, hiding beneath its boughs to collect myself.

Somehow, I'd thought the air would smell sweeter over here. It was all the same: the same forest, the same sky, the same warming sunshine.

Hazel's scent on the breeze, tantalizing as ever, potent as fuck, even here on the celestial plane... I wasn't sure if she slipped out of this otherworldly pathway to walk amongst the mortals once she left us, but dressed as a reaper, all in black and holding a scythe, I had serious doubts.

Had I not loved my pack as much as I did, our bond deeper than any in all the realms, I would have fled. Turned tail and run, deep into the forest, going, going, going until I was long gone. Abandon her, shirk her unwelcome sway over me so that I could be my own hound again, in control of my senses, my body, my mind.

Perhaps even my heart.

But I was loyal to Knox. A protector of Declan.

I would *never* leave them.

So, I padded after Hazel, slinking through the trees in her wake, tracking her with ease.

Until she disappeared.

Poof.

Into thin air.

To anyone else, this would have signaled the end. With no reaper to track, there was no mission. My heart drummed just a beat harder, adrenaline spiking, and I trotted after her, suddenly nimble and light on my feet, not stopping until I stood where she last had. Excitement made my mouth slick, my gut flutter, my chest tight. Finally, a chance to prove myself—to myself—beyond the confinements of the ward.

On our first day of training, Hazel had called us celestial beings. She had made an impassioned speech about it, in fact, suggesting we were akin to demons, reapers, even angels. While Declan had listened intently at the time, I'd let the words roll off me, instead focused on finding a way out of our new predicament.

But as it so often did, Hazel's voice found its way to me at night, playing over and over again on a loop inside my head, in my dreams.

And all that repetition, rehashing and dissecting every fucking syllable until I was exhausted enough to pass out, paid off in spades.

Because if we *were* celestial beings as she had so passionately insisted, then we had a magic all our own, magic repressed and denied by our torturers all our lives. Magic she had tapped into when she taught us how to cross from the mortal realm into the celestial plane. Magic driven by *intention*.

Fourteen days ago, I had teleported for the first time— from one room to the other, I moved through space with intention. Ten days ago, I'd disappeared from my bedroom and reappeared in the forest. It had taken a few tries, naturally, and there would be no passing through the ward, no matter how adept I'd become at transporting myself through the ether. But I could move as she did. Behind intention stood our freedom.

This morning, however, intention would unravel Hazel's best-kept secrets. Eyes closed, I fixated on her scent, on her face. I pictured her so clearly in my mind's eye that desire thrummed through me, quite involuntarily of course, and I had to fight for the intention. Center myself. Commit.

When I did, I left the forest behind and reappeared out in the great wide world, surrounded by soaring cityscape, her scent stronger than ever and her back to me as she strolled unseen through throngs of oblivious humans, the click of her little heels carrying through the celestial plane.

Her secrets, at long last, *mine*.

❧

As soon as the front door closed, its *thunk* echoing through the manor, Knox dropped his spoon, abandoning the pretense of ladling cinnamon-dusted oatmeal into his mouth, and then pinned me with a narrowed look.

"Well? Out with it, Gunnar."

I picked at the squishy crust of my peameal bacon, knowing I couldn't skirt him a second longer. Hazel had left us for the day—again—and my alpha had been waiting *hours* for a report on what I'd seen out in the real world. The confirmation that I could successfully teleport through the celestial plane had been news well-received, as I'd thought it would be, but the real curiosity came for *her*. All three of us *felt* for her. Interest danced through the pack bond anytime the reaper was around, and it wasn't just from Declan, as much as Knox and I made him feel that way.

My alpha wanted to know her. He craved her weaknesses and the chance to exploit them for the betterment of the pack. While he hadn't said as such in so many words, I could read Knox possibly even better than I could read myself.

Which was why I knew, right now, as he glowered at me from across the kitchen island, that his patience had run out. After sneaking back into our warded territory yesterday, barely making it in time and grateful as fuck that Hazel hadn't sealed the barrier behind her, I had insisted we *wait*. After all, she might overhear us, and even though it wouldn't arouse suspicions if neither Knox nor I spoke to her for the rest of the day, I'd pushed my own narrative that it was crucial to discuss my findings when she was gone—completely out of range.

And Knox had indulged me... until now.

In the meantime, I had wrestled with my feelings about what I'd seen yesterday, the various scenes burned into my brain forever. Her smile. Her tears. Knox intended to use her emotions against her, and at this time yesterday, I'd been completely onboard with that.

Today...

I ground my teeth together, looking pointedly out the windows over the sink. Hazel had repaired them recently, smoothing the cracks with a stroke of her hand. Declan had then cleaned them without magic, scrubbing each pane, standing up on the counters to reach the far corners as Hazel hovered around his feet, fretting that he might fall. Through the spotless glass, cedars swayed in the morning breeze, a near replica of the conditions I'd experienced yesterday. Cooler temperatures. Breezy but not blustery. Unfettered sunshine and a beautiful blue sky.

How strange, how fucking *irritating*, that everything around me could look the same, but inside my whole damn world had flipped on its head.

"Gunnar." Knox's tone left no room for more excuses. He had given me enough rope, but if I carried on further, I'd hang myself. Clearing my throat, I ripped my piece of cooked pork flesh in half, bringing the smaller bit to my mouth— where it stayed, just about touching my lips but never passing through. Not even its tantalizing scent could tempt me; my throat had been constricted and my mouth painfully dry since yesterday. No food could fix that. Not the pain in my chest nor the throb in my head.

"She goes into the city when she leaves," I said tersely. When I finally met my alpha's black gaze, I faltered, literally unable to refuse him any more than I already had. "Her first stop is a... school."

Porcelain clattered across the kitchen; even with his back to us, Declan was an open book, his fist around a white mug, his free hand jabbing at the buttons on the new coffee maker.

He didn't approve of this, none of it, and that hadn't mattered to me yesterday.

It did today.

I had no fucking clue as to *why*.

But it was driving me insane.

"A human school?" Knox asked, leaning back just enough to cross his burly arms. When I nodded, he arched his scarred brow. "Like the one from that television show?"

"No. The humans were younger. Much younger." Little round-faced cherubs, some bright-eyed, others shuffling along and weighed down by sleep, all escorted onto the grounds by their parents. I had never considered fathering pups of my own, but watching *her* watch them had stirred something strange in me. Unwelcome. Heartfelt.

Yearning.

Not my finest moment, to be certain.

"Did she leave the celestial plane?"

"No. She stayed hidden." Just as I had stayed hidden, always downwind from her, utilizing bushes and buildings and cars to my advantage throughout the morning. At first, I'd hidden because I knew I *had* to, but as time dragged on and it all unfolded, I did so because it was painfully obvious I had intruded on a private moment, something I both longed to fix for her *and* had no desire to become involved with.

Hazel had arrived at the school, a small kindergarten facility —according to the sign—in the downtown core, nothing more than a single-story house surrounded by a chain-link fence. Juvenile, soft colors splashed the walls. Flowers bloomed in well-kept boxes beneath windows and along pathways. Metal structures suggested the little ones were let out to play at some point, but our reaper lingered by the front door, standing on the big, two-toned circle at the entrance, waiting. Initially, I hadn't understood what the fuck she was even doing there—

and then, from my little hiding spot, I watched her come alive with the arrival of the children. Her whole gloomy demeanor brightened, her smile so wide that it hurt *me*.

"And what did she do?" Knox asked. I shook my head and dropped my bacon back onto my plate, the mound of food nowhere near as appetizing as past meals.

"She just... watched them." With that painfully stretched smile, she hovered in the celestial plane, *watching* as they trudged to the school. Some of the parents waited at the gate. Others walked their young in, hand in hand. The yard filled with chatter, the surge sudden and chaotic. Hazel took them all in almost frantically, as if not wanting to miss a thing, laughing at the childish antics that had made me roll my eyes —reaching out for unbuttoned jackets and unlaced shoes, her hand sliding through the child.

Almost like she wanted to *fix* them.

"And then?"

I said nothing, throat like sandpaper, unable to meet my alpha's eye.

"*Gunnar.*"

"And then..." Fuck, I'd never forget it, the way her expression crumpled as the yard cleared, her chin wobbling, her arms limp at her side. "And then she cried."

Declan whirled around, panic and rage ripping through our pack bond. "*What?*"

"She cried," I said. Not that I needed to repeat anything— Declan had heard me. Knox too. But I had no intention of clarifying or adding any extra detail. They didn't need to know that Hazel's knees gave out, that she didn't exactly *sob*, but the tears fell and fell and fell, splattering to the ground yet not one leaving a mark on the cement.

Distress pulsed along our bond now, from me and from Declan, and I tried—and failed—to rein my feelings back in as Knox glanced between us with a heavy sigh.

But I couldn't help it.

I'd *hated* watching her cry. Every physical whisper of sorrow across her features, from her crinkled brow to her trembling hands, touched me, made me palpably upset—so much so that I'd had to fight my instincts to pad straight to her side, exposing myself, and do whatever I had in my fucking power to make it all better.

While I still wasn't completely certain, I'd suspected for weeks now that the connection between us three and Hazel went deeper than that of a reaper and hellhound pack. We hadn't discussed it, but there could very well be an element of fate at play here; the urge to comfort someone *outside* of my pack had never struck me so fiercely before.

I didn't know what to make of that.

And there was nothing I despised more than to be out of control—physically, mentally, and, now, for the first time, emotionally.

Knox pushed his bowl away, elbows on the island as he said, "Did she stay at the school?"

"No, once the children went inside, she walked for a little while through the city," I told him, still feeling like I was collapsing in on myself like a dying star, Hazel's teary face refusing to leave my mind's eye. "She ended up at a food court inside a, er, *mall*, where she sat and watched the humans." Her focus on them had been almost unnerving, studying them with the same intensity that I and the others did when we watched humans on television. "And then..." *Fuck.* "And then she cried again, then she came back here."

"Huh." Knox tapped his finger on the island's smooth top, then absently traced it between splotches of varying grey tones in the stone.

"I think..." My words died in my throat. I had a great many thoughts swirling around my head, always did, but for once, I was unable to voice them. All my life, I had relished sharing my brilliance, telling others *precisely* what I thought of any situation. Here, I couldn't, not even when Knox's eyes narrowed, pressing me for my conclusion.

"She's lonely," Declan snapped, his words rising over the sound of water boiling viciously inside the kettle. Steam coiled from the coffee maker's black spout, as if fueled by my packmate's frustration. "Maybe Hazel is struggling to accept that, technically, she's dead. I think she goes out there every day to feel close to humanity." He looked between us, his stormy gaze pleading for Knox and me to see the reaper as he did. Little did he realize I was almost right there with him. Declan threw his hands up, churlish exasperation skittering through our bond. "And she's kind, and sweet, and she genuinely cares about them."

I rolled my eyes, more out of habit than anything. "Yes, yes, you've gone into great detail about her embracing that sick girl's soul during the reaping—"

"Well, apparently I *need* to," Declan growled, "because you'd have to be blind not to see her for who she is."

Outbursts from a hound so low in the pack hierarchy never went over well with other alphas, but Knox was the most diplomatic one I'd ever met. He usually entertained all opinions, but Declan had never been so outspoken before either—not until he met *her*. Another alpha would have put him in place, violently at that, yet Knox merely continued his distracted study of the island's countertop, dragging his finger back and forth, unfazed by Declan's words *or* the anger radiating from him toward us in our bond.

My lips twitched, threatening to rise into a snarl. I loved Declan, but he could take that anger and fucking *shove* it up his ass. I hadn't made Hazel cry. I hadn't condemned her to a lonely life of reaping. I hadn't killed her. And I certainly didn't relish her distress, nor the situation that caused it.

So. You know. *Check yourself*, as the humans said.

Knox had always been too soft on him.

"This has value," our alpha mused, a compliment that would have made me preen yesterday morning that fell flat today. Declan marched up to the island as the coffee maker dinged.

"Her suffering is not *value*," he snapped, his tone dangerously close to a challenge.

"No," I muttered, "but it's an angle."

"I don't like this." Declan crossed his arms, seething. "I don't like it at all—"

Knox held up his hand. "Declan, enough."

Without raising his voice, he asserted his dominance. Declan backed away, subdued as he checked on the bubbling water, and I bit my tongue, not liking it all that much either. After all, the desperation I'd experienced yesterday, the *need* to comfort Hazel, told me that I was already fucked. All that I had felt before seeing her weep paled in comparison to the storm churning inside me now —but I could hardly pitch a fit about it, nor did I dare go against Knox's orders.

"We don't have to *hurt* her to use this to our advantage," the alpha remarked, scratching at his beard, the gears whirring behind those unreadable black eyes. "If she's lonely, we can fix that, and in turn, get what we've always wanted."

Freedom. That was our endgame. The ability to exist in this world without bondage, to make our own decisions, to go where we wanted, when we wanted, untethered, uncollared, unleashed.

Only now, the thought of using Hazel to obtain it made my stomach turn. I glanced at Declan briefly, and my packmate simply glared back, like this was all my fault. And in a way, it was. Whatever Knox decided, my observations had been the precipitating factor.

Sighing, I shoved my plate away, appetite long gone.

Knox, meanwhile, attempted another spoonful of gloopy, cold oats, then dropped his spoon into the full bowl with a scowl.

"Horrid stuff, oatmeal," he muttered. Much to my surprise, he certainly didn't *sound* victorious, not like he did when we had found ways to fuck with Fenix or any of the other trainers. Instead, he wore quite the glare himself, one that topped Declan's and then some, as he snatched up the remaining stack of bacon from the plate in the middle of the island and shoved a slice into his mouth.

The terse way he chewed suggested that the cooked flesh, seasoned with salt and pepper, watched like a hawk by Hazel as it sizzled in the pan only a half hour ago, tasted the same as the oatmeal.

Horrid.

Absolutely fucking *horrid*.

11

KNOX

"I can't believe you've done this…"

"Hazel, why don't you sit down?" I gestured to the opposite end of the grand dining table where we had set a place for her—a plate, a wineglass, a set of utensils. Clutching her scythe harder than she had in days, the pacing reaper whirled around and stuck me with a glare that screamed, *Oh, now* you're speaking to me?

She needn't say it; it was strange, yes, for us to have an actual conversation. I'd done my best to avoid that this past month, given the last time we spoke privately had ended in disaster. *Inconsequential.* She wasn't, of course, inconsequential, not when she made all of us *feel* so fucking deeply, but making her despise me was just… easier.

"No, no, I think I'll stand," she ground out, swinging her scythe as she stalked back and forth. Declan shifted in place; seated to my left, his chair creaked beneath his awkward shuffling movements, his discomfort with this evening's conversation panging through our pack bond to the point of distraction. Thankfully, my beta had better control of his emotions. Even if Gunnar's opinion of Hazel had altered somewhat thanks to yesterday's outing, he had an exceptional poker face. Like me, he could keep his baser instincts in check.

Declan, meanwhile, made no effort tonight to hide his innate responses. He'd said nothing, not when Hazel set out our supper on the dining table twenty minutes ago, a feast of roast pheasant and sweet potato mash and buttery, garlicky green beans. Round little loaves of homemade bread piled high in the middle of the table. Three candles flickered around the basket courtesy of Declan's attempts to impress her with his homemaking skills.

But the pup had held his tongue, uncharacteristically so when it came to *her*, throughout all this—the arrival of our food, followed swiftly by Gunnar explaining that he had followed her into the real world yesterday morning. My second-in-command let it all out in agonizing detail, from her weepy visit to the children's school to her depressing sit-in at the mall food court.

Hazel hadn't said a word either until this moment, but her cheeks had grown darker and darker, and as soon as Gunnar concluded his tale, she'd shot up from her seat at the other head of the table, no longer squaring off with me. Now, she couldn't seem to stop moving.

"I think we should talk about this," I insisted, working hard to keep my voice even and calm, like I was soothing Declan after an incident with—well, fuck, *anyone* in Hell. Her flushed cheeks and accusatory glares threatened to throw me, riling me up from the inside out. With all the windows closed in the otherwise empty dining hall, her scent hit hard, raging like the sea.

Breathing through my mouth helped a bit, thank fuck.

"Oh, you think we should *talk* about this?" Hazel bristled as she rounded in place and marched back to the table. "Yes, let's *talk* about the incredible invasion of privacy and the ridiculous breach of trust. *Let's.*"

Declan wilted at my side; if he could, he probably would have hidden under the table for this conversation, but for the plan to move forward, we all had a part to play. Gunnar, meanwhile, showed no outward signs that her indignation affected him, his skin smooth and pale as always, lips in a thin line as he filled our glasses with a pungent red wine.

"Hazel, you must understand our position..." Reclined back in my seat, I threaded my hands together and let them rest on my chest. Above all, I intended to look relaxed throughout this conversation, refusing to get dragged into some ridiculous push and pull with Hazel's anger.

Hazel. Her name always left a strange taste in my mouth, as though I had craved it all my long life, even if it made me sick— like it was *too* good for me. But I'd watched a documentary recently wherein the human interrogators used a criminal's name repeatedly throughout the questioning to build trust between them. That was big for her—trust. If I could create it subconsciously, then we were doing better than expected. "After all, we were born and bred in bondage. Raised *for* servitude. In our cases, all three of us have suffered greatly at the hand that barely fed us. Gunnar simply wanted to know you."

"That's crap," she fired back, pointing her scythe at us so abruptly that Gunnar stiffened to my right, eyes on the blade. Hazel huffed a lock of that white mane out of her face, her free hand twisting in the shapeless black gown hiding her curves. "I know you're trying to find a way around the ward, and now you did, and now I'm going to have to—"

"What?" I tipped my head to the side, brows up in another silent challenge. "Punish us?"

Her cheeks ripened to scarlet. "Well, I mean, *no*, but—"

"Hazel, I think—"

"Stop saying my fucking name. I know what you're doing."

I bit back a smile. Her fire was exquisite.

She was right to smell like the sea, this ghostly reaper garbed in shadow, calm one moment, a tempest the next. Exhilarating, really, to find such a quality in a female.

"Fine," I said gently, hands up in mock surrender. "I simply think this is an opportunity for growth."

She shook her head with a scoff, the angles of her face catching the light of the overhead chandelier—a gaudy gold piece lit by three dozen candles, not electricity, the massive room cast in an eerie orange glow.

"This sets us backward," Hazel argued. "It's not growth."

"You wish to build trust? All right. Let's build trust together." Fingers twined together again, I directed both pointers toward the stained glass window behind her, the focal point of the room, the *feature wall*—fuck all those house renovation television programs. "And let's build it out there."

Her mirthless laugh made the hairs on the back of my neck rise. "*Fuck* no."

Declan exhaled sharply, fiddling with his fork and refusing to meet anyone's eye.

"Seeing you weep for the humans changed my perception of you, Hazel," Gunnar admitted, his honesty catching her— and me—by surprise. *Hazel.* He'd also watched that documentary.

The reaper stared him down for a moment, full lips parted, distracting, and then rolled her eyes and stalked away from the table.

"I see *you* now," Gunnar pressed as he rearranged his cutlery, his plate, his glass, positioning each piece at perfect angles, all straight and aligned with the table's edge. "Not just the reaper who paid for me, who I am contractually obligated to serve…"

More raw honesty. I glanced at Gunnar's sharp profile; if there was one hound better at masking their emotions than me, it was my beta. But perhaps a touch of earnestness was what we needed.

Because the goal *was* to earn her trust—truly. Then, when she felt for us, connected with us, cared for our well-being beyond her duty as a reaper, we would start to pull away.

And Hazel would let us. Because of all the trust, connection, and care. This moment right here was the start. No part of me wished to spend more alone time with her than necessary, not when she affected me like she did, but it was the best plan we had under the circumstances. Bullying our way out wasn't an option, nor could we breach the ward without her help. While we three had slowly expanded our horizons and learned more about our own brand of magic, magic that had been beaten out of us for years, we were nowhere close to outriding a ward.

Warding magic was complicated and highly specialized—not something any of us were about to master anytime soon, if ever.

Recently, a human proverb had struck a chord with me: you catch more flies with honey.

While I wasn't the honey type, I'd be a fool not to recognize the power in that sentiment.

And the honey route would shut Declan up, which, at this point, was an added bonus.

"I should have known something was wrong when you set a place for me," Hazel muttered as she scratched at her forehead with a frown.

"You *should* eat with us," I told her. She seldom ever dined with us, and while I had seen her nibble on food while she cooked, I'd yet to catch her take a whole plate just for herself. Hellhounds, on the other hand, thrived on sustenance. Feeding shaped pack dynamics, something that Fenix and other breeders actively sought to suppress. When Hazel's gaze snapped to mine, I flashed a patronizing grin. "Packs *bond* over meals."

Her eyes narrowed. From my tone, my posture, my quirked mouth, she probably sensed that I was goading her. Sometimes I just couldn't help it: that fire of hers was addictive.

But she held it in this time, swallowing the flames so that they boiled in her belly instead. My gaze tracked the would-be path, dropping from her lips to her throat, then slowly creeping down her supple figure to her hips.

Of course, she had nothing to say to that. The fetching creature had been trying to make us bond for a month now... How could she refuse such an offer?

I looked to Declan, for he had a part to play in this too—and now was that moment. When he did nothing, said nothing, his hickory-brown eyes fixed on his plate, my influence reverberated through our bond. Alphas were born, not made. I needn't say a word to spur my pack into action, but that internal pressure worked best when they actually respected me.

Old memories swirled across my mind's eye at the thought—of former packs with established alphas, packs who had turned on me because they chose *him*, packs dragged into violence and chaos as two alpha hellhounds fought for control. Fenix always did struggle to find a place for me; eventually, that place had been a tiny kennel where I was a pack of one for too many painful years to count.

"Hazel," Declan said softly, defeatedly, still staring at his plate, "please sit. Just hear us out."

Gunnar ceased arranging his cutlery, shooting his packmate an incredulous look from across the table before rolling his eyes in true Gunnar fashion. Honestly, you'd think

I had ripped out Declan's claws to force him to participate in this.

But my true focus settled on Hazel, who was also staring at Declan, wearing a strange expression. Affronted. Surprised. Possibly even a little hurt, though not nearly as shell-shocked as when she'd learned Gunnar had followed her into Lunadell.

None of it surprised me; the pair had connected during their first reaping, and now Declan was tidying the house in the evenings, without being asked, sweeping here and there, organizing what limited furniture we had under Hazel's watchful—affectionate, sometimes—eye. I had let it slide for the sake of our greater goal, but if I wasn't careful, he would grow even more unruly.

Nothing ever came between a hellhound pack and their mate—fated or not—except blood and death.

And the way Declan responded to her, the way Gunnar now *felt* about her, the way she plucked at our pack bond with nothing more than a smile, we were certainly headed down a dangerous path.

Slowly, dragging her feet the entire way, Hazel drifted back to her seat and settled into it. Scythe across her lap, she sat primly, her expression pinched and unreadable.

"This is an opportunity," I said. While I had no qualms looking her right in the eye, she seemed to prefer glaring at a spot on my forehead. So be it. "You want us to learn about the creatures we reap, then take us out there."

She scoffed again, this time with less venom. Disappointing.

"Why? So you can run away?"

"No. This is about building trust—"

"Trust *you* shattered by following me!" Ah, there it was— just a flicker, but enough to make the windows rattle and the candles shudder, orange light dancing around the room.

Gunnar and Declan looked up, foreheads crinkled, apprehension trembling in our bond. I held my ground, her outburst eliciting a pulse of desire inside me.

Desire that died when some of the dancing candlelight glinted in her eyes—her watery eyes.

This *had* hurt her.

She felt it more than I'd appreciated before.

Desire morphed to distress, a vice snapping around my heart, twisting, twisting, *twisting* as my hands curled to white-knuckled fists. My pack's attention snapped from the chandelier to me, sensing the abrupt shift through our bond, but I ignored them just as I ignored the empathetic ache in my chest for *her*.

"Let us rebuild it together," I proposed, no longer as smooth and casual as I would have liked, my words rough, my throat thick with fucking *feeling*. Perhaps the wine would wash it away, drag it back to the depths as the tide drowned all. My fingers twitched toward the glass, but I held firm. "Our history is a dark one, Hazel, full of violence and torture and teeth ripping into us."

Her eyes dipped to my face, jumping around the scars that marred me—*me*, a creature who could heal from just about anything but the cruelty of my past. I'd caught her studying them before, no doubt wondering what the fuck could scar a hellhound. If she ever wanted the stories, then she would have to agree to this—to me.

"You want us to trust you," I pressed on. "You want to trust *us*... Then you must understand we don't trust easily. It's earned, not given, and no *celestial being*, as you call them, has ever earned the trust of this pack before."

"Let us go with you into the world," Gunnar urged, his tone shockingly genuine. "Take us one at a time, and bring your scythe if you must. Let us explore humanity together. The materials you've provided us have helped learn human dynamics, their history, their current events, their slang... but it can only take us so far. If you want us to feel for them with the depth that *you* clearly do"—Hazel sniffed and looked away from him, her cheeks hollow like she was gnawing at them—"then we must walk among them."

The reaper looked to Declan, their connection more obvious than ever, and I frowned when the young hellhound shrugged, meeting her eye briefly before fiddling with his fork again.

"How do I know this isn't a trick?" Hazel's eyebrows shot up as her gaze jumped between the three us. "Some elaborate ruse to screw me over?"

It was, of course, but if we played our hand properly, we could all part ways unscathed. That was the difference here, and that technicality mattered.

"You don't know." I leaned forward. "But *you* have all the power—don't forget that. We outnumber you, yes, but we can never seriously hurt you." A nod to her scythe had her clutching at it again. "And *that* can kill us in an instant. I assure you, we are painfully aware of that."

So, really, what other option had we? The honey approach was our best bet—the one chance to claim what I had always wanted for my pack. We just needed to get on with it before Hazel's lure over Gunnar and Declan—and me—fucked everything straight to hell.

Hazel finally slumped into her chair, prim posture forgotten, nibbling on her lower lip for a moment and drumming her fingers on her scythe's staff.

"If we don't pass the trials at the end of October, you all have to go back to Fenix," she said sullenly. "I'll have to get a new pack and start over again... Or they'll reassign me to a smaller city. Either way, it's not what any of us want. I know... I know you don't want to go back, and you should know that I take this, this *promotion* very seriously."

Fear and fury collided along the pack bond from all three of us at the mention of a return to Fenix. It was another obstacle of the distant future: if Hazel *did* let us go of her own volition, putting our freedom over her ambition, would we be hunted down? Dragged back to Hell? Whipped and beaten—even killed?

Knowing and understanding the landscape of the mortal realm, every facet of it, was paramount.

"Yes, well, then we had better finally *do* something," I growled, unable to shake my rage at the thought of Fenix getting his hands on Declan and Gunnar again—taking them away from me, throwing them into packs who could kill them because of what they were: different, special, unique. With a deep breath, I finally caught Hazel's eye, holding it with an intensity that made her shiver. "Join the pack, Hazel, or send us back. In the end, the choice is yours."

I filled my plate in the silence that followed, using the giant serving spoon for the mash and the garlicky green beans. The others followed suit, taking only after I'd had my fill. A carving knife sat next to the whole pheasant, the bird roasted and basted, glistening with salty, crackly flesh. I ripped into it with my hands, taking the largest portion for myself before depositing cuts of cooked, steaming meat onto Gunnar's plate, then Declan's. The youngest among us saw to the bread, snagging three buns and doling them out, his head bowed and his gaze apologetic when it briefly met mine.

He knew he'd fucked up.

And I knew he would do it again for her.

The way they looked at each other across the table—it was inevitable. An unwelcome flash of jealousy prickled in my core, not because of how they looked at each other, but, perhaps, for the fact that they already had a bond. A silent conversation flowed between them, effortless, obvious.

Deep down, I'd always craved a mate, someone bonded to

me, to my pack, and vice versa. I would die for Declan and Gunnar, but I would suffer an eternity of unspeakable agony for my mate.

Only I'd accepted long ago that in my position, an alpha without a pack, then an alpha of a pack of misfits, that a mate was simply out of the question. That bond would forever be implausible for a hound like me.

To see it playing out in front of me now—*connection*...

Rolling my shoulders back, I ripped into my pheasant with a snarl, and the others hastily did the same, sensing my frustration within our bond.

"Okay."

We all stilled. Such a little word, said in such a little voice, somehow flooded through the room like a tidal wave. I lowered my greasy hands to the table and swallowed my mouthful of pheasant. Delicious, *delicious* pheasant.

"Okay?" I repeated gruffly. Shock plucked at our pack bond, shock mingled with relief and fear and exhilaration.

"We can... try it," Hazel said slowly, like she was working out every word as it came to the surface. "We'll do our regular training still, and I'll take you each out separately. But any issues and it's *done*. Do I make myself clear?"

"Crystal," Gunnar crooned, a familiar smirk teasing his lips. Hazel merely stared back at his wolfish expression, not blushing, not stammering as she usually did, and my beta's deflation reverberated through the bond.

Without another word, Hazel nodded and stood, then swept out of the room in a hurry. Declan downed his entire glass of wine in a single gulp. Gunnar poked at his green beans with a scowl.

And I savored our victory.

A victory that didn't feel nearly as powerful as I'd anticipated.

In fact, just like when I had learned all the new

information about our reaper, about her tearful excursions into the human world, this felt... hollow.

A pyrrhic victory.

We resumed our meal in silence, the unease of her departure entrenched deep in our bond, hovering over us throughout supper and long into the night. The only way I could get a wink of sleep was to remind myself that this was a necessary evil—that in freedom, there was suffering.

And if there was one thing this pack understood better than most, it was how to endure suffering.

How to fight through the pain.

No matter the cause.

12

HAZEL

"I really am sorry about all this…"

I stopped my swift march through the cedars with a sigh, closing my eyes for a moment. Declan and I hadn't said a word since we'd left the house, bathed in late-afternoon sunshine, the sky clear—perfect weather for what I had in mind for our first solo outing. But the day hadn't matched my mood, and a week after my pack told me they had sent Gunnar to spy on me, *breached* my ward, I still hadn't fully recovered.

And then there was Declan, his voice so apologetic, so sweet, like the first misting of spring rain after a bleak winter. For seven long days, I had been distant from my hellhounds, barely speaking to them, mulling over the best plan of attack for these day trips that they wanted into Lunadell. We had kept our conversations centered around training, and I'd become the house ghost, lurking in shadows, unable to bring myself into the fold.

Honestly, it had been a fucking miserable week. In just a month, I had come to appreciate their chatter, even if it was meant to rile me up. Most of all, I enjoyed having companions again—beings who were just *there*, so I wasn't alone.

We had almost lost that. Following me to Lunadell, *spying* on my most shameful ritual, was grounds for punishment. I could have sent them back to Fenix for much less; Knox and Gunnar took insubordination to a whole new level most of the time, even if they did everything I asked of them when we were training.

The potential loss struck a nerve, and it had taken me far longer than it should have to recover.

Declan's footsteps had fallen silent behind me. My sweet, helpful Declan. He had been instrumental in me agreeing to any of this; it only made sense that he was the first to go out, the one to set the tone for all future trips.

He didn't deserve the silent treatment.

Scythe in hand, I turned slowly and found him a good ten feet behind. Clearly he had been keeping his distance on purpose. Normally we walked everywhere together, our steps falling into an easy rhythm.

I hated to find him so far away, his expression tensed—like he was waiting for me to shout at him, maybe even strike him. Knox had had a point: the pack had never known anyone better.

And, damn it, I would be *better*.

"You don't have to apologize," I told him, gaze snagging on his hair, on the way the wind gently ruffled it. When he had first arrived, Declan sported a cropped haircut, neat and nondescript—militant, almost. Since then, it had grown out, the beginnings of a head of thick, obsidian curls on the horizon. It suited him better, the soft waves of black, so dark they were almost blue in the right light—so feathery that it deserved a good finger-combing just to reinstate some order. I gripped my scythe tighter, fingers itching to do the job.

The hellhound scratched at the back of his neck, and when he stepped forward into a beam of bright afternoon sunshine, I noticed a smattering of freckles over the bridge of his nose. All this time outside in the sun had been good for him—good for all of them. Even Gunnar sported a healthy glow these days, his porcelain skin a shade darker.

Very fair would be the appropriate makeup for him. Declan, meanwhile, had become the most exquisite golden brown—healthy, his cheeks fuller, his shoulders broader, his body somehow even more muscular than the first time I'd seen him naked and steaming from the shift.

"But I *do* have to apologize," he insisted, not stopping until we were a foot apart. "I feel like I guilted you into this, and it wasn't fair of me—"

"Declan, stop." I wrapped a hand around his wrist, my little squeeze forcing those big brown eyes to meet mine. Electricity skittered up my arm at the contact, and warmth bloomed in my cheeks when his breath stuttered. *Focus, Hazel.* "I can see the merit in this, in going out together, walking amongst the humans. It's a good idea... I just wish Gunnar and Knox had gone about it differently, that's all."

"But it hurt you."

I swallowed thickly. "It did."

"And that's why I'm sorry."

How could a man look so earnest without it being an act? I'd never seen it before, not when I was alive and not in the souls I reaped now. But something shimmered in Declan's eyes that I couldn't ignore. Maybe it was because they were so big—and maybe because it was *real*.

My heart lurched at the thought of hugging him, of following my gut and draping my arms around his neck again, breathing in his spicy, masculine musk.

"Okay, well..." I stayed exactly there, keeping the space

between us, my hand clasped around his wrist. "Sure, I accept your apology."

He nodded, his mouth twitching into a familiar smile—something warm and cozy, a smile that made the little butterflies in my tummy flutter to life. Birds twittered all around us, the forest alive in the throes of early autumn. They sensed us on the celestial plane, our presence unseen but palpable. Alone in our own little bubble, Declan and I simply stood there for a few painfully long beats of my heart, him a full head taller than me in my flats despite being the shortest in the pack. I was the first to look away, my eyes dropping to where we touched, heat flaring in my palm. Declan shifted in place, bringing that gorgeous body of his a breath closer, and I finally detached.

"I think you're going to like the spot I chose for today," I babbled, stumbling back a few paces and shouldering my scythe. My free hand still burned from the physical contact, aching to settle back against his skin, and I flexed it in and out of a fist with a nod toward the nearby ward. "Come on."

He kept his distance again as he followed me through the trees, though it wasn't quite as gaping as it had been a few minutes earlier. Good. While the events of last week had thrown me, I hadn't wanted our first trip riddled with tension—not with Declan. After all, I had chosen today's spot specifically for him.

For all of them.

I mean, no way would I let the pack decide where we went in Lunadell; I just couldn't allow them that kind of power. However, in my stretch of solo—depressing—downtime this past week, I'd given all three initial outings a great deal of thought, tailoring the location and the activity for each hound.

Gunnar had actually been the easiest.

And unsurprisingly, I still had no clue what to do with Knox.

But Declan's destination brought a smile to my face, and as I crossed through the tear in the ward, I hoped it would bring one to Declan's too.

Once the hellhound joined me on the other side of the magical barrier, I sealed it immediately. Before I'd learned Gunnar had followed me, had perfectly mapped my routine from morning to night, I made the trek to Lunadell daily. Since then, I'd stayed in the house, unable to go out there when the pack knew precisely what I was doing.

It was just too humiliating.

A grim reaper—sobbing in front of a kindergarten class, in a mall food court.

Pathetic. Alexander and the others would never let me live it down if they found out.

But never mind.

There would be no tears today if I could help it.

When I touched him this time, I went for somewhere safe: his shoulder, my hold featherlight and fleeting. The forest faded around us as I envisioned our destination, and in a flash of black, we were there. Declan staggered away before I could, a hand to his forehead, his cheeks flushed. Apparently, he still needed some time to adapt to teleportation—not that I could blame him. It had taken me a few weeks to find my footing at first, hopping between places, standing in one spot and materializing in another.

While we had left behind one forest, we faced another now, standing in a gravel parking lot at the cusp of a national park. Every spot in the lot had a car in it, typical for a Sunday afternoon, the trails and beaches full of families and nature enthusiasts trying to make the most of the mild weather before the rainy season. An outing into the city wouldn't have suited Declan; while the nature reserve was technically still within Lunadell's jurisdiction, it was vast. A full parking lot hardly meant anything with acres and acres of park at our disposal. Forest. Mountains. Sandy beaches dotted along the Pacific. It would be far less overwhelming than the downtown hospital where Declan had first reaped, and that was the point. His confidence had grown in the last month, but I didn't want to push him way out of his comfort zone.

A wall of pines, birches, and aspens greeted us, swaying in the coastal breeze, while wooden poles staggered along the rocky edge of the parking lot, connected by chains and broken only at the mouths of various forest paths. Behind me, Declan took it all in cautiously, eyes darting about, shoulders slumped—unsure.

"I thought we could spend the afternoon at the beach," I told him. "Humans come here to swim and relax, tan a little, kayak. It's really mellow… Something easy to start us off."

"The smell is overwhelming," Declan noted, nudging at the gravel underfoot with the toe of his Chucks. The pack seldom wore any of the shoes I'd acquired for them, but Declan had made an effort to put on every stitch of clothing possible for our outing today.

"Is it the forest?"

"Everything." He motioned to the nearby cars with a jut of his chin, then out to the mountains soaring up from a hazy horizon. "I smell the salt, the rust, the bark."

"It'll be stronger when we get off the celestial plane, so, you know, prepare yourself." I flashed a reassuring smile before drifting toward the nearest trail. The sign just out of the parking lot showed the paths we ought to take to the beach, a sandy playground that stretched for miles up and down the coast, cut into quarters by hills that jutted out into the ocean. For now, I decided on one of the smaller beaches, a spot that was bound to have a few clumps of humans, but, again, nothing to set Declan off.

The hellhound followed behind me at a distance, even along the dirt path through the trees. This time, however, it didn't strike me as purposeful; Declan stopped here and there, admiring certain sprigs of green drooping out of the forest, noting the slight changes in the autumn leaves, and pointing out shadows of woodland critters scurrying as far away from us as possible. I indulged him because it felt good to do so, and what should have been a twenty-minute stroll to the beach doubled before we knew it, and forty long minutes later, we paused at the end of the trail, the landscape an open canvas ahead.

A landscape that seemed to take Declan's breath away. He stood at my side, silent, lips parted, features slack as he took it all in.

"Have you ever seen the ocean before?" I asked, nudging at the rocky beach with the base of my scythe. About fifteen feet from the forest, the rocks gave way to soft, powdery sand, sand that eventually met the tide. Blue water rushed up the slope, tipped with white foam, the Pacific relatively calm today. Although it had been nothing but clear skies since this morning, black clouds gathered over the ocean way in the distance, a storm rolling in and finally giving the day's humidity some purpose.

"I've seen the Nile once," Declan told me after a brief pause, his gaze jumping between the humans scattered across the beach. They sat on blankets and folding chairs, couples and families and singletons. A pair on kayaks perched just beyond the shallows, their neon boats rising and falling with the waves. This was nothing new to me— watching humans just *be*. When I glanced up at Declan, surprised that he had seen such a famous river in person, he shrugged. "Back with my first reaper... You could see it from the house he stole for us."

Jealousy prickled in my cheeks at the thought of another reaper working with Declan, seeing what a beautiful creature he was inside and out. "What happened there—with your first reaper?"

"Fenix sort of shoved me into the pack just before they were chosen," Declan admitted, his lightly accented voice almost hollow as he surveyed the beach, the humans, the scraggly hills sandwiching it all in to the north and south. "The pack put up with me in Hell, but once we were out and had to prove ourselves, they turned on me."

"Turned on you? But—"

"I'm a runt, Hazel," he said with a cold chuckle. "Hellhounds don't tolerate weakness, and I think they assumed I'd make the pack weak. They didn't accept me, and they all made that known pretty, uh, violently."

I'd seen the scars up and down his sides, like more than one had ripped into him. Hellhound teeth were nothing to sneer at, their jaws powerful, their bite probably fatal to lesser beings. No one had confirmed it, not Knox with his scarred, rugged face, and not Declan now—but apparently the only thing that could scar a hellhound was another hellhound. From my understanding, they healed like shifters, but they *weren't* shifters, not in the traditional sense of this realm. Earth's shifters had been stolen and dragged to Hell, forcefully bred with the native hounds.

Hellhounds were another beast entirely.

And I couldn't imagine an entire pack closing in on all sides, no escape, fear immobilizing every limb...

Tears stung at my eyes, but I blinked them back before they surfaced. At no point did Declan need to think I pitied him, because I didn't.

But I could still grieve his past, what those monsters had done to him.

"Declan, I'm so sorry to hear that," I said, fighting to keep my words even and smooth, like this was any other conversation—fighting to keep my feelings a secret, one of the few I had left with this pack. "I'm so sorry for what they did to you."

He shrugged again, a little smile teasing his lips when a gaggle of human children erupted in shrieking laughter halfway up the beach. "It's done. It haunted me for a long time, until I..." His breath caught, and he cleared his throat with a shake of his head. "Anyway. If it hadn't happened, I wouldn't have found Knox and Gunnar." He went quiet again, smile dying, brows knitting. "And they... They're my family."

His sidelong glance punctuated the undertones of that statement, the words unsaid. Gunnar and Knox were his family—and he would always choose them. I couldn't change that, no matter how desperately it hurt to be on the outside of that sort of bond, so I forced a smile and squeezed his arm.

Just to touch him again, under the guise of comfort, to feel the electricity spark between us.

"I understand," I insisted. "Really. I do."

His eyes dipped down to my hand, where my thumb had unconsciously started stroking him in slow, deliberate back-and-forth swipes. When I realized what I was doing, how it might read to him, I hastily pulled away and focused on the humans enjoying the beach, my cheeks burning.

September brought moderate temperatures, and from the look of them, I'd dressed myself and Declan in the proper clothes to blend in. Sporting a pair of dark jeans, a black tee, and his off-white runners, the hellhound at my side looked very much the city dweller trying his hand at nature for the first time. I, meanwhile, could get away with my beachy black dress—loose, down to the knee, with short sleeves and a scooped neckline, it was as bohemian as I dared these days. With my feet wrapped in a pair of black flats, Declan and I made quite the gothic pair.

"Come on," I urged, working hard to ignore the fact that his warmth still lingered on my palm. "Let's go mingle with mortals."

I started off down the beach at a gingerly pace, stopping with a healthy distance between myself and the nearest humans to plant my scythe in the sand. There was no way I could bring it into the human realm without arousing a ton of questions, so here it would stay, on the celestial plane, until we returned.

I did it all the time, frankly. It wasn't like anyone else could swipe it without burning to a crisp.

Two steps away from my beloved scythe, however, I felt it again.

A faint ripple in the plane.

I stilled, listening, willing every sense to root it out. While not as strong as the shudder I'd experienced at the hospital with Declan, it was still *something*. Something I had never faced before. Something off-putting. Like the fabric of our surroundings quaked. A shiver sliced down my spine, and I crossed my arms, searching the beach, the forest, the towering hills for some clue as to what could possibly...

It had to be nothing. Because there *was* nothing—nothing to suggest anything on the celestial plane was off, nothing to give credence to my discomfort. All was as it usually was; maybe the ripple was just what happened when you traveled with another celestial being. After all, I had only walked the roads between worlds with reapers and souls before. Maybe it was my pack—maybe I just felt it when they crossed over.

I made a note to consult Alexander the next time we

spoke, then pushed it out of my mind. No sense in putting a dampener on what was supposed to be a positive outing.

Eyes on the scattered humans, I timed my exit from the celestial plane *just* right—when they all had their backs to me. It was a quick, easy slip, stepping from one dimension to the next, but the heightened hum of the mortal realm hit me hard as it always did. The human world was louder, brighter, the smells stronger and the ground at my feet grittier.

For Declan and the others, it must have been overwhelming—but going out here, walking amongst humans, was what they had *asked* for, and damn it, I intended to deliver.

"So, I was thinking we could just…" I trailed off when I turned around and found nothing—no Declan, no shaggy hellhound. Just the rustling forest, the overgrown path, the beaming sunshine. Fear bolted through me: this was *exactly* what I'd thought might happen. Bring the pack into the world, then watch them escape, one by one, until I was alone.

Again.

"Declan?"

Nothingness answered, the mortal realm sighing all around me. I stumbled forward a few steps, sand invading my flats, until Declan trotted out of the forest in his shaggy hellhound form. Relief made my knees weak, and I exhaled a sharp huff, swiping my hands through my hair.

Thank goodness.

He crossed the sand slowly, cautiously, sniffing at it with his tail low and his pointed ears extra perked. It shouldn't have surprised me that he felt more comfortable like this around strangers, but one of my personal goals for these outings, with Declan in particular, was to chip away at some of the past trauma—replace horrible memories with good ones.

"You just let me know when you're ready to shift back," I

said as he approached, that great head of his taller than me when I crouched down. While his eyes were still their usual red, in this light they had a brownish tinge to them that would *hopefully* allow him to blend in with any humans who didn't look too close.

But with a beast of this size, how could they not? Declan was a beauty, looking like a show dog with his silky black fur, fluffy tail, and sleek snout. If anyone asked, he was a mixed breed—perhaps a cross between a shepherd and a wolfhound, *something* to account for his size.

"No one here will hurt you," I insisted when he nosed along my feet, huffing at the sand that had spilled over their tops. When he straightened, I caught the end of his tail swishing back and forth on either side of him, and his mouth opened into a canine smile that I'd come to appreciate. Of the three, Declan was always the most expressive in his hound form.

Nodding, I straightened up and beckoned him to follow me toward the water. While there was no set plan for the day —I just wanted us to enjoy ourselves, let Declan taste the Pacific, bond a little—I figured it was safest to head toward the hilly area to the north. Most of the humans clustered down by the shore, with a trio of kids no older than ten running about, tossing a ball between them, and it would probably be best for everyone if we just watched for a while.

Kept our distance, this weirdo pair in black.

Declan padded along behind me, his shadow engulfing mine, bouncing with every step. A cooler wind billowed off the water in the human realm than on the celestial plane, making the hairs on the back of my neck rise—but maybe that was also because people were staring.

Should I have brought a leash for Declan? Was it beach law that he wear one? I hadn't even considered that beforehand. If I just kept him close—

"Puppy!"

I whirled around at the girlish squeal; the youngest of the three children peeled away from the rest, perhaps only four or five years old, and ran as fast as her tiny legs could carry her in Declan's direction, arms outstretched, greedy little fingers reaching for him. Her older brothers raced after her in her adorable pink overalls, all three sporting the same mop of chocolate-brown hair and near-identical green eyes, their cheeks sun kissed and alive.

The oldest caught his sister around the waist, scooping her up as she squeal-giggled in his arms, while the shorter of the two carried on a few paces toward Declan and me. Stiff as a board, the hellhound watched the trio unblinkingly, his fur rustling in the wind, his huge paws buried in the sand.

"Sorry," the eldest said when he looked up at me, his tone sheepish. "She really likes dogs."

"Can we pet him?" the next in line asked, lacking his brother's awareness of us—strangers at the beach, dressed a little differently from all the other adults, the dog by my side absolutely massive.

I'd never pet any of my hellhounds before—not in the way that these three intended. Tossing my braid over my shoulder, I opened and closed my mouth a few times, unsure if it was offensive to a hellhound's sensibilities to be fawned over like any regular dog. "Well, he—"

Declan answered for me, coming back to life suddenly, the bounce in his step even flouncier as he trotted halfway to the trio and plopped down in the sand. Even sitting, he towered over them, and as the middle boy cautiously approached, he dropped into a lie-down to even the playing field.

"I think that's a yes," I told them with a laugh, heart positively bursting at the sight. Declan had a soft spot for children—I'd thought so during his first field test, and his eagerness now to accommodate them without my asking only confirmed that suspicion. Tail sweeping across the sand, he even rolled onto his side when the littlest one approached so she could aggressively rub at his belly.

The eldest brother hung back after a few head pats, watching his siblings with eagle eyes as they stroked and scratched this strange, huge black dog. In a way, he reminded me of Knox: oldest, largest, concerned for the well-being of those in his charge.

I blinked rapidly, a rush of insight into Knox's character hitting me hard and fast.

Anyway.

This wasn't about my most standoffish hellhound—this was about Declan and how fucking amazing he was in every possible way.

"Does he want to play fetch?" the younger brother asked, eyes alight at the thought. He shot off before I could answer, and I was torn between telling him no, it was fine, and insisting that the little sweetheart in pink overalls not pull on Declan's ears like that. Not that it seemed to bother him, his tail still thumping contentedly against the sand.

The boy returned a few beats later, kicking up dust with every stride, a stick in hand. Slightly winded, he waved the thin bit of driftwood in Declan's face, then threw it with all his might. It sailed a respectable distance before plunking down on the beach. All eyes turned expectantly to Declan, the littlest one shrieking with giggles again. Declan's tail slowed, and he looked back at me, uncertainty in his reddish-brown gaze.

"Go get the stick, Declan," I told him, wincing at the slight baby-talk tone I adopted—like I was talking to a *real* dog. "Get the stick and bring it back! Good boy!"

The kids retreated when Declan stood, the eldest barely coming up to his head, but the apprehension disappeared when he gave a gleeful bark and trotted across the beach. I bit back a smile when he scooped up the stick and carried it over to us—because he would have had to be *so* gentle to hold the driftwood in his powerful jaws without snapping it like a twig.

My gentle boy.

My *perfect* hellhound.

He dropped the stick at the boy's feet, then bounced backward in a play posture, whining low and making a big show of watching the stick when the boy picked it up and threw it again. Then he was off, whipping across the sand and making the kids laugh when he did a dramatic dive, head over heels, to claim his prize.

This so wouldn't have happened with Gunnar and Knox, but Declan's playful personality, his shaggy look, his sudden hyperawareness of his massive form made him just right.

Across the beach, a man stood and plopped his sunglasses on his head, a hand over his eyes as he looked and looked and looked—until he found us. The kids didn't seem to notice their father searching for them, but I waved and he waved back. Even all the way over here, I caught the flash of his teeth as he smiled; then, as if knowing his kids were safe, he turned his folding chair in our direction and settled into it to watch after his brood, his wife dozing on the blanket beside him.

A deep, visceral pang of longing throbbed in my gut, and I crossed my arms, holding myself in a solo hug like that would push back the deep-seated loneliness inside. Because I so wanted what that man had—a partner, a gaggle of relatively well-behaved kids, a Sunday beach day beneath a gorgeous sky.

Normalcy.

I loved my life as a reaper—loved all that it stood for, loved the gravity of the role I now played in the universe.

After death, I'd been restless in Heaven, unable to find peace, always searching for something *more*.

It wasn't until I returned to Earth that I realized I was restless for life—for what that man had.

That was why I went into Lunadell each morning.

Even if all I could do was watch, play the shadowy spectator beyond the veil, at least I had a taste of normal again—just for a moment. Fleetingly, I could pretend that *I* was dropping off my children at school, meeting a friend for coffee, taking my dog to the park.

Toeing at the sand, I shook my head. *Stop it, Hazel.* I might have missed a normal human existence, but my life had so much more meaning to it now.

And in the end, that was what mattered.

Training my hellhounds mattered.

Shepherding souls mattered.

Not... *this*, no matter what my heart cried.

Slowly but surely, the game of fetch led us all down the beach—attracting onlookers, encouraging them to wander over to chat with me. Taking a cue from them, I eventually removed my shoes, toes in the sand, and made sure not to make physical contact with anyone. The old saying was true, after all: Death had a cold hand, and reapers were no different. I already looked like a washed-out version of the humans loitering around me, asking questions about Declan's breed, about his age, his temperament—no need to give them any further indication that I was different.

Eventually, Declan and the kids ended up in the surf. The oldest boy hurled the stick into the Pacific, and my hellhound charged in, fearless with his adoring fans cheering behind him. It was a sight to behold, his great black form bounding through the waves, barking and playing and *happy*.

Would other reapers have given him this chance?

All his past suffering—maybe its purpose *was* to bring him to Knox and Gunnar, and, in turn, me.

I had never believed in fate, even after death, but it was hard to ignore the chain of events that led us to this moment, to Declan playing, wild and free and content, and me being invited by the children's parents to join them for a beer like I truly was just another normal human.

It all felt so *right*, the day beautiful, the mood light, my heart so full…

Even with that storm rolling over the Pacific, inching ever closer across the horizon.

13

DECLAN

The humans had packed up and left at the first murmur of thunder.

At the time, I'd been almost sad to see them go, but now I was grateful for the solitude, for the privacy their absence gave Hazel and me. Two figures, alone on a beach much farther north than where we'd started. A reaper and a naked hellhound, soaked to the bone in chilly rainwater, riding out the storm as one.

A bolt of silver split the sky, skittering over the black. Temporary as it was, it illuminated the writhing treetops, casting the green in an eerie white glow that thrilled me far more than it scared me. Seconds later, thunder cracked so violently that they must have felt it in Hell. The storm crashed over the ocean, curls of white-tipped dark blue surging up to meet the sky in battle.

A good thing the humans had cleared out. As I blinked the droplets from my eyes, water sluicing down my skin and taking with it more than just the grit of the beach, I wondered if I could brave the waves. If one of those precious pups had been sucked away in the tide, victims to the ocean's fury, would I be strong enough to save them?

Another flash of lightning, this time brighter, closer, the thunder booming before the light died. Wind whipped across the beach, toying with Hazel's dress, her white hair even starker in the storm.

For once, fear evaded me. Loud noises and strange lights might have sent me running in the past, my heart racing, my nerves on fire, but not here—not now, not with her. Rather, I embraced it, succumbing to its primal call as the gale intensified.

Even in the form of a man, I felt my truest self come alive beneath the lash of light and the deafening *crack-boom* of the heavens. An hour in and the storm showed no signs of stopping, working its way inland. Did the pack feel it too— the summons, the power, the intensity? Out here, I truly was a beast, an animal uncaged, energy surging through my every limb.

A sheet of rain cut across the small beach we found ourselves on, dampening Hazel's scent, but even still—she was so much more intoxicating in the human realm. I always craved her, but standing here now, bare feet deep in wet sand, hair plastered across my forehead, raw, unbridled *energy* humming in my chest —I no longer possessed the will to stop myself from claiming her. No more suppressed desires. No more forgotten urges.

The next silver bolt split violently, twin streams engulfing the entire sky, thunder cracking in their wake. They lit up my reaper's face, her high cheekbones, her deliciously pointed chin, her ivory flesh.

Her wicked smile.

For she enjoyed the storm too, her shoes abandoned a few beaches back, her hair loose, her arms up as she danced in the rain. Jumping. Twirling. Laughing. Hazel was a wild thing in her own right, those beautiful eyes like beacons in the darkness.

Calling me home.

The next torrent of brisk ocean wind hit the beach hard. I braced against it, arm up to shield my face. Out of the corner of my eye, I caught Hazel embracing the gale like she would an old friend, arms outstretched, head thrown back. It wrapped around her like a lover instead, hoisting her black dress up her thighs, pasting the fabric taut over her curves.

She favored shapeless garments most days, but here, now, I had a moment to admire every delectable inch of her...

And she was a goddess.

A primal, wanton creature of the old world. The storm paled in comparison to her, and as I faced her direction, turning my back on the ocean, I truly saw her—for the first time, it seemed. No longer was this reaper my mentor, my protector, my guardian in this new life.

She was a woman.

A vision.

A dream.

She was *everything*—and I wanted her. Desperately. Not sweetly either.

A snarl echoed in my chest as I barreled toward her, and with a laugh she took off down the beach. We had been running since the storm started, something wild hounds in Hell did together. Race across their territory. Conquer the cruel terrain, bonding as a pack. She hadn't suggested it when the first drops of rain misted across the sand, and neither had I. As the humans fled, we'd broken off into a run —together, as one.

But we weren't running together now.

She ran.

I chased. Hard. Feet pounding the wet sand, my vision narrowed on her back, on the white mane blazing behind her like the tail of a comet. She wasn't *trying* to evade me. Hazel jogged. I sprinted. When lightning cut the sky again, my shadow consumed her, and she faltered with a glance over her shoulder, an echo of a laugh on her lips, her eyes wide.

Had she ever been hunted before?

Captured?

Consumed?

She deserved to know how it felt.

We deserved that.

I hooked her around the waist and dragged her flush against me, her back a perfect fit to the naked mold of my chest. She exhaled a shocked cry, bare feet hoisted off the sand, and her hands fell to my arm as I spun her around, away from the mossy grey rocks ahead. *No escape, sweet. You're not going anywhere.*

The beach betrayed me, sinking beneath my heel, and I lost my footing with a growl. We crashed to the sand together, her yelp drowned out by the earthshattering *boom* of thunder. She squirmed on top of me, and I rolled us—once, twice, three times down the gentle slope, not stopping until the surging tide was within reach.

Not until I had her pinned beneath me. Need tunneled my vision, the beach, the forest, the ocean blurred in my peripherals—Hazel's flushed features front and center, her chest rising and falling in uneven beats. Elbows in the sand, I caged her in with an arm on either side of her head, and her useless wriggling only made it so I nestled deeper between her thighs.

My lips hummed at the closeness to hers, our faces mere inches apart. Desire had my cock hard against her center, and she stilled when I made my affections known—physically, for the first time—with an insistent rock of my hips. I'd been so cautious before, savoring the spark of skin-to-skin contact with her yet never acting on it. But no more. No more sweet words and stolen glances and hands accidentally nudging whenever we walked side by side.

"Declan," she whispered, no longer the laughing, dancing goddess, no longer the queen of the storm. From the wary look in her eye, she straddled the line between goddess and reaper—torn between desire and duty.

I could work with that.

"Hazel," I growled back, daring her to protest. The rain muted her scent, muffled the sunshine, the dates, the *feeling* that filled me whenever I took a moment to breathe her in. So I closed the space between us, dragging my nose down the slender column of her neck, filling my lungs with *her*, with her exquisite scent mingled with stormwater and the ocean's rage. Her hands found my shoulders, fingertips cautiously pressed to their tops as I trailed down the hollow of her throat, smelling her, marking her with an openmouthed kiss that had her arching up.

She was always so cold, such a sharp, delicious contrast to the ever-present fire flashing through my veins. Tonight, she tasted of salt and freshness, not the sweet honeyed dates I'd expected, but I had the rain to blame for that. Her chest rose and fell with short, curt breaths, her back arching to meet my mouth, her hips ever so slightly undulating against mine. I growled when I met her soaked dress, despising the layer of fabric between us, desperate to rip it to shreds—to show her that I could be brutal like the rest of them, that I wasn't all wagging tails and skipping steps and happy howls in the surf.

"Declan—"

I'd issued the challenge—dared her to protest, to push back against me—but I couldn't stomach the thought of hearing the words. Snarling, I crawled up her figure and claimed her mouth for my own. Hazel squealed into the kiss; I'd caught her with her lips slightly parted, and I seized the opportunity without hesitation, tasting her as I'd needed to from the start, exploring her mouth and tangling my hand in her hair.

Trapping the white locks around my fist.

Tipping her head back so I could take what I wanted, drink my fill of her as our bodies rocked together. I found her bare beneath her dress, my cock nestled in her slick folds, so desperately close to uniting us that it fucking *hurt*.

Hazel moaned and shoved at my chest, but her protests died when I nipped at her lower lip hard enough to make her flinch. Shocked golden-brown eyes stared up at me, until finally they fluttered shut, her tongue suddenly chasing mine and her arms thrown around my neck. Nimble delicate fingers worked into my hair, smoothed down to cup my face.

This morning, I would have been satisfied with a kiss and nothing more.

But not now.

Like the riptide, there was no stopping this—no fighting it.

Desperate for more of her, her scent, her chilled flesh and her supple curves, my hand slipped between us, grabbed the neckline of her dress, and *ripped* the fabric clean down her body. I swallowed her indignant cry, then tore away from the kiss with a wolfish grin. Fire bloomed in her cheeks, skittering down her neck and flushing bright across her chest. Mesmerized, I traced the burn with one finger, not stopping until I reached her swollen lips, plucking at the lower one as she gasped for air.

Lightning made her blush even prettier. Thunder boomed in my heart now, coaxing the beast within me to the surface as I dragged my teeth down her neck. She arched up to meet me again, her moan a detriment to my self-control.

I had never shifted accidentally before. I had never lost control, turned from beast to man or vice versa without *intention*.

Here, I could have.

If I let the animal inside take over completely, there was no telling what would happen.

Little pieces of the beast escaped me, teeth raking her flesh, hands clawing at her exquisite body. Hazel accepted every rough caress like there was no other way to love, arching and moaning and writhing beneath me as I dragged my mouth down, down, down to the valley between her breasts.

Breasts still covered to me, black fabric stuck to each mound, her nipples pebbling through the material. Lips curled in a snarl, I wrenched her dress aside and dragged my tongue up the sinuous swell of her breast, licking the rainwater away. Her pale pink nipples matched her lips, equally tempting, equally swollen under my attentions. I closed my mouth around the little pink pearl, and she bucked beneath me, one hand twisting in my hair, the other pressed to her forehead—as if in anguish.

Desire and duty.

Which would win out?

I grinned against her skin, kissing my way to her other breast, needing to taste *every* part of her before the night was through. In the past, a spark always jolted between us when we touched, no matter how fleeting the caress. Now, the spark surged like the lightning, bright and brilliant, illuminating me from head to toe. I couldn't stop touching her, couldn't stop mapping the dips and valleys of her figure —couldn't stop *tasting* her.

Smelling her.

Marking her with my scent, marking me with hers.

And her scent was strongest in her core. I hurriedly crept lower, kissing and nibbling and nipping wherever her body begged to be worshipped, not stopping until I had the scraps of her dress shoved up her hips, her legs thrown over my shoulders. A bolt of light made the darkness into day, and I kissed her core in the thunder that followed, her heady cry drowned out by a single, intense drumbeat.

Here was my honeyed dates, my golden sunshine, my contentment. She tasted *divine*. My tongue swept between her folds, wet with rain and need. Every inch of her was as cold as the autumn rain—except for here. Her cunt was fire, a delicious, all-consuming heat that I just couldn't get enough of. Gripping her hips firmly, I yanked her closer and fucked her with my tongue. Hazel shuddered against my face, her thighs twitching, both hands in my hair, but she made noises I had *never* heard before from a female—wild and ragged and, frankly, a little squeaky—when my thumb found the little bundle of tender nerves at the crest of her sex.

That was where the pleasure lay, apparently. Right. *There*.

"Declan!" Roaring thunder threatened to drown her out, a poignant complement to the wind howling through the nearby forest—but I heard her. The sounds she made tonight, her taste, her body flush against mine... I would never forget any of it.

I settled between her thighs like I had finally found a home. She wiggled against me, pushed at my arms, shot up with a cry, and then flopped down on the sand—none of it deterred me. Her body was my temple, and I was here to worship until the ritual was *done*. I lapped at her center like a wretch dying of thirst after stumbling upon an oasis. My fingers and tongue traded places every now and again, allowing me to stroke her inner walls and taste that little bead that made her shaking turn violent. I enjoyed her as I never had a mate before, going on instinct, taking my time.

In the past, any physical gratification came from hurried trysts in dark corners, from the rare hellhound females in heat but ashamed to have succumbed to *me*. I thought I'd acted on instinct then, simply following my body's needs and desires like any male should.

But now I knew instinct. *Now* I felt fate. The three hellhounds in my past had used me just as I'd used them, our fucking shameful and quick. They'd needed relief, not chosen for breeding but still plagued with need. I'd gone with them for comfort, for acceptance—to quell the painful loneliness in my bones.

With Hazel, it was so much more than any of that.

She needed to know…

Hazel needed to know that if I had my way, I would never lick another female again, never worship a mate with every part of me, because this felt *right*. This was what I had spent my whole life searching for. She—

"Declan, *stop.*" Gone were the fingers twisting in my hair, replaced by both hands swatting at my shoulders. Panting, Hazel sat up on her elbows, face racked with worry as she very obviously avoided my gaze. Rain slaked over her gorgeous cheekbones, down between her breasts, and a flash of lightning illuminated all that you *didn't* want to see at a time like this: apprehension, fear, panic. She shook her head. "We shouldn't."

I pushed up with a growl, literally shaking at the effort it took to control the beast within. "Why not?"

Hazel looked lovely when she stammered, stumbled, stuttered for a response—because that told me she had no fucking clue either why we ought to stop. Her pale lashes fluttered, the color in her cheeks ripened, and I caught her by the hips when she tried to crawl back from me, fingers sinking in possessively.

You're not going anywhere, sweet.

"Don't you feel it, Hazel?" I asked as I prowled up her body, inch by inch flattening her back down to the compact sand, rain lashing at my back. She opened and closed her mouth, still fighting for a response, and her gaze slid from mine to my lips and back again. In a fleeting moment of softness, I brushed her wet hair from her face, curling it behind her ear with a trembling hand. "I have... The *pull* between us... I've felt it from the moment I first saw you, and I know you feel it too. Don't deny it for the sake of, I don't know, fucking *propriety*."

"I-I... I feel..." Her eyes dropped to my mouth again, her hands tentatively drifting up my chest, and that was answer enough for me. Forgoing any semblance of restraint, I caught her by the throat, fingers bruising into her jaw, and captured her in another searing kiss that made my cock ache and Hazel moan.

No more waiting.

Mine. All mine.

The tide surged up the sand toward us, ferocious as our kiss, constant as the fire between us, and I wrapped her legs around my hips at the next clap of thunder, then filled her to the hilt with a single, brutal thrust.

"*Oh!*" Hazel cried into my mouth, her back arching those perfect breasts into me, her hips shoved into the wet grit below.

Fuck. Her center felt as I always imagined Heaven might. In the deep, dank kennels of Hell, I had pictured warmth and acceptance, light and peace—comfort and an intense belonging that I scarcely believed existed in this world. But it was right here, in her, so hot and slick and tight, accommodating for me, for my liberties and my roughness, like we were made for each other.

Hazel deserved slow, sweet lovemaking—but I couldn't hold back. Couldn't get enough of her. Desperate to make the most of the moment, I retreated slightly and pounded back home, rutting hard and fast, grinding my hips to toy with that little bundle at the crown of her cunt, memorizing every breathy cry she uttered when I hit it *just right*.

She was all I could have hoped for in a mate, all that the others hadn't been. Attentive, her hands roving my body, the bite of her nails down my back the sweetest pain. Engaged, her hooded gaze locked on mine. Present, her hips rocking up to meet my every harsh thrust.

Mine—her mouth yielding to me, her body responding to me, her heart open to me.

My name on her lips would be my undoing.

I was so wrapped up in *her* that I barely noticed the slight shift in our positions—and suddenly I was rolling, my back colliding hard with the sand, the tide crawling up the beach within an inch of me. Hazel situated herself on top, her hands to my chest, riding me with her head thrown back and her full lips slightly parted. Backlit by lightning, glistening with rain, she was a vision.

Until she stopped. Until her hips stilled and her hands retreated, slithering down my body, and then up to cross over her chest. She nibbled her lower lip, brows crinkled, and shivered.

"Declan, I still think—"

"No, you still *feel*," I growled, propping up on one elbow as my other hand went for her swanlike neck. I'd learned that word recently—*swanlike*. While Knox and Gunnar watched yet another awful reality program a few nights back, I had sat with a dictionary and a thesaurus, rooting out words that fit Hazel in my mind's eye. Swanlike had been one of them. Divine another. Now, I needed additional words—for she was a wild thing, a goddess, and she deserved a whole book dedicated to her beauty.

I bucked up hard, driving into her, making every delectable bit wobble and bounce. Her hands snapped around my wrist in an attempt to loosen my hold on her, but I simply held tighter, anchoring myself along her throat as I pumped into her, relentless and hungry for her pleasure. Slowly, those grasping hands slid down my arm and found my chest again, then my thighs when she leaned back, rolling her hips to match my thrusts, both of us finding a familiar rhythm in the storm.

My free hand explored her, ripped her dress aside, revealed her to me as lightning struck and thunder clapped. It soon settled where we met, stroking her little button, swiping over it, circling around it, bearing down hard when she started to shake, my hips bucking harder, faster...

Until she lurched forward, stiff and shuddering for but a moment, her porcelain flesh aflame as she choked out my name. *"Declan..."*

Again and again and again. Her sex tightened around me, danced along my cock, and watching her come undone was the most beautiful thing I'd ever seen. The sight alone sent me sailing into the black. I thrust into her one last time and spilled myself inside her, a pleasure so sharp erupting through me that I felt it in my teeth. The world went completely dark for a moment, every cell in my body tensed and then not, a languid, lazy heat rolling out from my core.

When she pulled at my hand this time, it fell away from her throat. But rather than throwing it aside as I'd expected, Hazel pressed my hand to her heart, flat to her breastbone, where a ragged drumbeat stuttered beneath my palm. A weary smile crossed my lips, one that brightened to match hers. Even as the rain pelted our bodies, warmth swirling between us, I barely felt any of it; lovemaking had put us in a bubble, one I wasn't looking forward to leaving.

But we would have to go sometime. Knox and Gunnar were waiting on us, trapped inside the ward, eager to learn about the outing—eager to pick and prod and find a way to use it to their advantage in the future. I closed my eyes and gulped down a few deep breaths, the thought of sharing *any* of this with them making my heart sink.

This shouldn't be used against her.

Not only that, but during, I had thought of Hazel as *mine* —I had felt that possessive claim in my marrow. But she wasn't mine. The whole pack desired her; we all felt it in the bond, no matter how the others denied it or acted out to mask their interest in her.

In that moment, as Hazel climbed off me and settled at my side, her head on my chest, she *was* mine.

But she wasn't *only* mine.

And while that didn't frighten me, not an inkling of jealousy in my heart, I feared that the others may not give in to fate as easily as I had. That they would fight it, drag their feet—and in the process, hurt her.

Lose her.

That was a thought for another time though, when my mind was more functional and less interested in the way her soft breasts pressed to my sides, over my scars, how her supple figure molded so perfectly to mine...

How *anyone* could think with a naked Hazel at their side was beyond me, so why bother trying?

When she glanced at me, her smile faltering, I sat up and pressed a lingering kiss to her forehead. Her worries seemed to wash away with the rain, and she nuzzled back into my chest with a sigh, an arm wrapped almost possessively around my scarred torso.

And there on the beach, basking in a moment that would eventually expire, we held each other as the lightning struck and the thunder cracked, as the storm moved inland and softened, as evening became night...

Two hearts, beating as one.

✣ 14 ✣

HAZEL

Last night shouldn't have happened.

I shouldered my scythe with a sigh, striding across the busiest intersection of downtown Lunadell along the celestial plane, walking through people and the odd leashed dog like a ghost. Try as I might, I hadn't been able to stop my mind from drifting back to it—to the hammering rain, the booming thunder, Declan's teeth down my neck, his tongue between my thighs, his hand in my hair. Every fleeting image, flashing through my mind's eye like a flicker of lightning, set my body on fire at the memory alone. Seeing him this morning had been torture—seeing but not able to touch, forcing myself to be a proper reaper, a woman in control of the situation and *not* driven by lust.

But it wasn't just lust, was it?

Emotion had played a part in last night. Even in life, I hadn't been one to take a man to bed unless I truly *felt* something, and with Declan—with all of them, actually—I felt a little too much these days.

Still. Regardless of my body's needs, my heart's desires— it shouldn't have happened.

The end of the human workday made the streets and sidewalks of Lunadell's financial district a nightmare—had I found myself in the human realm, of course. Here, separate from them yet squarely in the thick of things, I could march through each and every one of them. The odd human might notice, a shiver spider-walking down their spine, but they wouldn't understand. And that was for the best. No sense in muddying an already complicated world with proof of the supernatural. Sure, it existed, but by and large, the general population hadn't a clue, carrying on through life like humanity was the planet's apex predator.

Chrome skyscrapers soared toward a hazy grey sky all around me, paired with trendy eateries, banks, investment firms—the works. Lunadell, like many major cities, had a substantial homeless population. At least once per block, a human lay on a dingy sleeping bag over a grate or the mouth of the subway entrance, the masses sweeping around them like they didn't exist. In a few hours, this section of the city would be a ghost town save for the bars, but even they closed early as the overworked humans fled the core for some respite in the suburbs.

I noticed a man with large hazel eyes in passing—like Declan's, though they lacked his intensity. And last night, *oh*, he had been *all* intensity. So unlike him. So raw and wild, like he just had to *have* me.

A man had never had to have me before—that kind of passion was intoxicating.

And wrong.

I shook my head as I breezed down another block, barreling through the crowds like they were nothing. It shouldn't have happened. Declan was in my charge—they all were. I was responsible for the pack's well-being. I fed them, clothed them, taught them...

Letting him fuck me into the sand... Wasn't that somehow taking advantage of him?

So, why didn't I feel guilty?

I knew, deep down, that it was wrong, that it most *certainly* couldn't happen again, no matter how desperately my body now craved his touch, and yet guilt was nowhere to be found.

And that made me feel shitty—that I didn't feel guilty when I should.

Shitty and distracted when today was all about *focus*. I needed to be present, alert. This wouldn't be a simple reaping, and if I kept drifting back to fantasies about Declan pounding into me, we might fuck it up.

And I refused to let Gunnar's first field test be a failure because of *me*. If he was going to fail—unlikely, given his annoyingly intense intelligence—he could fail all by himself.

So, I stuffed the memories of last night deep, deep down inside me, wrapping them up in my internal conflict, my emotions, my racing thoughts, and forced myself into the present. As I shifted my scythe to my other shoulder, my black reaper's robes billowing behind me, the hairs on the back of my neck stood on end.

The sensation came so suddenly, so sharply, that it ripped a gasp from me. I scratched at the nape of my neck, frowning. Even amidst all the human chaos here, I hadn't felt a single ripple in the celestial plane today—but now, out of nowhere, it was like someone was watching me.

Intently.

The unseen gaze burned into my body, and I stopped suddenly, whirled around, searching for a source.

But there was nothing.

Nothing and no one on the celestial plane within sight. No figures on the rooftops, no faces pressed up against tinted windows, no blazing demonic eyes peering through the sewer grates.

Just me.

And, well, Gunnar.

The hellhound had trotted along behind me since we'd left the estate; unlike Declan, he had been waiting for me in the manor's foyer already shifted, alert and ready, his whole body brimming with a stiff yet jittery energy that had been slightly off-putting when I first experienced it. Since then, he had kept his distance, that lean, muscular body of his seeming to glide, like he floated through the celestial plane, never so close that I felt his breath on my ankles, but never so far back that I panicked.

He slowed now that I'd stopped, nose going a mile a minute, taking in the hustle and bustle of downtown Lunadell, all of it slightly muted on the celestial plane. His fawny-tan coloring around his snout and up his paws glowed in the late-afternoon light, warmer than the day around us, comforting, in a way, given I'd memorized his every marking. This morning, worry made me paranoid that I would lose him, that he would bolt the second we arrived in the financial district, but here he was, focused, his body faintly aquiver. I had never seen him excited before; perhaps this was it, ears up, body sleek, nose working just as fast as his mind.

Would he act the same way for our first casual outing this Saturday night? I had something special in mind for him, given his love of music, but his past betrayal threatened to taint it already. After all, not only had he followed me into Lunadell, snuck past my ward, teleported on his own—but he had *watched* me in my most private, shameful moment, then brought it all back to Knox and Declan, sharing every detail.

I knew I had to let it go... I should have noticed him following me.

I shouldn't go watch school children and cry, but, you know, it happened—and would probably happen again.

So, for now, I did my best to keep my mind on the moment—again—so that Gunnar could make the most of his first attempt in the field. I'd been one hundred percent *there* for Declan; it was only fair to give Gunnar that same courtesy.

The pack's first individual reapings had been selected from a pool of offerings. I'd asked for someone gentle and soft, easy, for Declan. Gunnar's first soul, on the other hand, was the polar opposite—and I had asked specifically for *that* too.

Just as I turned away from the hellhound, true chaos erupted. Sirens came screaming into the city core from all directions, police vehicles and ambulances charging through the blocked roads, hopping curbs, horns blaring, and pedestrians scattering. Gunnar padded to my side, his red gaze utterly transfixed as the authorities converged on one location up the street—in an alley, in fact. Seconds later, gunfire erupted like fireworks, rising over the downtown hubbub. Humans shrieked as the shooting echoed through the streets, all of them fleeing, running through Gunnar and me, the block slowly clearing.

"This man is what they call a serial killer," I told him, grip tightening around my scythe's yew staff, the thrill of the impending reap looping in my belly. "He's killed a lot of people, and he does it because he likes it."

A quick glance to the side showed I had Gunnar's full attention, his bright red eyes pinned squarely on me, his body stiff. His head came up to my chin, a wall of trembling muscle at my disposal. In that moment, the partnership between reaper and hellhound had never felt so necessary.

"He's Hell-bound for sure," I mused, to which Gunnar snorted and nodded, both of us looking back to the gathering of police vehicles ahead. Red and blue lights washed over the surrounding buildings, and a few brave humans had started to gather at the scene, their phones out and recording. I rolled my eyes. "This man... He outsmarted human authorities for a long time. He's been killing for almost a decade—total narcissist. Psychotic. Thinks he's always the most brilliant man in the room. His soul won't be any different."

Gunnar gave a deep bark in response, tapping his front paws like he was winding up for a sprint. I pressed my lips together, fighting back a smile; for all his talk, for the ridiculous way he pressed his shirts, dressing the best out of the pack, using a fork and knife before the others—Gunnar was the yappiest of the three by a mile.

It was almost endearing.

"If he gets away, he'll become a very cruel spirit," I remarked. Souls had slipped my grasp before in the last ten years, but I had only worked small towns back then, and I could count my lost spirits on both hands. None of them had been as foul as this one, and if he got loose, he would take great pleasure in tormenting the living, just as he had done in life, for the rest of eternity.

Not on my watch.

And, apparently, not on Gunnar's. The hellhound paced forward a few steps, growling low, then looked back to me and barked in a *Come on, let's go!* tone that almost made me grin again.

Then he stilled, head whipping forward, snout pointing in the direction of the newly departed soul. Of course he could sense it. I had been creating soul-scent signatures for over a month now, putting the pack through the ropes so that when they faced a *real* soul, they would know it in an instant.

Even if I couldn't see a soul, I always sensed them. A bright, vibrant, humming energy released into the celestial plane, they were how I imagined stars might feel. Orchid-scented stars. Even now in Lunadell, other souls entered the plane, hundreds dying each day from this or that, but Alexander would see to them with his pack, managing the metropolis until me and my boys were ready to shoulder some of the burden.

For now, it was Gunnar's responsibility to focus on only *this* soul.

"Let's get him," I said. Those three words sent Gunnar into a gallop, and I jogged to keep up with him, sliding through the clustered police vehicles, both of us blitzing through humans in uniform. Already they had erected a barricade at the mouth of the alley, beyond the cars, and a crowd gathered in bolder numbers now, eager to get a look at who had died. Behind me, wheels screeched over the pavement; Kenneth Miller would be on the news this evening. No one needed to ogle his corpse now.

As we cut through the swath of officers, they parted for someone else: a sobbing woman with a black eye and ripped stockings, led away by two paramedics and men in suits, their copper badges hanging off their necks. Gunnar sniffed at them in passing, but none of the dozens of distractions deterred him. Good. A hellhound needed to act quickly. Not every death took place in a sterile hospital room; scenes of blood and guts and gore could easily distract the best of them.

Halfway down the alley between two buildings, the gap wide enough for delivery trucks to pass through on a regular day, Kenneth Miller had been gunned down. Knowing what I did about him, his life's story playing on a loop quietly in the recesses of my reaper mind, I suspected he had forced the officers' hands—he had chosen this, death by firing squad. Someone got him in the head, blood weeping from a wound in the center of his forehead. His glasses had fallen off, cracked at his side. A jagged hunting knife was in the process of being bagged by a rubber-gloved officer.

And the soul of a serial killer stood over his body, staring down at it with a cold detachment I so rarely saw in recently departed humans.

Gunnar paused on the tips of his toes some ten feet from the body, as if to take Kenneth in. Souls were a touch more translucent than their human forms, but otherwise they looked the same. In time, if they remained on Earth, they would rot and become the things of nightmares.

Kenneth Miller was an average fellow—but his type usually was. Tall, strong but not threatening, sandy-blond hair, and a full broom mustache. Still clothed in the outfit he'd died in, you wouldn't look twice at him on the street. Jeans. A grey tee. A black hoodie—a bit young for his forty-six years, but certainly not unusual. Worn sneakers.

A butcher in sheep's clothing.

I stopped at Gunnar's side, scythe prominent, *my* attire leaving no room for doubt: the grim reaper had come calling. Slowly, the soul lifted his gaze to us, first to me, then the scythe, before creeping over to Gunnar.

"Kenneth Miller," I started, my tone calm but assertive—stronger, perhaps, than my stature would suggest. It wouldn't be the first time a soul, particularly a *male* soul, didn't take me seriously because of my appearance. I held out my pale hand, palm up, and arched an eyebrow at him. "It's time to move on."

Head cocked, the man's soul studied us both intently for a moment, his mouth in a tight line, his forehead crinkled—and then he was off. A runner. *Of course*.

My heart skipped a beat, the chase always a little adrenaline-inducing, but Kenneth sodding Miller managed to actually surprise me. Rather than bolting down the alley away from us, he darted left, then crab-walked up the side of the building, screaming bloody murder the whole way, and somehow managed to twist his head fully upside-down like a demented owl.

So soon after death and well on his way to poltergeist territory, eh? Definitely damned.

I gritted my teeth as Kenneth went up and over the rooftop, disappearing, and then exhaled sharply, already annoyed with the stunt.

"Up," I ordered, striding over to touch Gunnar so that he could teleport with me—only he acted before I had the chance. The hellhound vanished before my eyes, so swift and fluid like he had done it a hundred times before, and for a brief second, my heart plummeted into my gut and out the other side.

Because what if this was it? What if *this* was his chance to flee, in the middle of chaos and turmoil, a soul on the loose?

Barking erupted from the roof—more like snarling, really, a gruff, harsh sound that resonated through the celestial plane. I leaned heavily on my scythe for a beat, relief making my knees weak, before teleporting up to the rooftop myself.

Gunnar had figured out teleportation before the rest of them. While I had no clue what other magic hellhounds had at their disposal, all the power denied to them and suppressed by their demon masters, I knew for a fact that Gunnar would discover—and conquer—it first.

I materialized on the roof's edge, taking a moment to assess the situation as it unfolded. Ahead, Kenneth Miller had broken off in a full-tilt sprint, blitzing across the flat, dusty surface, skirting air-conditioning units, and leaping from this building to the next.

And right on his heels, Gunnar, his body sleek and elegant, lean muscles rippling, charging after the wayward soul like a missile.

Impressive.

Beautiful, actually.

Gunnar needed a challenge. He needed mental stimulation just as much as the physical, and I had rightly guessed that selecting a soul who thought he was *better* than all of us would tickle his fancy.

Nothing like another giant ego to really spur a perfectionist genius into action.

Yet despite this being his first field test, Gunnar and I were still a team; he needed to experience how we would work together after we—hopefully—passed the trials at the end of October. So, anticipating Kenneth's continued blitz across the various midrise buildings, I teleported once more.

And arrived *just* ahead of him, catching him off guard four buildings over, my heels on the precarious side of the building, scythe aimed at his throat. The soul's mad eyes widened, and he reared back, my scythe's blade *just* missing his shoulder as he pivoted and beelined for the nearby service door into the tower. Gunnar turned on a dime and barreled through the grungy, locked metal door after his quarry.

Shouldering my scythe, I jogged after them, then paused in the dimly lit stairwell, cataloguing the scuffling of feet, the sudden collision of knees on stairs, the grunt of Kenneth Miller when he undoubtedly ate it—and Gunnar's ferocious snarls bouncing off the walls.

A small smile played across my lips.

Good.

Excellent—just as I thought he'd be. I'd requested these souls for my boys because I *wanted* them to succeed.

They needed to know they were *good* at something, that they were worthy, that they had value.

That they could do something I couldn't.

And that I needed them.

After all, had I been by myself, I could have caught Kenneth's psychotic soul, but in a city the size of Lunadell, without a pack corralling souls while I was off escorting someone else to Purgatory, we could have had another brutal poltergeist on our hands.

I found the pair five floors down on one of the dark stairwell landings, Kenneth on the ground and backed into a corner by a rather imposing Gunnar.

While the whole pack seemed to take a nod from their alpha's subdued attitude, Gunnar was without a doubt the most composed in a snarky, lazy sort of way. Although he had gone through the training motions over the last month, he struck me as a hellhound who did what he wanted, when he wanted, at the pace he wanted —unless Knox ordered otherwise. Seeing him now, in all his glory, cowing a rogue soul with every tool at his disposal...

It was almost... sexy?

I swallowed hard, ignoring the heat in my cheeks and the pleasurable twist in my belly. Intriguing. Not sexy— interesting. *Sure, let's go with that.*

"Well done, Gunnar," I praised, sauntering down the last few steps to join them on the landing. "Excellent work."

The hellhound backed off, but only slightly, still using his massive body to block Kenneth's various escape routes. He had already proven to be quick on his feet, adaptable and persistent. If Kenneth wanted to run again, he wasn't going to make it far.

And from the look in his eye, the slight tremble of that push-broom mustache, the soul of a serial killer at our feet knew it.

"Kenneth Miller," I said in my very best reaper's lilt, our eyes locked, "I'm here to take you away."

The fear in his gaze vanished, replaced by a raw fury that chilled me to the core—because that look must have been what his victims saw just before he butchered them. Cut them into pieces. Mailed parts of them back to their families. Defiled their corpses.

"Fuck you, *bitch*," Kenneth sneered, clawing up the corner to a crouched position. "I'm not going anywhere."

Then, for the first time in my reaping career, a human soul *spat* at me.

The wet blob landed on the hem of my billowing black robe, and, taken aback, the best response I could manage was to blink down at it. I'd been called all sorts of names, experienced every kind of emotion—but to be spit upon... Well, it was certainly new.

Gunnar snapped out of the lull before I could, charging at Kenneth, all teeth and muscle and *rage*, tackling him to the ground and snapping a hair's width from his face. Burly, almost demonic growls reverberated through the stairwell, and I felt their rumbling depth between my thighs.

Spittle painted Kenneth Miller's cheeks, and he cowered as far into the concrete as he could, a hand up to shield himself from Gunnar's wrath.

Surprise raced down my spine and pooled hotly in my core. Ever since our little talk in the dining hall, things had been strained between Gunnar and me, to the point that I worried it would affect today.

Yet here he was—defending me?

Defending my honor?

The fire in my cheeks exploded, scorching across every inch of skin as I lunged forward. A gentle hand on his raised hackles had the hellhound retreating, but just barely, allowing only enough space for me to kneel in front of the recoiling soul.

"Kenneth Miller," I said once more, every word punctuated by my hellhound's soft snarls, the gravity of the situation emphasized when I positioned my scythe's blade at his throat. "It's time to leave this realm and face judgment for the life you *chose* to live."

I cast Gunnar a sidelong glance, and without uttering a single command, he moved closer and slid into a lie-down position so that we were at roughly the same height...

Like he just *knew* what I needed.

As the former serial killer—and future flayed soul—started to weep at my feet, I wrapped my scythe arm around Gunnar, his heart thundering inside that great broad chest, and gripped Kenneth's sweat-stained T-shirt with my free hand, ensuring he wasn't going anywhere without me.

And together, we disappeared, headed to Purgatory without delay—where an awaiting Peter would drag Kenneth fucking Miller straight to Hell.

15

KNOX

The forest was quiet today.

And not the usual quiet of a sleepy morning, birds in their nests, squirrels in their trees, serpents underground. A gentle dusting of mist coated the ground as I approached the tree line, making my paws slick and muddying the natural scent of the wood. Not a single cedar moved, their usual whisper dead beneath a bleak sky. Had the familiar morning chorus greeted me, muted but present, I might have thought it was just the changing of the seasons—a cool day, a grey day, the clouds thicker than the air around me. It *could* all point toward a day better spent indoors, the overcast sky ready to shatter at any moment.

Only that wasn't the case.

Having spent the last two months inside the confines of this ward, I knew better. I knew *my* territory.

Better yet, I knew the telltale signs of danger.

The silence that greeted me as I crossed through the trees suggested a greater predator than any hellhound stalked the shadows. Something frightening enough to hush the entire forest.

Something worth dealing with—alone, while Gunnar and Declan enjoyed their breakfast.

A low growl rumbled in my chest at the thought of the spread Hazel had prepared for us today. Nothing out of the ordinary: eggs, crispy bacon, salted tomatoes, and sourdough buns. All good. All filling. All delicious and nutritious, the sustenance she provided making the pack *strong* in a way I never could before.

The food was fine.

The reaper was *not*.

For she had turned my pack against me—perhaps without even realizing it. In my study of her, the white-haired beauty had never struck me as the malicious type. She had likely coaxed Gunnar and Declan into her thrall unintentionally, but she'd done so all the same.

Declan had mated with her, as I suspected he would when the opportunity and the hunger presented itself. The likelihood of him abandoning her now was slim, which would make our escape harder than it was already. Gunnar, meanwhile, hadn't fucking shut up since his first field test, describing every bit of the hunt to me in agonizing detail, spending hours on the tablet researching a human murderer by the name of Kenneth Miller.

"I brought him to his *doom*," he'd insisted, shoving the screen in my face, forcing me to look at the dead eyes of a human I didn't give two shits about.

All my shits I gave to *them*—my boys, my pack—and Declan had fallen for a reaper, while Gunnar had fallen for the thrill of the hunt.

My beta hadn't said as much, of course.

Declan still refused to talk about it, but he had stunk of sex and *her* when they returned from their outing that violently stormy night last week.

Hazel had them, whether they would admit it or not. But

I knew it. And from the way she smiled around them, hopeful and earnest, her expression tinged with relief—she knew it too.

Which meant I would have to work harder to free them. A gilded cage was still a cage, after all.

But how?

How could I dissuade them when both hellhounds had what they craved?

And how long would it take for Gunnar to mount her, his and Declan's desire for the reaper clogging up the pack bond whenever she was within sight—within scenting distance, even. Packs shared their mates, and from the intense physical response she elicited from *all* of us, it was only a matter of time...

We had to get the fuck out of here before then.

Without my beta and his keen mind, however, I struggled to find the answer. Dozens of possibilities had already been nixed, not worth our time or energy, and the deeper Gunnar and Declan sank into her clutches, the less likely either were to propose anything new.

Frustrated, I patrolled the vast stretch of land inside the ward regularly now, headed out just after sunrise and returning once the pack had eaten breakfast. I needed time to *think*—and space to do it in without her scent and her eyes and her fucking smile muddling it all up.

The quiet had me tenser than usual as I padded into the green depths, taking the same route as always, a hint of a path worn into the forest floor by my enormous paws. Even on the celestial plane, I had grown accustomed to forest critters skittering away as I approached, but this morning there was no scrabbling of claws along branches or up bark, no warning chirps of little birds, no chaotic flutter of a dozen wings taking off into the sky.

Eventually, I reached the ward. Nosing along its base, I

followed it, careful not to get too close lest it singe a whisker. Nothing *smelled* out of place, but I felt it in my bones, the stillness in the cool, humid air, like every living thing around me held its breath, waiting for it to be over.

Whatever *it* might be.

I'd just scaled a fallen tree trunk, half inside the ward, its feathery top outside, when something finally caught my eye. A figure beyond the ward, small but distinctly humanoid. I glanced to the side, curious, then flinched back with a startled snarl, every part of me stiffening for a fight.

There, on the other side of the shimmering ward, was a woman—or, at the very least, a creature who had once been a woman. She hovered just above the ground in tattered clothes, a gnarled mess of tangled black hair snaking down her figure. But it was that face that startled me: deathly white flesh hung off to her bones, her cheeks sunken and worn away to the point that I could see her rotten teeth. Black beady eyes stared back at me, unblinking, and slowly she rotated her head to the side, studying me.

Possessiveness spiked in my chest, a need to protect my territory against outsiders forcing me right up to the ward, so close its burning magic heated my twitching nose. We stood toe to toe for a few slow beats—until she started screaming.

Her jaw elongated well beyond a human's natural reach, her tongue forked, her mouth dark—stinking, probably, like death and decay. A familiar callback to my time in Hell. She bellowed a high-pitched challenge, and not a thing around me moved, sensing her just as they sensed me.

She pounded her skeletal hands against the ward, each collision of her fist making the barrier shudder—but it held firm, even when she raked her broken nails across it. My hackles rose at the assault. Dead. A dead thing wanted in, unhurt by the ward's sting. I snarled back, not an ounce of fear in me, just anger, rage that this *thing* sought to take what was mine.

"She's a vengeful spirit."

Snuck up upon again; my hackles inched even higher. Now that I was aware of her, Hazel's presence bellowed just as thunderously as the spirit did, only it was a pleasant assault, one I could easily get lost in.

I steeled myself and cast the shrieking woman one last menacing look, a silent statement that her fury was *nothing* to me, then padded around to face the reaper.

Scythe in hand, Hazel wore her usual dour black attire, only she lacked the excessive material today, moving without her own personal wind billowing through the garment. Black trousers clung to her legs, leaving nothing to the imagination as they wrapped snug to her shapely figure. A loose black shirt hid the rest of her curves, the sleeves long enough to cover half her palms. Hazel supplied us with human clothing that suited our personas—mine muted greys and blacks and whites, finally large enough to fit me. Yet for herself, she always wore such drab pieces, like she wanted to retreat even further from humanity.

Without a breeze to carry her scent away, it hit hard with every step she took, salty and tumultuous as the sea, power churning below her calm surface. So heady. Enthralling.

I huffed her from my nostrils, holding my ground as she approached the ward, those keen brown eyes fixed on the squalling spirit.

"She'll be a poltergeist soon, something to torment and terrorize," the reaper mused, sorrow in her gaze and a rigidity along her jaw that suggested some internal conflict. "Give her time... She's almost there."

The spirit slammed her body against the ward now, screaming in a foreign tongue, desperate to gain access. When Hazel stopped in front of her, I turned as well, almost taller than the reaper when I rose to my full height. Deranged black eyes soon found mine again, and she fixated on me, hurling herself into the magical barrier, snarling, baiting me for a fight.

My heartbeat quickened. *Try me, spirit.* I was more than ready for her, almost *craving* a fight after weeks of domestic docility.

"Spirits can get stuck on one person," Hazel went on. Did she think I was hanging on her every word? Did she care anymore whether I paid attention or not? Quite against my will, my gaze slid over to her, to the delicate lines of her profile, down to her full lips as she sighed. "They can follow them to the ends of the earth, really. I've felt something strange out there lately... Like there's this, I don't know, disturbance in the plane. I've never felt it before, as if something's watching me." She planted her scythe in the forest floor, eyes narrowing at the spirit. "But I think I've finally found the source."

Another surge of possessiveness reared within me, anger burning in my chest, scorching up my throat, forcing my lips to peel back in a snarl—all at the thought of someone tracking Hazel, hunting her through the celestial plane. Out of the corner of my eye, I caught her studying me with a frown, as if she sensed my response, possibly even *saw* it.

No. With a deep breath, I settled. No, that feeling wasn't really about her. Protectiveness was in my nature as an alpha —Hazel was just caught in the crossfire now that she lived within my new territory. Nothing more.

"There are angel squadrons responsible for her kind," Hazel remarked with a dismissive flick of her hand. "All they do is hunt and eliminate rogue spirits, the ones who vanish before we can reap them. But, I mean, since we're here..." She gripped her scythe and lifted it into a defensive position, her stance shifting ever so slightly as she held it at her side—

like she was brandishing a broadsword. "We'll just dispense with her ourselves."

Together, then, we would roost the dead thing from my—our—territory. I exhaled a harsh breath, then licked at my jowls, the thought of battle making my mouth water. Despite my body's response, I could have walked away. Left her to deal with the spirit by herself: surely she was capable.

Indestructible, especially with her scythe.

But I wanted to see that thing wither with my own two eyes. Confirm its demise. Because if it got through the ward and Hazel failed to kill it, the tormented soul would latch onto the house—onto Declan, even with his newfound confidence. She would find the weakest among us and torture him because she *could*.

So, I retreated a few paces, allowing Hazel the space to align her scythe's curved blade right in front of the wailing spirit, a sliver away from the shimmering ward.

"Are you ready?" she asked with a quick glance my way. Had I been able to make more nuanced expressions in my hellhound form, she might have seen the *just fucking do it already* twist of my features. Instead, I offered a low, sardonic ruff, body tensed for a fight. With a nod, the reaper sliced through the ward, clean and quick.

And in rushed the screaming spirit—straight for me.

I braced for impact, but she hit so much harder than I'd expected, knocking me off all four paws onto the unforgiving forest floor. As soon as my side collided with mossy earth, I rolled and reared, snapping and snarling at her, my vision tunneled on the screeching banshee on top of me. Her gnarled black hair hung like curtains around my face, her flesh paper-thin, her clothing shredded beneath my claws. High-pitched cries filled the forest, finally sent the birds scattering. Deranged sounds poured from her dry lips, pained and twisted, like some unseen hand forced the air from her lungs.

Even still, as her talons sliced across my sides, I possessed no sympathy. If she could, she'd kill me. Already she watered the ground with my blood; fighting on one's back was a poor position for a hellhound. We were far better matched in face-to-face combat.

So, I arched and rolled, *finally* turning the tide in my favor, flipping the squawking spirit onto her back. My teeth found her throat in an instant, but no matter how I tore at her flesh, tasted dirt on my tongue, felt a rush of cold over my teeth, I couldn't harm her. And from the quirk of her mouth and the look in her black eyes, she knew it.

"Knox, *move!*"

The command made me bristle, but I followed it all the same, rolling to the side, pain blooming over my ribs, and shot up onto four paws again.

Just in time to see Hazel strike.

She was on the spirit in a flash, an executioner in black as she raised her scythe above her head, then brought it down like a gorgeous, deadly axe. The blade cut clean through the spirit's warped face, her elongated black mouth, her wild eyes, and the forest trembled when the celestial weapon *clunked* into its floor.

Silence exploded around us. The spirit remained for a moment, head split in two, limbs twitching, until finally her unearthly body dissolved into a white mist, then disappeared as the morning fog broke beneath the first few rays of sunlight.

Splat. Splat. Two droplets of blood fell from the tips of my stained fur onto the stone embedded in the dirt beneath me. As the skirmish became just another violent memory, the pain sharpened, made itself known in the various slashes

across my abdomen. I winced with the slightest movement—
no need to whine about it, for the pain was temporary.

Always temporary.

And more to come in the future.

"This is why our job is so important," Hazel remarked
shakily, scythe still stuck in the ground. She stared at the
spot the spirit had once lay screaming, everything about her
tensed. "No one deserves to become that... *That* is agony.
That is eternal torment. She could have gone to Heaven for all
we know, but she's been stuck here."

I didn't discount the role of reapers in the grand scheme
of things—just the brutal rearing of hellhounds destined to
serve underfoot. No soul ought to become what I'd just seen:
a shell of their former selves, all the light gone, nothing but
black emptiness inside.

But this changed nothing. Not between her and me, and
not my plans to get the fuck out of here.

Hazel removed her scythe from the ground with a soft
grunt, shouldering it like it weighed as much as a galaxy.
When she finally faced me, her pinched expression remained
until her gaze blazed across my sides. Then it all fell away,
replaced by a swift and sudden concern that just *couldn't* be
real.

"Oh, Knox..." She started toward me. "You're bleeding—"

My low growl stopped her dead in her tracks, and her
arms fell to her sides, her throat dipping with a noticeable
gulp. While deep down I craved her touch, longed to feel
those willowy fingers stroke my sides and heal my wounds,
there was a bigger game in play...

I just couldn't give in.

Finally, my skin stitched itself back together, shifter genes
kicking into high gear. I'd never been attacked by a soul
before; would her broken talons scar me too? Or would the

marks fade in this form and the other, left only to harden to scars in my mind?

The reaper's lovely features twisted with hurt at my rebuff, her cheeks flushed. And that hurt me too—pained me like it did to see Declan suffer under the hands of a demon, to witness Gunnar beaten and whipped for disobedience.

But she schooled her expression just as the wind returned to the trees, and I did the same, quieting my heart's longing and burying all those fucking feelings deep, deep inside.

"I'll be back for lunch," Hazel said stiffly, dressed for one of her morning excursions into Lunadell. Off to cry in a sea of human children, to weep in a half-full food court. We both knew where she was headed, which made the color in her cheeks brighter before she turned away and marched through the opening in the ward. Moments later, she sealed it behind her, and then she was gone.

In her absence, I rubbed myself against brambles and trees, rocks and underbrush, smearing the red on my fur across the forest.

Marked up my territory with blood and piss.

Made it my own.

Because after defending it for the first time, it truly belonged to me, and while we were here, no one and *nothing* would try to take it from me again.

Thanks to a vengeful spirit and a reaper's scythe, the land within the ward had begrudgingly become my home.

Our home. Me, Declan, Gunnar...

And Hazel.

For now.

16

GUNNAR

"What the fuck are you wearing?"

Something ridiculously uncomfortable. I held out my arms and rotated in a slow circle for the benefit of my pack.

"I believe it's called a... suit."

Seated in his usual enormous chair next to the hearth, Knox cocked his head to the side, then went back to the historical tome in his lap with a snort. Declan, meanwhile, continued his appraisal of my absurd outfit from Knox's bed, dressed in the most comfortable of all our attire—sweatpants and a loose T-shirt.

All of us had become more and more covered the longer we lived in these four walls, making use of the clothing that just appeared in closets and drawers courtesy of the reaper who seldom haunted this side of the house. In fact, the only time we were naked these days was before and after a shift, and even then, it was a quick hop into a cold shower to soothe the burn of the transition away, then into something soft that smelled distinctly of our individual scents.

This monstrosity was new.

It had materialized on a hook on the back of my bedroom

door this morning, and I'd have to be a simpleton not to assume it was for my outing with Hazel this evening. Well. Evening had come, and I'd been a dutiful hellhound by putting on this *thing* with some direction from the internet.

And it was… constricting.

"Looks like a nightmare," Knox mused from across the room before licking his finger and slowly turning one of the thick, yellowing pages. I huffed, spearing both hands through my rogue curls, my hair in need of a shearing.

"Couldn't agree more."

"I think it looks nice," Declan insisted. He crawled off the bed and padded over to me, holding the lapels of my jacket with a frown. Then, without warning, he buttoned my crisp white shirt all the way up to my neck. "Pretty sure all the buttons are supposed to be closed."

I smacked his hand away. "Well, now I can barely breathe."

"You look dapper, as the humans say," the youngest among us told me, his ease a contrast to my irritation thrumming along our bond. And it was me and me alone tonight that made the bond tense; Knox had been oddly settled since his bout with a vengeful spirit in the forest, and then Declan… Well, a good fuck would bolster anyone's confidence.

Bit annoying, really, this new Declan. I so despised being out of my element, and tonight, I was the *only* one struggling to find my footing in this place. Hazel had yet to tell me where we were headed for our first—and possibly only—non-training venture into Lunadell, and the rest of my pack seemed to delight in my ignorance.

"I think this is supposed to be in some sort of bow—"

"I am aware," I snarled, swatting Declan's hand away again when it reached for the loose black silk around my neck. A flash of teeth and a warning along our bond had the hellhound retreating somewhat, but the display did nothing to frighten away his smug smirk. Rolling my eyes, I went for the tie, looping it as I'd seen done on the online tutorials—and failing miserably to construct anything remotely like a bow. "It's meant to... do something..."

Declan's eyes twinkled with an unfamiliar mirth. "Yes, most things are."

"Oh, fuck off." I turned and stalked to the window, tussling with the bow tie. "You know, you've become quite insufferable since you rutted with her."

Knox's black gaze flicked up, catching the low flames in the hearth. We had yet to discuss Declan's new bond with Hazel—which astounded me, because for a hellhound pack, that connection was monumental. He had done what we'd all yearned to do from the moment we first saw her. And that changed things. It shifted the dynamic. Pushed Declan up the hierarchy. Gave him a different standing in our pack. Should a new member somehow find their way into our ranks, Declan was no longer the bottom hound.

Beyond all that, it implied a progression in Knox's and my relationship with Hazel as well, and the fact that we hadn't broached the subject in the twelve days since *it* happened told me we were on the same page: best just ignore it.

Hopefully, as we all bonded just a little more outside of reaping and training, she would find it in her heart to free us sooner rather than later.

Not that Declan would be all that keen to leave her behind.

And I...

Well, I rather liked the hunt. I craved that almost as much as I craved...

But never mind. There were greater issues at hand right now, namely this *fucking* bow tie that refused to loop like it was *fucking* supposed to—

"This is impossible," I announced curtly, two seconds away from tossing the damn thing in the fire. "Humans must purchase these things ready-made or *something*, because it simply cannot be done."

"Let me try," Declan offered, crossing the room with an irritating little bounce in his step. My eyes narrowed.

"Get away from me."

The bastard didn't even slow. "Gunnar, stop being stubborn."

"You can't be the best at *everything*," Knox added distractedly, squinting down at his book in the dim light, barely paying either of us any mind. I ground my teeth together; nothing screamed the change in our dynamic louder than *this*, right here. In the past, I'd seldom found myself ganged up on by Knox *and* Declan—Declan was rarely ever involved in any playful taunting, actually. But here, in my moment of weakness, they came together to poke and tease.

"Declan," I growled, pointing a stiff warning finger at him, "fuck off."

"You said that already," the hellhound muttered without missing a beat. "Just put your pride aside and let me try—"

"Why?" I caught him dead center in the chest and shoved, forcing him back a few feet—though that did nothing to wipe his smile away. "Are you somehow an expert in the art of bow tying?"

"Look, you don't know everything. Just stop being a stubborn dick—"

"Mind your place, Declan."

"Fuck off, Gunnar. Let me just—"

"Don't touch me!"

"Stop squirming!"

We wrestled with only a hint of seriousness; no one in this pack had ever come to physical blows with one another, and that wasn't about to change over a fucking bow tie. In our hellhound forms, we played roughly, jostling about, nipping at each other, and that seemed to translate to *this*, whatever this was, Declan doing his damnedest to get at my bow tie, me bodychecking him off...

And Knox fully engrossed in his book.

How the tables had bloody *turned*.

I had Declan in a headlock when a soft throat clearing stilled the entire room. Releasing my packmate, I swiped a hand through my hair, both of us straightening, panting as we faced the doorway.

In which stood Hazel.

Wearing...

Oh *fuck*, what *was* she wearing?

A pulse of slack-jawed idiocy quivered through the pack bond, all three of us ogling the reaper like we had never seen a female before. When she stepped into the room, however, the stunned silence turned sharply to lust, so much so that Declan actually staggered a few paces toward her, enraptured.

Like me, Hazel had dressed in black tonight, which was no big change from her usual palate. However, rather than shapeless robes and unflattering shirts, she had donned a *gown*. A fancy dress to pair with my suit. The garment had no sleeves, her arms and shoulders bare, her collarbones on display for the first time. A heart-shaped neckline curved over her bust, leading the eye down to a snug bodice adorned with glittering gemstones that caught the room's soft light magnificently. Fabric continued to cling to her delectable figure, over her hips, no doubt perfectly cupping her pert little ass, right down to her thighs. At her knees, the material flared to the floor. The reaper appeared slightly taller than usual, and the faint but firm click of her shoes was different than any we'd heard before.

She had dressed up for tonight.

And... She had dressed *me* up for tonight too.

I tried to gulp, but my mouth was just too fucking dry.

Cheeks flushed, Hazel looked between the three of us swiftly, clutching a gold strapless purse in both hands. Her white mane had been wrangled into an elegant knot on top of her head, exposing the beautiful lines of her neck, the slope to her shoulders…

Jealousy pounded through me out of nowhere, unexpected and *strong*, at the thought that Declan had touched her, tasted her, *fucked* her and I hadn't. The emotion throbbed through our pack bond before I could stop it, but I shoved the pathetic emotion deep, deep down inside me, even as Declan and Knox's gazes burned into the side of my face.

They understood the feeling. We were one, after all. But that did nothing to quell the sudden embarrassment, my face on fire, my palms sweaty.

"You look lovely, Hazel," Declan offered, shattering the terse silence that had stretched on since her arrival. She swiped at her hair, tucking a few stray strands behind her ear, her blush delicate—and intimate, having just received a compliment from a lover.

Jealousy and longing twined together like thorny vines around my heart, my hands curling to fists at my sides.

"Thank you, Declan," she murmured, her gaze darting to me. "Are you ready? The suit seems to fit well—"

"Yes, yes," I growled brusquely, stalking across the room and ignoring Declan's glare in passing. "Let's get this over with, shall we?"

The whip-sharp *snap* of Knox's book closing made me flinch, but no more than the ripple of upset across Hazel's lovely features. Our rejection hurt her; we had known that from the first week here, and yet we continued to do it despite our plan to win her over with kindness.

Well. *I* continued to do it. She and Knox seemed to have

found some begrudging mutual acceptance since the spirit encounter.

And Declan...

Smitten. Hopelessly besotted.

"Wait." She barred my path suddenly, stepping between me and the door. "Here..."

I stiffened when she tucked her gold clutch under one arm, then closed the distance between us in two long steps and stood up on her tiptoes to reach my bow tie. The looping fabric brushed across my neck here and there, but I couldn't tear myself away from *her*. Those eyes, those cheekbones— deliciously sharp enough to give my own a run for their money.

All these new phrases we had learned since settling here certainly made describing her easier.

And vastly more engrossing. An expanded vocabulary sent my mind racing in Hazel's presence, her sweet alyssum scent positively intoxicating, lulling me into a stupor if I let it. Her smell, her featherlight touch as she expertly crafted the perfect bow tie—it all made my knees weak.

No.

It made *me* weak.

Declan's chuckle had me steeling myself, and I darted around her as soon as she arranged the bow tie in place.

"Have fun, you two," my packmate called as I strode out of the room, the poignant *click, click, click* of Hazel as she followed me down the corridor setting my nerves on fire.

How I was going to survive tonight, I'd no idea.

Hopefully a human died wherever we went and we'd be forced to reap them together—because, honestly, that was the only way *we* were going to see it through to the end.

All the raw emotion simmering to a boil inside me died when Hazel and I materialized at the foot of the Lunadell Opera House. Still hidden away on the celestial plane, yet also surrounded by humans in fine suits and silvery furs and shimmering silk gowns, we stood before a great black building akin to some of the old cathedrals I had seen online and in the news—gothic architecture, they called it. Reminiscent, in some ways, of the stone towers in Hell, yet no part of me recoiled from the sight.

For this was a house of worship, and the goddess inside was *music*.

Hazel needn't explain an opera house to me. Ever since she had deposited that aging phonograph in the piano room, I had studied—in secret, mind you—the ways of music in the human realm. Genius creatures, these humans, who created such magnificent works. I had fallen in love with not only Beethoven and Mozart, but Debussy and Brahms, Shubert and Wagner, Vivaldi and Rossini.

Hell, John Williams made the list.

Even modern music with its synthetic beats had merit—because it was something new, something that elevated my heart and set my mind wandering.

Knox and Declan weren't privy to my fascination with humanity's rhythms, but Hazel knew.

And she had brought me here, to the steps of the Lunadell Opera House...

Guilt reared its ugly head as we ascended the wide-set stone stairs in silence, guilt for the way I had spoken to her back at the house, for the hurt I'd left on her with every snide remark. As I stared at her little feet, dress hitched just enough to reveal a pair of much higher heels than she had ever worn before, I acknowledged that the goal had always been to leave her...

But I needn't be so cruel in the process.

I needn't beat her down as so many had done to me, only with words instead of fists and whips.

She had chosen this place for me, for my love of human music, and it made me feel...

Too much.

Much too much.

Squaring my shoulders, I caught up to her, climbing two steps at a time while her dress only permitted her to scale the one.

"What show will we be enjoying this evening?"

She fidgeted with her hair, a shy smile on her lips, and nodded to the enormous posters stretching the full length of the main doors.

"It's a new one," she told me, "about the sacking of Rome."

"Excellent."

My praise brought the same flush to her cheeks as my scorn, but I still took it as a win. Lush red carpets and gold bannisters greeted us inside, the hum of countless human conversations in the foyer positively deafening. Despite looking the part, Hazel made no move to step off the celestial plane, and I stayed with her as we cut quite literally through the crowd. I lingered a half step behind, and it wasn't until we had cleared the curved staircase that I realized my hand, of its own volition, now hovered over her lower back.

Protectively, almost.

Possessively, certainly.

I shoved it in my pocket before she noticed, following her through curtained corridors, opulent and classist in every sense, until we reached a roped-off seating area.

"I came in during the night to put the sign up last week," Hazel admitted with an impish gleam in her eye, her cheeks dimpling as she sidled around the Out of Order post. "Wanted to make sure we got the best seats in the house...

Pretty sure nobody knows why it's unavailable, but no one's removed it."

"Clever girl," I crooned, following her lead into the small arched balcony, a pair of perfectly useable seats waiting. Velvet warmed beneath my fingers as I gave the back a cautious stroke, and I waited, again, for her to cross over into the mortal realm.

Only she didn't.

Hazel sat in her seat, and I sat in mine, both of us hidden from the viewing hall. To our left and right, guests filtered into the other balconies, just as patrons below filled the red seats. Gold angels, seraphim with their harps and archangels with their swords, cut up the walls and across the ceiling around the stage, which remained curtained off in more red velvet. A bit much, really, but for my first operatic experience, I wouldn't have it any other way.

Only I would have preferred to experience it on the human plane. After all, that was the point of these outings—to walk among humans, to see the souls we were bred to reap. To know them. To feel them. Every element would have been so much stronger out there, off the celestial, so much more grounded and *real*.

Still she made no move to cross over.

The reaper to my right merely studied those around her with a familiar intensity.

"Hazel?"

"Yes?"

Below, nearly every seat had been taken in the twenty minutes since we sat down. Above, a gaudy, over-the-top chandelier crept from the ceiling toward the audience like a groping hand, crystals shimmering, the gold arms looking especially polished.

"Why do you hide from them?" I asked frankly, shifting my intensity to her, to her elegant updo and her beautiful dress. Looking like that, Hazel deserved to be *seen*— worshipped, really, just as I worshipped music.

Beyond that, the men here ought to know what they couldn't have. Just the thought brought forth an immense satisfaction in my chest, a pleasurable tightness in my core.

The reaper shifted back and forth in her seat under the guise of making herself more comfortable, yet I knew it was just a distraction to hide her *dis*comfort.

From me.

Possibly even from herself.

She offered a half shrug, unzipping her purse and rooting around inside for fuck knows what—nothing, most likely.

"Because I'm dead," Hazel said after the silence between us became positively excruciating.

It was the answer I'd expected.

But it felt wrong—just as wrong as it had felt that day, when I watched her reach out for passing children, weeping. No matter what she said, how vehemently she denied it, Hazel longed to be among them again. She craved humanity. While she took great pride in her profession, her dedication to reaping souls a beautiful thing, she carried with her a hollowness that nothing but humanity itself could fill.

And that pained me more than I would ever admit—to Knox, to Declan, even to myself.

Frowning, I snatched up her delicate wrist, holding it between us, right up for her to see as her weak pulse fluttered against my palm.

"You don't *feel* dead," I stressed. Cold, yes, her flesh a delectable contrast to the ever-present fire of a hellhound. But she ate and drank, laughed at Declan's antics, sagged under Knox's ire—she sang in the shower, the rare time she took one, her voice lovelier than any of her old records. Hazel was the furthest thing from *dead* I could ever imagine.

The auditorium lights flickered from bright to dim and

back again, almost in time with her fluttering lashes as her gaze danced from my eyes to my lips, then to my hand snapped tight around her wrist. Hazel said nothing, but she didn't need to; her eyes insisted that she didn't believe me, that my words didn't put so much as a dent in her opinion. When the lights dimmed once more, slowly this time, I released her, and by the time blackness blanketed the hall and the stage curtains peeled open, she had both hands in her lap—and mine buzzed from the cool caress of her skin and the slow, tender waltz of her heartbeat.

Not dead.

Not with a beating heart.

Shaking my head, I sat up straight with a sigh and focused on the opera. Stage lights burst to life just as the pit orchestra started, and soon enough I, like all present, was lost to the music, to the story.

Naturally, I didn't understand a word of it, given the lyrics were in Italian—Hazel confirmed when I asked, her grasp of the European tongues shaky but passable. But an opera wasn't about a literal understanding of the words, rather the *feeling* invoked by the players. The score plucked at my heartstrings immediately. The flare of the costumes caught my eye, the whirl of the dancers stirring the beast within as I tracked them across the stage as a hunter tracks its prey.

Set pieces moved fluidly through the scenes, from the political pleas in the senate to the secret rendezvous of lovers in a midnight garden. Armies marched. Dogs bayed—*real* dogs on spiked leashes. Women wailed. The human spectators applauded throughout the first act, with each brief closing of the curtain, with each trail of the orchestra...

Magical.

Simply magical.

Perhaps an hour in, I finally tore myself away to whisper about the male lead to Hazel, that his vibrato was the best I'd heard in all the videos I had watched in secret, late at night while the pack slept.

Only the praise died in my throat when I found her crying. Not overtly weeping, of course. With her chin on her fist, her elbow on the chair's armrest, she consumed the dramatic rise and fall of the scene before us intently, tears streaking down both cheeks.

Perhaps I too had succumbed to the performance, suddenly drunk on the music, because I couldn't abide the tears this time. Couldn't ignore them as I had when I first stalked her through Lunadell. They elicited something foreign in me, a defensive rush for her well-being. I had never defended anyone but Declan. Hellhounds had been beaten before my eyes, killed in old kennels, and I'd felt nothing but relief that it wasn't me.

But her sorrow touched me.

Tormented me.

Set my body aflame and threatened to burn me alive in this very seat.

I reached for her with a trembling hand, and she flinched when I brushed the backs of my knuckles down her cheek. Her tears left an unwelcome warmth across her flesh, marring the reaper's usual chill. Hazel blinked back at me, then sniffled and let out a forced laugh.

"It's nothing," she insisted softly, despite the fact no one could hear us. Fuck, we could scream bloody murder and every soul here would be none the wiser. The reaper wiped at her face, removing all evidence of emotion—but her eyes shimmered in the stage lights, glossy and full.

It wasn't nothing.

It had never been *nothing*.

Teeth gritted, I faced her in my seat, every part of me tight —which she must have mistaken for annoyance rather than a desire to right whatever plagued her, because she blanched and shot up, sniffling again as she tossed her gold clutch on the seat.

"Sorry, Gunnar, go back to the show," she told me, an order that fell on deaf ears. "It's the music... It makes me emotional, that's all. It's beautiful."

It's not the music. Slowly, I stood, easily matching and then exceeding her height, even in those tall shoes. The sorrow I saw in her, sensed in her, *scented* on her, came from a much deeper well than an appreciation for the opera.

"I hated seeing you cry that day," I admitted hoarsely, honest with her for the first time. She slipped around the velvet-clad chairs, putting them between us with a frown. My feet longed to follow her, but I held my place—forced myself to be still, not to stalk or covet what I had denied myself for so long. "You cry too often, Hazel."

She sucked in her cheeks. "That's not true—"

"I hear it." It pained me to remember, to conjure up memories of weeping through her bedroom door, sniffling outside the piano room, shuddering breaths even as she crafted delicious meals for us alone in the kitchen. "In the house, I hear it... Sometimes when the others are asleep. Sometimes not. I hear you."

"I... It's not..." Lacking a clutch to fidget with, she went for her hair, mussing it rather than fixing it. Strands of white licked down her neck as she scrambled for a response. "I don't know what you *think* you hear, but it's not me. Reapers don't weep. *I* don't... You're wrong."

She ducked away before I could unleash the argument to prove that I was *right*. Darting around the posted sign, Hazel vanished into the dimly lit corridor outside our viewing balcony, and this time I *moved*, stalking after her swiftly and surely. In those heels, in that dress, she couldn't evade me for long, one of my steps accounting for three of hers. My gaze blazed down her figure, from the top of her frayed white knot to the dip between her shoulders, down to the shapely full moon of her ass.

You can't run from me, reaper.

She made it two balconies to the left of ours, following the curve of the hallway, headed—well, who knows where. Away. Away from my accusations, away from me. I caught her by the elbow before she took another step, my grip as firm as the clench of my jaw. Without her scythe, the reaper was certainly more... malleable.

Hazel let out a protesting gasp when I thrust her back into the wall, against the gold wainscoting that met tawdry red wallpaper. Her head collided against the wood, her shoulders, her hips, jostling her as I boxed her in, easily trapping her in place.

Only I had no plan from there. Grabbing her had been an impulse, a rare and fanciful moment in a life of patience and planning. Hazel tipped her head back to glare at me through watery eyes, the black shadows around her brown orbs purposeful—makeup that shimmered and glistened like her tears. The muscles along my jaw ached from the grit of my teeth, and I brought my thumbs to her cheeks, unsure of what I was doing until they made contact with her flesh.

Until they wiped her tears away. Not gently either. Aggressively, like I was determined to *never* see them again.

I hated them, those blasted drops. Hated what they meant, hated the sorrow they wrought within me.

"I know how it feels," I growled, bearing down when she clutched at my wrists and yanked hard, attempting to pull me away, to free herself from this cage. Something dangerous flashed in her eyes when her efforts did nothing—nothing but bring us closer.

And for once, I didn't run. Now that I'd touched her, tasted this intimacy like one sipped a fine wine, I couldn't stop. Needed more. *More.* My hips found hers when she tried to push off the wall, forcing her back, and before either of us knew it, my hand pressed to the hollow of her throat. I swallowed thickly, fingertips digging in right above her sharp collarbone. "I know how it feels... to be so desperately alone."

The sentiment was an unwelcome one, yet the words flowed from my lips like a pounding waterfall. Nothing could stop them. Not her scent. Not the quiver of her chin. Not the tears clinging to her lashes like diamonds.

"And now you've found us," I hissed, her body so small against mine—so small, yet so firm. *Not dead.* Definitely not dead. Heat soared in my core when she squirmed, her hands to my chest now, pushing, pushing, pushing. "And you want us so you don't have to be alone anymore, yet we fight you every step of the way. We snap and growl, bully our way through forced conversations, and still you *fight*." For companionship. For family, maybe. For a pack of her own. A lump settled in my throat, hot and heavy as the need brewing in my chest. I traced a line up her neck, and my thumb brushed the tip of her pointed chin. "Stubborn thing you are, reaper."

She shook violently now, as though touched by Death's hand all over again, but Hazel never once tore her eyes from mine. An unflinching stare from someone outside of the pack usually indicated the start of a fight—unless the lesser party blinked, looked away, bowed their head.

Neither of us blinked.

Music swelled within the auditorium, the desperate cries of the lovers rising with it, and I wrenched my hand from her throat, trembling a little myself. My palms flattened to the wall on either side of her head, and I waited with bated breath for a response.

But she gave me nothing.

Hazel wouldn't engage in this, wouldn't acknowledge

how her body had arched off the wall ever so slightly to press up against mine. I exhaled a strained breath.

"The music *is* beautiful, isn't it?"

What else could I say? I'd given her a piece of myself, acted impulsively, without care, for the first time in years, and for what?

Hazel's hands tightened, suddenly twisting the fabric of my suit jacket, as she rose up on her toes, our eyes locked—and kissed me.

17

HAZEL

Don't kiss him, you fool.

As a human, I had never just kissed someone, on a whim, with no forethought.

As a reaper, I had never kissed anyone at all—until Declan.

And we had done far, far more than kiss.

Which was *precisely* why I shouldn't have kissed Gunnar— shouldn't have stood up on my tiptoes, my feet aching in uncomfortably high heels, and most definitely shouldn't have yanked him down by his black suit lapels so that our mouths collided, stiff and firm. He exhaled a sharp breath against my cheek, his royal blues wide with shock, and I hadn't the gall to look away, so I stared straight into them, dragging out our closed-lipped kiss for as long as I dared.

His mouth was always so thin, twisted into a sardonic smile or a patronizing smirk.

I hadn't expected the softness of his lips, the way they molded so perfectly to mine despite the rigidity between us.

Pull away. It hasn't been that long. He's not kissing you back. You can pretend it never happened.

Just a peck. I could excuse a peck—forget a peck.

I couldn't forget the raw, masculine scent that flooded over me at his nearness, like he had doused himself in some heady cologne that modern men wore for their women. Spicy and woodsy, capable of making any girl swoon.

Only this wasn't cologne. That smell was Gunnar, pure and untainted, and it just… He…

Blinking rapidly, my entire face ignited as I ripped myself away, dropping back onto my too-high heels and hastily withdrawing my hands from his jacket. The opera carried on without us, Dontario and Isabella bleating sweetly for one another even as their warring families threatened to destroy their love, and I hastily racked my fuzzy brain for some sort of explanation.

His words had moved me.

Yes, all that about being lonely—about hearing me cry… Gunnar had, you know, *touched* me, and in a moment of weakness, I had decided to touch him.

How humiliating.

He'd never let me live this down.

Something else for him and Knox to exploit.

"I…"

His large hands slid across the wall, silencing what would have been breathless stammering on my part, and a chill raced down my spine when those hands found my hair. Goose bumps rippled across the sensitive skin of my neck, every sense heightened as one of his hands closed roughly around the bun I had taken great pains to perfect earlier, following a popular blogger's video tutorial so I could be modern yet classic for the night.

From the look in his eyes, the way his mouth lifted in a snarl, I still couldn't tell if he *liked* the updo, if my efforts mattered—not until he snaked his arm around my waist and dragged me into another kiss. His hand clawed at my hair when I gasped, sucking down his scent, my parted lips an open invitation for his tongue. Hot and curious, it explored my mouth, tangled with mine, claimed parts of me no one but Declan ever had before. The butterflies in my belly turned into a swarm of bees, buzzing and violent, dangerous in their numbers, and the rapid thrum of their wings skittered through my veins when Gunnar hoisted me completely off the ground. He slammed me into the wall, his hand tearing from my hair and skimming roughly down my body to my thighs, where he ripped at my gown, at the snug sequined fabric I'd thought was just *too* much for tonight.

Perhaps he thought the same—from the way he tried to tear it off, clawing through the sequins like a beast, not a man.

And that ferocity thrilled me.

Gunnar growled harshly into my mouth, his other hand also darting down to my leg, both ripping at the fitted material as our lips clashed, almost fighting one another for control. The kiss was so different from Declan—both steeped in passion, yes, but there was a fiery resistance here too, like he didn't *want* to kiss me but also couldn't stop.

Like he'd die if he stopped.

A familiar feeling, one that blazed furiously in my chest, between my thighs.

Something tore, rigid fabric finally giving way to raw hellhound fury when he finally wrenched my dress up my bare legs.

I hadn't worn panties since I'd returned to Earth to reap; back then, I'd thought no one would see, so why bother with the annoyance? A bra had become a necessity when I realized men—reapers, demons, souls—liked to watch my breasts bounce with every step. This dress had one built-in, cupping my chest brilliantly, crafting the perfect cleavage. But down below…

There was nothing there to stop him from—

Gunnar groaned when his fingers glided up my thighs and found nothing but *me* waiting for him. His knee shoved roughly between mine, forcing me open, and I snapped at his lip in response, earning another guttural sound that rumbled exquisitely in his chest.

He certainly wasn't shy in his explorations, not bothering to slow the kiss, to ask permission before his fingers smoothed between my slit. His whole body jerked when he found me wet, desire for him hot and heavy, and my back arched as those curious yet firm fingers stroked my sex, smearing the arousal onto my thighs—like he needed me to *know*.

Maybe with good reason.

Because I hadn't realized I... *wanted* him so badly.

All of them.

Sure, my pack was exquisite in every sense of the word. Not only were they intelligent and strong, witty and thoughtful in their own ways, but each one was positively mouthwatering. Gorgeous. Worthy of the attentions of Greek sculptors.

But I'd kept my distance, shoved aside my interest, forced myself to remain professional as I showed them the ropes of reaping.

Only this felt so... so...

Right. Gunnar brutalizing my mouth, caressing my most sensitive skin with those long, luxurious fingers...

It felt right.

As right as it had felt with Declan.

Which should make it—wrong?

While it might have been the norm for hellhounds to share a mate within their pack, it certainly wasn't how humans operated.

Only I wasn't human.

I was—

"*Gunnar!*" I gasped into his mouth when he thrust two fingers into me, rough and unhindered, my body taking him like it was welcoming him home. Still, it was a tight fit, and I parted my trembling thighs farther, twisting my hands into his hair with a moan as he harshly pumped in and out of me. He broke the kiss at long last, but only to drag his mouth along my jaw, to tease my neck with teeth and tongue as he pressed ever closer, threatening to smother me—if I were a lesser being.

But I could take it.

I could withstand him—*them.*

A domed alabaster ceiling greeted me when my eyes fluttered open, the sight reminding me, briefly, where we were, even on the celestial plane. As Gunnar ravished me with his mouth, his fingers, the hairs on the back of my neck stood on end—like someone was watching me. Again. But Knox and I had dispensed with that rogue spirit, so maybe it was just my own conscience suddenly aware of what I had willingly gotten myself into.

Again.

My hands left his soft dark curls, easing down to cup his face. "Gunnar—"

"*Need* you, Hazel," he snarled back, that ferocious tone shooing away my reluctance, quieting my conscience. Because I needed him too. *Now.* It pounded through me like a hurricane, fire snapping in my belly, my mind hazy with desire and my hands wandering with a mind of their own. Touching. Exploring. Claiming—roughly, my nails in play as they ripped over the suit I'd stolen for him, marked up the back of his neck so that he hissed and finger-fucked me harder.

After all the emotion swirling between us, the pent-up *feeling* that dogged me after discovering that he had followed me, exposed me—we needed a release, a chance to start fresh.

But was *this* the way to do it?

"*Oh!*" My core tightened, every muscle trembling as he dragged me that much closer to a climax with nothing but his fingers. Declan had been so reverent with his tongue, but Gunnar was frenzied, as if driven mad by lust, his bite beautiful, the pleasure fluttering through my insides sharp and painful and magnificent.

Vaguely, over an emotional solo from the orchestra's string section, I heard a belt opening, a zipper hissing. Gunnar hitched my torn dress up my hips with a growl, then scooped me up, both hands biting into my thighs, and pushed into me—hard and furious. I threw my head back with a cry as he stretched me, cock driving all the way to the hilt. Caging me to the wall with his lean, muscular frame, Gunnar slammed his mouth to mine, all fire, and his hand soon found my hair, my neck.

There was no tenderness in this hellhound—and I didn't want it. Caged in his arms, I craved his savagery, every violent thrust of his hips pushing me closer and closer to oblivion. With a snarl of my own, I bit back, yanking at his hair, his suit, my tongue and teeth far from passive in our kiss—a kiss that threatened to consume me, and in that moment, as he slammed me against the wall, fucked me with wild abandon, I was all too happy to be consumed.

I had no sexual preferences before this. Royce and I had fumbled about in a dark bedroom once, the man I thought I'd marry taking my virginity before we both left for the war. It had been hurried, like this, but awkward and painful too, full of nervous questions and uncomfortable chuckles. I'd thought all sex was like that—maybe it would get better with time, but barely.

And then *this*. Declan. Gunnar. Two hellhounds who had

opened my eyes to a world of pleasure I'd thought lost to me forever. *Taking* me. Begging to be taken in return, to match their passions, each separate but wonderful. Declan deep and raw. Gunnar violent and desperate.

More.

"Please," I whined, the word coming out in three long beats as he pounded into me, my entire body engaged, present. My heels dug harshly into his lower back as I tried to rock up to meet him, to play the tit-for-tat game as I did with our kiss, but he had me so pinned in place that it was impossible to do anything but hold tight and ride it out.

And what a glorious ride it was.

His mouth clamped possessively over the crook of my neck and shoulder, and I tore clean through his jacket collar when he bit down *hard*. Would he make me bleed? Spill my golden blood across his teeth? I moaned long and loud at the thought, raking my nails up his neck and into his hair. The sting of his bite was more pain than I'd felt in a long time, but it only served to heighten the pleasure rising inside me, making it sharper, more beautiful.

Without warning, Gunnar dragged me from the wall and carried me back to our balcony like I weighed nothing. He stalked with powerful, purposeful strides, taking me to the balcony's edge and depositing me brusquely on the gold bannister. Not that it would matter if I fell, but I clung to his shoulders all the same, hissing his name when he withdrew from me. Mouth set in a thin line, the hellhound grabbed me harshly by the hips, then flipped me around and bent me over the railing. I squealed at the sudden turn of events, scrambling for a hold along the balcony's edge, feet lifting clean off the ground when he pounded into me from behind.

The first act ramped up below, the stage awash with fire, both fake and real, with all the players coming together in a symphony of high sopranos and gorgeous tenors, deep baritones punctuating the calamity as it unfolded. I straightened up as Gunnar thrust hard and fast, pumping me into the balcony, and reached back to seize *some* control. My back collided with his chest, and his mouth found my neck, his vicious thrusts turned into focused grinding, hitting something inside me that made me want to sing.

"I *needed* you," he rasped harshly in my ear, nipping at my earlobe, one hand in my hair as the other arm cut across my body, bolstering me to him. "Needed you for *so* long..."

In that moment, I knew I needed him too, more than I had ever realized before. I needed all of them, and not just to maintain my position here in Lunadell. I needed them far beyond that, but the thought of voicing it made my eyes sting with unshed tears. So, I turned my head toward him, even as he ravaged my bun, fingers shredding it to thick white ribbons, and dragged his mouth to mine.

Hoping that the kiss said more than I could—hoping that it *showed* him that this moment of vulnerability did not go unmatched.

I came at the opera's sweeping crescendo, singers and instruments at a zenith, pleasure exploding through my every cell. The curtain fell seconds later, the hall silent for a beat until applause erupted from the humans below us, all around us. My climax maintained that sharp quality, scratching into my bones, tearing sounds from me that only seemed to spur Gunnar on until he too fell to pieces. His taut body stiffened, his mouth on mine, swallowing me whole as he spilled himself inside me with a groan.

The house lights brightened for intermission, and I clutched at the golden wood railing, heart racing but my mind blissfully still. Gunnar's harsh pants dusted over my exposed shoulders, soon followed by his lips as they trekked a lazy path across my skin. It prickled in response, and another wave of subdued pleasure washed over me when he gently pulled out and collapsed into the chair behind him. Tentatively, I went for my hair—a disaster beyond repair. No way would I cross into the human realm now, not when I probably looked so thoroughly used.

So thoroughly fucked.

The thought made my cheeks burn, and I shuffled back to my chair, perching on it and avoiding Gunnar's eye as best I could. Below, the auditorium swelled with voices, chattering humans coming and going, off to fetch drinks and snacks from the in-house bar, to discuss the new show in all the detail it deserved.

Gunnar and I stayed put, separate, and I scanned our surroundings as though the excessively lush décor was suddenly *so* fascinating.

Until he laughed.

Not cruelly, but rather in a weary, satisfied way that I couldn't ignore. Slumped down in his chair, he sat there, jacket ripped, hair askew, face flushed, and eyes twinkling. He hadn't bothered to tuck his spent cock back into his trousers, and relaxation seeped from his every pore, from his limp fingers hanging over the armrests to his easy smile.

Relaxation that became infectious in a heartbeat.

I flopped back in my chair, the aftershocks of a stunning orgasm leaving me weak and shaky, then pressed both hands to my cheeks when he laughed again.

The absurdity of what had just happened...

It *was* laughable.

A manic giggle fled my lips before I could catch it, and this time Gunnar snorted.

"Oh, *no*," I moaned, sinking deeper into my chair. "What have I done?"

"Again," he added. I closed my eyes, embarrassed and satisfied and comfortable in his presence for the first time ever.

"Again," I agreed. But he didn't let me ruminate, nor did he needle my brewing guilt with a few crude words. Instead, Gunnar yanked my hands from my face, and before I knew it, he had lifted me onto his lap, and soon that laughing mouth claimed mine.

And just as the second act started up, the lights extinguished, we delved deep into another *again*.

Again. And again.

And again.

❧ 18 ❧

HAZEL

"So... Is this when we fuck?"

My blood ran cold, and I stopped suddenly, which forced humans to peel around me on the sidewalk, thus creating an even wider berth than they had already given Knox and me, a few grumbling under their breath. Even with the hellhound loitering behind me as he had since we'd left the safety of the ward, I could *feel* his accusatory stare, his bitter grin.

The ice in my veins twisted around the ever-present knot in my gut. Because he wasn't wrong. On both Declan and Gunnar's off-duty outings, we had—fucked. Declan a week ago, Gunnar last night. The beta hellhound and I had stumbled into the manor with its recently fixed roof and fresh windows long after midnight, clothes torn to shreds, both of us drunk on sex and opera and each other. I'd then skipped breakfast, leaving the guys to fend for themselves, because I couldn't face Declan. Or Gunnar. *Or* Knox.

Being with my pack—intimately—hadn't felt wrong.

But I knew, deep down, it should.

So, somehow, guilt had finally gotten a hold of me, almost because it *should*, and I had let it drag me to a dark place, which put me in the worst mood for my Sunday afternoon outing with Knox.

An outing I still hadn't quite figured out yet. I'd thought it would just come to me when we stepped into the human realm in an alley near downtown Lunadell. Then, as the great mountain of a man trailed after me through the busy streets, I had hoped an idea would spark when we stopped in front of Lunadell's version of Central Park. So far, nothing.

And now...

Is this when we fuck?

Shame made my entire body boil. Guilt weighed it down. Frustration sparked a high-pitched whine between my ears, along with anger that I thought I *had* to feel this way.

Slowly, I faced him—and found the exact expression I'd expected. Surely Gunnar had filled him and Declan in on last night.

Of my three climaxes.

The old me, the human me, would have called a woman weak for succumbing to her base instincts, her most primal desires. My head screamed that I *was* weak, while my heart flipped my head the bird and demanded we go into the park —watch the children play. A few days into October, the weather was mild and the sun high. All in all, the perfect Sunday afternoon for a stroll.

And then there was Knox, the lone storm cloud threatening to burst.

We stared at each other for a very long moment, daring the other to blink first. Quite the pair we were: me in black jeans, black flats, a black peacoat like many of the humans. It *was* fall, after all, and even if the slowly plummeting temperatures didn't bother me, out here I needed to look like they did. Knox hadn't gone quite that far, but the dark slacks, the combat boots, the black long-sleeved sweater with the slightest of V-necks—exaggerated by his broad chest, defined pectorals, positively *rippling* muscles—suggested he had at least tried to blend in.

Only he was a giant, even in the form of a man. And I barely made it up to his shoulder. He'd trimmed his beard, combed his thick eyebrows, but the jagged scar that cut across his face, the permanent ink on his exposed forearms, sleeves jerked up to his elbows, told passersby that this was a creature *not* to be screwed with.

And beside him, me, diminutive in his shadow, white-haired and ghostly pale. No wonder the humans avoided us like we had the plague.

But Gunnar had been right: this was about integrating with humanity, teaching the pack about social values and mankind's modern mores. We needed to be *here*, not hiding on the celestial plane, walking through men and women like spirits.

I blinked first. To our left sat Lunadell Park, a sprawling patch of greenery in the midst of chrome and cement, tinted glass and metallic beams. Walking paths and bike lanes twined throughout the foliage and the city-maintained gardens. In its heart was a children's park, a kiddy pool— closed, no doubt, for the season. At this entrance, located at the north end of downtown, close to upscale shops, restaurants, and million-dollar town houses, was a fenced-in dog park. I nodded to it with a slight lift of my brow.

"Care to go for a run? I can find you a stick, or I'm sure someone will let us borrow a tennis ball..."

As if to emphasize my point, a gaggle of dogs started barking within wrought iron fencing; Knox didn't so much as glance their way, but his black gaze hardened.

"No? Nothing? Great." I had tried *so* hard over the last two months to never be short with them, to empathize, not just sympathize, with their predicament. But everyone had a breaking point, and Knox—and Gunnar—liked to push, push,

push. That little comment wasn't my breaking point, but I'd had enough. Arms crossed, a slouchy brown pleather purse hanging off my shoulder, I motioned to the café across the street with a flick of my eyes. "I'm going to get our coffees, then... Don't go far."

I shouldn't leave him alone, but where the hell was he going to go without his pack? Nowhere. None of them could cross the ward without me breaking it first, so, really, I had zero regrets abandoning him on the sidewalk and jaywalking across two semi-busy lanes of traffic just to get some space.

Space I needed to cool down in—otherwise today would be pointless. Declan and Gunnar had made their connections with me already; I'd felt the shift in our dynamic, an ease around the house despite my guilt. Knox was the last—and most stubborn—brick to fall. Today *had* to go well. We needed to go home unified.

And...

Well, sex was one way to go about it, much to my surprise, but unfortunately, our tension just wasn't the kind to erupt in a fit of carnal release.

More like a shouting match if he kept pushing me.

Although I seldom frequented cafés as a reaper, I went through the motions, same as any other body in there. Placed my order. Paid—I didn't steal *everything*, after all. Waited for the drinks to be made, breathing in the scent of cocoa beans and humanity. Listened for my name. *Hazel*. I took a to-go paper cup in each hand, the pumpkin spice lattes inside positively scalding against my palms, then flashed a strained smile at the distracted woman who held open the door for me on the way out.

Back across the street, Knox wasn't where I'd left him, but as instructed, he hadn't gone far. Following the gravel path into the park, I found him seated on a bench under an old oak, its leaves kissed by autumn decay. He practically took up the entire space, legs spread wide, utterly alpha in his stance, those thick arms stretched along the pine backrest.

He was watching the dogs in the little park within a park. Head cocked to the side, his dark eyes followed those in the bigger run, the edges of his mouth lifting when a few started to tussle.

That flicker of a smile extinguished when I entered his sightline, and he readjusted himself on the bench, allowing me a smidgen of space to sit beside him. Arms withdrawn, he accepted his drink without a word, and I slumped against the rigid bench's back, looking but not really taking in the dogs at play.

"Humans go wild for this every year," I forced out a few minutes later, neither of us indulging in the drinks yet. Both of my hands coiled around mine under the guise of warming them, steam swirling from the teeny opening on top. "Pumpkin spice latte... It's a seasonal treat."

Knox grunted, then leaned forward, elbows on his knees, latte in one hand, still somehow dwarfing me with his size. I sighed.

"Knox, when are we going to get on the same page?"

"Do you have something planned for today?" he rumbled, eyes tracking a human with a leashed dog jogging along the path in front of us. The golden retriever didn't look our way, but his hackles rose ever so slightly when he passed by Knox. Smirking, the hellhound shot me a sidelong glance. "Or will it just be straight to sex—rutting in those bushes over there?"

"*Stop.*"

I swiped at my hair, half-up, half-down, a few white tendrils stuck to my coat and tickling my chin. Even through that intimidating black mane, his neat facial hair, I noted the dance of his jaw muscles like he was gritting his teeth. Good. I'd take annoyance over smugness any day.

"No," I admitted after a beat. "I didn't plan anything for us, because I have no idea what you'd want to do." Declan had needed a soft place to fall, something simple to start out with. Gunnar's fascination with music was obvious. Knox, meanwhile, remained a goddamn mystery. "But I figured we should talk."

The hellhound huffed a cool laugh before bringing his latte up for a sniff. "Well, you guessed wrong, reaper. I don't want to talk."

Shocker. I rolled my eyes, shifting in place to face him. "Look, make fun of me all you want... Make all the sex innuendos you want. It happened. I don't care what you have to say. I don't need your permission to..." My face exploded with heat, the kind that beelined straight down between my thighs when he lifted his black eyebrows. "Never mind. We're in this together. Whether you like it or not, your pack and I... we chose each other." I held up a hand to stop him when he straightened, taking a breath like he was finally ready to argue. "No, we did. You saw the importance of reaping for yourself. And if you don't pass the trials at the end of this month, if you run away, you'll be taken back to Fenix—or maybe someone worse." The idea made me sick, honestly. "Maybe you'll be put down because you can't do your job—"

"Our *job?*" Knox's enormous hand snapped tight enough around his latte that the plastic lid popped off. With a growl, he clamped it back in place. "None of us chose this life—this *job*. We were bred into it. Manufactured centuries ago to serve *your* kind."

I'd thought about that at length before, and having spent the last two months with the pack, I felt even worse about it now than I had then. Honestly, I tried *not* to think about it, otherwise I would spend each and every day perpetually nauseous. "And I'm sorry about that. This isn't how I would have you get into any of this. You're my... You're my partners. We're a team. I want you to succeed."

"And what about what we want?"

"What *do* you want?" I crossed my legs, waiting for honesty—for the truth this time, after weeks of *Oh, we just want to go beyond the ward to learn about humanity, Hazel.* Right. Like I believed that was the whole story for a second.

A dogwalker with a pack of eight attached to a belt around his waist strolled up to the fenced-in park, on his phone, not noticing that the smallest of the bunch was dragging behind. Knox seemed more interested in them than me, going so far as to stand up when the little white fluffball whined and stumbled over his front feet. Fortunately, the brief pause at the gate allowed him to catch up, and soon enough they were all inside and off-leash, scampering about as their minder chatted with another human. Scowling, Knox returned to the bench, and I offered him a sympathetic look that he ignored.

"If I had to guess," I said softly after reminding myself of who he was, *what* he was in the grand scheme of things, "I think you want safety for your pack and security for its future. Food, a bed, respect... the freedom to come and go as you please." Knox spared me a glance, barely looking over his broad shoulder in my direction, a shoulder I battled the urge to touch, to rest my hand on so he could feel that I meant what I said. "I'm sorry you're in this position. Really. I am. From the bottom of my heart. I think it's foul how your kind came to be, and walking through Fenix's kennels was one of the most depressing things I've ever experienced.

"But my feelings, your feelings, our indignation—it doesn't change anything. Those running this world are more powerful than me and you. We're just a piece in the machine, easily replaced when it becomes faulty or makes too much noise. And if we fail the trials…" I finally did touch him, grabbing at his arm hard enough for him to shrug me off and give me his full attention, even if the brunt of his black stare made me want to shrivel up and hide under the bench. "If we fail, you're gone. Can you really afford to let Declan go to another pack where they'll attack him, put him at the bottom again because of his size—scar him even more than they've scarred you? Do you think he can survive that? And Gunnar… Do you want to see him in a pack where nobody appreciates him, where he's bored and aggravated, his talents wasted? I certainly don't. That would *destroy* me."

It wasn't the snide comments that would bring me to my breaking point—it would be watching this pack disintegrate.

"They're good at this," I pressed on. "Gunnar and Declan may have been forced into this life, but they are exceptional hellhounds—we both know it. You wouldn't tolerate them if they were any less, and they wouldn't have *sailed* through my field training otherwise. They're good. They could be great. And they actually seem to like reaping. Declan connects with frightened souls with nothing more than a look. Gunnar will never lose a soul, no matter how slippery they think they are." Everything around me blurred—Knox, the park, the dogs in the run—eyes suddenly stinging with tears—with passion. I let him see the shimmer but wouldn't let them fall. "They don't deserve to be taken away from this life, or from you, or, frankly, from me. I don't want to see that happen, and neither do you."

Knox studied me a beat longer, then looked away, back straight and eyes unfocused as he surveyed the park in silence. At least he hadn't snarled at me, sneered about circumstances we were equally powerless against.

At least he appeared to be mulling things over.

That was a start.

Mouth dry, I took a small sip of my latte, the sweetened coffee cooled just enough that it didn't scorch my tongue. The spice concoction wasn't anything new: ground cinnamon, nutmeg, ginger, cloves, a pinch of allspice. Humans had been baking fall treats with it since I was alive, long before even, but its popularity nowadays opened it up to ridicule.

I rather liked it.

There was nostalgia in the blend, memories of Mum's homemade pies, Dad's hot chocolates with a dash of cinnamon and cloves. It made me smile, the taste, the smell, and I'd hoped it might temper Knox this afternoon, but so far, his drink remained untouched.

"You know, I've tried to understand you, Knox," I told him with a shake of my head and a frown. "I've tried to get to know you—"

"Have you?" His patronizing laugh brought the heat back to my face, and I rolled my shoulders, once again preparing for a bout with him.

"Well, you aren't exactly an open book."

The hellhound shot to his feet so abruptly that the bench's thin wood panels literally bounced back into place without his massive body weighing them down. I gripped the metal armrest instinctively, latte jostling around inside the cup, my frown deepening when he looked over his shoulder at me—only barely, mind you.

"You want to know me?" he asked, growling out every word so low that I had to strain to hear him. "Quid pro quo, reaper. You first. Try to give instead of *take*."

I rolled my eyes again; I knew I shouldn't have let them watch *Silence of the Lambs* the other day. But fine. I wasn't exactly an open book either, but if someone asked about my life, the life before this, I had nothing to hide. So, shouldering my purse, I stood, then jogged after him when he strolled toward the gravel path. His pace was slow, leisurely, like he was waiting for me to fall in line, but those long legs carried him a great deal farther than five of *my* steps would have.

"Well, what do you want to know?" The little rocks crunched underfoot, and I slipped one hand in my pocket, ignoring the sudden outburst of barking dogs, their owners shouting for them to calm down.

"How did it feel to die?" He said it so casually, examining the trees—the first batch of non-cedars he would have seen, the last of the pack to leave our forested territory. I swallowed hard, throat dry again, and then chugged down half my latte to compensate. The sweetness that I usually enjoyed curdled in my belly.

"It… It felt like nothing," I told him as we followed the path's gentle curve deeper into the park, a pair of joggers zipping by us on the grass. "And, I guess, it felt like everything too. It happened so suddenly… They bombed us. I was in France for the war—"

"The Second World War?"

"Yes. I was an army nurse. We had a small camp set up for wounded soldiers, and the Luftwaffe did an air strike in retaliation for an English one… It was over before I even realized what had happened." I didn't remember *my* reaper, but I was told after, when I had accepted my scythe, that there were thousands scattered across Europe for the war. Reapers and their hellhounds, rounding up the millions who had died. A vague, fuzzy memory of the angel Peter remained, somewhere deep in my mind, along with the sensation of a frigid hand on my shoulder as we approached him and the gate. After that, nothing. Then paradise. Then —longing.

"Did you have a mate?" Knox asked, moving on without

pressing for any of the gory details. I arched an eyebrow up at him.

"This isn't *quid pro quo*, Clarice," I insisted. "I'm supposed to ask a question now."

We paused at a fork in the path. Left would take us to the outskirts of the park, to smaller paths that opened here and there to the sidewalk and the rest of Lunadell, surrounded by wilting fall flowers and hip-high stone walls. Knox turned right, herding me with his huge frame toward the playground, the tennis court, the kiddy pool.

He also straight-up ignored my comment, and I sensed this wasn't going to be a back-and-forth at all. But maybe I owed him something more than that. He was right, after all. Reapers took, took, took from their hellhounds. I could give.

Maybe this was his way of connecting with me.

So, fine.

"I had a fiancé," I told him after a group of women in spandex power-walked by us, chatting and laughing, a few pumping five-pound weights with each dramatic swing of their arms. "Royce. We grew up together… He lived just down the street. Sweet man. A good man. He was drafted when the war started, and I joined the nursing corps on the off chance that we could be together over there. He survived, I didn't. Death… let me reap him a few years ago when he finally died."

"Did you love him?"

I shrugged, studying the smattering of dead leaves hanging off a maple. "I thought I did."

"And do you *think* you love Declan? Gunnar?"

A little bump in the path caught me by surprise, but I stumbled more over the question than anything. Was that what this was all about? Rooting out my intentions with his packmates? I bit the insides of my cheeks as heat bloomed in my chest.

"I don't know." Might as well be honest. Knox's whole stern, silent, sexy brooding schtick had always suggested that he could sniff out lies anyway. "I care very deeply for them... for all of you."

There was no cool chuckle this time, but a deep, barreling laugh that scattered a handful of pigeons pecking around a garbage can up ahead. I stopped, every inch of me wound tight as Knox laughed in earnest for the first time in... Well, it was the first time *I* had seen this genuine amusement before, and it hurt.

It hurt that he still didn't believe me, that he could just guffaw away my feelings like they didn't matter, like they weren't real.

"Don't be like that," I snapped as he wiped under his eyes, his tanned skin flushed beneath all that rough facial hair, his mouth stretched so wide it might just fall off his face.

"Like what?" he asked through his tapering snickers. We had come to a standstill, and this time, when a cluster of joggers blitzed by us, one slowed to shoot us a glare over her shoulder—like we were the *biggest* assholes alive for just standing there. I stared back, unfazed, then shifted my fury to Knox.

"Don't be glib when I'm being honest with you." To his credit, the mirth dried up at that, and I resisted the urge to poke him, hard, in the middle of that broad chest—only because that wall of steel would probably break my finger in the process. If reaper bones could break, that is. No one had ever told me. "Don't be an asshole when you've made literally *no* effort to know me, to let me in. I've tried so hard with you—"

"I've been an alpha without a pack all my life," the hellhound stated, angling that enormous body toward me, closing the gap between us to a precarious foot. I stood taller and refused to be bullied by his size. His black gaze slithered down my face to my buttoned peacoat, to the latte caught in my death grip, then jumped back to lock with mine. "I was never violent enough to wrangle a pack. Never cruel enough, never crass enough. Never *enough*. Someone always cut in to take my would-be pack from me. I fought for them, but they chose a brute over me every time. I've been alone for as long as I can remember."

He eased in closer, and just before our bodies could touch, he crouched down to meet my eyeline. A cool, soft breeze toyed with his black mane, mussed my white one enough that a few strands caressed his cheek. Not once did we break eye contact, even as my heart boomed between my ears, as my knees locked and threatened to buckle.

Knox smelled like pure *man*. Raw, untamed, a wild thing —a summer storm ripping across the ocean.

The rest of the world fell away around us.

"And now I have a pack to call my own," he whispered, his breath warming my lips, that black stare verging on vulnerable. "I would kill for them. I would *die* for them. And you, reaper, *Hazel*, are trying to take them away just like all the others."

A whoosh of air ripped out of me, awareness exploding like Fourth of July fireworks. This was it—his angle.

I was like every other alpha in Hell.

That was how he saw me.

My lips trembled. Only I wasn't violent or crass. I was a woman, and his packmates desired me, connected with me, bonded to me in a way they simply couldn't with Knox.

I swiped at the white flyaways dancing between us, smoothing them back with all the rest as Knox straightened. Everything about him became hard again, the moment of softness gone, but my hand still found a way to his chest, settling over his heart, against his steely exterior.

"Knox..."

His gaze dropped to my hand, beneath which drummed a slow, steady heartbeat. Then, without a word, he pressed his over mine, engulfing it, and for a few precious seconds, we just stood there, frozen, hands together—until his fingers curled, and he peeled mine away from his chest by my thumb. He held it between us briefly, his skin like fire, before letting it fall. I jumped to, catching him by the wrist, unable to close my whole hand around it, and yanking hard, bearing down when he tried to twist away.

"I'm not trying to take them from you," I told him fiercely. "*You* are this pack's alpha, and I'm asking you —*begging* you—to expand your pack by one. To just... let me into it. That's all. I'm not an alpha. I know that. I'm not your master." I held firm, but keeping Knox in place was like trying to wrangle a snorting bull. "You don't serve me or owe me allegiance. We've been chosen, whether you believe it or not, for a greater purpose: to help souls. That's it. That's all this is."

He finally wrenched his arm away, half dragging me with him as he retreated with a snarl. "Pretty words, reaper."

The hellhound made it one long stride before I was in front of him, barring his path, shoving my shoulder into this stubborn runaway train.

"Take my honesty as you will," I snapped, eyes watering, latte trembling in hand. "It's on *you* now. I've said my piece, and I won't do it again."

I fixed him with one last look—one that said I was *done* fighting for his acceptance. He could take me or leave me, but now he knew my feelings.

And he knew the consequences if all this failed.

Still shaking, I stalked down the path as fast as my feet could carry me, not stopping until I reached the children's playground. Distantly, Knox's heavy, consistent tread crunched over the gravel underfoot; he wasn't exactly running to catch up. Ahead, children climbed the metal jungle gym, squealed down plastic slides, swung between thick rings. Parents hovered around the pebbly lot, seated on benches, standing at the wood stacks encasing the park's perimeter. More out of habit than anything, I drifted off the beaten path, watching them from the obscured safety of two towering maples.

Knox joined me a few moments later, after I had downed the rest of my cold latte.

"You watch them often, don't you?"

I shrugged, no longer in the mood for his quid pro quo bullshit.

"Because you want young of your own," Knox added. "You want a family."

The playground suddenly blurred, and I blinked back my tears, the familiar hollow ache in my heart sharpening painfully. "I guess. I've never really thought about why I do it... I just do it. Reaping is the most fulfilling life I can imagine, but it can be... lonely."

"Less lonely with a pack," Knox mused, and when I looked up at him, I found a gentle smile on his lips as he too watched the children play. "Or, I imagine, anyway."

"Yeah. It's been really nice to have you all with me... even when you're being an ass."

The hellhound huffed a soft laugh, then finally risked a slurp of his pumpkin spice latte. His handsome face twisted through a grimace.

"Hazel... This drink is shit."

In that moment, the hollowness in my chest lifted. A temporary respite, as usual, but welcome all the same.

I snorted and stole his latte for myself, which he surrendered a little *too* easily.

"Come on," I said with a nod toward the path. "It's after noon... I'll buy you a whiskey instead."

Shaded by the rustling canopy, Knox turned away from the whirling dervishes on the jungle gym, shadows playing across his features. "If you really want to hear my story, you'd better make it at least a double."

I tossed my empty latte cup into a garbage can with a grin. "Deal..."

19

KNOX

The Hazel of tonight was a far cry from the reaper of Sunday afternoon—the one who wore me down with words at the park, with but a simple touch of her hand to my wrist, and who had listened diligently to my life story at the bar after.

Back then, she had been a feminine thing, so soft and nurturing. Attentive. Kind. And not just with her words, but with her eyes too. I'd finally vomited up my depressing story onto the table between us, a tale that was nothing more than a series of failings and rejections, bounced from one pack to another until finally Fenix put me in a kennel alone with countless beatings along the way, and Hazel had simply listened. No pity. No judgment. She had just listened and kept my whiskey topped up, nodding here and there, smiling when appropriate, scowling the rest of the time.

That day, Hazel had been all that I'd needed her to be.

Something had shifted between us—even if my primary goal of freedom for the pack remained. Battling the rogue spirit together had changed the air around her and me, but *talking*, really letting it out, had made a world of difference.

Tonight, however, she was a new creature altogether.

Still feminine, yes, even with her shapeless black robe billowing around her, only hinting at the beautiful curves beneath. Compared to we three males, Hazel always possessed a womanly way about her that I had come to admire. But tonight, she was fierce too. Two sides of one coin, her many facets a secret pleasure to unravel. Strong, confident, focused, she strode along the quiet suburban sidewalk with a deep sense of purpose, the arched blade of her scythe glinting in the passing streetlamps.

I trotted behind her, in no hurry but not dawdling either. Gunnar and Declan had already reaped their first soul—and neither had shut up about it since. Supposedly it was a life-changing moment, that first reap, and a little tingle of excitement buzzed in my chest at the thought of finally experiencing it for myself.

And alongside *this* Hazel, at that. Stoic, determined, she looked every inch a warrior as we strode through the celestial plane. Quiet human houses passed by in my peripheral, single-level bungalows that had seen better days. Every so often, a car rumbled down the nearby streets. Suburban sprawl, Gunnar had dubbed it as we'd sat around the laptop, admiring the satellite photos of the neighborhood after Hazel had given us an address.

She hadn't done so for the others—told them in advance where they were headed. While I'd no clue what type of soul awaited me at 786 Clemments Street, Hazel had at least shared the location with all of us beforehand. Seated on the couch in one of the studies, sandwiched between Gunnar and Declan while I'd prowled about behind, she had typed in the address when prompted by my beta, my pack taking great interest in tonight's destination.

Two brief days had passed since our afternoon at the park, our evening at the bar. We hadn't fucked, nowhere close to it, and yet the atmosphere inside our territory had also changed.

For the better, Declan had mused, the young hellhound *thrilled* that we were all suddenly getting along. Hazel had been quiet these last two days—quiet but present, smiling more yet shy when the weight of the whole pack's attention settled on her.

But confident now.

Self-possessed tonight.

Utterly in her element.

It was a breathtaking sight. She had never looked more tempting, even with her back to me—*especially* with her back to me.

Perhaps this was why the others had enjoyed reaping so much. Maybe it wasn't the souls at all, but the surefooted stride of the reaper who had bewitched us from the moment we first set eyes on her.

Those online relationship articles had gotten one thing right: confidence was sexy as fuck.

We finally stopped at a house that looked like all the rest, the walls dark grey, the roof shingles black and gleaming from a recent downpour. A small vehicle sat on the cracked driveway. The grass, I noted, was far greener than the lawns on either side of the property, and the garden had been tended to by a loving hand, landscaped and prim. A red front door. A metal letterbox with newspapers sticking out its top. Ordinary.

"This is going to be a tense situation," Hazel said, the octave of her voice slightly different from her usual sweetness. Here, it carried the gravity of our task, and I jogged to her side, claws scratching across the sidewalk, and plopped down to observe. She gripped her scythe loosely, arm hanging between us, until the air exploded with the arrival of a new soul.

I stiffened, assaulted by the staticky surge humming within the celestial plane, deep and resonate, its vibrations rattling in my bones. Out of the corner of my eye, Hazel's hand coiled tightly around her yew staff, and she shouldered her scythe with a resigned sigh.

"You have to do what I say in there, Knox."

Faintly, over the explosive energy of the new soul and Hazel's calm but firm tone, I heard a man sobbing inside the house. Swearing too, using words that made some humans blush. My gaze shot to the door, up the steps and across the little wood porch. *Let me in. Let me see.* All that I was as an alpha came to the forefront, but just as I lurched forward, body primed for conflict, for action, Hazel stepped in front of me.

"She needs you," the reaper insisted, our eyes locked. "Comfort her. Protect her. She's terrified."

While I took in the words, I still found myself peering around Hazel at the house's front door. *Need to get in. Need to assess.*

"Knox, do you understand?"

I huffed up at her, then licked at my jowls with a grunt. Of course I understood. It was just... That new soul, the raised voice, the shuttered windows and locked door blocking my view.

Distracting, all of it.

"Okay, let's go, then."

I fought the urge to shoot up onto all four paws and bolt for the door, instead stalking along at Hazel's side up the stone path to the house. The soul's vibrations intensified, making every hair stand on end when we finally crossed the threshold. Pot roast permeated the air, same as the scent of meat and gravy and cooked vegetables that had often filled our own kitchen. That and cigarette smoke, a smell I had become familiar with at the bar the other day, humans puffing away at white sticks on the patio.

We entered a small foyer first, but Hazel veered right immediately into the bright white light of a living room.

I staggered to a halt in the doorway.

Not just a living room—but a murder scene too.

For there, on the floor, was a battered woman's corpse. Bloodied nose. Split lip. Black eyes—both of them swollen and bruised. Red hand marks around her throat. Blood down her torn blouse, her skirt hitched up to her bare thighs. One of her purple slippers hung off her foot, while the other lay in front of a muted television, the evening news plastered across the screen.

Behind her, a man on a chair. Average height, perhaps even slightly below. Average build. White-skinned, freckled, balding. He wore a sport jersey and a pair of blue jeans. A lit cigarette hung limply between two fingers, a breath away from the upholstery. Tears streaked down his cheeks. Blood marred his knuckles—*her* blood. Even on the celestial plane, I could smell it.

Jaw locked, I looked from the burning end of the cigarette to the small circular marks on the corpse's left arm.

Hazel, meanwhile, had already crossed the room, her deathly presence engulfing the whole house as she descended upon a cowering figure in the corner.

"Stupid fucking *whore*," the male muttered under his breath, words catching in his throat, thick and vile. The ring on his one finger matched the delicate gold bands on the corpse's hand. Humans exchanged rings when they married.

My hackles rose, a low growl vibrating in my chest.

They were mates, him and her.

The dead body, bloodied and beaten and violated—

"Amy?"

Amy. Amy's corpse smelled like blood and smoke, like the vanilla and bourbon candle Hazel had added to the TV room at the manor. Her scent was all over this space—the twin two-seater couches, the little pillows, the blanket folded neatly over the back of the armchair. Slowly, my gaze drifted to a kneeling Hazel, to the slim soul of a woman in the corner. A squeaky wail filled the room, made the drawn floral curtains shudder. Her mate didn't notice, smoking and staring at her corpse, cursing so softly that a human might have missed it, but my sensitive ears heard every fucking word.

"My name is Hazel, and this is Knox." She gestured back to me, and I forced myself to move, to march stiffly by the dead human on the floor. At least the damage didn't carry over to her soul; Amy was fresh and bright now, clean and well-groomed, her auburn hair in tight ringlets around an angular face with hollow cheeks. Hazel placed a hand on her knee, and the soul pushed back into the corner, made herself small, covering her head with both arms—like Hazel might strike her at any moment.

"Fucking worthless bitch," the male grunted. Out of the corner of my eye, I caught him flick his cigarette at the corpse, then stand and disappear through another door deeper into the house. A moment later, rattling glass accompanied the *whoosh* of a refrigerator door opening.

"We're here to take you to a better place," Hazel murmured, situating herself so that Amy couldn't stare at her own battered body. "I know it's frightening, but you're safe now..."

Strong *and* soft, this Hazel. A warrior with a gentle heart. As much as I longed to study her, reflect on her, I couldn't focus on anything—couldn't center my mind. Because there was all that blood weeping into the floor, between the wood panels, into the celestial plane. Then the vibrations of a new soul, sharp and vivid, deafening.

And the male.

I turned my back on him when he stumbled into the room

again with a beer bottle in hand, gritting my teeth when he cracked it open. The metal cap landed on the floor seconds later—close to where he'd chucked the cigarette.

Next to her body.

Amy sobbed and buried her face in her hands, shaking, shaking, *shaking* so violently that it made my heart physically hurt. I crept closer, sniffing at her arms, her hidden face, her hair. My tongue swiped across her neck—a neck marred by her mate's hands in the human realm, red and crushed—and instinct told me to hunker down, lie on top of her, make her feel safe and secure beneath me.

Security blankets. I'd read the phrase online, learned about compression therapy for humans who panicked like Declan once did, fighting for breath, heart racing, fear taking hold.

Only I couldn't do *any* of that.

Because the male wouldn't shut up.

Because that fucking piece of garbage had killed his *mate*.

And there was nothing worse, nothing fouler to my sensibilities, than the murder of one's soul mate.

Fate gave you a gift.

"Look what you made me do," the male grumbled from the armchair, kicking at her sprawled legs, her slipperless foot. "Fucking cunt, I told you not to push. All you do is push. And look what happens. Look what fucking *happens*."

With Hazel softly murmuring to the soul, cooing and coaxing her to lower her hands, I stood guard. Fury pounded through me when the male stood, his next kick landing on the corpse's side.

"I told you to mind your fucking business!" he bellowed, crouched over, screaming at the lifeless body as her soul wailed. Beer dribbled out the bottle, splattering over her bloody face, and he hurled it clear across the room. The shatter of glass had Amy's soul collapsing further in on herself; she dropped to the floor and rolled into a ball, rocking back and forth, sobbing.

I turned away from her, fixated on this male, this pathetic creature.

"Look at what you did!" He kicked her again, then stomped on her ribs. "Look at what you did, Amy!"

Snarling, I took a step toward him. Rage replaced the sorrow in my heart. I'd swallowed it for years, beat it back down; no matter how furious I became with the circumstances, with our surroundings, with the treatment of Gunnar and Declan, I rarely responded unless directly attacked. I protected. I stood between an abuser and the abused. Always.

But he wouldn't stop kicking her.

She was already dead, and still he pummeled her.

"Knox, let's just go," Hazel said distractedly. "We'll deal with everything in Purgatory…"

He broke her nose with his heel, crushing bone and cartilage, flattening it like a fucking cardboard box.

Centuries of subdued rage finally came to a boil—and I snapped.

With a roar, I charged from one plane to the next, leaving the celestial behind and hurdling headlong into the mortal realm. The bastard staggered back, off-balance and blinking hard at me like I was some drunken hallucination.

He should know what I was: vengeance, penance, instant justice for the brutal act of butchering his *mate*.

Time seemed to slow when all four paws left the ground, my body flying toward him, teeth bared and snarl rattling the windows. Distantly, Hazel's voice screamed through the planes, but with my heart drumming a battle cry, I barely heard it—didn't even acknowledge it.

We collided seconds later like an avalanche blasting over a lone pine tree, ripping it from the earth, root and stem. The fucker collapsed, slamming his head to the floor, cracking bone, and I went for his face, snapping, snarling, painting him with saliva as a wildfire blazed through my veins. Red eyes glared down at him, yet all I saw was red too, the hazy tinge of pure rage clouding my vision, focusing it on the screeching human beneath me. My claws raked up his chest, splitting him open, shredding him like a knife through butter. Hot blood spurted up my legs, but I pressed on, refusing to yield until there was nothing left of him, until he was just bits of flesh and bone and teeth on the fucking floor.

He deserved no less.

"Knox!" Hazel's cry came sharper this time, slicing through the fog. Footfalls clicked hurriedly across the hardwood to my left, even as I sank my teeth into the shrieking human's shoulder. "Knox, *stop*!"

No. Never. Never would I—

I stilled when the cool touch of a reaper's scythe settled against my throat. Human blood dripping down my jowls, I straightened and followed the staff all the way to her. She stood, paler than I'd ever seen her, eyes fixed on me, unnervingly still.

How dare she stop me?

How dare she rob me of this *one* justice?

I reared around the scythe, stabbing my front paw into the fucker's open chest until a rib cracked.

Hazel pressed in harder, the blade cutting through fur, its power extinguishing the fire within me as easily as one blows out a candle. This thing could kill me. Shaking, rage still pounding with every beat of my heart, I looked to her and wondered: would she thrust deep? Slit my throat with a hook made of stars?

Yes.

No matter her feelings, no matter our connection—Hazel would kill me to protect this human.

It was her duty.

And I had—infringed on it.

"Step back," she ordered firmly, and when I hesitated, she offered one last taste of her scythe's bite. Although it physically pained me, I slowly complied, taking a few stiff, furious steps away from the human.

The murderer who lay in a puddle of his own blood and piss.

"*Get back* on the celestial plane," Hazel growled, "and see to her soul. She is lost. She is broken. She is terrified." The reaper situated herself between me and the sobbing ingrate, peering down her nose at me, only a slight quiver in her lips suggesting she wasn't in *complete* control. That, like me, she was a second away from shattering. "Do your duty, Knox. *Now*."

Hazel spoke of *duty*…

This should be my duty: punishing the wicked.

Perhaps I ought to work in the pits of Hell instead, inflicting punishment onto damned souls.

No. My eyes slid to the growing pool of bright red blood. No, I couldn't torture the damned for eternity; I could barely stand to breathe the same air as *this* cretin.

"She needs you," Hazel told me, her flat inflection hinting that this was the last warning I would get before I found the scythe at my throat again. While I hesitated at first, eventually I turned, my innate protectiveness forcing me to cross between realms. Annoyance ripened at the fact that she knew my trigger—that I would always defend the meek. It was what separated me from other alpha hellhounds: the need to protect the smallest among us rather than pit the others against them.

Amy's soul remained in a tight ball on the floor, tearstained cheeks hidden behind her hands. I smelled the salty tang of sorrow as I approached, dropped to the ground, and positioned myself like a great furry black wall between her and her killer. While I would have preferred to focus on her, to lick her tears away, to nestle in so that her shaking body found warmth in mine, there was one big bloody distraction that I just couldn't ignore.

In the mortal realm, Hazel crouched before the battered male. She traced her hands along the wounds, sealing them with the same grace and ease that she sealed our ward. Slowly, the color returned to his cheeks, the life to his eyes. He eventually found the strength to sit up and skitter back, crashing hard into the nearby couch with a cry. Hazel studied him for a moment, then crept closer. Her finger found his forehead, even as he shrank away, and once she made contact, the vile creature at her feet stilled, eyes glassy, jaw slack.

"You'll forget the hellhound," she said, firm and in control again. "The name Knox will mean nothing to you. The last five minutes never happened." Her finger left his flesh—and she faltered. A heartbeat later, it was back, and her white brows crinkled. "But you will *never* forget what you did to her. You'll never forget this night. You will remember, in painfully vivid detail, until the day you die how you killed her, the look in her eyes when you finally choked the life out of her. And deep down, you will understand, Christopher Morten, that when you die, we'll be back for you. Knox and me, we'll be waiting," she whispered, "to take you straight to Hell."

Withdrawing her hand, she stood with a disgusted look, then wiped her finger on her robe, as if to rid herself of this Christopher Morten for good. The human lay there on the floor, dazed, and only came to when Hazel stepped inside the celestial plane and left him utterly alone in the house, with the corpse of his mate and the faint knowledge that he was damned.

My eyes tracked her every movement back to Amy, even if she wouldn't so much as glance my way. Hazel crouched at the soul's side, expression hard, while I remained a silent, looming presence. At no point did I utter an apologetic whine, nor did I growl out my frustration that she had stopped me from killing him, from punishing him for committing the foulest crime of them all.

Murdering one's mate...

I'd never forget it.

Never forget this night.

It made itself at home alongside a lifetime of other vile memories and would likely surface from time to time in the future.

And I then would remember how it felt to lose control.

How it felt to disappoint her.

"This is your last moment of suffering, Amy," Hazel murmured as she stroked the soul's hair from her face and took her gently by the shoulder. "I promise."

She then reached for me with the hand clasping her scythe, resting the rigid staff along my back.

And in the blink of an eye, we left the nightmare at 786 Clemments Street behind for good.

Anxiety rippled through the pack bond—mostly from Declan, which was nothing out of the ordinary, but also from Gunnar tonight, both of them fearful of my failure. Sighing, I threaded my fingers together, then tossed my head side to side, a noisy, satisfying crack thundering from my neck with each toss. Declan paused his pacing for a moment, his attention on me, face crinkled with worry, then resumed his back-and-forth in front of the manor's double-doored entrance.

If he went any longer, he'd wear a path into the tile. Gunnar, meanwhile, leaned against the opposite staircase from the one I sat on, still as a statue, that dark blue gaze drifting from the doors to me. Silence hung over the entire house—the whole property, even, the night deathly quiet, the forest still. Hazel had been gone for almost an hour now, and every faint creak of the settling manor sent fire through the bond from all three of us, each expecting our reaper to fly in at any moment.

It was exhausting.

While my pack wore clothes—Declan in a sweater and jeans, Gunnar in more formal trousers and a grey button-up —I sat naked. Dried sweat clung to my skin, and forest earth caked up my calves from the solo walk back. After we had deposited Amy's soul in Purgatory, Hazel had brought me to the property's edge, cut clean through the ward, then ordered me in. After closing it behind me, she vanished, no doubt off to deal with my impulsivity on a higher level.

Fuming yet *slightly* remorseful, I had trudged through the cedars alone, half as a hound, the rest of the way a naked man. Mud coated the soles of my feet and between my toes. The bitter fall chill had settled into my bones, and the battle lust had faded in her absence. A poorer alpha would have kept his failings from his pack, but living in such tight quarters, knowing the bond forming between the others and Hazel, it would get out eventually. Gunnar and Declan had greeted me at the front door, eager as pups for the news.

And I'd given it to them, every bitter detail. The excitement had vanished, and here we waited with bated breath—for my fate, for Hazel's *true* reaction to what I'd done to that fucker.

Gunnar had snarled and buried his fist in the wall at the notion of harming one's mate, even a hair upon her head.

Declan had raged silently, raw fury pulsing through our bond.

I'd known then that they had been thinking of *her*—of one of us, or some other bastard, truly hurting her.

And the longer I sat on these stairs, ass asleep and mind muddled, the more I'd considered that back there... I had been thinking of her too. Sure, I had a good two centuries of unbridled rage simmering in my heart, but the brutal murder of one's mate had been especially offensive. Hazel... Well, the others had given in to the connection between her and us. There was a very real chance that fate had set her in our path as *our* mate, despite the cruel circumstances of our meeting.

So, maybe, if I allowed myself such thoughts, I had reacted so violently because somewhere deep down, I imagined Hazel's lifeless corpse in Amy's place.

Maybe.

And that was a huge failing on my part, a weakness that I couldn't let rule me ever again.

The three of us straightened in unison at the sound of familiar shoes clicking up the front steps, across the porch. The copper knobs rattled faintly. One turned. Seconds felt like hours waiting for the door to swing open, and when it did, a weary Hazel appeared in its opening, her hair oddly flat, her lovely features taut. She used her scythe as a walking stick, easing inside and gently closing the door, her eyes on the floor.

Subdued tension flowed through the pack bond, all of us still and silent, but Declan was the first to react to the reaper's presence. He strode forth to meet her, oddly self-assured as he took her firmly by both arms. The slight jostling seemed to startle her, like she had *just* realized she was back with us.

It was good to see Declan confident after all this time. My pride in him warmed our collective bond, and Gunnar's thin lips twitched up slightly at the feeling, watching the pair just as intently as I did.

"Are you okay?" Declan murmured, stroking her upper arms with his thumbs, the closeness between them easy, natural, nothing about it forced. Hazel offered a weak smile and a slight nod in response, and his hands dropped to his sides, allowing her to pass unhindered. Gunnar then crossed the yawning space in a hurry, only to stop just short of her, his expression serious, that huge brain of his undoubtedly a blur—if the conflict ripping apart our bond suggested anything, at least.

Hazel paused beside my beta, then gave his right hand a squeeze. Since she had let them between her thighs, the reaper had gone to great efforts not to touch either when we were all together. She hadn't actively avoided them, but she'd maintained a respectful distance, her confusion and discomfort at being shared between hellhounds obvious. Yet now, the intimacy between the two came easily, nothing more than a simple caress settling Gunnar and Declan as I never could.

The evidence of that shone in our pack bond. As soon as they connected, the anxiety eased. It didn't vanish completely, but we all seemed to find comfort in her company. My fingers twitched in her general direction, as if they too sought to caress her, but I stayed put, watching it all unfold from the stairs in silence.

"We have a strike against us." She sounded exhausted. Concern bolted through the pack bond, though Hazel seemed not to notice. She tapped her scythe's staff against the tile once, twice, her frowning deepening. "I... I have a strike... for allowing one of my pack to attack a human."

"He's fine," I growled back, gruff and tired myself, in need of a cold shower and some time in front of a roaring fire to really think. That *Christopher* fuck should be the last thing on our minds; he didn't deserve to occupy a single second of consideration in this house. "You healed him and erased his memory… What more could matter beyond—"

"Don't you *speak* to me." The reaper finally looked my way, her face pale, her eyes rimmed in dark circles and glittering with unshed tears beneath the foyer's ancient yellowing chandelier. Scowling, I finally stood, towering over all of them as my fist went rigid around the wood bannister.

"Hazel—"

"How *dare* you force my hand?" Her voice cracked through the accusation, and she stormed across the room and up the stairs, not stopping until she had the added height to her advantage three steps up. Eyes I had come to know so well as of late sparked with gold, with fire, the weight of their glare like a lead anchor threatening to drag me under—drown me. Hazel's lips trembled, the pack painfully silent below as we faced off.

"How *dare* you make me raise my scythe to you?" she demanded, lifting her godly weapon as if I'd forgotten its sting against my throat. "I could have killed you! I wouldn't have had a choice!"

In her eyes, I found turmoil. Rage. Anguish. Fear.

"He deserved to be punished," I said roughly.

"He will be punished," Hazel fired back, white-knuckling her scythe, her other hand in a dainty yet powerful fist. "But not by us. That's not our duty. He wasn't our charge or our responsibility… *She* was."

"And she deserved to see him brutalized." If it was the last thing that woman's soul witnessed on Earth, she ought to see him suffer. Her arm sprinkled with cigarette burns flashed across my mind's eye, the handprints on her corpse's throat, and a growl rumbled in my chest as I squared my shoulders, ready to *fight* for this. Amy should have watched me rip that fucker apart at the seams—

A tear cut down Hazel's cheek. She made no move to brush it away, and my heart twisted harshly at the sight.

"Don't you *ever* put me in that position again, Knox," she hissed. And that was that. Hazel marched up the stairs, her scent coarse and violent like a raging sea, and then disappeared to her wing of the house. Moments later, as I made a vow to never make her choose between me and duty again, her bedroom door slammed shut, its echo carrying throughout the building.

Once again, Declan reacted first. He jogged up the opposite stairwell and paused on the landing. Darkness filled the windows behind him, a starless night observing our drama. Briefly, it seemed like he meant to follow her, but indecision thrummed through our pack bond, and he went left instead, up to our wing, our doorless bedrooms, his shoulders slumped and his emotions messy. They played across our bond openly, his love for me colliding with his desire to comfort her.

Although my knees didn't give out, I found myself sinking back to the stairs all the same, squatting there with my elbows on my knees, my head hanging low. After a lengthy sigh, Gunnar wandered over, his footfalls softer than usual, tepid and cautious. He sat at my side, our bodies touching as they often did in our hound forms, the pack accustomed to sleeping together, keeping each other warm in the pits of Hell.

Tonight, his presence offered a silent support. We sat like that for some time, feeding off each other, coming down from the high of the night as one and settling the chaos along the pack bond. Our calm would eventually work its way to Declan.

"Knox?"

I grunted. Even with my eyes closed, I felt Gunnar's gaze burning into the side of my face.

"I would have killed him," he admitted softly. With a weary grin, I raised my head just enough to meet his eyes and then patted his knee.

"I know, Gunnar. I know." Had the others been in my place tonight, they would have struggled to control their primal impulses too. Mates were sacred. Precious. Honored. Fated and rare.

Our mate...

Well, I was finally starting to think—acknowledge, admit, accept—that ours just might be celestial.

And if anyone did to her what that fucker did to Amy...

No one would be able to stop us.

❦ 20 ❦

HAZEL

At precisely ten after ten the following morning, someone knocked at our front door.

Hands buried in a sink full of dishes, I paused and looked over my shoulder with a frown. Beside me, plate and towel in hand, Declan also stilled. Because... who the hell had gotten through the ward? Had Gunnar locked himself outside?

I mean, we never locked the doors, but...

Another knock, sharper this time, three curt raps of someone's knuckles.

Declan lowered the half-dry plate to the counter with a breathy growl. We hadn't said much this morning, but he hadn't left my side since I'd started on breakfast two hours ago. Even without an in-depth conversation about last night, about how shaken I still was from the whole thing, his presence soothed me, and we had been working alongside one another in a companionable silence since the pack had finished eating, clearing the kitchen island, putting leftovers in the fridge, washing the dishes by hand.

In times like these, I preferred the monotony, the normalcy of cleaning one's dishes, getting your hands wet and sudsy rather than snapping your fingers and finding the space around you sparkling clean. Last night, with Knox, it had all happened so fast—

The third knock sounded the most impatient of them all. I accepted the offered dish towel from Declan, still staring in the general direction of the front door, and wiped my hands dry, then tossed it on the counter and strode out of the kitchen. Behind me, there was a very soft, *very* faint *whoosh* of the shift, and before I'd even reached the foyer, I found a trail of discarded clothes and a shaggy hellhound at my heels. Declan trotted after me, hackles up, and nosed at my hand in a way that was reassuring—not like he was seeking comfort, but rather reminding me that he was here. My heart skipped a beat at the thought. My Declan. Always there for me when I needed him, even if we didn't say a word.

Gunnar and Knox were already on the landing by the time I marched into the entrance foyer, beams of sunlight slanting in through the enormous windows and filling the cavernous space. It wouldn't last. From the look of the grey sheet the sun fought so valiantly through, we'd soon be neck-deep in another autumn storm.

Raising a hand, I wordlessly summoned my scythe. It whizzed through the house, straight to my palm like good ol' Thor beckoning his faithful Mjolnir, and I gripped it tight as I grabbed the doorknob and twisted it open.

Alexander's handsome face greeted me from the other side. I blinked, stunned at his presence, that soaring model-esque figure filling the doorway. We hadn't seen each other since my first month with the pack, back when I relied on his guidance in the early days of their training. Had our higher-ups ordered him here this morning? Had they alerted him to last night's fuckup?

It had happened so fast. Knox's ominous presence hovered behind me; I hadn't been able to look him in the eye yet, so furious that he had lost control, so hurt that he'd broken our fragile trust *again*, so disappointed in myself for not noticing the signs in his body language—not realizing at the house that he had been about to—

"Morning, Hazel."

"Alexander, hey." I stepped aside to let him in. Declan inched backward, but he remained so close I could practically feel his slow, steady breath on my neck. "Is everything okay?"

Are you here to take them from me?

Nobody upstairs had been thrilled with the incident, but it wasn't the first of its kind, nor would it be the last. To some, hellhounds were wild animals. It was therefore expected that they might lash out, especially the alphas.

I had just gone with it, accepted their reasoning with a strained smile, even as my heart splintered apart, and then returned home with a word of warning rattling around my brain.

If he does it again, put your scythe to good use, Hazel. That behavior is unacceptable.

Even in the melodious voices of angels, it was a statement I never, ever wanted to hear again.

Or act upon.

Because…

Well, Knox… He… He and I—

"There's been a building collapse in Lunadell," Alexander remarked, sweeping into the foyer like he owned it, wavy golden locks swooped back like a crooner straight out of the fifties. Dressed in a fitted black suit, his bright blue gaze flashed over my pack with mild interest; he had never approved of my choice. His scythe had a ribbed edge on the blade, the kind that tore innards apart after it sliced through flesh. That blackthorn staff was taller than me and stiff as a board, whereas my yew followed the natural, subtle curve of tree bark.

"Gas line explosion. About seventy-five dead." Alexander trailed off, eyes suddenly unfocused and very far away. "No. Seventy-six, now." Blinking rapidly, he cleared his throat and smoothed a hand over his hair. "We need all hands on deck, I'm afraid."

Before I could get a word in edgewise, Alexander snatched my hand, and the second we touched, he transferred to me all that Death had given to him. Faces, names, life stories, and cause of death—mostly fatal crush injuries, but a few heart attacks and suffocations peppered the array. Seventy-six new souls destined for Purgatory. Some would go up, others down, and they needed us. *Now*.

"Yes, yes, of course," I said absently when our hands parted, shaking mine out as a headache tingled behind my eyes. It was more information than I'd ever received in a single go before; I could hardly imagine how it felt to reap wars. "My pack has done field tests already... We're happy to help."

Seventy-six was far too many even for Alexander's pack of eight to contain, and after a building collapse, the influx of souls, it would be utter madness on the celestial plane. He couldn't do it without us.

Apprehension prickled in my belly when I spotted Gunnar and Knox making their way down the stairs, both stone-faced and solemn.

"Knox stays," I announced—not because I wanted to, but because after last night, I felt it *had* to be said. Gunnar and Declan could work just fine without him for now. The alpha stopped halfway down the stairs, every inch of him hardening, and our eyes met for the first time all morning. My eyebrow twitched up, daring him to try me after what he had put me through last night, after the sheer panic I'd suffered at the thought of using my scythe to subdue him.

Sure, Christopher had deserved to die—painfully, brutally—for what he'd done to his wife. But that wasn't our place. Lucifer doled out penance for sinners; we were just bounty hunters, really. Glorified handlers. To kill that bastard would have been stepping *way* out of bounds, far above Knox's pay grade.

Someone else would have killed *him* if he'd ripped that human apart.

So, he had forced *me* to—

"No, we need everyone," Alexander insisted as he checked his wristwatch. I rubbed between my eyebrows, willing myself to stay in the moment, to stop getting lost in Knox. The reaper to my left then shouldered his scythe and flashed a smarmy smile. "Don't worry, Hazel. My alpha can keep them in line."

My three hellhounds bristled at the comment, Gunnar's eyes narrowing, fur rising off Declan's back; Knox clenched the bannister so harshly that the wood splintered. Right. Like hell that was going to happen. No one would "keep them in line" but me.

And Knox.

If he could fucking behave himself.

"No time to waste," Alexander muttered, shooting me a knowing look before peeling back toward the door. "Let's move out."

I understood his urgency, but this was my pack's first *real* experience. With this death toll, I couldn't hold their hands—paws—nor could I be on top of them at all times.

Trust. Did we have it yet?

Declan, I trusted implicitly.

Gunnar—to some extent.

Knox...

Knox was forever my wild card, and as he and his beta descended the stairs and stalked across the foyer to join

Declan and me, I hoped, prayed, that he could keep it together today.

That he could redeem himself and last night's incident might just become a distant, awful memory.

"This is a big deal," I said as Gunnar and Knox stripped down. Gunnar's nudity had my cheeks flaming, and I looked at Knox's forehead, like I always did, to not get lost in the peaks and valleys of his muscular frame. Frustrating as it was, *embarrassing* as it was, their quick shift from gorgeous naked men to enormous black hounds made it easier to give succinct instructions. "With me, you three. Am I clear? Do *not* leave my side."

Beyond all the tension between us, all that had happened, this my first outing with the entire pack—past the ward, into the real world. If they had been waiting for a chance to bolt, this was it.

Declan licked at my hand in acknowledgement. Gunnar trotted out the front door with a determined, focused air about him. Knox held his ground for a beat, and when I looked into those red eyes, I found a glimmer of understanding. Acceptance.

But maybe I was just reading into it, seeing what I wanted —*needed*—to see.

Maybe my personal feelings clouded everything, and in the end, when they scattered immediately after we touched down in Lunadell proper, everyone would see I wasn't cut out for a pack.

And I'd be alone.

Again.

My throat tightened at the thought, and I hurried out, Declan and Knox at my sides, Gunnar leading the way across the soggy grass to the forest.

Whatever was about to happen would happen.

There was nothing I could do to stop it. So, with a deep

breath, I centered myself, studied the new faces of dead humans crystalizing in my mind's eye, and threw caution to the wind.

This would inevitably go down as the worst accident in Lunadell—possibly even the whole province—to date. Chaos assaulted us the second we materialized on the cusp of the cordoned-off downtown strip, located at the edge of the financial district, straddling the line between that and a lower-income section of the city. Half a skyscraper remained, like someone had taken a block of cheese and cut jaggedly down its middle. While not the tallest building in the city, the explosion took a substantial hit to it and the buildings nearby. Shattered windows. Debris everywhere.

Blood. Sirens. The crackle of walkie-talkie relay between first responders.

And screams.

So many screams. Seventy-six dead, but how many more were injured?

How many would *never* recover from this day?

On the celestial plane, much of the calamity was muffled, but combined with the onslaught of new souls, snapping and sparking and sizzling inside the demolished building, it was a lot to take in, even for me. I swallowed hard, assessing the damage quickly, clinically, assuming most of the newly departed were clustered in the eight exposed floors near the base of the tower. With the structure weakened, the levels above had toppled too, the building much like a stroke victim.

Horrible. Just awful.

My pack clustered around me, sniffing the smoke-ridden air that filtered from the human realm to the celestial plane.

Knox had situated himself between us and Alexander, looking taller and more regal than I'd ever seen—like a true alpha.

"Now, you, beta…" Alexander snapped his fingers at Gunnar, then pointed to the yellow police tape stretched down the street. Ambulances and cruisers filled the space on this side of it, humans sprinting about and carrying bodies. Distantly, the roar of incoming firetrucks drowned out a nearby woman screeching on a gurney, her leg shredded to the bone, paramedics tending to her as they rushed her away from the disaster. A young officer ran clear through Alexander as the reaper said, "I want you on the perimeter. Send the little one in with my four—"

"Alexander." I planted my scythe so that the staff cut in front of Knox, creating a little barrier of my own. "You don't give orders to my pack. We'll contain and subdue so that you can reap."

We faced off for a moment, two celestial beings with nuclear weapons at our sides. Even now, months after I had been promoted to Lunadell, he *still* wasn't thrilled to have me here. I might have looked to him for help with the hellhounds at first, but I knew how to reap—I was damn good at it. And these days, I knew my pack. Mostly. He might have had more experience in this territory, his pack over twice the size of mine, but he wasn't my superior. No fluffy white wings, no cowl and skeletal hand—no bossing me and mine around.

Behind him, his pack was already at work, immense black hellhounds moving through the wreckage. Two had a gaggle of human souls sequestered at the base of the tower, and they circled the sobbing figures like sharks.

"Fine," Alexander muttered, shouldering his scythe. He took a half step back, then paused. "But consider pairing your alpha with mine… so he can see a *real* alpha at work."

Knox flashed a hint of teeth, a low warning rumbling in his chest. Alexander shot him a pointed look, then me a smirk before disappearing into the fray.

Smug twat.

"Ignore him," I said as I stepped in front of Knox and faced my pack, waving off the rest of the wandering hellhounds as well. "Ignore all of them. We're here to do a job, just like Alexander's pack, and we're here to *help* lost souls. Period." I focused on Knox, pushing last night out of my mind as best I could. "I want *you* patrolling the perimeter. Nothing gets in or out. If you see a soul past that yellow tape, you bring them back."

Much to my surprise, Knox sat. Literally just… plopped down, waiting, staring at me without a hint of his usual boredom. Maybe he had learned his lesson—and the anxiety knotting in my gut could just fuck off already.

"Gunnar, Declan, you're with me," I carried on, glancing between the pair. Gunnar studied the building, red eyes darting this way and that, no doubt cataloguing every minute detail. Declan, meanwhile, shuffled in close to me, tail wagging ever so slightly. Good. *That* was the attitude I needed from both of them. "Declan, I want you with frightened souls. The ones who are too scared to even move. Find one, sit with them, wait until they are reaped. Don't leave their side." He offered a little yip and a snort, tail wagging faster. I nodded, sensing his eagerness. "Okay then, Gunnar, you're on runners. Anyone who starts to bolt, herd them back in. I know Alexander's pack will be doing something similar, but this is where you shine. Nobody gets beyond the lobby on your watch, clear?"

The hellhound tapped his huge front paws, claws clacking on the pavement, his lean figure brimming with jittery energy. Ready to work. I swallowed my smile, pleased to see each one heeding the call in their own way.

"Okay then... Let's do this."

Knox trotted off without a backward glance, headed straight for the yellow *Caution* tape, the white and orange cones along the perimeter of the accident site. With the other two watching me, waiting for the go-ahead, I lingered just a few moments to watch him pad around the outskirts. Knox sniffed at the ground, at the cones, at the first responders, then disappeared behind a few police cruisers.

You have to trust him. That's all you can do.

I sighed softly, tapping my finger on my scythe's staff.

Please, Knox... Please don't screw this up.

"Right." I motioned to the crumbling tower just as another fire broke out, flames bursting through a tenth-story window. Humans screamed and ducked for cover. "Let's get to work, boys."

And work we did. For their first venture into the gritty world of reaping, Gunnar and Declan needed no guidance beyond my initial instructions. Two floors up, Declan sniffed out a terrified soul under a desk, her human body crushed beneath an array of collapsed office equipment and ceiling. Shock and fear made her incapable of speech, incapable of any movement at all, and without hesitation, Declan crawled under the desk and plunked his head in her lap. It was a tight squeeze, but he did it.

Best of all, he did it with the confidence of a hellhound who had been doing this for centuries, not weeks. Even with Alexander's pack roving about, muscular pit bull-looking hounds who never met my eye but whose tails shot up around *my* pack, Declan didn't show so much as a whiff of his previous self. The Declan of ten short weeks ago would have hidden behind Knox, low to the ground and whining, searching for the best escape route available.

Today, he just got to work.

And it left me beaming.

Gunnar, meanwhile, strutted about the wreckage as I'd expected: snooty, assertive, calculating. He left my side only a few minutes after Declan, vanishing from sight and reappearing in the lobby—half of which you could see into from the upper floors, the rubble piled high and crawling with human rescuers. One of the souls herded into the group by Alexander's circling hellhounds had slipped free, and before either of the bulky hounds could respond, Gunnar was just *there*, guiding the soul back with gentle nips to the heels. He lapped the whole group, souls and hellhounds, with a few assured barks, then vanished again.

I nibbled my lower lip, grinning when I caught Knox's distant figure still patrolling the outskirts, moving at a steady clip around the wreckage.

Who needed a pack of eight, ten, twelve hellhounds when three perfect ones would do?

Unfortunately, even with all of us combing through the tower, skirting fires and sidestepping corpses, ignoring wounded humans because we *had* to, the task was monumental. Alexander could only reap one soul at a time, which left a lot of management for the rest of us at the site. With our brief bit of tension shoved aside, he and I fell into a competent rhythm without ever once going over the game plan. I spoke with each and every soul, calming them, assuring them, informing them what had happened and where they were going. It saved Alexander time when he reappeared, took their hand, and whisked them down to Purgatory.

For the better part of an hour, we reapers and our packs were a well-oiled machine, shuttling some fifty fresh souls away for judgment. Twenty-eight to go—two more had died from their injuries since we'd arrived. Declan had found one of the most recent dead down at a gurney; I spotted them in passing, the soul on an empty stretcher, numb, vacant, staring at the thickening clouds overhead, and Declan snuggled in beside him, his head on the soul's chest.

Despite the catastrophic nature of the accident, everything on *this* side seemed to be going smoothly—until Knox caught my attention. Insistently. Noisily. Barking, barking, *barking*, the sounds rougher and more aggressive with each passing second. A howl erupted from somewhere down below, and as Alexander grabbed the most recent soul I'd soothed, he shot me an annoyed look.

"I'm sure he's fine," I ground out, refusing to badmouth my alpha in front of him, all the while hoping that Knox hadn't lost control again.

Another hoarse howl. My confidence in him plummeted, and I teleported from the fifteenth floor to the street, scanning the organized chaos.

And finding him nowhere.

"Knox?"

Heart in my throat, I jogged around a few bulky vehicles. Since we'd arrived, police had pushed the crowds way, *way* back, well beyond the initial cordoning, allowing a few blocks of space for them to work.

"*Knox!*"

At the far end of the interior accident zone, I finally found him in a sprint, headed straight for an alley between two brick apartment buildings. He moved effortlessly, like a great black shadow, paws barely touching the ground with each stride, and I cursed under my breath when his snarl reverberated across the celestial plane.

What now, for goodness' sake?

I cut the distance between us in an instant, teleporting to the mouth of the alley, fury in my chest and fire on the tip of my tongue that he would do this to me *again*.

"Knox!" I shouted, scythe at the ready. His name bounced off the brick walls, buildings looming tall on either side of the narrow corridor. The hellhound slowed, and just as I was about to rip him a new one for abandoning his post, for ignoring me, I saw it.

Saw *him*, actually. A man in black—dragging one of our newly departed souls down the alley. His thin arms locked around the squirming soul's waist like a bear trap, and when she shrieked, eyes wide and wild, he clapped a hand over her mouth.

A hand with a symbol cut into it, too bloody now to identify with any certainty. In fact, he was *covered* in runes, every exposed bit of flesh artfully sliced and diced and bloody beyond repair. My arms fell to my sides, stunned.

What…?

Who…?

Knox shot off in a burst of speed, powering down the alley at a gallop, leaping at the figure just as he had Christopher.

Only he didn't make contact this time, didn't tackle the villain and rip open his chest with claws tougher than steel.

Because the ground opened up and swallowed the bloody creature and the soul whole. Gone. A familiar eerie ripple shuddered across the celestial plane, and a shiver cut down my spine, the cold hand of fear gripping me once more after weeks of quiet.

Confounded, I staggered deeper into the alley, eventually breaking into a run and coming to an abrupt halt where I had last seen that terrified soul. A huge red symbol had been painted across the concrete at our feet, stretching the width of the alley, intricate in its design and bloody in its origins. Brows furrowed, I crouched down and traced the circle with my eyes, inside of which was a smattering of runes from a number of cultures, many of which even I didn't recognize.

This was old magic. *Very* old.

And totally not in my wheelhouse.

Panting, Knox stalked to my side and shifted back, the heat rising off his body hitting me like a hurricane.

"What the fuck was that?" he demanded, voice low and harsh. Sweat beaded on his forehead and trickled down his handsome face, steam coiling between us. I shook my head, totally at a loss.

"I have no idea."

"I saw him walk her out of the wreckage by the hand," he growled as I tentatively pressed my fingertip to the markings at my feet. Hot and wet, the metallic tang was so painfully obvious that it made my stomach turn. A quick sniff confirmed it: blood.

"Was he a reaper?"

"He was dressed like one," I muttered, wiping my finger on the ground with a grimace. "But no, he wasn't. Reapers don't... We don't deal in blood magic." I nudged at the nearest sigil with the base of my staff. "We don't need to."

"But he could touch the soul. Carry her. Take her."

"Yeah..."

"Demon?"

I looked up at him, at the storm in his black eyes and the hardness around his mouth. "I don't... I don't know."

Beneath the blood and the carvings, that *thing* was attractive enough to be a demon, but that was hardly definitive. Plenty of supernatural creatures were gorgeous; it was a predatory advantage.

Speaking of gorgeous predators...

Still radiating heat, Knox shuffled closer to the sprawling bit of floor art in front of us, nostrils flared through a few deep sniffs. He then swiped two fingers through the circle, effectively breaking it—and most likely its magic—and *licked* his fingers.

"Oh, Knox, no..." I tugged at his wrist. "Don't—"

"It's human," he rumbled, bringing his fingers closer for another sniff. "Human blood."

My belly flip-flopped, the heat rising off him suddenly a little *too* hot for comfort. "That familiar, eh?"

Knox rolled his eyes and smeared the blood on the ground. "Is that really what you're worried about right now?"

"Well—"

"It smells like them," he said dryly, which pushed the nauseating churn inside me down to an unsettling tremor.

"Tastes like them?"

"Like Christopher, yes," the hellhound stated without hesitation. Ah. Right. Last night. Knox sat up on his haunches as he surveyed the alley. "These markings... They're on the celestial plane."

"Seems that way." I couldn't imagine something like *this* lasting long in the human realm, not when it looked so obviously Satanic—in a pop culture-y, horror movie sort of way, at least. Based on the empty metal trash bins lining the corridor between the two buildings, I assumed someone had been by today to empty them; something this large, so obviously in blood, so palpably wicked even to humans, wouldn't have survived long.

"So that bastard was celestial?"

"Probably," I said with a sigh, tapping my scythe on the pavement as I worked through the very limited list of beings capable of utilizing this cosmic pathway. Angels, demons, gods, reapers, hellhounds... It certainly narrowed the list, but there were still *thousands* in the demonic category alone, and searching through them would amount to searching for one specific needle in a mountain of identical needles.

Knox shot up with a snarl, his powerful thighs in my peripheral view briefly before he stalked away. "*Fuck.* I should have gotten to her sooner."

"This isn't your fault," I insisted as I stood, wiping my finger one last time on my flouncy black sweater. While there were bigger issues afoot now than Knox mentally berating himself, I couldn't let that slide either. He might have been completely at fault last night, but this... This was something else entirely.

The hellhound made it halfway down the alley before I caught him by the arm.

"Hey." I planted my scythe and held tight, using it to anchor us when Knox tried to just barrel on ahead. He stopped with a growl, and I pressed my fingertips hard into his forearm, into the sweat and corded muscle, around the twisting and twining veins. "This isn't on you, Knox. You did everything right."

Slowly, he turned in place, wearing the same guilty look that he had last night when I returned to the house. "I watched him drag her beyond the tape. I should have stepped in sooner."

"You didn't know."

"But I should have."

"No, you shouldn't have," I argued, digging my nails into his flesh until he finally met my eyes. "It's nobody's fault. Well. I mean, it might be..." Someone set that thing loose on the celestial plane, and if he was a free agent, then *he* was responsible for whatever devilry he committed. "But not you. So, stop it. Right now."

His lips twitched. "You think an alpha obeys commands, reaper?"

I smirked. "I think an alpha can listen to *logic*, yes. And what's logical, going forward, isn't beating yourself up... It's working together to make this right."

The tension in his shoulders lessened, as did my hold on his arm, when he finally nodded. "Yes. We need to find her."

"We need to find *him*."

Whether *we* was me and the pack or someone actually

sanctioned to tackle this kind of thing was a different issue. I had zero experience with another celestial being stealing souls, but suspected it was something for Heaven to handle. They had the resources, after all, and a whole arsenal of bored angels just chomping at the bit for a good hunt. Once we had reaped the final soul from the collapsed tower, I'd be headed upstairs—twice in less than twenty-four hours, at that—to file an official report.

A brief silence blanketed the alley, and before I knew it, my hand had slid down his forearm, over his wrist...

And then his fingers tangled with mine, loosely threaded together.

"How are Declan and Gunnar doing?" Knox asked as we both studied the sudden turn of events, neither of us pulling away.

"Great. Perfect, actually," I told him. "You're all naturals at this."

Knox scoffed, his hand more open than mine, so big and firm, like he was scared he'd crush me if he squeezed back.

"You're a protector, Knox." My skin was so pale next to his, so deathly white, faint gold veins a stark contrast to the deep blue wisps weaving along his arm. "You had a moment last night, and you learned. We both did. And now it's done."

Shattering glass and screeching tires punctured the silence, and we broke apart in unison. My hand wrapped around yew. His fell to his side, tensed, as if purposefully stretched open. I swallowed hard, then nodded toward the street.

"Come on. Twenty-seven souls to go before we can call it a day."

I'd just crossed onto the sidewalk when he called my name.

"I *am* sorry," Knox said, lingering right where I'd left him when I looked back, "for the position I put you in at that house. It won't happen again."

A flush warmed my cheeks. "Forgiven."

Together, we hurried back to the carnage, more souls in need of our care—and a mystery gnawing at my insides, the fear in that kidnapped soul's eyes threatening to haunt me for the rest of my days.

DECLAN

The pack stilled at the sound of the front door gently shutting downstairs. Scattered across Knox's bedroom, the three of us looked to the doorless opening. Hazel had been gone for most of the day; after we had cleared the crumbling skyscraper of all its departed souls, she dropped us off here, then vanished. Knox had been the one to fill us in on what they'd seen—on that fucked-up creature who had stolen one of *our* souls.

She had gone to Heaven to make a report, apparently, and now, almost nine hours later, she had finally returned, the sweet little *tip-tap* of her flats echoing through the house. Weeks ago, she would have left us to our own devices after our evening meal, but none of us had eaten, the pantry untouched in her absence. Dread frayed at the pack bond for hours, and now, as her scent thickened in the air, her footsteps grew louder, relief flooded my connection with Gunnar and Knox instead—from all sides. Relief, excitement, worry.

Because something foul was wandering the celestial plane. Hazel had sensed it for weeks, all the way back to my training at the children's hospital. She had chalked it up to that rogue spirit, but from what Knox had described, the bloody beast today was much, *much* worse.

And the thought of her, out there, alone, had us all on edge.

Never mind that she had her scythe. Never mind that she was an immortal being, celestial, divine in her own right. The three of us fretted over her like she was made of glass—and that was fucking telling.

Gunnar and I knew it: Hazel was our fated mate—we three were destined to find her, claim her, love her. The physical intimacy shared between us and Hazel had sealed it. At this point, we were just waiting for our alpha to stop being a stubborn ass and get with the program already.

Knox shot to his feet as soon as Hazel appeared in the doorway, and concern pounded through our pack bond at the state of her. She had never looked so exhausted, dark rings around her eyes, her hair staticky and wild. Traveling up to Heaven seemed to take a greater toll on her than the usual teleporting, and she had done it twice now in less than two days.

Leaning heavily on her scythe, she shuffled into the room with a sigh, and before anyone could tell me otherwise, I was at her side, an arm around her waist.

"Are you all right?"

She nodded, stabbing the end of her scythe to the floor so that it could stand tall and proud without her. "Just tired."

A low throb of longing rippled through the pack bond, and Gunnar and I did our best *not* to look at its source. Even though we had both tasted Hazel, caressed her bountiful curves, kissed down to her marrow, there wasn't even a whiff of jealousy between us. That was the way with bonded hellhound packs like we three—or so I had always been told. I'd never been fortunate enough to have a mate for myself, but now I finally understood why: fate had been holding off until I met the reaper nestled to my side.

Gunnar had proven to be less physically affectionate than me, preferring to verbally spar, his tone snarky but flirtatious. The only one still desperately craving her—and fighting it hard—was Knox.

"What did they have to say?" our alpha demanded as I walked Hazel to his bed. For the first time since we had mated, she let me hold her, as if just too wiped out to fight it anymore. While her reluctance hurt, I understood it: humans didn't share mates, and she was sensitive to both my and Gunnar's feelings. It was all unnecessary, of course. There was no bad blood between him and I, no tension, no competition. Innately, we each understood how the other responded to our mate, how we longed to care for her.

Hazel just needed time to accept it.

Seated on the end of his bed, she rubbed at her cheek and shook her head. "They think it was most likely a demon, even without the blood being black."

"A demon collecting souls from Earth—directly?" Gunnar's eyebrows shot up as he settled on the bay window ledge, arms crossed. Seconds later, his foot—wrapped in fine Italian leather, a gift from Hazel for his successful first field test—started to tap, a tell that his mind had begun to race. "Is that usual?"

"I've never seen it," Hazel told us. She inched away from me when I sat beside her, and I swallowed the pinch of hurt, instead easing back on my elbow and stretching the other arm out behind her on the bed. Her gorgeous mane unfurled down her back in an explosion of white, and she fidgeted with it absently, bringing it over her shoulder, then fluffing it back. "Demons *can* collect souls directly after death, but only if they've made deals... Humans can sell their souls for something in life. I always thought it was rare, but apparently not."

"That *thing* wasn't a demon." Fire poker in hand, Knox crouched in front of the hearth and stabbed at the dying embers inside. One harsh breath sparked a flame, and he fed it with the kindling from the nearby basket. "I know demons... He wasn't one."

Well, that settled it. If Knox said it wasn't a demon, it wasn't a demon. I certainly needed no further proof, though Gunnar appeared lost in thought—like he hadn't even heard our alpha's declaration.

"I didn't think he was a demon either," Hazel admitted softly. "He didn't *feel* like a demon. Maybe kind of looked like one, but—"

"Did you tell them about the carvings?" Firelight danced across Knox's scarred face, sparks exploding in the hearth as the flames gobbled up the little twigs and bits of crumpled paper. A blazing dot of orange settled in his beard, and he extinguished it with a flick. "The symbols on his body? The blood sigil on the ground?"

"Yeah, yeah, all of it." She shuffled back deeper into the crook of my arm as she readjusted her position, seated on one bent leg, the other hanging over the bed's edge—not touching the floor, probably, the short little thing. Affection squeezed my heart at the thought, danced along our pack bond, my feelings eliciting something similar from Gunnar. Our alpha exhaled sharply—did he think we were *both* struck by puppy love now?—but remained focused on Hazel as she said, "I had to fill out a ton of paperwork. Heaven is so ridiculously bureaucratic. But, yeah, I wrote everything down. I even drew whatever I could remember..."

She tucked her hair behind her ears, shoulders slumping, folding in on herself. I swallowed hard, fighting the urge to just grab her and yank her against me—because I could hold her up. Last night with Knox had taken a lot out of her already, and now this? *Let me shoulder the burden, sweet.*

"I don't know," she muttered. "I did what I could. They said they'll take it from here, so…"

"But you have doubts?" Gunnar asked, to which Hazel sighed again, as if at a loss.

"I just don't know how to feel right now. This is something I've never seen before, and I've been reaping for ten years. I *don't* think it was a demon. His blood was red." She shook her head, frowning. "But I have no clue what else it could be. All I know is that he stole a soul, and he could be… hurting her, and I just… I want…"

Justice. Her heart was too big to carry this darkness alone. I finally sat up and pressed a firm hand between her shoulders, then slowly stroked up and down, massaging her.

"I'm sure the angels will find her," I insisted, wishing I could drain away all the fear and stress with my touch alone. "They'll make it right."

Knox scoffed, sliding the iron poker back into its cannister noisily as the fire snapped and hissed. A warm orange hue filled the room, paired with the white lamplight from either side of the alpha's bed, and shadows danced across all our faces—mine the only hopeful expression present.

"Agreed," Hazel said, her gaze tangling with Knox's, the pair locked in a private, wordless conversation while Gunnar and I smirked at each other. Good. It was nice to see them bonding, slow and laborious as the process might be.

A monstrous gurgle suddenly echoed through the room.

Three sets of eyes whipped to me, and Gunnar rolled his.

"For fuck's sake, Declan, just go eat something already."

My face ripened with embarrassment. We had worked through our usual lunchtime today at the tower, and after we'd returned, the whole pack had been too anxious about

Hazel to do much more than pace and speculate. Apparently, mine was the only belly to complain about it.

"Oh, sorry..." Hazel stood in a hurry. "I should have realized that you—"

"We are more than capable of feeding ourselves," Knox interjected before I could. Female hounds in Hell usually minded the young and patrolled the internal territory; males were solely responsible for providing food. Hazel's concoctions tasted *way* better than anything I'd ever eaten, but she wasn't expected to wait on us anymore. We knew the layout of the house, where to find everything. We could feed ourselves. She just... She made everything taste so fucking *good*.

"We wanted to wait for your return," Gunnar added. "Food has been the last thing on our minds today."

Hazel nibbled her plump lower lip for a moment, slowly looking between the three of us as color blossomed in her cheeks. *Fuck*, did I ever love her blushes. For a deathly pale reaper, she was so wonderfully prone to them. That lone left dimple suggested she was fighting a smile, and interest throbbed through our pack bond. All three of us delighted in making her happy.

No denying it anymore.

"Okay, well, I should probably get started on something anyway—"

"I was thinking..." Shuffling to the end of the bed, I ignored the sudden rush of saliva at the thought. "Pizza."

"And what, pray tell, is *pizza*?" Gunnar asked, nose crinkling.

"It's that round bread with the cheese and tomatoes," Knox said absently, nudging at the fire with his foot, pushing a log an inch to the right—like that would make a difference. Grinning, I scrambled across my alpha's bed and grabbed his tablet off the little side table. A few swipes of my finger and I had the most appetizing pizza imaginable on the screen: Meat Lover's Extravaganza.

"We can order it online from one of the shops in Lunadell," I said as Gunnar crept closer. As soon as the tablet's screen light illuminated his features, I could almost sense him drooling. "Then we go and pick it up."

After all the shit we had been through in the last twenty-four hours, I figured we could do with a treat—something out of the ordinary, something new and exciting. When I looked to Hazel, I found her mirroring my grin, her gaze warm.

"Yeah," she murmured. "It seems like a pizza sort of night, doesn't it?"

Reaching out, I snatched her hand and tugged her back to the bed, where she plopped down beside me in a flourish of silvery-white hair and a whoosh of the sweetest dates. Gunnar joined us a moment later, the pair of us like sentries on either side of our reaper. As we scrolled through the online menu, Knox abandoned his precious fire, and soon enough loomed over the three of us, arms crossed.

Not a hint of a scowl anywhere.

In fact, when I peeked up at him—stealthily, briefly, not wanting him to know that I was studying *him* for a change—I swore I saw a smile. It was faint, barely there through his coarse black facial hair, but *real*.

And in that moment, our pack felt whole.

Complete.

Comfort pulsed through our bond; the others must have sensed it—that feeling of belonging. A piece had always been missing, and now we'd found it.

Now we'd found *her*.

"I think we should make yours an extra-large," Hazel mused, dragging a delicate finger across the tablet screen, oblivious to the moment unfurling around her. "And we should probably get a couple… Four at least."

"I rather like cheese," Gunnar said as we built our own pizza through the website—the first of many, it would seem. "Can we double it?"

"What is Brooklyn pepperoni?" Knox demanded, reading it all upside down, totally invested for once, his head cocked to the side and black brows furrowed.

Gunnar snatched up the tablet. "Fuck me, we can put cheese in the *crust*?"

"Is it different than the regular pepperoni?" Knox huffed, his question still unanswered.

"Hazel, are anchovies what I think they are?" I asked, hesitating over the little button that would add them to our pizza. Fish, were they not? *Blegh*.

"Oh my God, you guys…" Hazel giggled, the sound sweeter and more beautiful than anything in this realm or the next. Warm, raw affection thrummed through our bond in response. "One at a time."

An eternity later, Knox, Gunnar, and I had eight extra-large, extra-cheesy, extra-meaty, Brooklyn-pepperoni-laden pizzas to split between us, while Hazel had a single small, thin-crust, cheese-and-onion pizza to her name. Then, for the hell of it, because no one—including Hazel—had sampled a molten chocolate mud cake before, we tacked four of those onto the order as well.

What followed felt so… natural. Hazel and I venturing into Lunadell, strolling along the human plane to the pizza shop—hand in hand. Paying for the enormous stack of boxes, boxes that I insisted upon carrying by myself. Slipping back onto the celestial path to steal four eight-packs of beer for all of us to share. Laughing. Talking about anything so long as it had nothing to do with reaping or that creepy fuck from earlier today.

Coming home to find Gunnar and Knox had set the dining table with plates and cups—which were forgone immediately for the chilled cans of beer. For the first time, Hazel sat with us for a full meal, Knox at the helm, the rest of us bunched around him at one end of the long table. Sharing slices. Clinking beer cans for a toast. Rehashing the day's huge reaping—gossiping about Alexander and his pack of stuck-up hellhounds.

Hazel's rare and beautiful laughter filling the room.

And as I polished off my tenth slice, nowhere near full, I realized that in all my long life, I couldn't remember a time I'd been happier.

❧ 22 ❧

GUNNAR

I had never seen so many humans in one place before.

Sure, the tower had been crawling with humans, dead and alive, but this was something else entirely. Wall-to-wall people packed into the dimly lit space, music pounding to the point of pain, its bass reverberating in the red brick walls. Sweat mingled with the vast and varied scents of alcohol—both of the sweet and acrid varieties—and then the perfumes, the body odors clashing and colliding, blending and growing into something pungent. How anyone came here for *fun* was beyond my understanding, but that was the purpose of tonight.

Fun.

To celebrate Knox's first successful reaping—an incident that had been so standard, so pedestrian, that even Hazel hadn't all that much to say about it when they returned. An old woman had died in her bed, and there was Knox and Hazel to escort her safely and comfortably to Purgatory. Apparently, she had been a dear, sweet and uncomplicated, greeting death as a friend with a peaceful smile on her crinkled features. The one tidbit that had sent Declan and I into fits of laughter was the fact that this old soul had had the audacity to grab Knox by the face—red eyes, huge teeth, and all—and squish it, then kiss it like she did with her tiny Pomeranians.

Hazel hadn't been able to contain herself either when she'd shared *that* delicious moment with us, much to Knox's chagrin.

Still, our alpha had completed an important part of his training—and we as a household had bonded deeper over the last few days than we had in the last two months. Thoughts of abandoning our reaper were becoming faint, few and far between, yet Knox still wasn't ready to drop it *completely*. He would. As soon as he tasted her, he'd never want to leave.

I would have thought the turn of events sinister, witchcraft of the highest order, if Hazel wasn't so fucking sweet. And personable. And perfect for *us*.

She was wearing red tonight.

My cock rather liked the color on her, standing at full attention the moment she had drifted shyly into Knox's bedroom while we were getting ready for the outing. Even now, an hour later, desire scorched through my veins, and every sensual sway of her hips promised that I wouldn't get through the night without at least half an erection tenting my trousers.

Mind you, most of the human men present must have been plagued by something similar—because fuck *me*, all these females in short, tight little outfits, their hair styled, their faces dewy with makeup… It was a delectable tease that no man could resist. Nightclub had to be code for a mating pit; I was sure of it.

Standing on the outskirts of the writhing mass of humans, I couldn't recall how we had settled on this particular venue. *Sampson's Corner*. The most popular club in Lunadell, according to its website. All I remembered was that yesterday Hazel wished to celebrate the fact that her entire pack had passed the most important step in our training: the first field tests. Knox had suggested pizza again. Declan had proposed an outing into the city. I had requested something with music.

And now here we were. This certainly *was* music by its most basic definition, but I could hardly understand the jumbled words—though what did come through was overtly sexual.

At least the drunken humans seemed to like it, occasionally screaming along to the lyrics, especially the females. While it wasn't a locale I would frequent, the building itself was suitable enough. After waiting in a line outside on the sidewalk for about twenty minutes, Declan insisting we get the *full* human experience, we had been granted access to Sampson's Corner, a three-level nightclub in the heart of Lunadell. The main floor had been just as packed as this, only it served as a spot to drink and chat—if one could even hear conversation over the din. Above that was a rooftop patio illuminated by countless strings of light, and this here, in the basement, was the pulse of the club—its dance floor, its busiest bars, and a few shadowy corridors spiderwebbing off into fuck knows what.

Not my scene. Certainly not Knox's either. Declan only seemed to enjoy it because Hazel hadn't stopped smiling since we'd arrived. But, at the very least, the drinks were tasty; loitering near one of the brick walls under an obnoxious black speaker, I gulped down half the mixed cocktail in my plastic cup. Vodka and some other concoction, something sweet and tangy, a smooth blend that oozed inside and warmed my gut. Knox was already onto his third scotch; I spied my alpha at the bar, towering over the humans around him and sticking out like a sore thumb with all that hair.

But we looked the part, each sporting the same uniform

as the other males: jeans and a button-up, all in dark, muted colors. Hazel, meanwhile, stood out like a fucking beacon. Swirling my cocktail in the plastic cup, I scanned the crowd slowly, taking in the array of colors and sizes, textures of female hair and expressions on the males' faces, until I found her and Declan.

Neither knew what the fuck they were doing on the dance floor, but when the humans jumped and threw their arms up, so did they.

It was rather endearing, actually. This was Hazel's first experience with a modern-day nightclub, same as us, and she appeared to be having a good time. Cheeks flushed a light bronze, her eyes glittered like starlight beneath the club lights, her white waves wild and free. Each bounce unleashed a cloud of her scent, hitting all three of us hard despite the maelstrom of other smells in the windowless space.

And that *dress*. Ruby red, sleeveless, to her midthighs. Skintight and slinky, every curve on display. The neckline arched delicately over her ample cleavage, her breasts propped up tonight as if to fit in with the other females. Hazel needn't try to look like anything or anyone but herself; my body responded just as eagerly to her in shapeless reaper robes as it did for that dress.

Speaking of eager... Desire throbbed through our pack bond when she flipped her hair, then spun in place, laughing freely, head thrown back in wild abandon. My cock stiffened, and I adjusted it as discreetly as I could in the darkness, not needing the entire club to know I had a raging hard-on.

Declan coiled an arm around her waist, dragging her flush against him so that his mouth found her neck. She arched into him, her fingers trailing through his hair before she spun out, cautious as always not to show one of us more physical affection than the other. A smirk tugged at my mouth, and I downed the rest of my drink. She needn't worry about such things; I could watch Declan *fuck* her, right here, right now, without an ounce of jealousy.

Well. Maybe a bit. Because I'd want to be in the thick of it with them.

But a pulse of possessive annoyance thrummed through our bond when another male wandered too close to her, sidling up behind Hazel like he was about to grab her. Declan moved in before I could, locking eyes with the human briefly over Hazel's head. Ten seconds of unbroken eye contact had the male backing off—all without the reaper noticing.

Good. Looking like that, so damn scrumptious, positively delectable, Hazel would attract the attention of every hungry male present.

But she was *ours*.

Although I had no interest in jumping around the mass of sweaty humans, Hazel's smile was just too beautiful to ignore. I sauntered forward, eyes locked on her, eager to nibble down her throat just as Declan had—

Until I felt it.

A breath on the back of my neck.

I stiffened.

Desire gave way to heightened vigilance, and I whirled around, searching for the source with a keen eye and flared nostrils, finding nothing but the brick wall and a few cobwebs rustling in the corner beneath a speaker. An air vent broke up the red pattern, metallic and dark grey—a possible source for the rush of air, only this had felt purposeful. If I hadn't felt that vent's breath before, why now?

Tossing my plastic cup aside, I rotated slowly in place, studying the club with more intention than I had previously. Eyes pierced me from all sides; someone was watching.

But who?

Humans filled the space to bursting, and they were all looking for something. Another human. A drink. A distraction. The odd one glanced my way occasionally, but their quick scan was nothing compared to what burned into me now. I stopped on my third cautious circle, every sense on fire, and glared at the brickwork.

Nothing.

Nothing but a good seven feet of empty space between me and the wall, the vent, the speaker, the shivering cobwebs...

Without a care for who might see me, I crossed between realms, leaving the mortal behind for the celestial.

And came face-to-face with a bloody man.

Our noses mere inches apart.

Both our eyes widened. Surprise punctuated the sudden meeting, replaced swiftly by adrenaline, the urge to *fight* hitting me for the first time—ever. Hellhounds in the past had always thrown the first metaphorical punch, but as I stared into the green eyes of a *man*, this thing who wore the flesh of a human covered in bloody symbols, I pulsated with aggression.

I wanted to rip him apart.

Because how likely was it that there were *two* such creatures afoot?

A shock of inky-black hair sat neatly styled atop his head. A strong jaw. Pale skin—probably from blood loss. Anemic, lean, slim, his body reminiscent of human fashion models. Half the bloody runes on his angular face appeared to be scarred over, carved into him long before tonight. One just below his left eye seeped red, fresh and angry.

Was this the thing Hazel and Knox had seen?

The wretch Hazel had fretted over for days, fearing for the soul he'd stolen away while we had all worked so diligently to save them?

I cocked my head to the side, the obnoxious music muffled on the celestial plane, the tangled scents of humanity dulled.

"Tell me, creature," I crooned, my thin smile making him gulp. "How fast can you run?"

Because I can run much, much faster.

The threat hit home, forcing a few choked stammers out of him. Every inch of exposed skin bore the brunt of his blood magic, yet he appeared well-dressed and modern in a fitted blue suit. The tip of a neatly folded checkered kerchief stuck out his breast pocket.

A beast of this world, then.

I lunged. He staggered back into the wall—and clear through it. An enormous red symbol illuminated the moment he made contact, painted onto the brick, a cluster of distinct sigils encased in a massive circle. It swallowed him whole, the brick suddenly fluid and flexible, but then firm to my tentative touch. Bloody. Red stained my fingertip when I pulled it back to inspect, the scent metallic enough to make my mouth water, to compound the battle-lust inside.

The air sizzled with a strange buzz, unfamiliar even with my extensive experience on the celestial plane. Unsettling, this new sensation.

Highly unwelcome.

Fury suddenly raged through our pack bond.

"Was it him?"

Only Knox could produce something so profound through our connection, something that could cut me off at the knees and divvy me up into little pieces. I shrank instinctively as he approached, striding through the celestial plane as the nightlife carried on without us. Distantly, I spotted Declan and Hazel; my packmate's anxiety hitched, intermingling with Knox's wrath, and an uneasy look flashed across his face. Hazel, meanwhile, appeared totally oblivious, her expression jubilant, joyful, dancing her little heart out.

"Not knowing precisely what he looked like to you, I believe so," I remarked with a nod to the bloody symbols on the wall. Knox took it all in hurriedly, a lone, fat ice cube jostling around his glass tumbler of scotch.

"Demon?"

"Hard to tell." Having stared into the eyes of many a demon, I should have known in an instant. Instead, indecision percolated around my skull. That angular face reappeared in my mind's eye, clear as day, the bloody carvings slightly muddled, and I plucked at minute details, highlighting them, emphasizing them. I did it frequently with memory work—usually it made things clearer. Not this time. "He... He had no scent."

"Yes." Knox sniffed at the artwork, scowling. "What I thought as well. No ash. No hellfire. No blood—save what was leaking out of him. Not black either."

"Agreed."

A confident swipe of his fingers through the exterior circle broke the barrier, any lingering magic rendered useless. "Human blood again."

"I don't think he was human."

"No. They've no access to the plane."

"Not many do."

"Gods do—"

"And they bleed gold like angels."

Knox grunted in agreement, then stepped back to stand alongside me, the pair of us examining the symbology in silence. Frustration gnawed at me; I so despised not having an immediate answer for any and every problem we faced. Most of all, I loathed not being able to steer my alpha in the right direction. He looked to me for guidance, for confirmation that his decisions were the right ones—the *best* ones available. Here, we were equally at a loss.

And, frankly, that pissed me the fuck off.

"It's a portal," I mused. Given our lengthy stint in Hell, I suspected Knox knew that as well as I, but *sometimes* working through problems aloud had its benefits. "Personalized to him, most likely. Even with the circle unbroken, it did nothing when I touched it."

"Blood magic," Knox muttered.

"As Hazel thought, yes."

We both sought her out, turning and watching her dance with Declan. Right then and there, she appeared so ordinary. Well, not *ordinary*. Stunning. Magnificent. Beauty beyond compare. But without her scythe, her robes, her sullen demeanor, she seemed... young.

Free.

It was a good look for her.

Longing strummed through the bond, and I knew Knox shared my sentiment: she deserved to look like that more often.

"If he *is* a demon, perhaps he's hiding his scent, his lineage, maybe even his blood through the carvings," I said slowly, softly, working through it for myself as I went along, "and then we both know that when they get a taste for someone, they obsess."

A muffled snarl echoed from my alpha, tip to tail, fire sparking in his dark gaze. "You think he has a taste for her?"

"Or you." I shrugged. "Why else would he be *here*, watching us?"

Glaring, Knox shot back his whole drink, then tossed the glass aside. It collided with the brick, shattered on impact, shards raining down at the base of the useless portal.

But... why would a *demon* need a portal? They could access the celestial plane with the same ease as Knox and me—

"She goes nowhere alone," Knox declared. When my eyebrows lifted incredulously, he cleared his throat, a whiff of uncertainty in our bond—hastily quashed by a hellhound who seldom questioned his own judgment. "For her own protection."

"Ah. Yes." I swallowed a grin. "Of course."

"We don't know what that thing is," he carried on, for once unaware of my teasing, "but blood magic is old and foul... accursed. It *could* harm a reaper."

This time I let my amusement shine, peering at his gruff profile with a smirk. "Unlikely. Reapers are quite indestructible, but until we get a firm answer on what he is, we *should* keep an eye on her."

When my alpha finally tore his gaze away from Hazel, frowning, I offered him an innocent shrug and a hapless smile. "I suspect you will be wholly up to the task, Knox."

He rolled his eyes at the implication. Declan and I had been cajoling him as subtly as we dared lately; we all *felt* one another's desire for her, and no amount of glaring and brooding from Knox could make us ignore that. As a pack, the bond highlighted our deepest desires, our strongest impulses, our sharpest feelings.

He felt for her just as strongly as we did, perhaps even more as alpha.

If he didn't, he would have offered Hazel up to that bloody lurking *fuck* in some ludicrously orchestrated scheme just to be rid of her.

Then, in her mysterious absence, oh, look at that... our *freedom*. What a funny coincidence.

Instead, his first thought was to guard her. Protect her. Like she was already our mate, all of us on the same page at last.

Not that I had a problem keeping a closer eye on the most beautiful woman in the entire fucking galaxy, but as a reaper, she *was* virtually untouchable, especially when her kind were said to heal like shifters. I hardly feared for her physical safety.

And yet, demons were expert torturers. One needn't skin a victim alive to scar them for eternity. A few choice words, day in and day out, would do the trick.

As we crossed back into the human realm, sticking to the shadows to not draw attention to our sudden reappearance, I thought it best we told Hazel of the carved man's celestial loitering tomorrow. After the dancing, the laughing, the drinks, the news would absolutely ruin her good mood. Tonight, she deserved a moment's reprieve from a life of death and darkness.

"Come on," I mused, nodding to the dance floor as Knox grimaced, like he already knew what I was about to say. "Let's go not let her out of our sight, shall we?"

I then cuffed him by the sleeve and dragged him, quite literally, onto the dance floor, which, if Knox's expression said anything, was akin to the foulest pits of Hell.

Until Hazel tumbled into him, a little off-balance in her heels.

And when he caught her, steadied her, Declan and I exchanged a knowing look: the end was near for our alpha, and if he just let himself, he was going to love it.

23

HAZEL

I couldn't remember the last time I'd danced.

It had to have been during the war—on a bit of downtime, someone with a radio, me and the other nurses in my unit whipping out a jitterbug, maybe even a jive. But since I'd come back, there had been no dancing for me. Rarely any laughter. Music came in passing, or when I had the odd moment to sink into my old records.

Tonight was brand-new for me, just like it was for them.

And as I hopped onto a barstool in the far corner of the underground club, perspiration on my brow and my thirteenth drink in hand, I couldn't help but wonder why I hadn't done this sooner.

Maybe because I hadn't wanted to do it alone.

We never used to dance alone. Never. Always with a partner, something that had been painfully absent since my soul returned to reap.

At Sampson's Corner, I had three.

Well, two willing partners and a hulking reluctant one.

My lips wrapped around the little red straw bobbing in

my cocktail, and I slurped back a drink that tasted almost identical to apple pie. Sweet yet tart, with a dash of cinnamon and a hint of spice. Delicious. Thirteen deep and only now, after midnight had come and gone, was I starting to feel the tingly effects of alcohol. *Tipsy.* That was what one of the girls in the bathroom had said, how she described her level of inebriation.

I hadn't been drunk since the war either. In fact, none of us were even sure a reaper *could* get drunk. Shortly after we had arrived at the nightclub, Declan suggested we give it a whirl—test my limits. Had tonight taken place two months ago, I would have staunchly refused, possibly even seen it as a ploy: get me drunk, toss me aside in a moment of weakness, then make a break for it.

But Declan matched my every drink with one of his, and slowly, as the hours sped by, his cheeks had become rosier, his gorgeous woodsy browns less and less focused, his moves on the dance floor less precise.

Not that said moves required much precision. It was an awful lot of bouncing around these days, screeching to mash-ups of popular songs. Those humans who *did* snag a partner danced far closer than we would have back in my time; some even looked like they were fornicating, grinding hips and writhing together, sweaty clothes the only thing keeping them from actual sex.

Gunnar had given these modern moves the odd try, but never with a straight face. His snark had suggested he couldn't take any of it seriously, a notion I echoed even with all the booze circulating my system. He had five drinks to go before he caught up with me and Declan, and Knox...

Well, Knox was two ahead, favoring the club's scotch selection, and yet somehow seemed the most sober. As the four of us settled into a corner, the hellhounds loitered around me and the humans gave us a wide berth on this side of the bar. Hardly surprising. While we dressed the part of clubgoers, Knox's size alone was deterrent enough. Drunk men navigated the crowd of scantily clad women all night, but only two had had the courage to approach me.

Not that they ever got a word out, mind you.

One look from Knox had sent them scampering.

But none of that mattered. Knox had been scowling at them tonight, not *me*. Declan had no qualms in looking like an absolute loon on the dance floor, shamelessly copying the humans around us. And Gunnar had been pleasant, quippy, always there to catch me should I teeter off-balance in shoes I usually shunned.

Tonight, in this basement, surrounded by so many humans it should have felt stifling, it was easy to forget. Forget the stress of training and the impending trials. Forget the shifting dynamics between me and the pack. Forget the bloody beast who had stolen a soul. Forget the fact that I *hadn't* danced in ten long years, that I hadn't smiled this much in just as long.

For the first time in a painfully long time, I could be present. I could enjoy the moment.

And if all the other drinks on the menu were this delicious, I could—maybe—get drunk. Then I might just forget *everything*—for a night, at least.

"Tequila time!" Declan announced in a singsong voice, wriggling between Gunnar and Knox and plopping four dangerously full shot glasses on the bar top. When his packmates offered him near-identical raised eyebrows, he shrugged and flashed us all an adorable smile. "I heard the humans say it on that show… The one where they travel and party—"

"Every reality show on that network, then?" Gunnar said

with a slight roll of his eyes. I leaned in for an experimental sniff, confirming that the crystal-clear liquid in the glasses was, in fact, a very strong tequila.

"Where are the salt and lemon wedges?" I asked, certain that the bartender would have offered them. Halfway down the crowded bar, I caught one of the servers in all black sweeping quartered lemon wedges off the counter with a scowl. Declan, meanwhile, scratched at the back of his neck, briefly just a lost, tipsy little puppy.

"Do we need those?"

"Next time," I insisted brightly. As if that was the go-ahead he needed, the hellhound distributed the shot glasses amongst us, and after a somewhat sloppy cheers, we threw them back together. Fruity richness tangled with the almost painful bite of pure, paint-stripping alcohol, and while I hastily sucked down some of my apple pie cocktail to dull it, Knox chased his shot with a gulp of scotch. Gunnar made a face as he set his empty glass on the counter, nudging it away like he was officially *done* with tequila for life.

The ringleader of tequila time shuddered, his face puckered; Declan danced from one foot to the other, coughing, chasing the aftertaste away with nothing at all. Poor darling.

"So, tell us, Hazel," Gunnar said, the three of them boxing me in on the barstool, barricading off this dark corner with their impressive, sculpted bodies. No amount of clothing could mask such perfect Adonis figures. "Is this reminiscent of your human days?"

I snorted. "Not even a little. We had dance halls, but the dancing now is so different. Most of the time, for us, we had live bands, and we… You didn't dance alone." Royce had been a good dancer—quick on his feet, his narrow hips catching the beat as he led me through the steps. Something twisted in my gut at the memory, and I went for my cocktail. "And there were always dances we did, steps to follow. You weren't really making it up as you went along."

Still noticeably reeling from the tequila shot, Declan accepted what was left of my cocktail with a grateful smile. "Do you remember any of them?"

The ache in my core sharpened like the twist of a knife. I stumbled a little over the answer, staring at my drink in Declan's skilled hands, the liquid level falling, falling, falling —gone.

"Every last one," I admitted, hoping none of them heard my slight fumble over the pounding bass.

But my pack heard everything. *Everything*. Everything that I didn't want them to, especially the subtext. Their hurried glances told me they were discussing my depressing omission between themselves, through that mystical pack bond that connected them forever. A part of me wished I could tune in to their frequency.

Be one of the pack.

Without it, I would always be an outsider.

Always.

Declan hopped up on the barstool beside me, setting my empty drink aside and stretching an arm along the counter so that it almost wrapped around me. His proximity was such a comfort, even if we weren't touching, and I found myself gravitating toward him, our knees nudging together, my body settling into the crook of his arm.

"Well, come on, then," Gunnar interjected, his smooth lilt rising over the roar of the nightclub. He stepped back, which opened our little huddle up, then offered me his hand. "Teach me one of your favorite routines."

I cocked my head to the side, shoving down the memories of a life gone by—a life that would never be, so there was no point in dwelling on it. "I don't know. This music doesn't exactly lend itself to the Lindy Hop."

"Indulge him," Knox insisted. He handed his empty tumbler to Declan, who set the glass next to mine on the bar top, sixteen scotches deep and steady as steel. "I need something more interesting to look at than *them*."

He gestured to the crowd of selfie-snapping, uncoordinated-dancing, sloppy-face-sucking humans on the other side of the squared off bar with a thrust of his chin. Disdain riddled his features, and had we not reaped together yesterday—had I not watched that decrepit but sweet old soul smoosh Knox's huge hellhound face in her hands—I would have worried about his opinion of humanity.

But Knox just had standards.

And no one here met them.

My eyes dropped to Gunnar's awaiting hand, to the sheer size of it compared to mine, smooth and pale, long, lean fingers outstretched. Like Declan's, they were *exceptionally* talented in their own right. The thought of them stroking my slick folds, pumping in and out of me as the third act of the opera raged on, elicited a painfully hot blush, one that I did my best to hide behind my hair.

"Well, the Lindy is a tough one to learn if you don't know, you know, your side of things." Slowly, I slipped my hand into his, and he escorted me off the barstool and into the scarce bit of space between the bar and the brick wall. "I can teach you the foxtrot... That's a pretty easy one."

Gunnar arched a dark eyebrow. "You think I want *easy*?"

"I think you need easy," I fired back, relishing the pleasant burn of his hand around mine, the safety I felt inside it. "Prove me wrong and I'll step it up a notch."

As always, Gunnar was up to the challenge, exceeding my expectations and then some. He picked up the footwork after a single demonstration, moving slowly through our first attempt, then faster on the next, finally steering me around like he had been born to foxtrot. What we really needed for a dance as smooth as silk was a ballroom. All his lean lines, his effortless control of those long limbs—Gunnar was built to move, to follow a routine and execute it flawlessly.

Declan, on the other hand, struggled to find his footing when his turn came, but we all blamed it on the booze. Apparently, reapers had a stronger tolerance than hellhounds, because he and I had downed the same amount, but he just couldn't make it work. His feet were all over the place, the pair of us tripping over each other, laughing while Knox and Gunnar chuckled from the sidelines.

It was a blast.

And when the sweetest hellhound of my pack finally toddled off to get us all another round of drinks, my lone credit card in his pocket, I had a suspicion about him...

That he was better than he let on.

That he fumbled around to make me smile, to make me double over in a fit of giggles at his clownery, my cheeks sore from laughter.

No one had ever done that for me before: embarrassed themselves on purpose.

I mean, if that *was* his game, anyway.

Maybe he was just hapless and sweet and naïve and innocent—and made love like *none* of those things, masterful when the time called for it, in control and dominant when I needed that.

Multifaceted. I huffed a few strands of hair out of my face, hands on my hips as I watched him disappear into the swarm of humans at the bar. Yeah. Gunnar was precise and meticulous. Knox consistent and resilient. And Declan— never one-dimensional.

I could work with that.

I could *love* that.

Them.

I… I could love them one day—no question.

A thought that made me giddy.

A thought that, tomorrow, I would blame on the liquor.

Relishing the buoyancy, just for now, I spun in place to Knox, unable to picture him gliding as effortlessly as Gunnar through the foxtrot—but eager to see him give it a go all the same. "Your turn, alpha."

He held up those huge hands, declining my offer with a slight shake of his head and a quirk of his lips. "I'm afraid the foxtrot requires skill that I don't possess."

I let out a bark of a laugh. "Bullshit."

Right on cue, we fell into one of our usual stare-offs, only this one wasn't riddled with an undercurrent of tension and strife, both of us struggling for dominance. It was still a standoff with one winner, one loser, but the stakes weren't all that high. In fact, his black eyes almost glinted with a mischief I expected from Declan, and I nibbled my lower lip, peering up at him through my lashes with a playfulness of my own.

Knox refused to fold, his great burly arms crossed, and no amount of coaxing would change that.

But for the first time in our relationship, I had an inkling that maybe, just maybe, I could get him to *bend*, just a little.

And that was progress.

A hand suddenly smoothed up my back, tracing the ramrod line of my spine to the nape of my neck. Heat blossomed *everywhere* as Gunnar closed in, his body looming behind mine, his mouth teasing my ear as he whispered, "So… Am I ready for something more challenging?"

I swallowed hard, my throat bobbing beneath his elegant fingers, and found Knox's mirth dead in the water. Instead, he watched us intently, that black gaze blazing a path from Gunnar's hand on my neck up to my lips. The intensity of his complete focus *and* the wall of muscle barring any escape at my back...

It made me want to run.

And it made me want to *melt*.

"We... We have the records at home," I stammered, breath catching when Gunnar's fingertip whispered across my chin, scorching a path like a wildfire cutting through a field. Any second now, it would bring down the whole damn forest. I rolled my shoulder back, nudging him away as best I could, and while he retreated, he didn't let go. Instead, he dragged his parted lips up to my temple, and out of some sense of skewed morality, I railed against him, twisting out of his grasp, my heart thundering. "I-I can teach you how to really swing there... with the right music."

His tongue flicked out to wet his smirking lips. "Ah. Were you a *swinger*, reaper?"

Too late. Even with the added distance between us, the wildfire was off, ripping through me unchecked, unhindered, setting every inch of me ablaze.

"I... It means something different these days," I stammered, relieved to finally spot a returning Declan, arms overloaded with drinks, out of the corner of my eye. "To swing... It—"

"I know what it means," Gunnar purred, slouching against the bar to let Declan pass, his mouth positively sinful, his eyes twinkling like he really did enjoy my fumbling now. And why wouldn't he? Gunnar *had* me—because, by the modern definition, I was a swinger. I'd slept with him and Declan...

And I'd loved every second with them both.

"Come along, reaper," Gunnar urged, pushing off the bar as Declan set out the drinks on the counter. He caught my hand before I could slip away, then yanked me flush against him. Chest to chest, the hellhound maneuvered me with ease, a hand on my lower back while the other steered mine to his shoulder. He fell into the steps I'd showed him, which left me no choice but to let him lead, and the hellhound steered me around in an easy waltz, his royal blues locked on mine. "Teach me how to *swing*..."

❧ 24 ❧

KNOX

They kicked us out at two in the morning.

By four, we had finished an enormous platter of waffles and fried chicken at an all-night diner.

At four thirty, we returned to our territory, and as soon as the three drunk fools under my charge stumbled through the ward, the sky split open with a vengeance.

Having witnessed the changing of the seasons, summer bleeding into autumn, August and September trailing ever further behind us, I had categorized all the usual storms. There was the light misting that drizzled all day, bringing with it humidity and an ever-present damp. Then there were the days where it rained on and off in great heaving bursts; just when you thought it was over, *crack*, there went the sky, pissing down fat droplets that hammered the windows and threatened Declan's rooftop patchwork.

There were storms that built over hours, the sky slowly darkening, the winds reaching a howl only after a creeping escalation.

This was a tempest, a sudden and violent downpour. Hazel shrieked at the first explosion of rainwater, the droplets small but plentiful, relentless and cruel. Thunder crashed somewhere far off, possibly over the distant mountain range. Bright white light lashed against a pitch-black sky, the skittering bolts powerful but fleeting. The cedars did what they could to shelter us from the assault, some of the taller ones bowing to the wind, their piney branches dancing.

After a night *full* of humanity, from their smells to their noises, their drunken slurs to their clumsy stumbling on the streets of downtown Lunadell, the storm was a welcome reprieve. I would take damp earth and sodden brushwood over Sampson's Corner any day.

Gunnar and Declan agreed, apparently. Glee blasted through our pack bond from both as soon as we set foot on our territory again, and the alcohol was fuel to the fucking fire. One moment they were drunkenly heckling each other with words—and then words turned to fists, the pair scuffling and shoving each other through the forest. At the next flash of lightning, Gunnar ripped his meticulously cared-for shirt clean down the middle, then hurled the torn fabric into the awaiting boughs of a cedar. Declan followed suit, and before I could reprimand either, they shifted, shredding their trousers in the process.

I slowed my march through the soggy trees with a sigh, wishing those two would just drag their intoxicated asses to bed. But to see them roughhousing, playing, nipping and snapping their teeth at one another, Declan's tail up and wagging, Gunnar's encouraging barks bouncing off the landscape...

Well, it made my heart full.

I couldn't remember the last time they had felt free enough to just—*be*. Hellhounds. Members of the same pack, bonding, strengthening their connection through a bit of rough-and-tumble play. Like two pups who had finally found each other in their shadowy den, I'd never seen them act this way.

So, I let it go. Inside the ward, they were safe, contained. They'd find their way back to the house eventually, when the liquor left their system and their bellies howled for food.

I already dreaded the impending headache. While I had downed more than the rest, it seemed I could handle my alcohol better than all of them—and that included Hazel. Who knew a reaper could get drunk? Not me.

With Declan and Gunnar off to fend for themselves, I looked to the last member of our group, eager to herd her inside and into bed.

Especially with that *fuck* lurking in the celestial plane. He couldn't cross the ward, but that didn't mean he wouldn't try. And in her current state, Hazel was no match for blood magic, scythe or not.

And that scythe was precisely what I found where I had last seen the white-haired reaper. Leaning against a barren cedar trunk, the hook forged in starlight looked so inconspicuous. Safe, powerless without its soulmate. My brows furrowed. Where the fuck had she gone without it? Not that it mattered—no one could touch it in her absence if they wanted to keep their hands. But after that thing had followed us to the nightclub, I certainly didn't like the idea of her wandering off, drunk and alone, unsteady on her own two feet.

Her two *bare* feet.

Because there were her fucking shoes, twin black heels, tucked neatly beside her scythe and already filling with rainwater.

"Hazel?"

The pitter-patter of rain answered, and my frown deepened. A flash of red suddenly caught my eye, teased me, darting between the trees, up and down like she was climbing through the underbrush. Honestly, it was like minding a bunch of pups...

"Hazel," I called, voice drowned out by what felt like a purposeful clap of thunder. I glared skyward, then started off toward her. Faintly, the smell of ocean spray and salty sea air tickled my nostrils, her scent calling me home.

I found her headed east, cutting clear across our territory to nowhere. Her scent snagged on trees and scrub, a beacon through the storm, a dotted path for me to follow even when I couldn't see her. Eventually, she must have grown tired of wandering, because she stopped in a slanted clearing, standing atop the scraggly grey boulder in the dead center of the lopsided circle—dancing. Arms up. Bare feet threatening to shred on the rockface.

Her smile was beautiful, her laughter like a hymn.

But given the hour, the weather, I wasn't feeling all that worshipful.

"Hazel, get down," I boomed over the roar of rain, catching her eye with a wave from the tree line. She paused her dancing for a moment, hair slicked down her neck, her back, that sinfully snug red dress of hers drooping to expose a black lacey cup over her right breast. I swallowed hard, my mind darting to salacious places—like what was *under* that lace.

"No," she called back. The reaper threw her hands up in time with the next lightning strike. Brilliant white light illuminated the clearing, cast her in an angelic glow. When it vanished, she was a temptress once more, a dangerous creature in red, a threat to my self-restraint.

Fighting a smile, some traitorous part of me loving her defiance, I stalked into the clearing, careful over the slippery patches, the forest floor turned to muck. "We should get out of the rain. Come along."

I motioned for her to get down, but she shook her head, rising up onto her tiptoes, graceful as a ballerina.

"I love storms," Hazel insisted, running her hands up her neck, over her face, into her hair. "They're so... powerful. Don't you feel it?"

"What you feel is drunk," I said flatly as I picked my way around a few other rocks, mindful of the slope that led down into a shallow ravine—which the storm would flood within the hour, if it hadn't already.

"What I feel is *alive*," she countered, "and it's *amazing...*"

Yes, I imagined it would for someone who dealt exclusively in death. But the charade had become tiresome. When I finally made it to the boulder, I could *just* reach her ankles.

"Hazel, get down and let's get out of the rain." As soon as I had her, I'd teleport us straight to the house, shove her inside—see her to her bedroom, where she would undoubtedly crash. I was doing this for her own fucking good.

Yet she still scampered out of reach, defiant to the last. "Why? Because the wet will make me sick?" She snorted, her face lighting up. "I'll catch a cold?" Another snort, one that sounded more mad cackle than anything. "*You'll* catch a cold?"

"Yes, yes, hilarious," I muttered. Lightning seared across the black, and I used Hazel's intoxicated fascination with it to finally snare her. With her eyes up, I lashed out and caught both her ankles, then yanked her off the boulder. Light as a feather, she tumbled and squealed into my arms, then wiggled out in a fury immediately after.

Before I had the chance to really *feel* her. Hold her.

"Knox!"

"I'm not in the mood for you to be difficult," I growled, catching her by the elbow before she scampered off again. It was a bald-faced lie, of course; the alpha in me adored her fire, just as I had from the first day we met. But I couldn't give in to that, couldn't let myself succumb like Gunnar and Declan. I had to be stronger—for them. "Let's go."

Hazel twisted and squirmed in a futile attempt to get me off her arm. "I'm not ready to go back yet."

"Well, I *am*, so—"

"So, *you* go back, then," she argued as the pair of us skated clumsily across the muddy clearing.

"Not without you," I said distractedly, more focused on finding the best exit through the trees at the perimeter. The most solid muddy path would be best, as the muck rendered my fucking boots useless, and something without a lot of scraggly underbrush would benefit her bare legs.

Hazel, meanwhile, delivered a well-aimed kick to my shin. "Oh, what, *now* you want me around?"

I frowned down at her, seconds away from asking what the fuck she was talking about, only to be dragged into a clumsy brawl in the mud as the reaper tried to shake me loose.

"Hazel, for fuck's sake—"

She slammed her shoulder into my chest, the hit hard but nowhere near painful. It did knock me slightly off-balance, however. On an ordinary day, that wouldn't matter, but here and now, my feet encased in stupid human shoes, I lost my footing in the forest sludge. My left foot gave out, sliding sharply backward, but rather than releasing her, I yanked her with me, the pair of us stumbling down the little rocky hill and into an exposed cedar trunk. The tree stopped our descent, my back taking the brunt of the fall, and I whipped around before she could wriggle away, pinning her to the bark with a snarl.

"Stop this," I ordered, knowing full well the glaring reaper only took orders from Death. "Right this instant."

"Get off me," she grunted. Her dainty hands slapped at my arms, and I pressed down on her chest, right at the base of her throat, to trap her in place. My hand almost stretched the full width of her, palm to her chilled flesh, one fingertip a breath away from her thundering pulse.

Hazel kicked at my shins again, missing on the first attempt but nailing me much harder on the second. I winced and held firmer, only then realizing I didn't need to blink the rainwater out of my eyes anymore. In the shade of the old cedar, we found a shelter from the storm hammering the rest of the forest.

She seemed to realize it too, her arms falling to her sides, her breath coming in hard, stuttering pants. The pause heightened the way she felt against me, cool and solid, beautiful, fire blazing in her golden-brown gaze—a fire that threatened to consume me. I licked my lips, desire spiking, no doubt flickering through our pack bond straight to the others, and no amount of deep, steadying breaths could quiet that rising need. As if sensing it, Hazel nudged halfheartedly at the arm pinning her to the tree. Those cautious fingers then crept up my wrist, my forearm, before leaping to my chest.

The quiet is dangerous, warned a gruff voice at the back of my mind, one that grew softer and softer, its protests falling on deaf ears when Hazel's gaze flitted from her hands on my chest, up to my lips, then directly into my eyes.

The voice was right: there was danger in the quiet. Time stilled around us, the moment suddenly far too intimate.

Was this how she had hooked Gunnar and Declan?

My teeth gritted at the thought, but her fingers shyly toying with the end of my beard drop-kicked doubt clear out of sight.

Because Hazel had never felt malicious to me. The quiet didn't read as a trap—not in her cautious yet open expression, her hesitant exploration across my soaked shirt. It all seemed so natural, so right, the way it unfolded between us.

And maybe that *was* the trap.

Her full lips parted with a soft breath, damn distracting, fucking up my train of thought so *she* was all that was left, occupying every crevice in my mind, threatening to steal away my heart...

My hold on her went lax, and she slipped around my hand easily. Instead of running, the reaper closed in on me, eyes never once leaving mine. She fisted my shirt collar, twisting the damp material, and then used it to hoist herself up— straight to my lips.

The kiss took me completely by surprise, so much harder than her supple mouth had ever hinted at. She crashed into me without hesitation, all the tentativeness gone, throwing an arm around my neck like she knew precisely what she wanted. Standing stock-still, arms up but refusing to lock around her, I let her do what she pleased, unable to tear my gaze from her face.

From her thick, fluttering lashes, how they splashed across her pale skin. White on white, yet somehow contrasted too. Starlight. She was fucking starlight.

Despite the height difference, she fit perfectly to me, snug, her curves soft and pliant to the wall of muscle I had perfected into armor. With a sharp breath, I finally responded, my hand shooting to her hair as if to yank her off. Only instead of pulling her away, my fingers threaded through the mess of silvery white, and suddenly I was crushing her to me, my lips parting.

Our first kiss was still hard—rougher now, tongues tangling, teeth crashing. I slammed her back into the bark again, hips grinding instinctively when her legs parted for me. Every bit of exposed flesh glowed luminescent in the storm, her skin soft and cool—but her mouth shocked me. It was so fucking hot, a perfect home for all that fire, and as she locked her ankles behind my back, I couldn't help but wonder if her cunt blazed even hotter.

Only I shouldn't wonder about that.

Shouldn't give in to the primal beast inside, to the lust flooding my veins and warping my thoughts...

I ripped my mouth from hers, from the first kiss in my many centuries that had ever made me *feel* something. "No, Hazel... No."

It killed me to stop. Loss throbbed in my chest, the disconnect physically painful, but what hurt the most was watching her face fall. Cheeks flushed, hair mussed, eyes wide with confusion, Hazel opened and closed her mouth a few times, but nothing came out. Her fingers, meanwhile, dug sharply into my shoulders, ten individual little knives leaving me with a whole host of new scars.

But I couldn't give in.

Had to... Had to keep my wits about me, especially with that blood-magic fucker skulking about.

I went for her legs, trying to untangle myself from them, but she held tighter, eyes shimmering, fighting to stay open —as if holding back tears, anguish that would streak down her cheeks if she dared blink. Guilt twisted in my gut, but I shoved it deep, deep down, like always, not wanting to hurt her but knowing my duty had to remain elsewhere. We had already detoured so far off the beaten track, the path to pack freedom, and it became bumpier and bumpier with each passing day.

"Hazel—"

"Don't you want me?"

Her choked whisper shredded my heart to pieces, and I stiffened. "What?"

She studied me for a tense beat, and then she sucked in

her cheeks. Fury replaced heartache in a flash, and Hazel blinked hard, tears careening down her cheeks, so distinct from the rain. A stiff flourish of her hands brushed the streaks away before she shoved at my chest, hard, that seductive tentativeness dead and buried. I set her down with a soft clearing of my throat, a throat that felt too tight, and any attempt to shove down the lump that had settled there was like swallowing a mouthful of bees, stingers and all.

As soon as her bare feet touched the ground, Hazel shouldered her way around me and stomped into the clearing —her dress hiked up, especially at the back, high enough to reveal the tantalizing curves of her ass. Just the bottom bit, nothing too scandalous, and yet my cock, roused from our kiss, shot to full attention at the sight.

Fuck me. Teeth gnashing together, I took a moment to readjust my trousers. Constrictive things. Would have been better to just be naked. Desire threaded with my own anger as I stalked away from the cedar, and rain pelted me from all sides as soon as I left the safety of those piney boughs. I glared at her retreating form.

"What?" I demanded, my voice cracking across the clearing and making her stumble. "Are you angry because I won't *fuck* you like Declan and Gunnar did?"

Hazel whirled around, her furious gaze catching the lightning that cut overhead.

"No," she snapped, one hand tugging at the hem of her dress, the other motioning between us. "I'm angry that you keep pretending there's nothing here. We don't have to *fuck* to accept it—or at the very least acknowledge it."

"Stop. This is nonsense." If only there had been a slight wobble to her words, *something* I could latch onto and blame on all those drinks. "*Drunken* nonsense that you'll regret in the morning."

Those busy hands fell to her sides, coiled in tight, trembling little fists. "Fuck you, Knox."

And then she was off again, marching toward the tree line on the other side of the slanted clearing, like she had some true destination in mind. I could have stayed right here to stew in my thoughts, in my ridiculous feelings—in the truth behind her words. There *was* something here, something between us that I simply couldn't deny anymore.

Affection.

Acceptance—of my role as alpha, of the strengths of my miscreant pack.

Desire.

But...

But that didn't matter.

It simply couldn't.

Rolling my eyes, I carried on after her. No matter how irate she was at my rejection, no matter how my traitorous body desired her, I would still get her back to the house, safe and sound. I would see her to her bedroom door, possibly even a bathroom so she could clean the mud from her taut calves, her milky thighs.

A cluster of shrub and close-knit trees slowed her, and I'd caught up just enough to snag her by the elbow when the forest floor gave way beneath her feet. Hazel slipped about a foot down the decline, headed for the ravine, before I snatched her up and steadied her. While I hadn't expected gratitude, her violent wrenching away had my eyebrows shooting up—

And then she slapped me.

Clear across the face.

The blow landing out of *nowhere*.

A sharp, pleasant sting echoed across my skin, and renewed desire pounded through me, made my hands quake, my cock ramrod straight, my vision narrowed.

"Go back to the house, Hazel," I growled, low and dangerous, words laced with an unspoken threat. Not of violence—but of a loss of control.

She rolled her shoulders back, lifted her chin, and inched up on her tiptoes. "*You* go back to the house."

I concentrated on my breathing as she marched off again, willing my body to settle—ordering my mind to let go of the notion of fucking her into the mud.

Really though. Rogue spirits had to be easier to corral than a drunk reaper.

Sick of this back-and-forth, sick of her effortless sway over my own damn body, I caught up with her in three long strides. This time, however, when I snatched up her arm with the intention of hauling her all the way back to the manor kicking and screaming, the forest had other plans. Hazel reared back as if to strike me again—and the mud gave way, forcing my foot to take a hard right down the ravine. My knee buckled. I flailed. Hazel scrambled to grab a tree branch. I fell.

And dragged her right down with me. My back hit the scraggly floor hard, and before I could catch *anything*, we slipped and rolled and tumbled all the way down the slope— a slope that steepened, laden with unseen rocks and mud and leaves sticks and oh *fuck*, whatever that was actually hurt a bit. Over and over we flew, and still I refused to let her go.

Not even when we finally hit the gully at the bottom. The ravine's base squished beneath me but had yet to flood. Overhead, the cedars bent and swayed, shielding us *barely* from the sheet of rain. Having taken the brunt of our descent, I sat up with a breathless groan, Hazel strewn across me, her dress around her hips and her hair like a spider's nest. The reaper pushed up, both hands on my chest, and blinked at her new surroundings, momentarily dazed.

But as soon as her gaze landed on me again, that hand

was up, palm out, ready to hit me for some cardinal sin. I caught her before she swung, a snarl humming between us. She fought me, silent and fuming, our fall just a brief pause from whatever *this* was between us. To her credit, she was far stronger than she looked.

I was just stronger.

Capturing both wrists, I managed to roll and pin her, then shoved a knee between her exposed thighs when she tried to kick me. Her throat dipped delectably when my cock pressed against her belly, hard and insistent, but a heartbeat later she bared her teeth and *fought*. Squirmed. Wriggled. Thrashed about.

Little did she realize, her fire only made everything *worse*.

The union of an alpha and his true mate, his fated mate, was said to be a violent one. Harsh enough to draw blood. That wasn't the case with *every* female; all my past trysts had been hurried and in secret, neither of us a mating pair.

For an alpha's mate was the only one who could handle his power, his strength.

The only one who could stare down the savagery within and survive.

The only one who could laugh it off—and slap him across the face.

How long could I refuse her? How long could I face all the evidence and *still* walk away?

Scowling, I released her and sat up on my knees, pointedly *not* looking at her exposed sex, her bare stomach, the swell of her hips. Just as I was about to climb off and stand up, Hazel rose onto one elbow, then grabbed my shirt collar with her free hand. The fabric tore when she yanked me back down, and ruled by the beast within, I fell into a biting kiss that wrenched a snarl out of me again.

For a creature who looked so breakable, Hazel was resiliency personified, her bones forged of the same cosmos as her scythe. She withstood everything I had to throw at her, every rough caress, every probing sweep of my tongue. Her nails raked down my neck and under my shirt, and I met the searing pain with a hiss, my fingertips sinking into her thigh.

Did reapers bruise?

Fuck, I hoped so.

Even if it all came crashing down right this second, I would have loved to see marks on her pale flesh tomorrow.

She matched my ferocity with one of her own, biting and snapping at my swollen lips, tugging at my hair, arching up beneath my much larger body.

Hell, she even managed to roll me onto my back, catching me off guard at just the right moment to flip me into the sodden earth. Settled on top of me, Hazel ripped her mouth from mine, one hand on my throat, the other my chest, her molten center writhing over my constrained cock. Her tongue swept across her full lips, that once furious gaze muddled and complicated. Then, without a word, she staggered off me, half-naked and tromping through the ravine.

I blinked the rainwater from my eyes, bereft without her. Hazel's scent lingered in her wake, a clear-cut trail through the darkness, and I shot to my feet, every sense zeroed in on *her*. It had been an age since I'd hunted anything properly, but through the rain, beneath the flash of streaking white and the doldrum echo of thunder, I stalked her. Hunted her. Pursued her across the ravine.

Hazel stumbled along like she'd forgotten she had left a predator behind, yanking her dress down and attempting to untangle her hair. Slow and steady, she picked her way through the soggy terrain, her back to me—a fatal error.

Don't you want me?

Blood pounding in my ears, I finally answered. In a few monstrous strides, I was on her, hooking an arm around her waist and hoisting her off the ground. She squealed my name, legs flailing, and I lurched forward with my teeth to her neck—let her go at the foot of a fallen tree that sliced across the valley. Hazel stumbled a little once her feet found the forest floor again, but I refused to give her so much as a second to reorient; I shoved her forward, bent her over the tree trunk. A green sheen coated the bark, moss growing, but it was solid enough to withstand the weight of a gasping reaper.

Her hair spilled over her shoulders, and my hands frantically found the top of that red dress—grasped it, ripped it clean in two. Pretty as it was, delectable as she looked in red, it only got in the way. Next came the black material that wrapped around her chest, that hid away her breasts. It opened with a snap of the clasp, lace splayed on either side of her like wings. Lips lifted in a growl, I tangled one hand in her hair, holding her down, while the other went for my cumbersome trousers.

Hazel kicked back at me blindly, squirming in place and swatting halfheartedly at my forearm. I stretched her neck back, practically salivating at the sight of her folded over before me, ass up, sex ripe for the plundering. Logic switched off when I dug my cock free. The internal monologue that had plagued me since birth, the one that assessed risk, that always pushed me in the "right" direction for the sake of others around me *finally* fell mute. More beast than man, I let desire win, just this once.

I parted her legs with my knee, spread her softest folds with my fingers—and plunged into her with a single, brutal thrust.

Everything went black as I sank down to the hilt, her wet inferno engulfing me whole, welcoming me home—the perfect fit, a lock requiring a very specific key.

A key crafted by fate.

Well, I suppose—key*s*.

Her long, breathy moan brought the world into color again, and her dulcet soprano cry met my gruff baritone rumble in perfect harmony. Hazel arched her body up, rising to meet me even with my hand twisted ruthlessly in her hair. Delicate shoulders met my chest. Her heat tightened around me. Her lips tumbled open. Her hand found my hair.

And sank in, gripped firmly, wrenched like she was spurring on a stallion. I snarled in her ear and bucked hard, earning another moan that would rattle around my skull for eternity. My teeth found her neck just as my hips found their rhythm, the pair of us falling into a dance that somehow I had always known—for which I'd spent my life waiting for the right partner. It came easily, naturally.

Roughly.

Harsh and violent, Hazel gave as good as she got. Sure, I was the one who pounded into her from behind, taking her with a brutality that would have splintered a lesser creature to pieces. But she rocked back to meet my every thrust, tipped her head to the side to offer her flesh to my greedy mouth—neck, shoulders, jaw, lips. Nothing was safe. Nothing off-limits.

I still wasn't sure if she could bruise, but I could mark her skin, evidence of our union scattered across the luminescent white in angry red lashes.

She accepted my savagery and responded in kind, raking her nails across my neck, up my sides. My hair became her new obsession, a prop for tugging and twisting, her grip its harshest the louder she moaned.

As her lovely body tightened, her pale pink nipples pearled and her full lips parted, her eyes slowly drifted closed. I memorized every quiver, every quake, sensing her nearing her breaking point, the cliff's edge in sight as her cunt choked my cock each time it slammed into her.

I fisted my hand firmer into her messy mane, dragging her

back so that my mouth found her ear, my pace never slowing. No mercy. Not for an alpha's mate.

"I *do* want you, Hazel," I snarled softly, pumping harder as her hands scrambled across my body for something to cling onto. "Don't you understand? I fucking *want* you. I can't. I shouldn't, and it's killing me."

"Have me," she sang sweetly, glancing over her shoulder as much as my rough hold on her hair would allow. "Knox, I'm yours—*oh!*"

Her face screwed with pleasure, and I nearly lost myself in the way her body rippled around me. Heat flashed in her cheeks, then skittered down her beautiful figure in a telling flush. Bent over the fallen tree trunk, she shivered and shook in my arms—and still I offered her no mercy. Not when my own release was a breath away. The beast within surged, taking control as I slammed into her once, twice, three times more.

And as I spilled myself inside her, pleasure surging and threatening to cut me off at the knees, I yanked her head to the side. Bared her throat to me. Instinct guided my mouth to the crook of her neck and shoulder—and I bit down hard, a sound reverberating in my chest that even *I* hadn't heard before. Something primal and raw. Guttural. Possessive.

Whether it frightened her or not, Hazel took every last brutal moment of it, her breath falling in stuttering gasps, her body warped for my purposes.

For my mark.

That was what I was doing, what I had never done before: marking a mate.

Mine.

Ours.

Tentative fingers walked up my cheek, buried into my hair. Softly this time, she held me to her, even after my teeth left her flesh. We stayed like that, some tragic statue in the forest, my harsh breath gusting over her neck, our hands in each other's hair. Stinking of one another, scents entwined. Sex and sweat mingled with the storm. As the beast retreated and the man seized control, I knew I needed to *move*, but I couldn't.

I wanted to stay like this forever, buried in her, my mark on her skin, her hand in my hair and her supple body tucked neatly to mine.

If only hellhounds were permitted such luxuries.

Slowly, as my self-control came trickling in, I eased out of Hazel and stumbled back a few paces. Lost in her, I hadn't noticed the changes around us: the rain had downgraded from a battering to a misting, and the sky stayed a dreary dark grey, not a hint of flickering light to be found. As I scrubbed a hand over my face, thunder grumbled very, very, *very* distantly, heard only to those with heightened senses. Water squished soundly underfoot, and I made a halfhearted attempt to do up my trousers, my movements as sluggish as my mind.

Hazel, meanwhile, straightened in front of the fallen tree trunk, her back to me, body glistening from the dripping rain. She picked through her torn clothes, leaving the tattered dress where it was but reattaching the black lace around her breasts. A hint of modesty, our roles reversed—her mostly naked, me fully clothed. I scowled down at myself, then ripped clean through the shirt buttons, wrenching off the soaked fabric and tossing it aside. Next came my boots and socks so that I could feel the mud between my toes—feel more *myself*.

In a matter of moments, I too stood naked, skin coated in the cool watery mist. Hazel's gaze swept up and down my figure almost appreciatively, and her lips lifted in a gorgeous little smile.

Only I couldn't bring myself to smile back.

All of this had been... a loss of control, fueled by scotch and whatever the fuck she had gulped down for the last six hours.

I'm yours, Knox. It was just heat-of-the-moment talk. And that pissed me off.

I held up a hand when she drew a breath, looking like she had something to say.

"Tell me you're mine in the morning," I growled, knowing full well she would run from this just as fast as I would in the harsh light of day. "When you're sober, tell me."

Her mouth opened and closed a few times before her arms crossed and her expression pinched.

"I *am* sober," Hazel snapped back, "and it *is* morning, you stubborn twat."

No longer in the mood to fight, physically or verbally, I started a shaky climb up the nearby hill, in need of a cold shower—and then to brood in front of the hearth in my bedroom.

I made it halfway up the slope before a certain someone, who had been soundless in her approach, kicked my left leg out from under me. Embarrassment flared hot in my chest when I lost my footing again and skidded through the mud, not stopping until I grabbed at a sapling. Hazel loomed over me, arms still crossed, but much to my surprise, her glare was gone.

She wore the same expression that she had when she'd listened to my stories, to my pathetic, depressing history at the bar all those weeks ago. Compassion. Understanding. Awareness.

But not pity.

I gritted my teeth all the same, a snarl rumbling low inside me as she sauntered down the hill.

A snarl that quieted when she held out her hand and arched an expectant brow.

Take it, you fuck, her eyes ordered.

And I did. Without hesitation, I clapped onto her hand, and she helped me to my feet. All it took was a touch, the return of skin-to-skin contact, and the anger faded, the urge to brood and berate myself for giving in... gone.

The beast resurfaced, shoving aside the logical man in favor of seeing to my marked mate's comfort. Wordlessly, I scooped her up and threw her over my shoulder—to spare her pretty feet from the mud and the grime and the wet.

To hold her.

All the way back to the house I carried her. Up to her bedroom door where I set her down, where she kissed me on the cheek and said a soft, sweet good-night.

Where we went our separate ways and settled on opposite ends of the house.

And seated before my fireplace, I knew: we might be separated by physical distance, by wood and concrete, by brick and tile, but in a very real sense, with that mark on her neck, her scent tattooed across my skin—Hazel and I would never be apart again.

25

HAZEL

At about seven o'clock, the nighttime lamplights around Lunadell Park switched on, adding a soft yellow to what had been a rosy sunset. Seated on the same bench under the same old oak that Knox and I had maybe, sort of, kind of came to an understanding a few weeks back, I watched evening descend on the city that in less than three weeks, I would be responsible for reaping. Alongside Alexander and his pack, *we* would be responsible for the two million souls who called the metropolis home.

It was a lot of pressure.

Having a hellhound pack of my own, breaking boundaries with every single one of them, developing *feelings* that I had never had before—not even for Royce, who I'd promised to marry after the war...

It was just a *lot*. In general. Overall. The desire to perform to the highest standards at one's job followed you into the afterlife apparently, but so did feelings, emotions, physical needs. And when I'd snapped awake out of a brisk two-hour nap this morning, Knox's bite still achingly present on my skin, it all hit in one big, jumbled nuclear strike. I'd needed space, needed to get out. Needed time to think and reassess. A reaper *shouldn't* sleep with their entire pack, right? It was a working relationship, like that of an army platoon or a naval crew. We were supposed to be professionals, doing the most important job imaginable.

And I'd crossed a line with all of them.

Or had I?

As I stood, the park quiet, the crinkly, crackly autumn leaves rustling all around, I still didn't know the answer to that. Alexander made his hellhounds sleep in barracks outside of the main house, but I had come across other reapers on my few exhausting stints to the heavenly cities in the last few months. Most of the old-timers had insisted their hellhounds were family, that they would die for them—figuratively, I suppose. None of us were clear on whether we reapers *could*, in fact, die. But the sentiment stood: not every reaper saw their hellhound packs as property, as just another tool for reaping, a ladder rung in their climb to bigger and better things.

So why did I feel so—off? *Still.* After sitting and thinking and obsessing on this damn bench for the last twelve hours.

Casting one final look around the park, at the empty dog runs, the quiet bike paths, I slipped into the shadows of the oak and left the human realm behind. My scythe stood waiting right where I'd left it, planted in place at the foot of the tree, its staff cool and familiar when I wrapped my fingers around it. With a sigh, I brushed a bit of nonexistent fluff from the blade, polishing it with my slouchy long-sleeved shirt—procrastinating, not wanting to return and face the three hellhounds I had...

Well, exchanged intimacies with.

That was one way to put it.

None of them had made me feel guilty about it, and Gunnar had once told me that packs usually shared a mate.

But still.

The whole situation was strange, even for me—a woman who had died in 1943, then come back in the early days of the twenty-first century to collect souls for Death. I should be used to strange by now.

Only this strange was personal, intimate, my heart taking all the risk.

Because last night—this morning, whatever—I had told Knox I was his, when in reality, I could say the same to Declan and Gunnar. I felt for each one differently, cared for each hellhound for their individuality, all the while adoring them as a whole, a unit, a pack.

"Ugh." I speared a hand through my hair, gnawing at the inside of my cheek. All these thoughts—I'd been through them before. Repeatedly. Round and round my mind went, all day, on that bench. Each time I considered handing the pack over to another reaper, perhaps after they had passed the trials, every cell in my body fought tooth and nail against it. My mouth dried up. My chest tightened, some unseen hand taking my heart and *squeezing*. Light-headed, flustered, uneasy —I couldn't let them go.

Yet giving in to whatever we had, this connection between the four of us, made me weak-kneed and uncertain. Happy too. Thrilled, actually, to consider the bond solidifying between myself and the boys.

But...

"Oh, just *go*, Hazel," I muttered. I couldn't put it off any longer. Ignoring the whispering ripple that shuddered along the celestial plane, I teleported away from the park in the blink of an eye. Made a pit stop at the ward. Crossed through that and sealed it up. Just the sight of the forest brought a rush of fire to my whole body, memories of Knox, so masterful and domineering and *good*, knocking the wind out of me. Clinging to my scythe, my one consistency, I materialized in the alpha's bedroom.

Where I found an empty space and a dying fire. Downstairs, cutlery clinked, and the tap water ran; swallowing hard, I teleported down to the kitchen, appearing suddenly enough to make Declan drop the plates in his hands.

"Hazel!" Midway between the island and the sink, the stack of ceramic hit the tile with earth-shattering force, disintegrating into a hundred little pieces at Declan's feet. Knox and Gunnar were at the island, the alpha in his usual spot lording over everything, Gunnar at the opposite end picking through whatever was left in the breadbasket after the meal. Such a little breadcrumb vulture, that one. Both stared up at me with the same startled expression as Declan, only Knox was the first to bounce back.

"Where the fuck have you been?" he demanded, rounding the island and stalking over to me. If we were perfect strangers, the sheer size of him would have sent me running. But I knew him. I knew him better now than I did twenty-four hours ago, so I held my ground, scythe at my side, refusing to be bullied.

Gunnar rose to his feet at the island, his regal features twisted into something unreadable.

"I... needed time to think," I said slowly. While I didn't scuttle to the other side of the kitchen or hide behind Declan, I still leaned away from Knox's towering figure, especially when his eyes narrowed.

Hard to believe that just this morning those black orbs had been soft as liquid gold when I'd kissed his cheek at my bedroom door.

"Have you any idea how worried we were about you?" the alpha pressed, the depth of his snarl making the hairs on the back of my neck stand up. I finally planted my scythe between us, just for a little added security, and shook my head.

"What?"

I'd left the property dozens of times in the last two and a half months—my absence wasn't a cause for alarm. Peeking around the mountain of a man in front of me, I looked from Gunnar to Declan for an explanation and found the latter silently picking up the largest pieces of broken plate. He too wore an expression that I couldn't quite read, his dark brown eyebrows furrowed, his beestung lips pursed in a concerned frown. Huffing, I snapped my fingers, and in an instant the plates materialized next to the sink, whole and intact, the floor around him spotless.

"That *thing* followed us to the club last night," Gunnar told me, and my belly bottomed out at the news. "I pursued him, but he disappeared through another portal."

"Oh" was the best I could manage, my already too-full brain sluggishly working through the news under Knox's accusatory glare. "Well. No one told me that—"

"We would have had you been here this morning," the alpha remarked tightly. When our eyes met, I couldn't help wondering if he was just annoyed that I'd, what, disappeared on him after last night? He eased to the side, finally allowing the others access to me without a wall of alpha muscle in the way. "Instead, we found an empty bed and *nothing*."

Yeah. Maybe a little bitter, but worried overall. I practically felt it, the concern tainting the air around us. Sure, anger mixed in there too, but every one of his features suggested his harsh tone came from a genuine place.

And that made me feel things.

A lot of things, actually. My eyes prickled with tears at the mere *thought* that Knox was so worked up about my safety...

"Okay, well, I'm fine," I insisted, hating that Gunnar didn't look like he believed me, that he shared his alpha's infuriated concern over my well-being. And Declan... He looked torn between hurt and relief, his feelings out in the open as he leaned back against the counter with his arms crossed. At no point did he glance my way or meet my gaze, and that stung. "I didn't know about the demon, or whatever he is, but I only felt a weird little ripple toward the end of the day, before I left the park, and—"

"What were you doing at the park?" Knox tipped his head to the side, making up for Declan's lack of eye contact by never once taking his eyes off me. It was a welcome change of pace, all this concern rather than blatant disdain, but I had survived for ten long years on my own as a reaper; I didn't need to be monitored.

"This third-degree inquiry is a bit ridiculous," I said tightly. "It's none of your business."

Knox scoffed. "*You* are our business, reaper."

The notion carried between all three of them, in the slight lift of Gunnar's brows to the little nod from Declan.

"Right." I'd be the biggest asshole on the planet if I threw that back in their faces—especially when I no longer questioned it for a second. "Look, I'm sorry. Really. I get it. I just needed some time to think. The trials are coming up in a couple weeks, then this guy is clearly following us around, and... and... *us*..."

Mouth set in a thin line, Knox brushed my hair away from my neck, exposing the bright red mark he had left there. I flinched out of reach and dragged my hair back over my shoulder, hiding it away, and crossed to the island.

"What about us?" Declan asked, his words soft and uncertain. Planting my scythe beside me, I licked my lips and scanned the measly supper leftovers—procrastinating, again.

"Yes, do go on, Hazel..." Gunnar settled on his stool and threaded his fingers together, then steepled them in front of his smirking mouth. "What about *us*?"

Three expectant gazes settled on me like a ton of bricks, the pressure slowly but surely crushing me into the floor. Confusion churned in my belly, made my mouth dry, and I picked at the little bits of leftover—grossly overcooked—steak strips on the serving platter in the middle of the island.

"I… I don't know, okay?" The weight refused to lift, resting squarely on my shoulders as all three hellhounds waited for something better than indecision. Heck, *I* needed something more than indecision, but clarity had evaded me all fucking day. "I've never been in this situation before."

"And what situation is that?" Knox asked gruffly, lingering right where I'd left him between the island and the door. I popped the bit of steak in my mouth and chewed for a thousand years—yep, definitely overcooked. Had Gunnar shouldered Declan out of the way at the stove again?

Once I swallowed, difficult as it was, I couldn't just go on picking at their scraps.

"A situation where—" I shrugged, struggling under their scrutiny. "—I've, you know, been with… had *feelings* for, uh… more than one man, and I—"

It was then I noticed my hellhounds were each grinning to some degree and exchanging quick looks between themselves. I scowled, a hand on my hip. Sure, I preferred a grin to a frown, but my suffering wasn't for pack entertainment.

"It is *not* amusing, I assure you," I said, bristling. Gunnar's smirk sharpened.

"It's a little amusing."

"No," I gritted out, snatching up a lone honey-glazed carrot and popping it in my mouth. "It's not. It's stressful. And confusing. And… I don't know what to do about it."

"Why is it stressful?" Declan asked, his palm to his cheek, smile dampened for the time being—like he was really trying to *connect* with my predicament. Classic Declan. In that moment, all I wanted from him was a hug.

"Yes," Knox drawled, cutting through that tender feeling with a huge, unnecessary dose of snark, "don't you want us?"

Shoulders tensed, I shot him a withering look. *Don't you want me?* Nice. Throwing my words from this morning in my face. The alpha merely smirked back, a challenging flicker of his scarred eyebrow daring me to call him out.

But that wouldn't help anything—or change the direction of this conversation. Getting into a sniping match with Knox was just another way to put off a resolution to this. To us.

"I mean..." I swallowed hard, the lump in my throat like a rock. "Obviously I *do*—want you, all of you—and that's the problem."

Knox's smug expression faltered.

"I see no problem," Gunnar insisted, straightening in place and clapping his hands together—like my omission meant it was all done and dusted, problem sorted. Unfortunately, it just wasn't that simple. I flashed him a weak smile.

"No, of course you don't, but I—"

"Hazel, there's no problem for us." Declan strolled from the sink to the quartz island, arms crossed, those beautiful eyes so warm and comforting—begging me to believe him. "No jealousy, no competition. We aren't fighting for you... Well, I suppose we'll fight *for* you, if you get my drift, but you aren't a prize. It isn't every hellhound for himself. We all care very deeply for you. I've thought you were our fated mate from the beginning, and now these other pigheaded fucks are finally realizing it too..."

Gunnar shot his packmate an eyeroll, while Knox's low warning growl suggested he didn't enjoy his stubborn streak being called out by anyone. I, meanwhile, fidgeted with my shirtsleeve as a rush of heat hit me, made my head spin. *Fated mates.* It was a term that carried a lot of weight in the shifter community, and while hellhounds were different than shifters, a class of their own, apparently the mythos was transferable.

This pack of three believed Fate had created me for them —and them for me.

In their eyes, we were destined to find each other.

And from the way we met, after all they had been through, my ten long years of miserable loneliness... Maybe Declan had a point.

But...

I shook my head and pushed away from the island, leaving my scythe where it was as I strode across the kitchen. "I'm sorry. I-I still need to think."

Blitzing by Knox, I made a beeline for the door—only to find it instantly blocked by Gunnar. He'd teleported in a flash, tall and imposing, that lean figure managing to fill the entire doorway, his elbows pressed to either side of the frame.

"We *want* you, Hazel," he rumbled, tipping his head to the side as I stuttered to a halt. The look in his eye had morphed from confidence to hunger, those royal blues darker than I had ever seen them. Even the smirk that lifted his thin lips was a different shade, no longer smug but primal. I stumbled back a few paces at his first prowling step forward, and he motioned to me, then the others with such certainty it made my head spin. "And you want *us*. What, exactly, is there to think about?"

"I... I..." A low whine stretched between my ears, my head full of staticky nothing. "I, uh..."

His smirk turned deadly. "Hmm. Yes. That's what I thought."

"You all want to leave," I insisted, blurting out the suspicions that had been on my mind since the very first day.

Some might call it grasping at straws—I saw it as the final tethers that needed to be cut before I could truly give in. My eyes danced wildly between the three, heart thudding hard. "You want to go, be free, get out of this life—"

"Is that what we said?" Declan's voice whispered in my ear, lightly accented but deep, seductive, so unlike his usual self. I jumped when his arm snaked around my waist; all of them were getting so good at teleporting—or had he just closed the distance between us without me noticing?

Either way, he was here, hard and firm at my back, refusing to budge when I retreated into him. His free hand found my hair, and my skin prickled when he swept it back, baring Knox's mark to the world. He nuzzled it, his breath soft, the fleeting caress of his nose, his lips, so warm, so soothing, like the Arabian Gulf on a summer's day.

I blinked hurriedly, trying to shake off the lull crafted by his caress—because Gunnar still prowled toward me, slow and surefooted, while Knox watched on, the weight of his gaze crushing.

"Yes," I whispered, looking to Knox, "that's what you said. You want to leave—"

"Maybe once." The alpha gestured to his neck. "Not anymore. You and I mated—officially. That mark... What else has scarred your reaper flesh?"

I exhaled a shallow breath when Declan nibbled just under my ear, his thumb sweeping over the red bite on the dip between my neck and shoulder. "Nothing, but—"

"Then we're fated, and it's as simple as that," Knox told me. The sneer of the past had fallen away, his voice calm yet assertive, talking to me like we were finally equals. "If you're fated to me, you're fated to them. And if we leave, we leave together."

"You should really take that and run with it," Gunnar mused, close enough that I could feel the heat emanating off him, even through that thin navy sweater, his crisp black trousers. The hellhound snagged a finger under the hem of my shirt, gently at first, then gave a sharp tug, claiming my full attention as he closed in on me. "He's been mulling it over all day... Practically paced a hole into the floor in front of his damn fireplace." Gunnar glanced back at Knox, grinning. "The alpha has *finally* made his decision."

Knox's black stare narrowed, and he issued another warning growl, one that, again, was ignored by his smirking beta. My brain still struggled to compute, to just jump on the same page as them with nothing more than a few words and a novel scar as proof—and the fact that Declan had gone from soft, barely there pecks to a firm, openmouthed kiss that dragged up my neck to my ear certainly didn't help. I squirmed against him, needing the space to process, but he only held tighter, his hand smoothing possessively down my belly to my thigh.

"Tell me, reaper..." Gunnar walked two long fingers up my torso and between the valley of my breasts. He took his time, tracing my collarbones, swirling around the hollow of my throat, before snatching my chin so roughly, so suddenly, that I squeaked.

Warmth bloomed in my cheeks, made worse by the flood of need aching between my thighs. Declan scraped his teeth gently over Knox's mark; Gunnar closed in, our bodies a breath apart. Sandwiched between two hellhounds, I struggled for control, arms limp at my sides as they touched me, possessed me. Gunnar nudged my chin up, tilting my head back against Declan's shoulder.

"Tell me," he urged hoarsely, "what do you need to think about?"

"I..." It wasn't fair. How was I supposed to form a coherent sentence with both of them touching me? I pressed my lips together, closed my eyes, sucked down a steadying breath—none of it settled me. When I looked up at him again, I found Gunnar staring intently at my mouth, like he wanted to kiss it, bite it, fuck it... maybe all three. *Oh no.* "I-I..."

"I-I... *I*," he parroted back at me, singsongy and mocking as Declan chuckled against my skin, cupping me between my thighs. The only thing separating his firm hand and my damp sex was a slip of cotton, my black leggings suddenly *too* flimsy for my liking. Gunnar swiped his thumb over my lower lip, flashing his teeth with a predatory grin. "Go on, Hazel. Tell us."

He allowed me two stammering syllables before he pounced, slamming his mouth to mine with a snarl I felt in my bones. I arched up on my tiptoes with another squeak, eyes wide, hands floundering, pushing him away, pulling him closer, indecisive as ever. His kiss set my body on fire, rough and furious, a kiss to claim me, mark me just like Knox had. A jolt of white-hot pleasure shot from my clit to my nipples when his tongue slipped into my gasping mouth, the delicious burn amplified by Declan's sharp nip at my shoulder.

Just like they did in training, the pair worked in perfect unison, exemplified exceptional teamwork, to strip me naked in under a minute. Declan went for my shirt, yanking it up my body with a frustrated growl when it caught at my chin. Gunnar broke the kiss to allow the slouchy fabric to pass, then slowly worked his mouth down my neck as Declan unhooked my bra. By the time it had snapped free, popped off, exposed me, Gunnar's wandering mouth found a nipple to claim, and he did so harshly, all teeth and tongue and fiery pressure that made me squirm. His hands dropped to my black leggings, and before I knew it, he had them wrenched down my thighs, and he fell to his knees to finish the job, guiding them down my legs. Declan steadied me when I shuffled from one foot to the other, stepping out of my last stitch of clothing.

Role reversal was a hard pill to swallow; it just seemed so ridiculously unfair that *I* was the only one naked when there were three men with *perfect* bodies in the same place at the same time. A little mewl of disappointment bubbled up my throat, but Declan silenced it before it could spill out, twining his hand into my hair and stretching me back so that he could capture my mouth. His kiss was sweeter than Gunnar's, less fire, more slow, deliberate passion, our mouths immediately parting, consuming each other equally.

My whole body jerked when Gunnar's tongue swept between my folds, but Declan refused to let me break away. While my hands quickly found Gunnar's sturdy shoulders, his packmate held me in a kiss that could last a lifetime— even when Gunnar nudged my legs apart, his tongue swirling around my clit. A long, low moan tore out of me, humming between Declan and me, and I squealed when Gunnar had the nerve to hoist me up onto his shoulders so that my exposed sex was *literally* in his face.

I struggled harder, embarrassment ripening in my cheeks, made so much worse given the fact that this was unfolding in front of Knox. Out of the corner of my eye, I caught the alpha watching intently, his black eyes somehow darker, like the deepest pits of the oldest galaxy, where starlight goes to die. Somehow I still felt him, his gaze ripping across my naked figure, just as firm as Declan's mouth, just as sure as Gunnar's hands digging into my thighs.

A shocked cry snagged in my throat when Gunnar *really* got to work, feasting on me like a starving man. His tongue thrust into me, his nose nuzzled at my most sensitive parts; for a hellhound with such sharp, quick wit, it was no surprise that he was as good with his mouth as he was with everything else. Fingers. Cock. The last time we came together, it had been the latter. Declan had shown how skilled he was with his tongue, and now *Gunnar*…

My eyes fluttered shut, lost in bliss, in agony, the physical sensation of being touched, taken, possessed, maybe even *dominated* by two men unlike any pleasure I'd ever experienced.

My mind shut off. All the issues that had bounced around in there all day—silent. I had no clue how this all came about, how we went from a much-needed conversation about serious things to… *this*. To carnality and wanton desire, to tongues working me over like never before. But here we were —and it unfolded so naturally that it made my heart strangely full.

The three of us moved on instinct, my hips slowly, tentatively rocking against Gunnar's mouth. His hands had found my ass, kneading it, cupping it, while he fucked me with his tongue, then drifted up to toy with my clit, every sweep of his tongue sending a jolt of fiery pleasure from my core to—*everywhere*. Declan refused to let up on our kiss, deepening it as he held me up for Gunnar. I felt limp and useless between them, until the hand that had been buried in Declan's soft brown waves finally got to work.

Intuition drove me, a gut feeling that made me move without question or hesitation. While my other hand occupied itself in Gunnar's black curls, twisting hard when he pinched at my thigh and chuckled against me, my free hand dropped to Declan's sweatpants. Slipped under the loose waistline. Delved into his black briefs, the elastic snapping snug against my wrist. I found him hard and straining, and one pump of my fist had the hellhound at my back groaning. His masterful kiss faltered, and I smiled against his mouth, savoring the way his knees *almost* buckled as I stroked his cock, velvet steel in need of some serious attention.

In that moment, I had them both at my disposal: one hand guiding Gunnar's frantic pace between my thighs, the other stroking Declan into oblivion, his cock swelling further in my hand.

But just as fast as I'd seized control, I lost it. Gunnar switched things up on me out of nowhere, replacing his wicked tongue that had been thrusting in and out of me with two long fingers. I bucked, moaning into Declan's mouth, when he zeroed in on that sensitive little spot along my inner walls. Meanwhile, his mouth latched onto my clit and refused to let up, no matter how hard I yanked at his hair, the thrill of both combined with Declan's hand kneading my breast just *too* much.

My climax hit hard and fast, utterly ruthless in how it throbbed through me, burned me from head to toe. I arched and shuddered, riding out the pleasure as the levies broke— and neither hellhound stopped what they were doing. They pushed me in their own ways; Gunnar pumping his fingers in and out, sucking at my clit like he wanted to punish it, while Declan wrapped a hand around my fist and stroked his cock for me when I lost my teasing rhythm.

With great difficulty, I finally tore my mouth from Declan's, gasping for air, my cheeks hot and my brain fuzzy. The best orgasm of my life made everything hazy, and I needed Declan to hold me up when Gunnar set both my feet back on the ground—my knees just refused to work. My sweetest hellhound wrapped an arm around my waist and scooped me up.

"You're so beautiful when you come," he rasped in my ear, and little licks of fire lapped at my sex, his voice enough to set me alight again. Gunnar shot to his feet and stalked to the kitchen island, ripping his button-up clean open in the process. I flinched when Declan tweaked one of my nipples, a twinge of pain mingling with the pleasure overdose pounding through my system, and I could almost feel him smiling against my neck when he added, "We're going to make you do it again and again, sweet... One for each of us, at least."

The best I could manage in response was a hapless moan, my gaze briefly darting over to a brooding Knox before shooting back to the island at the sound of a calamitous crash. In one swift motion, Gunnar had swept everything off the surface, cups and serving trays and knives clattering to the floor. His elegant hands dropped to his trousers, unbuttoning them, unzipping them, kicking them and his briefs off with a sneer. Like Declan, his cock dropped forward, hard and insistent, and I licked my lips, swallowing down a brief moment of panic.

For some reason, I hadn't even considered that I'd be taking care of *three* of those beasts...

I should have.

But now that I'd come to terms with it, I almost relished the challenge.

Without a word, Gunnar hopped up onto the island and settled on his back, a god on his altar, all porcelain skin and greedy eyes.

"Bring her here," he ordered gruffly, but Declan was already on the move, steering me and my useless legs to the island. The hellhound all but threw me onto it, and I scrambled to arrange myself so that I wouldn't trample Gunnar—even if the look in his eye suggested he'd be all for it. With his lean, gorgeous body stretched flat across the island's counter, I was able to crawl over him, but he caught me by the hips before I'd made it very far, holding me over his length. It nudged at my slick entrance, teasing and torturous, as Gunnar cocked an eyebrow and murmured, "Just where do you think you're going?"

Before I could answer, he thrust up, spearing me almost as effortlessly as he had made me come. I folded forward with a cry, body spreading to accommodate for something much bigger than his two fingers. My hands scrambled up his chest, searching for balance until our hips collided. Every muscle across his torso strained, like the task of holding still took an intense toll on him. The effort stretched all the way up to his mouth, set in a thin line, to his jaw clenched hard.

A part of me wondered if he was waiting for me to adjust, allowing me a few precious moments to *breathe*. Little did he know, I didn't need it. Lower lip caught between my teeth, I rocked back, then rolled my hips forward, loving the way his short black eyelashes fluttered ever so slightly. The slight quirk of my mouth—*got you, Gunnar*—had his eyes narrowing, and I felt him bend his knees behind me, plant his feet, then *slam* up into me so firmly that my teeth chattered.

"*Oh!*"

Growls sounded throughout the room, all three alerted to my yelp and closing in like a pack of wolves circling their wounded prey. Knox's heavy footfalls seemed to echo with every step, slowly making his way to the island as Gunnar pounded into me. My hands anchored themselves on his shoulders, and while I could have ridden him to my heart's content, this was a ride that required you to just hold on for dear life—and that was what I did. Barely. The lingering aftershocks of that first climax sparked into something different, something sharp and punctuated, prickling through me with a vengeance.

Suddenly, Gunnar stilled. The hellhound caught me by the chin, his one hand finally abandoning its steely hold on my hip. It slid down to my throat, carefully guiding me forward so that he could gently capture my mouth in a kiss that made my toes curl and my heart skip a beat. In a delicious contrast to the way he'd ravished me, his mouth set a sweet, soothing pace, like a balm to a burn, and I moaned softly when he eased out of me.

A hand pressed to my lower back, hot and firm, and suddenly Declan replaced him, filling me with a slow, deliberate thrust that had my hips arching and my eyes rolling back in my head. He pumped in and out of me gradually, another balm to Gunnar's roughness, before pulling out and nudging at a different hole entirely. I stilled, breath catching as I shot up and away from Gunnar's gentle kiss.

"Easy, sweet," Declan murmured, planting a few delicate kisses up the path of my spine, between my shoulders, at the base of my neck. "Relax... I won't hurt you."

While I wasn't a virgin before the air strike stole my human life, I hadn't done—*that*—before. But sandwiched between Gunnar and Declan, I trusted them. Of all three, Declan was the least likely to handle me harshly, and that was what I needed for my first time.

Slick with my arousal, he eased into me inch by inch, pausing whenever my breath caught or my nails bit into Gunnar's shoulder. They both kissed me in the meantime, Gunnar along my neck, brushing over my parted lips, across my flushed cheeks, and Declan down my back, along my sides, nibbling at a few ticklish spots that made me exhale soft giggles.

It was a tight fit. A little painful, even as a reaper, but the pair handled me gently, stroking me, kissing me. Declan's fingers eventually found my clit, massaging it so tenderly that I almost came again from that alone. When he had filled me to the hilt, his packmate took hold of my hips again, and my eyes rounded in shock when he eased into my sex.

Both of them—at the same time?

I let out another helpless moan, trapped between them and loving every second of it. Somehow, they made this work without a word shared between them, but I couldn't help wondering what the trio felt along their pack bond. Was it as tangled as my brain, hazy with lust and desire and affection—the beginnings of love?

I desperately wanted to know, but every thought evaporated when Gunnar thrust up fully, claiming me once more. Declan rocked in and out of me with slow, deliberate movements, steady and unfaltering in comparison to Gunnar's rough, hurried bucks of his hips. They stayed true to themselves, mindful of each other as they had their way with me, and once more I was left to play catch-up—to hang on for dear life and hope I survived.

At one point—a time that could have been seconds after they both filled me, minutes, *hours*—Declan wrapped my hair around his hand, then gently lifted my head up.

"Tell us how you feel, reaper," Gunnar ordered, his smirk both knowing and mocking, confident and playful. Sometime in the last however long I'd been trapped between them, Knox had pulled up a stool next to the island, and he continued to watch the display in silence. He cocked his head to the side when I shakily met his black eyes, one strong arm stretched possessively across the end of the island, just over Gunnar.

A teasing twist of my nipple had me yelping, dragging me back to Gunnar's question. How did I *feel*?

Overwhelmed.

Enamored.

Adored.

Desired.

My incoherent babbling response showed just how useless my brain was with both of them thrusting into me under Knox's watchful eye. The trio grinned, Declan's affectionate smile lingering in my peripherals, the grind of his hips harder now, slowly but surely catching up with Gunnar's rough thrusts.

"What?" Gunnar tapped a finger under my chin. "I don't think any of us quite got that…"

"We want to hear you, sweet," Declan whispered into my ear, and I let out a feeble whimper. How did they expect me to form actual sentences right now? Seriously. This was just cruel.

Swallowing hard, I forced my mouth to move. "I feel… I feel…"

"Say it," Knox rumbled. Trembling, I collapsed onto one elbow, my head to Gunnar's chest, everything down south wholly occupied.

"I feel full," I whined, embarrassment burning in my cheeks when a chorus of baritone chuckles arose around me. As if that declaration was all they needed, Gunnar and Declan pumped faster, harder, the three of us rocking back and forth on the island countertop—an island that I would never be able to look at the same again.

Not without remembering how it felt to be so—*full*.

It felt heavenly. Overwhelming, sure. But wonderful too. Like I was complete in the best way.

And it only got better when Declan reached between Gunnar and me to find my clit. He stroked the little bundle as best he could, the angle awkward but my hellhound determined. With Gunnar catching something *delicious* on my inner walls with every harsh thrust and Declan toying with me relentlessly, I came with a little half shout. Eyes clenched shut, my body tightened, tightened, tightened, the pleasure sizzling, until it all just broke apart, an avalanche of ecstasy rushing over me, demolishing everything in sight.

Both Gunnar and Declan groaned as my core clenched and my sex rippled with another stunning orgasm, and I vaguely felt teeth on my shoulder in the fuzzy aftermath. Declan's hand clamped over Knox's mark on the opposite side, his pace quickening, his grunts more like growls as he pumped into me. As if accommodating, allowing his packmate to take the spotlight, Gunnar had stopped moving completely, his hands on my hips—practically *lifting* them up for me because every muscle and bone in my body had dissolved into jelly.

Teeth that had just grazed and nipped before now sunk into my flesh when Declan pounded once, twice, three times, then stilled against me, his body shuddering through a climax of his own, his bite searing. Weakly, I lifted a hand to twine into his hair, relishing his teeth on my skin.

I should have been satisfied: two climaxes and another mark on my body? A mark that would likely be permanent, just like Knox's... That should have been enough. But as Declan licked across the tender wound on my shoulder, slowly inching out of me, I wanted *more*. I craved Gunnar's release, his face twisted in an almost painful bliss. I'd seen it before. I'd fought the memories of both him and Declan, the snapshots of our most intimate moments popping up at inappropriate times.

As of this morning, Knox had been added to my memory bank, although his was more of a physical recollection, given he'd been behind me at the time. But I wanted to see it. Slowly, my gaze drifted over to the alpha, to his obsidian stare and his scarred face, to a mouth that had tainted this reaper's flesh when nothing else had ever left so much as a scratch.

"Insatiable, this one," Gunnar rasped, and heat flared through me from top to bottom when I realized he'd caught me staring at his alpha—ogling him, fantasizing, reminiscing. His sly mouth quirked, and before I knew it, he had us both up and seated. Declan's arm wrapped around my waist, and he tenderly hoisted me off the counter, the pack once again communicating without a word. Gunnar hopped off shortly after, taking over from a flushed Declan. Over my shoulder, I caught my sweetest hellhound leaning against the island, his brow sweaty, his cheeks pink, his full mouth lifted in the most beautiful smile.

But I was forced to look away when Gunnar steered me toward Knox—when he took my hands and placed them on his alpha's waistline. Knox's cock strained against his trousers, and weak from two climaxes, my uncoordinated fingers struggled to get the button open, to wrench the zipper down. I managed—somehow. With an elbow propped on the island, the alpha simply watched me peel his trousers aside, then free his cock with trembling hands.

His cheek twitched when I circled a finger around the engorged silky head, and the huge hand that had once sat loose on the counter tightened to a fist when I risked stroking his thick shaft.

"Come on, Hazel, we can do better than that," Gunnar murmured in my ear. He dragged his tongue down the column of my throat, over Declan's mark at its base, before he cuffed me on the back of the neck and guided me down.

Instinct took over again; I parted my lips, taking Knox into my mouth an inch at a time, not stopping until he nudged the back of my throat. He snarled softly when I eased off and swirled my tongue around the tip of his cock. The alpha drew in a ragged breath, nostrils flaring as I bobbed up and down slowly, and the hand that had sat uselessly on his lap all this time found its way to my hair.

Tonight, he was shockingly gentle with me, all the brutality and pent-up frustration from the forest gone in the way he played with my hair. In fact, I swore I felt him twirling it around one finger, all the while watching me, never once pulling his gaze elsewhere.

Not that I could look away either. As soon as our eyes found each other, I was done for, not able to think—just move.

Gunnar's presence disappeared behind me, the absence of

his hellhound heat, his cock nudging insistently against my thigh, leaving me rather exposed. Bent over in front of an alpha, a chill skittered down my spine, and like the ripple in a pond, it flared out, little goose bumps rising across my arms and legs, up my neck.

Out of the corner of my eye, I spied Gunnar hopping up on the kitchen island, his knee brushing my shoulder, his shaft sticking straight up at the helm of his thighs. Having two of them watch me taking Knox's cock in my mouth was almost too much, and my sex ached with need once more, desperate to be *full* again.

As if sensing my wants, perhaps even seeing them in my eyes, Knox smoothed his hand from my hair to the underside of my chin. Gently, he lifted me from his shaft, and we moved in tandem, like dance partners expertly flowing from one step to the next. With his support, I climbed into his lap, my hands going for his shirt before we floated effortlessly to the next bit of footwork in this dance. Lower lip caught between my teeth, I dragged his thin jumper over his head, needing to really *feel* him, the coarse hair on his chest, the steel beneath his flesh.

Knox let me manhandle him—let me throw his shirt aside, brush his thick black hair over his shoulders. He let me cuddle up to him, cup his strong jaw, *kiss* him so deeply I swore I tasted his soul.

Only he didn't have a soul.

None of us did.

But in that kiss, there was something more inside him, something that bonded us together—and I craved it with every fiber of my being. I kissed him hungrily, greedily, not even breaking when he steered my hips over him, aligned our bodies so that when he slammed me down, I took him all in one swift stroke.

I felt Gunnar and Declan's interest in our union, in the

way they shuffled about behind us, the low growls, the rush of heat turning this kitchen into a goddamn sauna. Between them, I had been putty in their very skilled hands, something to be molded and taken, my pleasure dispensed at their discretion. Yet with Knox, I had some control. So much larger than me, he could have easily thrown me about, pinned me here and there, set the pace that best suited us.

But he just sat there, taking my desperate kiss in stride, one huge hand on my lower back as I swirled my hips. Pleasure tingled in my core, and my belly looped deliciously when my clit brushed up against him with every rock of my body.

"Hazel…" I'd never heard desperation drip from Gunnar's lips until now. Only that could tear me away from Knox's firm mouth, and I found his beta studying me, stroking himself, waiting. Licking my lips, I leaned over to taste the head of his cock, taking just that in my mouth and smiling at the sound of his pleasurable hiss. Knox took over the motion of our bodies, both hands rocking my hips, grinding me down against him so that the exquisite build I'd felt between my thighs remained unbroken.

Where Knox had been gentle and indulgent when I used my mouth on him, Gunnar was as rough as he had been before, one hand in my hair, holding me as he pumped into my mouth. My gaze darted up to his royal blues, and I found every inch of him rigid, mouth in a thin line, jaw gritted. I wrapped a hand around the base of his cock, my lips colliding with my fist as I took him faster, deeper, his hips bucking up hard to take advantage.

He spilled himself into my mouth minutes later, a hot burst of salty essence dribbling down the back of my throat. I coughed and arched against the sudden onslaught, but he snatched up my free hand before I could push at his torso, in need of a breath, his shaft buried deep. Pain cut through the pleasure building in my core; his teeth had found my wrist, and as he shuddered and jerked into my mouth, he marked me like Declan and Knox with a bite.

"Gunnar," Knox growled, and the hellhound finally eased up on my hair. I sat up with a shaky gasp, eyes watery, and found my wrist still clamped firmly in Gunnar's mouth. Gold blood dribbled down my forearm, and when his eyes fluttered open, they locked on me, so vulnerable, so open. I'd thought I had tasted Knox's soul in our kiss before, but here, I swore I saw Gunnar's in his eyes. Beautiful.

And Declan's soul…

I felt Declan's soul in his touch.

All these souls that didn't exist—*depth*. That was a better word for it. I experienced the depth of these three hellhounds in a way I never had before, but I desperately wanted to again.

When Gunnar finally released me, he kissed the wound on my wrist, licked at the ichor staining my pale flesh. Once, his smirk had made me bristle; tonight, I found it endearing. I grinned back, then slowly retracted my arm, cradling it to my chest, eager to examine each of the three marks sometime later in the mirror. Would they be as individual as the hellhounds who gave them to me?

God, I hoped so.

Soundlessly, Gunnar slid off the island, and as soon as the space cleared, Knox shot up, carrying me with him. All this time, he had seemed like a passive participant, keen to just play the voyeur while his pack had their way with me. But as he pinned me up against the smooth edge of the island, I realized that wasn't the case at all.

Knox had just been biding his time.

Letting his pack feast first for once.

He wasn't passive—he never would be.

And I'd never fully be in control with him, no matter what he let me do to him, how he let me kiss him...

I let out a startled cry at his sudden ferocity, at the way he hooked his hands under my knees and lifted me, spread me open for him. The shifting angle allowed him to plunge deeper. Trapped in place, I threw one arm around his neck, while my free hand clung to his shoulder. His first thrust was brutal, verging on violent—and I fucking *loved* it.

"Kn-nox," I whimpered breathlessly, digging my nails hard into his flesh and wishing I could mark him up like he had me. He snarled back, teeth to my neck, pounding into me with the force of a late-summer storm, the kind that felled trees and tore shingles from rooftops. After Gunnar and Declan, my body ached, the pain almost pleasant, but when Knox was through with me, I wasn't sure when I'd be able to stand again.

Even the island struggled to keep up with him, the wood creaking, the quartz groaning, all of it threatening to crack right down the middle the harder he drove into me. He should have frightened me, but I found myself whispering, *begging*, for him to go harder, faster, deeper—*take* me. And Knox complied. Vigorously. In fact, this felt like one of the few things we had ever agreed on.

My third climax came like an explosion, sudden and vicious, destructive in the best way. I cried out in his arms, scoring my teeth across his rugged pectoral and teetering on the verge of a breakdown. Pleasure had me seeing stars, stars that snapped and burned behind my closed lids, Knox's name spilling from my lips over and over again until he stilled. Unyielding as my scythe, the alpha stuttered to a halt against me, buried deep inside, practically slamming me *through* the island, and his body trembled as he spilled himself inside me. Buried against my neck, his mouth hovered over the mark he had made this morning, and the

346

bloody scars left by Gunnar and Declan tingled—as if sensing a kindred spirit.

It was only when Knox eased out of me and carefully set my feet on the ground that I broke. My knees buckled, my hands flailed out for the counter, and the alpha caught me before I hit the floor. Silently, he scooped me up and set me back on the island, my chin dropped to my chest; I just didn't possess the strength to lift it anymore, everything inside totally liquified. Moments later, something warm and soft slipped over my head, and I vaguely felt someone maneuvering my arms through sleeves.

Knox's black jumper was *far* too big for me—it was practically a dress. But it smelled like him. It enveloped me in the softest hug. I never wanted to take it off, but it wasn't enough to stop me from shivering. Even my teeth chattered, the lack of hellhound skin contact leaving me cold, well and truly freezing, for the first time since I had returned to the human realm like *this*—dead yet not, my touch frigid and my heartbeat slow.

Gunnar stepped in with his trousers, both him and Knox manhandling me, sliding the luxe material up my legs. I tried to protest, insisting that I'd ruin them, stain them with what was dripping out of me, but that seemed like the furthest thing from anyone's mind—so I let it go. As soon as Knox gathered my hair and arranged it over my shoulders, keeping the wisps away from my face, Declan materialized out of nowhere in front of me with a mug of tea in hand. Steam spiraled off the surface, a little string hanging over the side of the cup.

I accepted the drink with a tired smile and wrapped both hands around it, the sleeves of Knox's jumper covering my palms and muffling the burn. Earl Grey with a splash of milk and sugar—a favorite that had followed me into the afterlife.

"You all right, sweet?" Declan asked, his hand on my

knee. The pack hovered around me like they never would have at the start of all this, directly in my personal bubble, either touching me or within an inch of it. Exhausted, sore, satisfied, and a little dazed, I struggled to find the words to answer—but I knew what I wanted: to dive into a pile of hellhounds, all of us snoozing on top of each other, just like they had been the first time I set eyes on them.

But this would do for now. Three gorgeous, naked, sweaty, muscly men eyeing me warily, waiting with bated breath for a response.

They certainly knew how to make a girl feel wanted.

After a tentative sip, finding the tea much too hot but delicious all the same, I nodded. "Yeah. I'm okay."

"Are you sure?" To my right, Gunnar watched on with a furrowed brow, arms crossed and a dribble of my gold blood on his chin. Blowing on my tea, I wiped the ichor away with my thumb. Of the trio, Gunnar was somehow the most vocal lover, someone to set the pace, lead the way—and I appreciated that about him. He was an instigator, and given I had never done this before with more than one man, I needed someone like that.

"I think so," I managed. Knox curled his arm around my hips, my butt, and I leaned into the embrace with a weary sigh. Everything still felt full—most of all, my heart. Having them all so close to me in the aftermath, my body experiencing sensations I hadn't since I was alive, taking in the concern in their eyes, the affection... It was a lot to process.

And yet my mind was blissfully empty for the first time all day, like I already knew the answer to every question, comment, and concern from my nagging inner monologue.

My vision blurred, only clearing when I blinked sluggishly and sniffled, refusing to let a single tear fall.

"Is this how it's supposed to feel?" I asked hoarsely.

Gunnar's frown deepened, and Declan moved closer, standing between my knees and stroking the tops of my legs with his thumbs.

"What do you mean, sweet?"

"I mean... being fated," I managed, fighting for every word, my body suddenly craving sleep—with all three of them around me. "I feel... whole. Is this... how it's supposed to feel?"

Gunnar's expression lifted as he exchanged a quick glance with a grinning Declan, and Knox cleared his throat, holding me just a little tighter.

"Can't tell you, reaper," he insisted, his tone gruff as always—but a little light twinkling in those midnight-black eyes. "This is the first time *we've* been fated to anyone."

I risked another sip of my tea as Declan murmured, "But it feels right, doesn't it? Like this is how it was always meant to be?"

The drink scorched down my throat, burned my tongue, and I didn't care. If the pack continued to look at me like they did right now, every day, for the rest of our days, I honestly wouldn't care about anything ever again.

"Yeah," I said softly. Gunnar swooped a rogue lock of white behind my ear, smirking.

"Then... yes, I think this is how it's supposed to feel."

Only one little thought worried me. "Is that how you guys feel too?"

"I can't speak for anyone, but it's how *I've* felt since August," Declan insisted, holding his hands up innocently and stepping back when Gunnar rolled his eyes and Knox growled. "Just saying... I've been waiting for the rest of you to catch up for ages."

I brought my tea up to hide my smile, breathing it in as Gunnar swatted at his packmate.

"We get it."

"You all said it was puppy love, but here we are—"

"Shut up, Dec…"

Declan swerved dramatically to avoid another smack and then flicked Gunnar dead center in the chest, which kicked off a little shoving match that made Knox sigh before nuzzling his face into my neck, over his mark, not bothering to stop the playful squabbling.

I watched on without a thought in my head.

Just a fullness in my heart.

An ache between my thighs.

Three permanent marks on my skin…

And my favorite tea in my belly.

❦ 26 ❧

HAZEL

"Wow. So that guy is just... takin' a shit on the sidewalk, huh?"

"Declan." I pursed my lips, trying not to laugh—a task made infinitely more difficult when Gunnar snorted, both him and Declan watching the human who had *no* idea he wasn't alone... shitting on the sidewalk. To be fair, he couldn't see *us*, and it was a relatively empty part of Lunadell, the sun only just inching above the horizon, the city still asleep. Based on the cloud cover, we were in for another grey autumn day, the end of October within sight, the trials looming ever closer.

"Focus," Knox ordered, his beastly tone snapping Declan and Gunnar back into the moment. Three sets of eyes landed on me, and after a week of nonstop sex, sometimes with just one of them, usually with the entire pack, I no longer felt their intense weight on my shoulders. And thank goodness —*finally*. After all, we were here for work, not play. With only a precious seven days before the four of us had to prove ourselves to an archangel with a stopwatch and a clipboard, these test runs were serious business.

Although… The human to our right taking his sweet time pushing out the longest shit in the history of mankind sort of took the edge off. Clearing my throat, I smoothed a hand down my reaper's robes with a sigh.

"Okay, you guys know the drill," I told them in my best serious-reaper voice. "There are five orbs scattered around Lunadell with soul-scent signatures. Your job will be to herd them back to *that* building." I pointed to the nearby structure, a warehouse amidst dozens in the city's south-end industrial zone. "It's where our tester will be waiting for you. On the day, we'll be using real souls, so I've charmed the orbs to react accordingly. They'll run. They'll hide. They'll attack. You have forty-five minutes to wrangle all of them back as a unit."

While today was just a practice, something to get the pack familiar with the exact landscape they would be tested on in a week's time, I wanted them to do well. *Needed* them to succeed. After all, the bite marks on my shoulders and wrist still hadn't healed, and by shifter lore, we were fated. These were *my* boys. The thought of Heaven sending them back to Fenix so they could wait for another reaper to select them, train them all over again, made me want to vomit. Failure just wasn't an option, and while we might have spent the last week in a bubble of sex and food and murmured conversations in front of a flickering fire, I had seven days to get *my* pack as ready as possible for the biggest test of our lives.

And this practice run was just for the first exam on the first day… They would have seven trials to complete under an angel's watchful eye, and when the time came, all I would be able to do was sit back and watch. For the next week, I could step in as needed, give guidance where possible, and do everything in my power to ensure my boys passed with flying colors.

After that, the real work began—but they would be with me for the rest of their lives, just like Fate intended.

That was all that mattered.

"I'll be waiting for you on the roof," I added. "My scythe is planted there—use it for direction. They'll try to trick you during the real trials, get you all turned around in the city's core so that you can't locate the drop-off point as easily. So, get more accustomed to its power, to the aura it gives off here. You might be able to sense me across the celestial plane, maybe even feel me, but one of the trials is proving you've bonded to my scythe. That when it calls, you come running."

Knox's lips thinned at the sentiment, and he crossed his burly arms in a sullen silence. While we might have bonded officially, his mark the deepest in my flesh, he still wasn't thrilled with any of this. The very idea of proving his pack's capabilities to an angel offended him, but at this point it was a necessary evil we just had to get through.

We hadn't discussed it, but despite his brooding, I really hoped he understood that this was all temporary. In a week, there would be no one to interfere, no one to judge or monitor us. Beyond the standard rules of reaping, we would be on our own.

I gave his bicep a gentle squeeze, which earned me an annoyed nostril-huff and a scowl. Across our little huddle, Declan met my eye, and even though I *still* couldn't feel the pack bond like they could, I sensed his reaction to his alpha's mood, practically heard his sweet lilt whispering around my head.

He's fine. Just ignore him.

I gave him a barely discernible nod, the corners of my mouth *just* kicking up—for him, for his kindness, for the way he was always there to reassure me with nothing more than a look.

353

"All right..." I clapped my hands together, then lifted a prompting eyebrow. When no further questions came, I motioned to the pack with a grin. "Let's do this, then."

The trio started to strip down, efficient and careful with their clothing. For once, I didn't look away—didn't bother to hide my obvious interest in their physical perfection. My eyes wandered, wild and unchecked, over every pronounced ridge, every torso of rippling muscle. Broad shoulders, even my lean, sleek Gunnar. Toned, powerful thighs.

Yum.

Gunnar caught my eye during my very obvious perusal, and his knowing smirk had me blushing ever so faintly.

"Is there a *reward* for a job well done, reaper?" he drawled, sweeping his gaze up and down my body just as openly as I had his. After a week of carnality, you'd think they would be satisfied, that *I* would be satisfied, but it seemed like we could never get enough of each other. One hellhound would finish with me, bodies slick and spent, and then another would sidle in to pin me against a wall or bend me over a table. As a group, we'd finish up, everyone attended to, but then someone's nuzzling would turn salacious, and *bam*, it would start all over again.

I shrugged innocently. "Maybe. Do a good job and we'll see, won't we?"

The look he exchanged with Declan told me we most certainly *would* see, whether the pack succeeded or not. Knox, meanwhile, appeared to be scoping out our surroundings, hands on his hips, his stance protective. Swallowing hard, I resisted the urge to drag my tongue up his back, between his rippling shoulders—I didn't want to distract him. The instinct to observe his surroundings was a good one, one I didn't want him to lose for the sake of a little flirting.

But the street was empty, the human shitter in the next realm gone, probably in search of breakfast. Warehouses and storage facilities lined either side of the two-lane road, a few vans parked here and there, unmanned and silent.

"You have forty-five minutes," I told them, dipping into my most professional tone as I checked my rarely used wristwatch. As if taking that as a cue, the pack shifted in unison, three gorgeous male specimens on two legs morphing to three handsome hounds on four. I curled my hands into fists so that they didn't bury themselves in Declan's shaggy fur; it was just *so* sinfully soft that I almost couldn't help myself. Clearing my throat, I tracked the third arm on my watch, tick, tick, ticking ever closer to the twelve mark. Once it hit, I snapped my fingers. "*Go.*"

And they were off in a hurry, Knox at the helm, Gunnar and Declan fanning out behind him. Hands clasped behind my back, I watched them charge down the street with an affectionate smile, one that stretched all the way down to my heart. I could have followed them, teleported around the city to track their progress, but it was best to let them do their thing without my scent distracting them.

Because apparently it did.

A lot.

And apparently, I smelled different to each one of them, which had made my eyes water with happy tears the first time they told me.

As soon as the last tail disappeared around the corner at the end of the quiet street, I nodded. No need to follow them —because I had such faith that they would blow these practice tests out of the water. If anything, at this point I just wanted to see them in action.

Anyway.

Curling my loose hair behind my ears, I started off toward the warehouse across the street, atop which I'd wait for their return with all five of my tricky soul orbs.

Only suddenly—I felt it.

A ripple in the celestial plane.

A shudder in the air around me, pungent enough that it made my stomach turn.

Halfway across the pothole-ridden road, I whipped around—and found a demon staring me down.

At least... a possible demon. With all that red blood weeping from sigils carved so precisely into his pale flesh, I had my doubts.

Demons bled black, black as that familiar head of oiled-back hair, a hint of stylishness that matched his charcoal-grey suit. Only his cuffs were frayed, his leather oxfords scuffed. That red blood could be a symptom of magic, something to disguise his true nature.

The pack and I had discussed this at length.

We'd also assumed Heaven would have dealt with him by now. I mean, I had filed a report with them ages ago. They had a whole department for exactly *this*. In theory.

And that theory was the only reason Knox had agreed to leave me alone today, to even participate in the test while I stood waiting on that rooftop all by my lonesome.

I shifted my weight between both legs, sizing him up, this somewhat attractive creature who had stolen one soul out from under me already.

"What are you doing here?" I demanded, a measured gravitas behind every word—something to tell him that *I* had the authority in this realm. The man tipped his head to the side, squinting his left eye when blood dribbled over his brow and into the bloodstained white. A fresh pentagram had been carved into his forehead, a few extra flourishes added inside the circle to suggest this was more than some human Satanist bullshit.

A cool October wind cut down the street suddenly, strong enough to rattle a few windows in the mortal realm. Here, it only tickled the ends of my hair, whispered across my skin.

Fine. If he wasn't going to talk, then I'd just have to *make* him.

"What do you want?" I stalked toward him, a hand raised to summon my scythe. It sat waiting for the pack on the warehouse roof, but my palm prickled with its response, already whooshing toward me.

Only it would never reach me.

The second my foot pounded the concrete with my next step, up sprang a wall of orange light. I yelped, surprise knocking me off-balance, and stumbled back into something that *burned*. The yelp morphed into a startled squeal, the back of my black robe singed, the scent of burned hair making my heart pound just a little faster. All around me, orange light shot up and split, swiftly forming four walls of bars—and a roof to top it all off.

A cage.

Of light.

Of *magic*.

My first instinct was to teleport out—but that got me nowhere, my efforts wasted. Nor could I cross out of the celestial plane. The shimmering bars seemed to mute my abilities, and a tentative touch had me hissing and shoving my fingertip into my mouth as the flesh sizzled and blistered.

"What do I want?" The creature's voice echoed around the confines of my cage, like a dozen different voices of varying pitches were *shrieking* at me. I winced, then flinched back when I found him right up against the bars of my makeshift prison. He wrapped his hand around a staticky beam of orange light, staring at me, totally emotionless. "I want *you*, Hazel."

Without the drama of all the different voices, he sounded strained. Hoarse. Like he had been screaming all night for *many* nights in the recent past.

My heart sank.

He knew my name.

"Stop. You don't have to do this," I insisted firmly.

"Yes," he muttered, his back to me, dragging my cage with one hand. "Yes, I do."

The creature hauled the cage up the street—headed straight for a portal painted across the pavement, one that bloomed red out of nowhere, the color sharpening with his approach. It hadn't been there when we'd arrived; I was sure of it.

Nothing had been out of place.

It had just been a quiet street...

I gave it one last go—tried to summon my scythe, to teleport out of here. My scythe had made it to the street level; it lay on its side in front of a garage door, useless, unable to hear my call anymore. While I felt the familiar pull of teleportation, I stayed put, a tension headache splitting my skull in two, streaking from the base of my spine right up and over, settling between my eyes.

The cage didn't extend underfoot, the road exposed beneath me, but a frantic pulse of my own magic only cracked the pavement—barely. And if I didn't keep moving, the bars would smack into me from behind, burning me down to, what, the bone?

Yes, I'd heal—but how quickly and to what extent was the question. Magic of this kind was so far out of my repertoire; souls had been my life for the last ten years. I knew the magic of the celestial plane inside and out, but not this. Not something capable of searing my flesh.

Damn it. The bloodred portal in the ground loomed closer and closer with each of the creature's shuffling steps, and my options were running painfully thin.

"Look, you don't have to—" A savage baritone reverberated off every building around us; I whirled around to find Knox charging down the street, teeth bared, that huge hellhound body racing like a furious storm. Unable to stay still, I backpedaled, eyes wide and heart leaping into my throat. "Knox!"

The creature picked up his pace, and I stumbled again to avoid the magic's bite, only to lose my footing and slam into the bars on the other side of the cage with a cry. Knox barreled toward me at full speed, and behind him two other enormous shadows ripped around the corner. My boys were here. They wouldn't let him—

The ground disappeared from under me the second I crossed onto the portal. The cage plummeted. The pack disappeared, their snarls distant, *so* very far beyond my reach...

And I fell screaming into the black.

27

KNOX

I *knew* this was a bad idea.

Knew it in my gut from the moment Hazel had proposed it yesterday. She shouldn't have been left alone. Of *course* no one had dealt with this bastard yet. Shouldn't have come. Shouldn't trust anyone else to protect our mate—

Paws pounding the pavement, I skidded to a halt over the bloody portal, an intricate series of runes that had *not* been here when we'd first arrived. I had made sure of that, but I should have given the area a proper patrol. Should have done more. Should have been better...

Nothing happened when I stomped over the marks. Not when I dug at the bright red inscriptions, the scent of fresh human blood so briny I tasted it with every heaving breath. Raking my claws over the ground, I snapped and bit at the spot where she had last stood, her final fleeting moments before the portal opened and the ground swallowed her whole. Hazel's scent lingered, but even on the celestial plane, the morning breeze threatened to sweep it away.

Howls erupted from the rest of the pack, despondent and furious in equal measures. Rage and confusion and fear tore through our bond, and I shifted back to the sound of Gunnar and Declan's claws scratching over the pavement.

Gone.

She was gone.

He had taken her—our *mate*.

Ours.

Fate had given her to us on a silver fucking platter, and I'd been too damn stubborn to see it all this time. And now, after just a taste of paradise, it was gone. Ripped away.

"What happened?" Gunnar demanded, sweat glistening across his pale flesh after the shift, his chest heaving, his aura quivering with fury. "What the *fuck* just happened?"

Declan nosed around the sigil frantically, searching her out in his hound form and whimpering when he came up empty.

"I should have known—"

"You did know," my beta growled. "You said it... We shouldn't have assumed someone had taken him out."

Declan shifted onto two legs at our side, his fear palpable but his presence strong. Focused. Unlike the time before Hazel, fear seemed to center his mind rather than send him spiraling into a panic.

"We couldn't have known," he muttered, swiping his hands through his hair. "This wasn't here before. I swear, I didn't scent it—"

"He set a trap," I told them, toeing at the spot where I'd first seen that horrible orange cage shoot up from the earth. "As soon as she walked into it, she sprung it. This was planned. He was *waiting* for us."

Rage made every word labored, so furious with myself, with *him*, that I could barely see straight, never mind trying to think my way through this.

We were alone.

Someone had taken our reaper, our mate, and we were unmonitored for the first time in our very long lives...

Never before had the pack been left to ourselves outside of a cage.

I glanced up and down the empty street, jaw clenched when a car ambled by on the road running perpendicular to this one.

"Her scythe..." Declan uttered the discovery like it pained him, and I watched him sprint over to the boxy grey warehouse to the left of the road. He slowed as he approached the locked garage door. Sure enough, there was Hazel's scythe—just sitting there, useless, so far from its partner, from *its* fated mate. Did it feel the same sting of loneliness and loss that we did?

"Don't touch it, Dec," Gunnar called, halfheartedly trailing after his packmate, stopping at the concrete curb, arms limp at his side. The look he shot back to me said more than words ever could, but I *felt* it. For a hellhound who usually had all the answers, he hadn't a clue where to go from here.

Neither did I.

A month ago, I would have ordered us to run. Teleport out of Lunadell—go north, into the wilds, find an abandoned wolf or bear den. Settle in for the winter. Hide our tracks. Regroup. Head somewhere new come spring...

Now, just the thought of leaving this *street* gave me fucking heartburn, fiery pain searing up from my gut, burning my throat, my chest.

I had felt her panic. I'd never really *felt* Hazel before, but since we had mated, I—and the others—had experienced flashes of her emotions, her physical sensations. Given we'd spent the last week fucking, really cementing our bond, it had mostly been her pleasure. But today, I felt her panic, her fear.

And I'd come running.

But not fast enough.

Just fast enough to watch her fall.

All my rage pounding through our pack bond was aimed squarely at myself, for *my* failing, but that wasn't productive. If I sat stewing, nothing would get done.

"Gunnar." I motioned to the bloody sigil smeared across the road. "Guard the portal. He may come back for whatever reason."

My beta hopped to without hesitation, stalking toward the portal like he wanted to murder it.

"Declan," I called, directing our attention to the base of the garage door, to *the* most powerful weapon just sitting there. "Guard her scythe. No one can touch it, but someone might try."

My packmate crouched over it, not touching it, but close enough to bite an intruder's fingers clean off if they tried to get around him. A furious concentration knitted his brows—almost made him look intimidating. Amidst all the other emotion storming through my insides, a wisp of pride shone bright; I always knew he had it in him.

Strength.

Declan was stronger than anyone had ever thought; he had just needed the chance to prove himself.

Well, the time was now—for all of us.

"And what will you do?" Gunnar asked, planted squarely in the middle of the portal. I had no doubt that should it open, he would plunge headfirst into the darkness to find her.

"I…" What *would* I do? Shaking my head, I looked to the west, to the coastal territory of the other Lunadell hellhound pack. "I'm going to fetch that reaper."

"Alexander?"

"Yes, perhaps he can…" Everything inside me knotted at

the thought of asking for help with this. "Perhaps he can do something we can't."

Disgust ripened in the pack bond. Each one of us loathed the idea of someone else, particularly another male, stepping in to rescue Hazel. After all, what sort of hellhound pack couldn't protect their own mate? Pathetic. Relying on another? *Pathetic.*

But what choice did we have? If this was blood magic and he wasn't the demon Heaven insisted he was, then this might be way out of our realm of understanding. Alexander was a pompous prick, probably the kind of reaper to shove a hellhound's face into its own shit just to prove a point, but right now, he was our only option.

I turned away from the pack, seconds from teleporting, when agony sliced through my body. Up my midback, to the right. Like a blow to the kidney, painful beyond anything I'd ever felt.

As I collapsed to my knees, wheezing, clutching at the would-be wound, I knew in my heart that that pain was *hers.*

"Knox!"

Gunnar shot to my side, and when I peeled my hand away from what should have been a gaping wound, we found my usual tanned flesh—unmarked, uncut, unharmed.

The fucker was torturing her.

Out of the corner of my eye, I caught Declan jogging in our direction, only to stop at the edge of the road. I waved him off, my order one that needn't be said: stay with the scythe. Still, his concern rippled through our bond, and I could all but hear his hellhound form's low whine at my distress.

"It's fine," I rasped, my breath slowly coming back, the pain ebbing—but barely. "I'm fine."

"She isn't," Gunnar muttered. His hands skimmed along my forearm, like he was about to help me up, but he retreated at my low growl, leaving me to stand on my own. My beta rose swiftly and looked me dead in the eye. "The pain was Hazel's... I felt it too—a little, anyway."

I had been literally sliced open before, cut up and cut open for the amusement of demons; this agony had felt like someone had taken a blade and shoved it in as deep as possible, then *twisted*, just to make sure their victim was down.

To make sure Hazel *stayed* down.

Rage threatened to cloud my vision, but I blinked hard, trying to focus on the task at hand and not the fantasy of ripping that cut-up *fuck* into little pieces with my bare hands.

"Stay here until I return," I snarled, the shift already upon me. Gunnar clapped my shoulder, a brother in arms to the very end, and stepped back.

"Hurry, Knox."

Nodding, I dropped from two legs to four, claws hungry for that bastard's innards. Hazel had told me where Alexander and his pack lived, and we had scented them out every time she took us into Lunadell. Teleporting to the property line would be a breeze.

Convincing him to help us find her, hopefully, would be just as simple.

If not, a certain reaper would taste my wrath long before the fucker who took her.

Eyes closed, I vanished from the scene of the crime, every second precious.

Praying, for the first time in my life, that we weren't too late.

28

HAZEL

I came to with that sickening sense of waking up in an unfamiliar bed, in an unfamiliar room—the kind where your heart lurches and your mind races the second you regain consciousness.

Groaning softly, I stirred but struggled to lift my eyelids. They had never felt so heavy before, not even after a night of drinking and very, very little sleep.

But even without looking, the rest of my senses confirmed at least a few things.

I was sitting upright, my head drooped to my chest, the strain in my neck and back suggesting it had been hanging for some time.

My wrists and feet were bound to the chair with something cold and cutting—barbed wire, maybe?

And I was... groggy?

Yep.

For the first time in my afterlife, I was *groggy*. Disoriented.

As a reaper, I'd felt invincible for the last ten years, but as I threw my head back, wincing at the *thud* when it smacked into the chair's solid wooden back, I made another frustrating realization.

My invincibility was a product of the weapon I wielded, gifted to me by Death—and the fact that I spent all my time with human souls. Frightened human souls at that. Sure, the odd demon crossed my path, but for the most part they were bound to Lucifer's laws. Angels bound to Heaven's decrees.

Reapers were neutral territory. We were fucking Switzerland in the war between Heaven and Hell.

The rest of the supernatural world had stayed off my radar…

Until a carved-up psycho trapped me in a cage, dragged me through a portal, and stabbed me in the back with *something* that hurt worse than death. I shifted in place, my butt asleep, and grimaced at the flash of pain in the middle of my back, just off to the right.

He must have drugged me.

I sucked in a deep breath, damp earth flooding up my nostrils, accented by a cold metallic bite reminiscent of wet rocks. Finally—*finally*—I forced my eyelids up. They slid back down on their own accord, and I spent an embarrassing amount of time battling with them.

My eventual victory came with a depressing view.

Bound, like I'd suspected, to a high-backed chair at the head of a long stone table, I found myself in a cave of sorts— or, at the very least, deep underground. Slate grey surrounded me from every side: floor, walls, ceiling. Shadows collected in the corners, the surrounding cavernous space black enough that I'd have been screwed if I couldn't see in the dark. Candles flickered across the table, and an eerie glow cast everything nearby in a nauseating orange. With some difficulty, I tipped my head up—and found a skull-encrusted chandelier hanging over the table.

Great.

Just perfect.

Psychotic and disgustingly dramatic, my captor.

As I tried to lubricate my too-dry mouth, my sandpapery throat, I saw to my wrists. Simple twine coiled around each, binding me to the chair's armrests, but any movement felt like razor blades slicing through my flesh. I bit back a whimper as a thin stream of gold erupted from beneath the tawny thread, and I stilled with a stuttering breath, not in the mood to test if this rope could carve through a reaper's bones too.

Refusing to just sit here and wait for whatever rubbish that bastard had up his sleeve, I resorted to magic. However, like in the cage, nothing happened. A pulse of energy had the skull chandelier above rustling a little, and as I glowered up at it, I realized *why* I couldn't get a foothold, magically speaking: sigils. Dozens of them carved into the ceiling, all sorts of ancient warding and protection symbols etched deep into the stone. A few I recognized, but most were foreign to me. Based on my inability to perform, I assumed there was at least one to muffle *my* magic—or any magic outside of the carver's brand.

Fantastic.

This day just kept getting better.

Footsteps clicked primly behind me, and I straightened, each soft *tip-tap* like thunder. They moved slowly, purposefully, in no hurry to greet me at this twisted banquet table. Heavy too, the gravitas palpable. The air around me thickened with *power*, and it didn't surprise me one bit to find it wasn't the fucker in his meticulous, albeit frayed, grey suit, his slicked black hair—but a much larger figure in reaper's robes, the hood drawn, its back to me as it strode leisurely down the length of the table. I swallowed hard, ignoring the weight of its presence…

And the scent of violent death suddenly permeating the room.

It sat gracefully at the other end of the luxurious stone table, the dancing candlelight stilling to perfectly straight peaks of light in its presence. Slowly, the figure lifted skeletally thin hands to its hood and peeled it back.

My hands clutched at the armrests as I battled with my lingering brain fog. This being may have donned a reaper's garb, but *he* wasn't one of Death's servants—not from the look of him. Cheeks so sunken they peeled open to bone and sinew. Blazing yellow eyes that stared unflinchingly back at me. No eyebrows, no eyelashes. Thin lips. Thin skin too, translucent and stretched over his skull.

Like a corpse—only he radiated power, control.

Magic, even.

No doubt the artist behind all those symbols.

"Hello, Hazel." A rough, grating voice skittered across the table, and suddenly the fiery tips of the candles moved again —frantically, like even fire wanted to get away from him.

"I don't know you," I said flatly, peering down my nose at him—refusing to let an ounce of fear show, "but you seem to know me. Hardly fair, is it?"

The creature chuckled, the sound making the hairs on the back of my neck rise, every gut instinct in me screaming *run*.

"And why is that not *fair*?" he rasped.

"I appear to be the guest of honor," I remarked, each word clipped, annoyed, like this was just one big bother. "I'm seated at the head of the table, after all. Surely you owe me the courtesy of your name—and the reason for my being here."

And maybe an explanation for *why* I was tied up in unbreakable twine, a binding that continued to grate into my wrists. Gold rivets dribbled over the armrest, and my heart skipped a beat at the first dull *plop* of a droplet hitting the stone floor.

My captor settled into his own high-backed chair, elbows on the armrests, fingers steepled together. His thin mouth twisted up and to the left, those yellow eyes never once leaving my face. Hard to read, a face that looked like faded silk stretched over bone, but something told me that if I made a wrong move—pissed him off—I'd know it. Instantly.

"The humans knew me once as the Ferryman," he drawled. "They left coins in the mouths of their corpses to pay for passage through the beyond."

The Ferryman?

I bit the insides of my cheeks, the fog finally lifted, my mind racing through all manner of supernatural entities who might fit the bill. Not a demon, then. Certainly not an angel. Not a shifter, not one of the fair folk. Not beautiful enough to be an elf, not humanoid enough to pass as a phoenix.

Ferryman.

Coins.

Passage to the beyond—

"Charon?"

Those yellow orbs practically shimmered in response.

A *god*, then.

One of the ancients.

Awesome.

One of the few species to rival angels, gods were so hit-or-miss when it came to their power.

But clearly this guy was packing.

Damn it.

From my vague recollection of Charon, he served the Greek god Hades, and like me, transported souls into the afterlife. Unlike me, the souls found him on the shores of the rivers Styx and Acheron; with the coins placed upon their bodies in death, the proper burial rite of the time, humans had once paid for passage in the Underworld.

"Yes," the god murmured, gently touching his steepled fingers to his lips, "Charon. So seldom uttered in this age…"

"What do you…?" I shook my head. While his identity was now clear, the rest of it was still a tangled mess. Why *me*? "I don't understand."

"It's all right, dearie," he crooned, straightening at the sound of new footsteps echoing from the dark depths behind me. "You will—momentarily."

The footfalls came faster, a lesser stride, shorter legs, and were accompanied by a very distinct feminine whimper. I tried to look around the chair's back but couldn't quite get the right angle.

And then he stepped into the light—my kidnapper, my bloody shadow. Still in the same grey suit, he strode forth with his once pristine black hair slightly ruffled…

A soul on his arm.

My eyebrows knitted, confusion and fear twisting together inside me.

She was young, the soul, no more than sixteen or seventeen. Lovely but withered, she shuffled along at the man's side, and I noted fresh carvings across his pale flesh. Red painted his face. Black ringed his eyes. Not a demon. *Definitely* not.

Mouth hanging open, struggling to make sense of the situation, I watched on expecting the bastard to seat the soul in one of the table's empty chairs. Instead, he escorted her down to Charon, who wrapped his spidery fingers around her hand and gently guided her onward. He arranged her expertly, silently, so that she sat directly in front of him on the table, her aura shivering. The soul cast a tentative look back at me, her maroon curls spilling down her back, her periwinkle-blue hospital gown missing its bottoms.

Charon then stood swiftly, towering over the seated soul with what he probably thought was a serene smile, but any stretch of that mouth read as predatory—he could never look *sweet*, never lull anyone with his handsomeness. His yellow gaze flicked to me as his hands started to explore her, meticulously mapping the curve of her shoulders, the lines of her waist, right down to her knees, her calves, her feet.

There was something so overtly sexual about it that I felt bile clawing up my throat.

"*Stop*," I growled. The soul trembled with fear, whereas I shook with rage. "Stop this, Charon."

"Oh, simmer down, reaper," the god murmured, sweeping the soul's hair so that it all gathered over one shoulder, exposing her thin neck, her bony shoulders. He walked his fingertips slowly along the curve there with a reverent sigh. "She's here for me... just like you."

And before I could get another word in, he tore into her. Literally. His mouth slammed to her neck; his spindly fingers pierced her gut. Screams filled the cavernous space, bouncing off rock and slate, a choral verse from me and the soul.

"*Stop!*" I screeched, fighting my restraints with every bit of strength I had left. Tears may have blurred my vision, but not enough to skew what he did to her. Charon tore flesh from bone, ripped chunks of hair from her scalp. He consumed her viciously, like he alone was a pack of lions feasting on a fallen gazelle.

Only this gazelle endured every brutal second of it, wailing, begging, screaming for mercy—until he plucked out her tongue, ripped out her throat. When she fell silent, I screamed louder, my throat shredded, my wrists sliced down to bone as I fought my shackles.

It could have lasted a matter of minutes or hours—I had no idea.

But he ate her.

Every last part of that soul passed through his laughing mouth, crunched between his gnarled teeth. When he licked the remnants of her essence from the stone table, I slumped in my chair, exhausted, horrified, weighed down by immeasurable grief.

Because there would be no afterlife for that poor girl. No Heaven. No Hell. Just—nothingness, rotting away inside this monster's belly until he too met a gruesome end.

And as he flopped back into his seat, his smile beyond wicked, I vowed that there would most certainly *be* a gruesome end.

One way or another, he would feel her pain.

What I wouldn't do for my scythe—

"Did you know gods can retire?"

Somehow it didn't surprise me that he sounded like nothing horrific had just happened. "W-what?"

"I didn't," Charon mused, picking at something—soul?—between his teeth, "but Hades did. Went off with his little wife when Lucifer offered to buy him out—take over his domain. Too many souls going to Hell these days, apparently, and he needed the real estate."

I blinked back at him, still numb with anger, with shock.

"At first, that fallen angel let me stay on, the spoiled prick," he continued with a sigh. The god wove his hands together and set them on his slightly rounded belly. "I maintained my post—escorted souls and all that. But then he realized I was, well, *skimming* from our supply."

"You were eating them," I clarified tersely. No sense in mincing words anymore, not after what I'd just witnessed. Charon shrugged, unfazed by my tone.

"Yes, and ol' Satan doesn't like to share his toys. He banished me from his realm, put a price on my head... I had to go. Had to ward up, as it were." Charon lurched forward, on his feet so suddenly that I jumped, and his palms slammed onto the table where that poor soul had met her end. "But I'm *hungry*, Hazel, fucking ravenous. And once you've had *soul*, you can't just go back to burgers and fries, you know?"

"No, I *don't* know," I sneered, fighting the quiver behind my words. "You're despicable. Those people deserve an afterlife—"

"Humans are nothing but sheep," he bellowed, the landscape around us shuddering, the chandelier swinging. A few of its candles extinguished, and one of the skulls fell and shattered as soon as it hit the table. "They are but *livestock* for the rest of us!"

A barbed and sudden pain stabbed between my eyes, and I folded over, gritting through the agony as the world around us quaked. It dissipated, but not until everything stopped shaking. Flashes of light danced behind my lids, and with a heavy heart I straightened, forced back into this absurd conversation, and found Charon leering at me.

He enjoyed my suffering.

Got off on it, just like he did with the souls.

Ugh.

"What's he got to do with it?" I demanded, nodding toward the silent bystander at Charon's side, to the man riddled with carvings who had haunted me and the pack for weeks. Those terrible yellow eyes narrowed, and Charon floated back down into his chair in a flourish of black robes. His chuckles hissed across my skin and made the candles tremble.

"Who—Richard?" The god shook his head and snorted. "Richard is a warlock. He killed a member of his coven... The *gravest* sin, eh, boy?"

Through the blood, I caught the clench of Richard's jaw, and he turned away without a word.

At least he had the decency to appear *somewhat* ashamed of all this.

"You see, with the bounty still active, *I* can't go out there and hunt for myself, and no demon would fetch souls for me," Charon remarked, sounding bored again as he picked at his nails. "None of them want to get on Lucy's bad side, so Richard acquires all my meals. He too is a wanted man, and my wards grant him immeasurable protection. Symbiotic parasites, we two."

"Warlocks can't go on the celestial plane..." I pressed my lips together, realization hitting like a freight train. "But all the runes on him, the blood magic, gives him access—"

Charon met my deduction with a round of sarcastic slow claps.

"Yes, yes, well done." His pale forked tongue flicked out, a serpent tasting the air, and he fixed that yellow gaze squarely on me. "I'm afraid despite his prolonged life, bolstered by magic, the *work* takes a lot out of him. My warlock has an expiry date..." Charon's mouth warped into a cruel smile. "But reapers don't."

29

DECLAN

What was a reaper without her scythe?

Crouched over the universe's most powerful weapon, I studied every detail, all of it reminding me of Hazel. From the slight curvature in the yew staff up to the beautiful bow of the blade, the symbols etched into the star-forged metal mysterious and ancient, elusive and lovely.

But without a reaper to *use* the most dangerous weapon around, what was it? Just a stick with a hook on top?

And what was Hazel without it? Could she defend herself? Before Knox had disappeared to find Alexander, we had all felt it—a pulse of pain in our backs, a sign that our mate was suffering. Through marking her, we had cemented the bond, played right into fate's hands, and now we were paying for our failure to protect her. Every flicker of agony that *we* suffered here would have been amplified tenfold for Hazel, and that fucking killed me.

Most recently, a sharpness jolted between my eyes, up the center of my skull. Gunnar had felt it too, prowling around the bloody portal, grimacing through it while I gritted my teeth so hard, I swore they were on the verge of cracking.

Frustration rippled through the pack bond. It had taken us—*them*—so long to realize that Hazel was perfect. Witty, kind, intelligent—breathtaking beyond measure. My alpha and beta had shared an intense physical attraction to her from that very first moment, same as me, and yet they fought it to the bitter end. Then we had one blissful week together, all of us fucking and eating and laughing and *talking*, and then...

And then that thing took her away.

My frustration turned ragged, harsh, stabbing through the pack's shared bond so suddenly that Gunnar stopped his frantic circling of the portal. His eyes settled on me, curious yet understanding, but I continued to stare down at the scythe, jaw clenched, all the muscles involved positively aching. Because Knox had left me in charge of the scythe, arguably the most important thing in Hazel's world—outside of us, hopefully—and I wasn't going to let it out of my sight.

Wasn't going to let some demonic cut-up fuck materialize in front of me and whisk it away somehow or summon it with his own brand of warped magic.

A teeny, tiny part of me also thought that if I stared hard enough, picturing her beauty, those soulful brown eyes, her full mouth, the sharp angles of her cheeks—maybe she would reappear. Maybe the scythe's power would sense our bond and, I don't know, fly her back here.

Nothing yet, but I'd keep trying until someone said otherwise.

Because, really, we had nothing else going for us. The portal was dead. Our territory was still warded up, and the only way inside was with a weapon none of us could touch if we wanted to keep our hands. Hazel's pain shuddered through me, through all of us, like a fading echo—and that was a fucking tease. We could feel her.

But we couldn't touch her.

Couldn't help her.

Can't save her.

I glared up at my forehead like I was glowering at the little voice who dared utter such a depressing thought. We *would* save her.

Somehow.

Alexander, maybe, would know a way to—

Knox reappeared in the middle of the unlined road suddenly, a reaper at his heels. In the human realm, the day had started, trucks ambling up the street, a few garage doors open. Sunshine warmed the otherwise chilled landscape, golden beams trickling through the celestial plane to stop my breath from fogging in front of me.

Life carried on as it always did—like our world as we knew it hadn't crumbled to pieces in a second.

Gunnar ceased his stalking as soon as our alpha appeared, still in his human form, his mouth set and his black eyes *furious*. Seconds later, two other hellhounds arrived as hounds, the larger one radiating alpha energy, both looking to their master for guidance.

"Fan out," Alexander ordered, waving halfheartedly around the industrial park. "See if you can find a scent."

I glanced toward Gunnar, who folded his lean arms and scowled. Surely, they could smell that fuck already—like a rotted corpse, the ground stained with human blood. But the hellhounds did as they were told, burly and muscular, every step powerful.

Reminiscent of my old packs, actually. Typical hellhounds, the sort that wouldn't fit in with *our* pack. Three months ago, just the sight of them would have sent me cowering straight to Knox, my sole protector in a lifetime of pain and misery. I would have then hid behind him, waited for the threat to pass. Today, I stayed crouched over Hazel's scythe, heartbeat elevating just a touch when the unfamiliar alpha sniffed in my direction.

Gunnar had already taken a few steps toward the garage, positioning himself squarely between me and the other hounds. Affection threaded through our bond from my end—until I realized he was probably guarding the *scythe*, not me.

Because he knew I didn't need his protection anymore.

"So, you say he took her through this?"

Pretty militant-looking, this reaper, with his blond hair slicked back and up, styled like the Superman guy from that one movie. I had seen plenty of his type over the years, striding through the kennel like he owned the place, peering down his nose at packs through those horrible black bars—no better than the dirt off the soles of his pristine loafers, hellhounds. The reaper who had taken my old pack on long before I found Knox and Gunnar erred more toward Hazel: kind, thoughtful, devoted to the job. It was the pack who had disowned me, not him.

With his fitted black suit and cold blue eyes, Alexander probably wouldn't have even entertained the *idea* of me, let alone allowed me to live on his grounds and serve him.

"He trapped her in a cage," Knox said stiffly, his tone suggesting their interactions so far hadn't been pleasant. Subdued fury simmered through our bond as he stalked after Alexander. "It was like a ward in nature... Sprang up from the ground and she couldn't cross through it, couldn't use her magic. Couldn't even summon her scythe after it had her."

Pausing at the outer circle of the portal, Alexander finally glanced to the scythe at my feet. He tipped his head to the side, observing the weapon for a moment, then poked at the bloody sigils with the base of *his* obnoxious scythe, its staff thick and rigid, its blade jagged. A weapon for war, making Hazel's seem so soft, so powerfully feminine by contrast.

I much preferred hers.

It didn't need to *boast*.

It just did the job when called upon.

When nothing happened after Alexander's cautious prodding, he nudged at the portal with his foot—just the toe of his shoes, which he then examined with a grimace.

Like he was worried he'd scuffed them, that the blood might stain the leather.

Gunnar exhaled sharply, annoyed.

"Huh," the reaper muttered. We all waited with bated breath for more, but when Alexander shrugged one shoulder and turned away from the last place we had seen our mate, Knox lost it.

"*Huh*?" he snarled, his huge hands in fists, looming over an already tall reaper by a few menacing inches. "Is that all you have to say?"

"What would you like me to say?" Alexander positioned his scythe defensively in front of him, his face calm, his tone bored. "From what you've told me, a demon bested a reaper today—and that's her own fault. I mean, she lost her scythe, for fuck's sake. Am I supposed to pity her?"

Rage pounded through the pack bond, snarls and growls rising from the three of us. Gunnar had started to pace back and forth again, prowling about like he was assessing the best angle to get at Alexander's throat. Knox, as always, remained a block of unreadable muscle, imposing in every way that counted, his fury detonating like a bomb under the surface.

To his credit, Alexander seemed to realize he'd said something stupid. His little half-smile fell away, his body stiffening, and his hand tightened noticeably around the scythe. He glanced between the three of us, indifferent in the way his eyes swept over me. I might have been crouching, but I shook with raw anger, and if he got near me, I'd rip his fucking face off.

This wasn't Hazel's fault.

It was our fault, if anything. We hadn't protected her—we hadn't fought hard enough for our mate.

"No matter," Alexander said with a sniff, readjusting his suit like he had actually done something to rumple it. "I'm sure she'll figure it out… Or I suppose you'll be getting a new master soon. It really makes no difference to me." His bright blue gaze slid over to me, then down to the weapon at my feet. "Perhaps I should take that… for safekeeping."

Another burst of rage thrummed through the bond as Knox shook his head. "It isn't yours."

With a dismissive little chuckle, Alexander stalked toward me, eyes on the prize. "No, but I'm the only one here who can potentially handle it. Can't just leave it lying around, can we?"

Gunnar was in his face in three long strides, but a jagged scythe to the throat had him begrudgingly moving aside. Our alpha trailed after the reaper, no doubt biding his time, weighing all the possibilities before acting—a classic Knox move, the reason he was better than any alpha out there.

"Insolent bunch, this pack," Alexander muttered, his upper lip curling as he studied each one of us. "Really… What the fuck has Hazel been doing with you?"

"You can't have the scythe," I said firmly, hating the way her name sounded coming out of his mouth. "It's hers."

Wearing a patronizing smile, Alexander marched toward me totally unfazed. "Stand aside, hellhound."

Knox shifted, morphing from fearsome man to snarling hound in an instant, and I followed immediately after. Hackles raised, I stood over the scythe and bared my teeth, my message clear, my fear a distant memory.

But nothing about me seemed to put Alexander off; he kept coming, despite Knox and Gunnar closing in behind him, the sounds of his baying hounds echoing through the plane after they undoubtedly heard our war cries. I snapped my teeth at him, crouched protectively over Hazel's most prized possession, refusing to yield—

Until he clocked me across the face, using his scythe's rigid staff to knock me off my feet. The blow fell harder than any I'd suffered before, and I went down with a yelp, toppling head over heels twice before sprawling in a furry heap. A loud whine screeched between my ears, and when I rolled onto my side, the world was just a little off-kilter.

A storm of black charged for Alexander, Knox's guttural howl making the nearby van windows rattle, and Gunnar blitzed toward the reaper like a missile. Alexander's two joined the fray, snapping at heels and feet, bullying their way between their master and my packmates. Blinking hard, I struggled to my feet, wishing adrenaline would dull the pain in my temple where the staff had landed.

But I could endure pain. I'd proven that time and time again. Teeth bared, I charged forward and fell in line beside Gunnar, barking and lunging at the other pair of enormous hellhounds.

"*Fuck!*" Alexander reeled back suddenly, stumbling away from the skirmish and shaking his hand. He hissed, examining the seared red flesh with wide, furious eyes.

Apparently even reapers couldn't touch a scythe that didn't belong to them. Triumph pulsed through our bond, and we closed ranks around Hazel's scythe, the three of us backing over it as Alexander's pack withdrew, looking to him for further instruction.

The reaper scowled at us, his face pale, his hand stained like a bad sunburn.

"Useless, all of you," he spat, pointing his scythe at us. "There will be *consequences* for your disobedience."

Dry amusement trembled through our bond; sure, blame your fuckup on *us*, you dick.

"And your fucking reaper deserves whatever she gets," he added, and all the humor died, replaced again by a swift and deadly venom. If we could get him away from his scythe, that prick wouldn't leave the industrial park with his head.

Knox prowled a few paces toward Alexander, stilling when the reaper lunged forward with his scythe, stabbing it into the space between them. Two feet closer and that blade would have plunged right into Knox's chest.

"Be seeing you all *very* soon," Alexander hissed before vanishing from sight. Thick with tension, the air around us fell silent, deadly, two packs of hellhounds squaring off. We outnumbered them, but they were here on their master's orders; would they follow through?

The alpha's red eyes swept over us, his hackles lowering, that great square head of his a near match for Knox. The hound at his side glanced up, his muscular body tensed, waiting. Gunnar and I padded forward, the scythe still within reach, but stopped when the alpha exhaled, his nostrils flaring, the breath long and loud.

And—resigned?

Fuck that guy. I could almost hear it, almost feel it rolling off the hellhound pair in resentful waves. The alpha huffed again, this time at Knox, the sound specific and pointed, then disappeared, his beta following shortly after.

Knox was on me the second they were gone, nosing at my face, snuffling around my ears, searching for an injury. If there was one, it was deep inside. Not a drop of blood hit the ground, and I was ready for more.

"I'm fine," I insisted after I shifted back, the heat of the

RHEA WATSON

change steaming the air around us. I stayed on my knees, letting my alpha continue his inspection until he was satisfied that nothing was broken. The welt on the side of my head stung like nobody's business, but that would pass.

Gunnar shifted beside me, then crouched and inspected my left while Knox finished off at the right.

"Are you sure, Dec?" he asked, brushing my hair away from the tender skin around my temple. His keen eyes narrowed, both of us coated in a sweaty sheen as he scrutinized whatever Alexander had left there. "That was a solid hit."

"Really, I'm good." I shrugged my packmate off with a quick grin and smoothed my hair back down to cover the bruising as best I could. The blow continued to ring between my ears, but there was no getting around that. "Stings a bit. Head's ringing. But I'm fine. I'm ready to go."

Knox's human form appeared in the corner of my eye, and he ruffled my hair briefly, then clapped me hard on the shoulder. Even though he wasn't smiling, his eyes flinty and his scared brow furrowed, I knew he was proud of me. I felt it in our bond—and in the way his hand lingered on my shoulder in a hard squeeze.

"Well, so much for Alexander," Gunnar muttered as he sat back on his heels, arms wrapped around his knees. Knox let out something between a scoff and a snarl.

"He didn't give a fuck from the second I told him... I think he just wanted Hazel's scythe."

I bit the insides of my cheeks, our collective rage in the bond making me see red. Needing the distraction, I stood and stepped over her scythe, back to my sentry's post behind it as the others rose alongside me.

"Bastard," I growled, Alexander's scent still lingering along the celestial plane. Fresh and clean, his suit must have been recently laundered, the smell suddenly tainted with burnt flesh. *Good. Hope it hurt, fucker.*

"What now?" Gunnar's uncertainty was palpable. Of the three of us, he was the least likely to ask that question.

Which meant we were on the verge of screwed. I scratched at the back of my neck, searching, searching, searching for *something*. But then the headache started up again, the one I swore linked with Hazel. Someone was hurting her; the pain played through our bond and across Gunnar and Knox's faces too—but Knox most of all. He grimaced and pinched the bridge of his nose, eyes clenched shut.

"Now," he said hoarsely, "we get out of here."

My heart pitched into my gut. Leave? But... this was where we had last seen Hazel. Her scent—

"Her scythe will be fine where it is," Knox carried on. Gunnar's and my confusion in the bond must have said more than words could. Our alpha folded his arms and motioned to our surroundings with a nod. "No one can touch it—not even that uptight fuck. But he'll be back, probably with his whole pack, and potentially an angel."

"That could be beneficial," Gunnar said softly, and I agreed. If anyone had the power to take down whoever stole Hazel, it was an angel. Knox seemed less convinced, his expression hardening, and I instantly understood why.

"Unless they all share his... attitude," I offered. If the angel saw us as lesser beings, as *animals*, then they wouldn't care what we had to say. They would just take us out for standing up to a reaper—and then it would all come crashing down.

"We find safe ground," Knox told us with one last backward glance at Hazel's scythe. He fell silent for a moment, his gaze roving the blade like he was memorizing it.

Like this might be the last time he ever saw it. Something cold gripped my heart at the thought.

But the moment passed. Knox rolled his shoulders back and tossed his head side to side, cracking his neck, gearing up for a *real* fight.

"After that, we find that fucking coward who took her," he growled, "and we bleed him until he talks…"

❧ 30 ❧

HAZEL

"I won't reap souls for you, Charon," I said, unable to keep the trembling fury out of my voice. What he was asking me to do… It was blasphemous. I had come back to this world with a sacred duty: to guide, protect, and escort wayward souls to their destiny. There was nothing this sick shit could offer me that would entice me to reap souls for him to *eat*.

The screams of that poor girl still echoed through this awful place, faint but present, reverberating in the darkest corners, in Charon's predatory smile.

"Come now," he crooned. "What does Death give you in exchange for your service? *Nothing*. I can pay you—in anything you desire."

"I don't reap for a reward." I let my head thump back against the chair, my answer final. "Find another warlock to do your dirty work."

The old god stared at me for a few beats, his smile slowly fading. Beside him, Richard shifted his weight from one leg to the other, nervously glancing between the two of us. Apparently, I had said the wrong thing. The stretched flesh across Charon's barbed chin quivered, and he launched out of his seat onto the table. Kicking candles aside, he stalked to the middle of the stone surface, glowering at me.

"If you won't take a reward, then perhaps you'll take *punishment.*"

I tipped my head to the side, refusing to give him anything that he could use against me. "Are you... threatening a reaper? You know we're basically indestructible—"

"Is that what you think, *girl*?" he sneered. Charon vanished with a delicate little *pop*, then reappeared in front of me so suddenly that I squeaked, heart in my throat. He shoved my chair back, and I hit the ground hard, pain dancing through my skull. Slowly, the god dragged his hands up my body, from my bound ankles to my knees, down my thighs—just as he had the soul. The same hungry look glimmered in his yellow gaze, and I squirmed, nauseous at the sight, at the feel of his spidery hands roving my body unchecked. They went wherever they pleased: one up my belly, over my breasts, the other coiling around my neck and *squeezing.*

He might not be able to kill me—hopefully—but he could absolutely hurt me.

"You reapers are nothing more than souls in titanium wrapping," Charon hissed, his hand locking tighter and tighter around my throat. My lips parted, my eyes widened, and I shuddered in disgust when he delved under my robes— when his papery cold touch found my skin, pinched at it, plucked at it.

"F-fuck y-you," I forced out. He could do what he wanted to me; I would *never* collect souls for him.

"If you don't reap for me, then I'm going to peel your wrapping away, one strip at a time, and make you my fucking Christmas ham!" he bellowed, spittle raining down on my face, the edges of my vision tinged black. I struggled against my restraints, the ropes slicing deeper, cutting grooves into my bones.

The pressure eased just enough for me to draw a full breath, and I hurriedly filled my lungs, unsure when I would get the chance again. Charon cupped my chin, the rage melting from his bony features, giving way what he must have thought was a sympathetic expression—forced concern.

"What do you have to say to that, Hazel?"

His whisper smelled like rotted flesh. I twisted my head to the side with a grimace and scanned the darkness, the rocky walls, Richard's blank stare. If my choice came down to me or them, my soul or the souls of countless innocents, I knew where I stood.

Looking Charon square in the eye, I lifted a challenging brow. "You want to eat me… *Do it*, then."

I braced for rage, for fury, for more screaming and spitting and groping and splitting headaches. What I hadn't expected was disappointment. Apparently, my refusal to fight was just *so* pitiful. Charon clambered off me, scowling, and with a snap of his fingers my chair whooshed upright at whiplash speed.

My captor strolled to the other side of the table, kicking scattered candles and their silver stands out of the way as he went, taking his sweet time to settle into his chair. He appeared to be mulling over my response, reassessing, changing tactics. I swallowed thickly, unsure what else I could sacrifice that was bigger and more meaningful than my own soul.

"You don't care about yourself? Fine." Charon leaned back in his seat and wove his hands together again, resting them on what I suspected was a very bony, hollowed-out chest. "I should have expected that… Pious, pretentious bunch, you reapers." The corners of his mouth crept up. "But what about your hellhounds?"

My heart skipped a beat, and Charon's whole being seemed to blossom when the color drained from my face, leaving me cold and numb. I schooled my features as best I could, but that vile smile told me he had found the perfect button to press.

And he was going to stab it with everything he had.

"Ah, yes, your *pack*," he sneered with a few breathy chuckles. "You know, your pack was the reason Richard chose you and not that other reaper... The blond with the penchant for designer suits."

"Alexander," the warlock loitering in the shadows muttered, and Charon waved him off, annoyance flickering through the god's smugness.

"Yes, yes, that one. He had *eight* hellhounds, and you only chose three."

"I went for quality, not quantity," I gritted out, to which Charon snorted.

"Well, all that quality sealed your fate. Imagine my delight to discover *two* viable reapers in the city where I chose to settle... Richard selected the weaker of the two, the one with the smaller pack, the inexperience. He's been monitoring you all for quite some time now... Set up traps all over that industrial park today, didn't you? Look at him..." Charon flicked his gaze in Richard's direction, mock pity in his voice as he said, "Can't you see how *exhausted* he is? All that hard work—"

"And how did Richard know we would be training there?" I demanded. Today's test had been decided on a whim, something that had always been on the agenda, but had only come to me last night as the first practice test to run.

"It's where the trials take place in Lunadell," Richard said dully, only after Charon prompted him with a dramatic roll of his hand. I sighed; this god was such a fucking diva.

"And you know that—how?"

"Tortured the information out of one of Alexander's hellhounds," the warlock told me, "then we killed him."

I slumped in my chair, wrists on fire, ankles aching—heart breaking. Some poor hellhound had had to die for all this to come to fruition. But given Charon's peculiar appetite, his obvious insanity, I shouldn't have expected any less.

"So, new deal..." Charon leaned forward, the table clear between us, our staring contests no longer buffeted by twitching candlelight. "You reap for me, or I kill your pack. One at a time, starting with the little one. You'll watch me pick them apart until they're no more than scraps of fur between my teeth—"

"My boys will rip you to pieces," I snarled, knowing I needed to say something, to stand up for my pack—even if I didn't totally believe it. Charon and Richard had magic on their side. Wards and spells and sigils. My pack had... themselves. Brute strength and coordinated hunting strategies. Their silent bond. And that was it. Without my scythe, we were at an obvious disadvantage.

Hopefully they realized that.

Hopefully...

Hopefully they were long gone by now, despite everything, despite the trio of permanent marks across my body. This was their opportunity to get the hell out of Lunadell.

But I knew in my heart that they wouldn't go.

Because they loved me.

And I loved them.

And that love would be their undoing.

The room swam, and if I blinked, I'd give myself away— I'd damn them all. So, I looked up, focused on the skull chandelier. Had he killed *humans* to make that? To acquire souls? It wouldn't surprise me if Charon farmed them and ran his own slaughterhouse—

"You cherish them, don't you?" the god asked softly. "I can smell them on you... With your hair back, I can *just* about see the mated marks on your—"

"You're pathetic." Disgusting. Vile. And as soon as I got out of this chair, I'd rip *him* apart—feed *him* to something ancient and terrible. My insult didn't land; Charon merely gazed back at me like the cat who'd caught the canary.

"You *love* them," he whispered. "Not like that other reaper... He didn't bat an eye when one of his pack went missing, did he, Richard?"

"No, Lord Charon... I chose the smallest. The reaper was unfazed."

My opinion of Alexander had faltered since this whole hellhound business started, from the way he spoke about them at the kennel to the methods he'd suggested I use to discipline Knox, Gunnar, and Declan in the beginning. But now? Now, my respect for him had reached rock bottom.

"How will you feel, Hazel, when I make the wolves howl?" Charon tapped one long, sharp white fingernail on the table, grinning. "When I pull out their fur, pluck out their eyes, carve out their hearts—will you mourn?"

I pressed my trembling lips together, struggling to not react, to pretend just the *thought* of my pack in pain didn't gut me.

Charon clapped his hands together, positively giddy. "Well, I suppose we'll just have to see, won't we? Run a little experiment... See if my working hypothesis has *merit*. Richard!"

The warlock dragged himself from the shadows, walking like he bore the weight of the world on his shoulders, his eyes circled in blood and exhaustion.

"Bring the pack here," Charon ordered, never once looking away from me, "and let's test this little bitch's mettle."

"You won't find them," I said, hating when the tears finally spilled down my cheeks, the floodwaters too high, the levies broken. "They're gone. Without me and my scythe, without my wards, they would have left. Taking me means they can escape this life for good."

Charon let out a hauntingly callous sound that made even his warlock cower.

"We've been watching, stupid girl. Richard's told me how they *look* at you," the god sneered as his lackey retreated into the darkness and disappeared. "They haven't gone anywhere, but they should have… Those mongrels are going to wish they ran when they had the chance."

31

GUNNAR

"Please don't hurt me—"

"Fucking *move*."

The sniveling little shit had better be grateful that holding a knife to his throat and shoving him along the celestial plane was *all* I had done to him. But the day wasn't over yet. The night was young—and I could still easily slit his throat with his own blade.

Ever since getting my hands on the villain who had stolen our mate right out from under us, it was obvious he wasn't a demon. He bled red. He cowered and whimpered. He hadn't sensed me sneaking up on him in the hallowed halls of the children's hospital where I'd found him skulking about— perhaps searching for another soul, maybe another reaper, to add to his filthy collection.

In hound form, I had crept low, channeling all my fear and fury into stillness and precision. I'd been on top of him before he knew what hit him, knocked him down, pinned him to the floor. Shifted and stole the blade strapped to his ankle, held it to his throat, threatened to hang tight if he dared teleport away.

But he couldn't teleport.

He needed a portal.

Because the fucker was a magic-user—distinctly from the human realm. The carvings on his flesh allowed him to walk the celestial roads, but beyond that, he was an ordinary fuck well versed in magic and mischief.

And ugly crying, apparently.

"Please, please don't—"

"If I have to listen to another pathetic word from you, I'll gut you right here and be done with it," I growled, holding him in front of me at an arm's length. From the size and curve of the dagger I'd nicked off him, it was used for skinning.

Skinning *what*, precisely, was another question altogether.

Late in the afternoon on a weekday, Lunadell Mall had been hit by the early dinner-rush crowd. Teens free from school and adults scurrying away from work flocked to the food court, to the shops bursting with Halloween decorations. The holiday was but a week away, and already I was sick of the explosion of orange and skulls and pumpkins and pointy witch hats on every fucking corner.

Still, the kitsch had been a pleasant distraction from Hazel's kidnapping, albeit a temporary and brief diversion. If I let myself *think*, really sink into my thoughts and feelings about what had happened this morning, I'd collapse. Fold in on myself. *Fail*. Again. So at Knox's directive, I had given myself over to the hunt. For hours, we two had combed through Lunadell, sniffing out the rat bastard in my grasp while Declan maintained our safe haven in the middle of the mall food court, guarding the elevated dining platform so that we had a territory to return to for status reports.

"Why are we here?" the fucker asked over his shoulder, bloodshot eyes nervously darting about, his hands up helplessly at his sides. Hands capable of such impressive magic, even *if* he required a portal.

Strange, that he had allowed himself to be taken by a creature like myself who possessed limited magic, who had only brute strength and a dagger at his disposal.

"Shut up," I muttered, giving him another shove for good measure, preferring that he stumbled here and there. The blade in my hand edged into his throat, and he let out a strangled sob, moving forward without a word.

A mall food court *was* an odd place for a base of operations. All of us had been mindful of Alexander's warning, and should he return with his pack and an angel by his side, we were fucked. It wouldn't matter that he had tried to steal Hazel's most sacred possession; all the higher authorities would know is that *we* had snapped at a reaper, disobeyed a direct order— perhaps the bastard would even spin it to imply that our pack had something to do with Hazel's grisly disappearance.

We couldn't have that.

Unable to breach the wards around our current territory, Declan had suggested a public place as a safe haven, and Knox had agreed; if the cavalry *did* show up, all we needed to do was cross from the celestial plane into the human realm and risk exposure for *everyone*. All these unassuming humans going about their day, fetching dinner, shopping with their friends, were the perfect shields.

I had brought up the mall. With Hazel on the brain, the memory of her sitting on the very same raised platform in the middle of the food court, watching the humans weeping, so painfully lonely, was all too fresh in my mind.

Perhaps that was why this place bothered me; it wasn't the Halloween decorations in every storefront window, but the reminder that I had once tailed my mate here, spied on her, did nothing as she sobbed into her hands—as she *begged* for companionship.

The huge tiles slated together on the floor, grey and faintly glittery. The fountain in the middle of the mall, in which human children threw coins. The fake greenery around pillars. The silent moving staircases between floors. The multilevel food court, some clumps of booths sunken into the ground, others propped up on podiums, surrounded by producers of fried, greasy nonsense. Humans flocked to them, to the fat and the salt and the false coloring.

I much preferred Hazel's cooking.

Everything about this place brought me back to that day when I'd followed her, and now here we were again, searching for her scent, trying desperately to find the trail that would lead us back to our mate.

Shoving my prisoner along, we followed the corridor's curve into the food court, the sudden burst of chattering humans and smelly food vendors an assault. But the man in my grasp didn't flinch; perhaps he lacked heightened senses. Yet another clue into his origins.

Knox had already returned to base camp, the alpha standing with Declan in the center of all the chaos. Humans occupied a few of the tables on our platform, but the teens seemed to prefer the booths to the smattering of two- and four-seater tables. My packmates muttered to one another, close in proximity, their expressions tense. Had they discovered something in my absence? Nothing of note rang through our bond, but those *looks* suggested my capture wasn't the most promising news of the day.

They parted on my approach, eyes narrowing at the bloody bastard, our high-value prisoner. We'd all stayed naked, clothes long since abandoned. After all, it would be even *more* shocking for three naked men to materialize in the middle of this food court should opposing forces provoke us.

"Found this one sniffing around the hospital," I announced as I steered my captive up the steps to the platform. The fucker's lips parted and he drew a sharp breath, but before he could utter one miserable word, I cuffed him hard by the back of the neck, lifted him off his feet, and hurled him to the floor. He crashed in a heap before me, crying out for mercy and shielding his face as the pack closed in. Declan and I knelt on either side of him, the blade back at his throat, while Knox lorded over everything, a menacing giant to the figure on the ground.

"Please, please," the man whimpered, a few of the many bloody incisions on his face splitting open as he spoke, "I'm just as much a victim as your reaper. *Please.*"

"What's that supposed to mean?" Declan growled, eyes flitting to me, then Knox, then back to the pathetic creature on the ground, belly-up and cowering.

"She's alive. I swear it, she's alive—"

"We *know* she's alive," I said coolly. While the admission was music to my ears, it didn't mean anything. The pack could sense our mate—and that was the problem. "Alive and in pain, right? We can fucking feel it."

So that *he* could feel it too, I nicked the blade's tip over what little unmarked flesh remained on his throat. His skin split and wept red, and I forced a cruel sneer, like I relished my addition to his collection of carved runes. In reality, I was falling apart inside, racked with such fear, such worry, that it threatened to drown me.

"She's being held by a god," the man told us, shaking in his perfectly polished shoes, that grey suit too fine a material for some useless nobody. "I don't know his name, but he found me after I fled my coven. I-I killed another warlock... It was self-defense, I swear, but the code is strict, and they would have killed me—"

Declan cut off the fucker's rambling with a good, solid

punch to the face. The crunch of bone suggested a broken nose, and his upper lip split on impact, the air around us saturated with iron.

"Stay on topic, asshole," Declan ordered, so confident and poised—so unlike the hellhound I had known all these years. While our captive might have been ranting, he had given us plenty in just a few words. An ancient being of unknown power had Hazel trapped. *This* shit was a warlock, a creature who had no business on the celestial plane but was clearly proficient in magic of all kinds. I pressed the dagger to his flesh, not breaking it, but hard enough that one deep breath would slit his throat.

"Where is Hazel?" I asked, a sudden calmness thrumming through me, a *focus* to silence the fear inside.

"My n-name is Richard," the warlock replied, another off-topic response. Blood smeared across his front teeth, dribbling in from his busted lip. "And he made me... He carved the symbols so I could collect souls for him—as payment for his protection. He wants her to do it now because I... Being on the celestial plane—I'll die soon. My body can't take it."

Another warning slice to his flesh silenced him, and this Richard pressed his eyes tightly shut, squeezing out a few tears. Crocodile or not—I couldn't say.

"Tell us where she is," I ordered softly. "Better yet, take us to her."

"Of course, of course..." The warlock's eyes snapped open, the madness fleeting but present. "He sent me out to fetch his dinner, but I had hoped to find you all instead. I don't want to die. If you kill him, we'll be free. Her and I. Please. I'll take you." Boldness struck, and he sat up on his elbows; I let him, both of us painfully aware that he had information we so desperately needed. "He's holed up in

Luna Pass, the mountain range north of the city. Inside... It's warded, but I can get you through."

"Then let's go," Declan snapped, shooting up and taking hold of Richard's arm. "We don't have any more time to waste."

We hauled the warlock to his feet, the blade remaining at his throat. A flicker of excitement plumed in my chest, but as eager as I was to find her, hold her, *hurt* the villain who dared hurt her, I couldn't get ahead of myself. This journey was only just beginning—and Hazel was still very far away.

"Knox," I started, "do you think—"

"I'm not coming with you."

A beat of intense stillness echoed through our bond, squashing all of today's noise to nothing. Knox had been strangely hands-off during our brief interrogation, and to hear the certainty in his voice now, like he had just been biding his time to say—*that*...

A huff of disbelief whooshed out of me. "What?"

"This could lead to our death at the hands of some god," Knox remarked, gruff and unnervingly firm, his arms crossed. "We have an opportunity here. Go. Get out of all this for good. Start a new life."

Declan and I exchanged fleeting, frantic looks across Richard. The warlock all but hung between us, weak on his feet, head drooped—and, as far as I was concerned, inconsequential for the time being.

"W-what are you talking about?" Declan adjusted his hold on our prisoner, shaking his head. "No, we have to find Hazel."

In the human realm, time ticked on, the food court slowly filling, lines building in front of the vendors. So ordinary out there—so normal.

"Ever since you two came to me, my priority has been

your safety, your freedom," Knox insisted. "That is what an alpha is supposed to do—"

"It's different now," I argued, incredulous that this was even a discussion, "and you know that. She's a part of our pack. Someone has kidnapped a member of our pack. They're *hurting* her. Our mate. We can't just leave her."

Seldom did I struggle to get a read on a situation, especially when it came to Knox and Declan. Not only did we share the pack bond, but I had been studying their moods and expressions for years now. Declan had grown these past three months into a stronger hellhound, the abuse of his past finally fading, allowing him to blossom into the packmate he was always meant to be. Hazel had changed Knox, broken down his walls, made him a little softer. I understood all that. Recognized it. Catalogued it, saw the root of the subtle but distinct shifts in their personalities.

But this?

I didn't understand this.

Didn't understand *him*—my best friend, my brother-in-arms, my alpha.

I knew how he felt about her because I could fucking *feel* it. Literally. How could he even entertain this train of thought anymore?

"No."

Since arriving in Lunadell, we had watched a lot of television, movies—and I had read a great many books. The weight of that one word—*no*—hit me as I imagined a bullet might, shot at point-blank, straight to my heart.

Declan seemed to crumble beside me, a stray shot hitting him too.

Knox didn't even blink.

"I've given this a lot of thought since she was taken," our alpha said, his words lacking inflection, emotion. "We should seize our freedom while we can. This could easily be a trap."

"So what if it is?" I shoved the warlock into Declan's arms, and for the first time in my life, raised a weapon to Knox—the dagger, square to his chest. My arm trembled as he stared me down, his aura overwhelming, and I dropped it to my side and stepped back. "If it's a trap, then we'll spring it and *fight*."

Never had either of us gone against Knox. Conflict shone bright along our bond, Declan's mingling with mine, weaving together, stronger as one.

From Knox I got... nothing.

"We leave," he said flatly. "Head north—"

"I'm going to get Hazel."

Declan's declaration possessed the strength Knox and I had always wanted for him. Not once did his words waver. He stood tall, overpowering our captive, staring back at our alpha like he was seconds away from shifting—attacking, even. Certainty pounded through the bond now, confidence. He had made up his mind.

And it could shatter our pack.

I swallowed hard, but the lump steadily growing in my throat refused to budge.

"You love her, Knox," I whispered, pleading with my eyes, unable to fathom ever begging the huge hellhound before me for anything. "You're mated. Declan and I are mated to her. *She* is who Fate chose for us. Don't do this. Don't walk away under some misguided sentiment that no longer applies."

"I've made up my mind." Knox took a step back, away from us, away from the life we had fought so hard to build. "If you don't follow... then I am no longer your alpha."

Fury sparked amidst the conflict brewing in my chest. "Don't make me choose between her and you."

Because we both knew who I would pick—who I would always choose now.

Knox said nothing.

He had always reminded me of a mountain: strong, steadfast, rising above all those around him. Today that felt truer than ever, for today he felt cold, stoic, ice-capped and untouchable.

Tears filled my eyes, anger and frustration and misery and heartache crashing about inside. How dare he make me choose between him and my mate?

Our mate.

How fucking *dare* he?

"Gunnar..." Declan placed a gentle hand on my shoulder, his eyes fierce, his voice steady. "She's suffering. We have to go."

I focused on Knox. *Look what you're making me do. Look at what you're doing* to *me.*

Again, he said nothing. Just stared back, his gaze obsidian, black as the deepest pits.

Betrayal. I'd never felt it so profoundly before—and I had been fucked over a great deal in my lifetime.

"Goodbye, old friend," I said hoarsely, struggling through every word. "You'll regret this as soon as we leave."

I knew that for certain.

"No, Gunnar," Knox rumbled as I grabbed hold of Richard. My alpha offered a slight shake of his head, then a weak and resigned smile. "Not this time."

My nails gritted into the warlock's sleeve, and Declan grabbed hold of my free wrist so that we wouldn't lose each other in transport. Just the two of us now.

Hot tears streaked down my cheeks, but when I cast Knox one final look, he had already turned away, his back to me as he padded down the stairs. The food court blurred around us, and I jabbed the tip of the warlock's dagger into the nape of his neck.

"Take us to her," I demanded. *"Now."*

32

HAZEL

I had traded the chair for a cage.

Knees hugged to my chest, butt numb from sitting on stone for hours on end, I stared at the angry orange shimmer of my cell, the bars staticky and sizzling. As soon as Richard had left, Charon dropped the dramatics—like he missed having an audience. With a wave of his bony hand, he reconstructed the cage I'd arrived in, then dragged me inside by the back of my chair. Once all the orange bars slanted into place, effectively trapping me, muffling my magic more than it already was, my bindings had disappeared. As had the chair. As had Charon.

And soon enough, it was just me in this awful cavernous pit. Charon's threats had hit home, and the wait to see if Richard found my boys was *agony*. There was nothing else to do but worry—sit there and ruminate in silence. Sure, I'd attempted to teleport, to attack the bars with whatever magic I had inside this reaper body. Nothing. The plethora of runes, the fierce sting of the magical enclosure, was enough to beat me.

It would be enough to beat *them* too.

A part of me wished the pack had run off as soon as I was taken. Maybe if this had happened a few weeks ago, they could have saved themselves. But I knew without question that the three hellhounds I'd fallen for were still in Lunadell, looking for me, searching frantically. Every so often, I felt—something. A shiver of panic skittering down my spine, a whisper of fear on the back of my neck. Before they had left their marks on my skin, I could have chalked it up to my own panic, my own fear.

But mine roiled in my gut. The feelings that danced down my spine, tingled on the back of my neck... I was starting to suspect they belonged to *them*. By shifter lore, we were bonded.

So, maybe, just maybe, I could feel them in a way I couldn't before.

Maybe inch by inch, I was being let into the pack bond they all shared.

What a time for it to happen—when I wished they were far away from this nightmare.

Somewhere in this godforsaken cave, water dripped, dripped, dripped. A kind of consistent, delicate torture that would drive me mad one day. For now, it reminded me that there was a world out there, that it went on without me... and that my boys could too.

Unlikely, but—

A brilliant blast of light flashed down one of the nearby corridors, its rounded mouth briefly illuminated bright white. Magic hummed through the air, thickening it, and I shot to my feet when a pained yowl reverberated against the stone. I knew that cry, that deep, angry, pained cry.

My heart sank.

My boys had come for me.

And they'd tasted Richard's magic.

I rushed toward the bars on the left of my cage, hissing and whimpering when I accidently brushed one, the burn as intense as ever. Footsteps thundered down the narrow offshoot from this great room, followed by the sound of claws on stone, barks and snarls that were so obviously Declan—

A violent snap of metal.

A high-pitched yelp that cut straight to my marrow.

"No!" I cried, burning my hands again as I tried to get closer, to *see* what that bastard was doing to them. Not that I wanted to see—but I *had* to. I had to know. They were here because of me, and whatever happened to them deserved to haunt me for the rest of my miserable days.

Silence blanketed the cave for one, two, three painfully long beats—and then the most agonizing wails I'd ever heard shattered the quiet. *Declan.* I knew the sounds they all made, could detect the minute subtleties between each bark and howl. And that was *my* Declan.

A figure appeared in the corridor's opening, moving along haltingly, his back to me.

Richard.

I'd thought him a victim of Charon, same as me, until I realized he was hauling something by a chain into this main cave.

At the end of which—Declan.

A shrill, shrieking Declan in his hound form, being yanked along by his back leg, around which was an enormous bear trap. The teeth ripped into his flesh and stained his shaggy fur red, leaving a trail of it in his wake. He struggled hard against the restraint, twisting and clawing at the ground, trying desperately to stand and toppling back down with every hard jerk of the chain attached to the trap.

"Declan!"

Charon had lit dozens of candles when I last saw him, a crowd of enormous white, flame-tipped columns littered around the cave—I now realized it was so I could witness every gruesome detail. The metal trap caught the light here and there, highlighting the runes carved into it, and I clapped a hand over my mouth to muffle my sob.

Those markings probably prevented Declan from shifting.

I'd heard of shifter traps before, inked in magical sigils to keep the captured in their animal forms. Maybe they were easier to control when they couldn't access opposable thumbs.

"You bastard!" I screeched, wishing I could slam my hands against the bars of my cage, make my fury known with more than just my voice. "Please, let him go! He doesn't deserve this—"

"Please, please," Richard parroted back to me, mocking me in a singsong tone. Fresh blood dribbled down his face, and not just from the sigils carved into it. My pack had roughed him up a bit. Good. From the horrible twist of his mouth, that cruel smile he wore as he yanked Declan into the cave, hopefully whatever they had done to him *hurt*.

Declan reared up suddenly, lunging for the warlock with a mouth of razor-sharp teeth that could strip flesh from bone, but Richard snapped the chain hard, wrenching Declan's wounded leg sharply to the right. He stumbled with a whine, more blood splattering the stone floor, filling the air with a metallic tang that I tasted with every breath. That bear trap had such vicious teeth, so sharp and jagged, intended to score into the bone.

I knew that feeling, knew precisely what Declan was going through, my wrists painted with dried gold blood, my previous wounds healing slowly and tenderly. Aching with every slight movement. Limiting me. Maybe even scarring me.

Panic made my throat tight. This time, when Declan lurched forward, Richard clocked him across the face with the bulky end of the chain, and I stifled another sob when my sweetest hellhound tumbled down and didn't get up.

"You don't have to hurt him—"

"No, he doesn't," an unwelcome voice crooned, slithering into the cave and up my spine. I whipped around and found Charon floating in from another dark tunnel, casual and cruel in the way he carried himself. The god drifted by my cage, barely shooting me a sidelong glance in passing. "But I'm afraid *you* made that choice for us, Hazel."

Before I hurled the curse seething at the tip of my tongue, Gunnar charged out of the corridor to my far left. Teeth bared, eyes blazing, he blitzed straight for Richard—but a lazy flick of Charon's hand threw him off course, sent him flying into the wall with a yelp. He hit hard, his back bowing backward to the curve of the rocks waiting there to catch him. I pressed a trembling hand to my mouth again as he crashed to the ground, whining, dazed.

It killed me to watch this, my heart broken, my mind frantic with so many scattered thoughts that it was impossible to think straight.

The one thing I could do from in here was look for Knox. My warrior in black. The unfaltering pillar of this pack. My eyes darted around the cave, jumping from dark opening to dark opening, searching for his familiar silhouette—either as a man or as a hound.

And I came up short.

Gunnar pushed shakily to his feet and sprinted for Richard, but a blinding bolt of staticky white light hurled him into the wall again, his back taking the brunt of it *again*. Hit it just right and his spine would snap—I was sure of it. Trembling, I searched for Knox a little longer.

But he wasn't here.

He... hadn't come.

I didn't have the energy to be furious with him too, but how could he let Declan and Gunnar go after me alone? We needed the strength of the whole pack to take down Richard and Charon, to combat their dark magic when I had my personal supply cut off.

And... What Knox and I had shared... what we had all experienced over the last week, I thought he...

Hovering at the leftmost corner of my orange cell, I shook my head. It didn't matter. He wasn't here, and that was that. *Stay present.*

"So, what do you have to say now?" Charon peered over his shoulder at me. "Will you reap?"

I bit the insides of my cheeks, relishing the way the pain centered me, then forced myself to match his smile. "*Fuck you, Charon.*"

With a gentle flourish of his hand, he created a long, thick black whip out of thin air. A sharp silver tip capped it off, and he yielded it with expert precision, cracking it at his side.

"Let's try this again, shall we?"

I screamed when he lashed out at Declan, striking him three horrible times across the back.

"Stop!" I sank to my knees, hands in my hair, powerless. Charon whipped Declan once more, eliciting a harrowing screech from the hellhound, blood spattering stone like some fucking abstract painting. "Stop! Please, don't hurt him!"

Gunnar shot up again with a snarl, and Richard hit him with another blast of magical electricity.

"I think it's your turn to beg for mercy, dog," the warlock sneered as Gunnar pushed onto his side, then snorted and blinked hard. His brilliant red eyes found me, piercing as ever, and he shook his head ever so slightly.

Don't give in.

I swore I heard him, clear as day, inside my head. Maybe I

was delusional at this point, but the strength in his gaze emboldened me, gave me courage.

For how much longer, I wasn't sure, not when I watched him get up only to be knocked back down—over and over and over again. Declan crawled around, dragging that awful chain behind him, screeching when the whip made contact, the lashes ripping his skin. Their intensity seemed to sharpen, hitting harder with every strike, and I tried so damn hard to be strong.

But I couldn't endure this.

Couldn't let the hellhounds I loved suffer for my stubbornness.

And yet I couldn't condemn innocent souls to *him*, to be torn apart and eaten by a sick god while his disgusting little sidekick watched.

Dragging in a ragged breath, I turned away from the violence, frantically searching once more for something I could use to help—maybe even to harm. A rock. A fallen candle or its silver stand. *Anything.*

My knees gave out when I realized there was nothing. Nothing I could reach. Nothing I could summon. I crawled to the far right of my cage, hands scrambling over the ground, desperate for the smallest token—

Two orbs glittered in the darkness dead ahead of me. I stilled, Declan's shrill cries louder than ever, the singe of Gunnar's fur making me gag. Leaning to the left, then right, then back again, I stared hard at the dark mouth of a rocky opening that would have only been waist-high on me, narrow and unassuming, sequestered off to the side. Ignored, most likely, by a certain god and warlock.

Something caught the light depending on how I leaned, reflected it back at me.

I had seen that reflection before: Knox sitting in the

corner of his room, next to his hearth, keeping watch while his pack slept in his bed that first night.

My heart soared, and I pressed up as close as I dared to the shimmering orange bars, squinting as a massive humanoid shape came into focus, filled the entire opening, black mane and all.

"Knox?"

33

KNOX

This pain was going to kill me.

Stop my heart—*bam*.

But not until I let it. Not until I had done what I came here to do.

"Knox?" Hazel's choked whisper grated my frayed nerves. I hated to even guess what she'd thought of my absence—where her mind had gone, thinking I had abandoned her, the pack, everything. The look in Gunnar's eyes had been torturous enough, but the thought of my mate's heart breaking because I wasn't there…

That was the pain that would finish me off, not her scythe chipping away at my flesh.

Over the course of the day, I'd had a theory. A theory that could have either panned out or wound up a miserable failure. No matter the cost, I'd needed to try. Needed to throw that damn warlock off the scent. Needed Declan to play along, to make my beta, my second-in-command, a piece of me, believe I had betrayed everything we now cherished.

As it stood, the theory had worked.

To a degree.

Hot blood coursed down my arms in rivers. Dripped on the floor. If that fucking god wasn't so busy getting his rocks off with the whip, he would have smelled me. Rage rooted me in place; Declan's cries were so familiar, and for once I couldn't rush to his side and bully back his abusers. He had to take it, and so did I.

I readjusted my grip, the slightest movement wrenching further agony from *everywhere*. My flesh—on fire. My heart— clamped and choked and twisted. The pain was in my bones, my teeth, driving into my skull with a ferocity I had never experienced. It *would* kill me; that much I knew.

A scythe imprinted on its reaper.

With such power, it could never fall into the hands of a stranger.

It fought back. Scorched flesh. Turned bones to dust.

So too would be my fate. But not yet.

Hazel was my mate. We were one, two sides of the same coin. My alpha bloodline gave me strength unparalleled by other hellhounds. I could endure. The scythe knew me the moment I clamped my hands around it. It *knew* me—but still it resisted.

Yet it had the decency to bring me to her, to cut through wards like a hot knife through butter, and for that I would be grateful until my last breath.

Keeping to the shadows, I crawled out of the tunnel I'd followed for miles, deeper and deeper into the mountain range. Hazel's scent had guided me most of the way, but Gunnar's suffering and Declan's cries had hastened me along even when I could barely move myself.

The god was laughing now, no longer baiting Hazel with her pack's misery. Declan's back had been shredded to ribbons, and Gunnar took far longer to rise after each burst of the warlock's magic. And my reaper watched me, still as stone, crouched at the base of those angry orange bars —waiting.

The edges of my vision blackened. Charred flesh hung off my fingers, whittled down to bone. Blood splattered the floor, leaving me light-headed but determined. I used the ridges of the stony wall for guidance, leaning against them as I shuffled along, inch by inch to my final destination.

Up close, the magical cage burned my eyes, too bright, too violent in the way its magic sizzled. But I held firm, steadfast, until the pain won out and I collapsed a few feet away. Hazel slipped a delicate arm through the bars, her pain reverberating through me when the orange wisps snapped at her skin.

Her wrist...

Covered in gold.

Metallic and salty—reaper's blood.

A snarl lifted my lip, baring a pathetic flash of teeth, and I roused whatever remaining strength I had to pass the scythe to her outstretched hand.

"Hold on, Knox," Hazel murmured as she wrapped her fingers around the staff—relieved me of my last burden. "Hold on..."

As soon as the scythe left my possession, my body gave out. My head cracked hard on the ground when I slumped, arms outstretched before me, the full damage on display. Both hands were but tattered flesh that hung like strips of charred fabric off too-white bones. Blood pooled in front of me, all around me. I blinked slowly, breathed slowly, the darkness around my vision sharpening and taking root. Here to stay, the shadows.

Difficult as it was, I forced my gaze up so that I could watch her in action. She looked complete with her scythe, and she got to work without a backward glance at our enemies. Mouth set in a determined line, Hazel cut herself free from her cell, slicing through the jittery orange bars, carving a door where there was none. No flash. No dramatics. She did precisely what she needed to slip out without causing a commotion, and once she did, she dropped to her knees beside me, my blood seeping into her reaper's garb.

Scythe forgotten at her side, Hazel cupped my face with both hands, just holding me. Time slowed around us. Her eyes shimmered with tears, and for the first time all day, her relief throbbed through me instead of her pain. Gently stroking my coarse scruff with her thumbs, she lingered, her outline getting fuzzier.

"Don't let go," she whispered. "Stay with me, Knox. Stay with *us.*"

I swallowed hard, my eyes blinking in uneven beats, and watched her snatch up her scythe. She rose elegantly, practically gliding with every step, and wielded her weapon like an expert assassin, like she had been raised with a broadsword in her hand.

The cave fell silent. The god's laughter died.

Difficult as it was, I needed to see—needed my last living memory to be of *her*. Pain lanced through me as I dragged my useless body along what was left of her cell, hauling myself around so I could witness a reaper's justice.

Gunnar lay on his side, panting hard. His red gaze slid from her to me, and desperation vibrated through our bond. I did my best to nod, to let him know I felt it—that I understood. He had chosen her in the end, but it had killed him.

It killed me too.

Chest rising and falling slowly, Declan had stopped squealing, left in a heap of blood and fur behind the towering god, this creature of stretched flesh and gaunt cheeks and bony hands. His black robes mirrored Hazel's, only he wore them like fraud.

Neither said a word as they faced off, but that blasphemous yellow gaze acknowledged her scythe with a slight widening. Hazel rolled her shoulders back, and one step forward forced the god into action. His hand shot up—but so did hers. The air sharpened, hummed with magic, invisible to all but its users. Hazel's crashed with his, both their arms jerking at the collision.

Yet she was the one to advance. The reaper closed in on the god with slow, precise steps. Footfalls echoed suddenly; *Richard* had taken it upon himself to engage in the battle, to uneven the odds.

Gunnar caught him by the heel, clamping down viciously and rolling the fucker off his feet.

Silent, a predator in her own right, Hazel stopped within an arm's length of the god. All the ancient runes on the ceiling, the sigils carved into stones throughout the mountain—no match for that scythe.

It ended in an instant.

Hazel threw her hand to the left, the thrust of tangled magic forcing her opponent to veer left as well. The god stumbled, his eyes rounded, nostrils flared.

In that split second of imbalance, she struck, swift as a viper. Hazel slashed her scythe up and diagonal, cutting clean through him from his hip to his shoulder, then across that narrow neck to rid him of his head. Three pieces of an old god tumbled to the ground, falling like thunder, his golden blood sprinkling like rain.

Face ashen, Richard booted Gunnar in the head, then took off running. Hazel gave him a five second head start, then flung her scythe. The blade whirled, round and round, slicing through the air—and decapitated our final foe before he escaped into the tunnels.

I slumped onto my side, a soft smile teasing my lips.

My warrior goddess.

She would protect them when I was gone.

She would protect *herself*.

And that brought me peace.

Hand up, Hazel summoned her scythe back to her, then saw to the metal mouth snapped around Declan's leg. With a single swift strike, she shattered it. Gunnar stumbled to her side in his human form, blood leaking from his nostrils, hair askew, eyes bloodshot, and helped free his packmate of the last chains Declan would ever wear.

Good. That brought me peace too.

My eyes closed slowly, and when a whoosh of air rushed over me, it took everything I had left to open them again. Darkness crowded in from all sides, but I could still make out her beauty. Frantically, Hazel checked me over, stopping at my hands with a sob.

I smiled weakly, touching a bony finger to the center of her chest.

"I have never loved you more, reaper, than this very moment," I rasped. Tears cut down her cheeks, and she shook her head fiercely.

"No, Knox, don't go. I can't follow you if you—"

"Tell them..." My hand fell, but she caught it, bone and all. The creeping shadows narrowed my view to just her eyes, and I wouldn't have it any other way. "Tell them..."

That I loved them too.

That I could die in peace knowing my family was safe.

Tell them.

And finally, it all went black.

34

HAZEL

Lightning cut across a foreboding sky.

Thunder cracked, rattling down to the deepest roots of the oldest cedar.

Rain pummeled Lunadell, threatening a flood of biblical proportions.

A frightful Halloween night: great for the ambiance, miserable for the little ghosties and ghoulies trudging door to door with pillowcases in hand. In years gone by, I had watched them, chosen the best and busiest suburb in whatever city I found myself in so that I could stand amongst all the children on one of their favorite nights of the year—a night where strangers were *obligated* to give them candy. I could hardly fathom such a thing. If we had shown up on our neighbor's doorstep in masks when *I* was a child, someone would have pelted us with an apple or a potato, maybe even shooed us off with a broom to the side of the head.

No. The years had become kinder for children. I so loved to be among them, even if it made me weep. But tonight, there was no place I would have rather been than right here.

Well, perhaps not *right* here. Standing beneath the boughs

of a few cedars clustered together at the tree line, I squinted against the rain. It hadn't been pouring when I'd left Alexander's estate, yet now, a maelstrom, seemingly out of nowhere. His pack had moved into the main house in his absence, so at least they had more protection than the ramshackle barracks situated at the cusp of his sprawling seaside property.

I had no idea where he went or what had become of him, but no one upstairs would even utter his name—always *that one*, they said in reference to him, rolling their eyes. In the few days since the business with Charon and Richard, the truth had come out, my story backed by the individual retellings of my pack.

Alexander had tried to take another reaper's scythe. Rather than help, he had indulged in a few of the deadly sins —and now he was gone. His pack had been temporarily transferred to me, and on Halloween, of all nights, I had gone to speak with them for the first time. Militant bunch, that lot. Focused. Highly trained. Obedient to their alpha. Nothing like my pack, except for the fact that they listened to me. As our higher-ups searched for Alexander's replacement, a suitable reaper to formally take over his hellhound pack, they were under my charge.

And from my succinct conversation with the alpha, for once as a man and not as a hound, that seemed to be a blessing in disguise.

Another streak of lightning skittered across its stormy backdrop, illuminating my house atop its slight hill. Thunder rumbled, unfurling over the landscape like waves crashing on the shore, and I stepped out of the forest, head down, scythe at my side, and made my way home. Mud squished underfoot, the air warm but cooling with every hour, threatening to turn the rain freezing. By morning, the first breath of November would leave the ground hard.

Smoke plumed out of our now working chimney. The patched roof would keep out the wet, the damp, the frost, and soft yellow flickered from the second-floor windows in the pack's wing. Despite the rain seeping into my bones, I hurried along with a soft smile, up the steps, and through the front doors.

A puddle gathered instantly at my feet, lightning illuminating the foyer before I had even closed the doors behind me. Thunder vibrated in the wood as I bolted the entryway, locking us all in for the night. It had been three *long* days since Charon—since Knox had picked up this very scythe and put his life at risk for all of us.

We should have been preparing for the trials tomorrow morning; instead, we had another week to recover.

Squeezing the rainwater from my hair, I planted my scythe at the front door and peeled off my drenched black robes. My muddy flats came next, every article of clothing shed by the time I reached the landing between the twin staircases. My wing to the right, the pack's to the left.

I went left; I would never go right again, not as I once had.

The lamp on Declan's bedside table was on, but his bed sat empty.

As did Gunnar's. I frowned in the doorway—until a wiry, luxurious shadow sidled into the corner of my eye. A glance down the hall had me grinning again: arms crossed, lips quirked, Gunnar leaned against the doorframe at Knox's bedroom.

My cheeks warmed under that unfamiliar gaze. Everything else about him was the same: a statuesque figure corded with subtle strength, his skin pale, his lips thin and passionate, his limbs long. He stood before me in a slouchy pair of grey sweatpants, his chest bare and toned. But those *eyes*. Once a dark, lush blue, they had lost their sheen during Richard's attack, and now, as if they had absorbed some of his magic, sparked with a startling bright blue, forever humming with electricity. In a way, they suited Gunnar better, but it would still take some adjusting to on my part.

"You're all wet, reaper," he mused as I padded over to him. His crossed arms loosened, and I rose up on the tips of my toes for a teasing little kiss. Our mouths lingered a breath apart, and his pursued mine when I eventually dropped back down, his chuckle tickling between my thighs. A firm hand cupped my chin, holding me close, and Gunnar cocked his head to the side, a few chocolate-brown curls falling over his new eyes. "I suspect this won't be the last time I tell you that tonight."

I arched an eyebrow. "Promises, promises…"

His touch was like fire, and I cuddled into his chest, my lower lip caught between my teeth, and basked unabashedly in the heat.

"Did all go well with Alexander's pack?"

I nodded, trailing my fingers over the muscular curves of his arm. "My pack now—until they find a suitable replacement."

"You should be the only reaper in Lunadell," he murmured into the top of my head, his hands locked behind my back. "You can handle it."

"No, I can't." Pushing up onto my toes again, I stole a quick peck, then danced out of reach when the hellhound snapped at my lips. The solid *clack* of his teeth colliding sent a shiver down my spine, a promise for what was to come glittering in his eyes. He had said it more than once in the last few days that I ought to be the only reaper—that I should just take Alexander's pack and reap Lunadell on my own. But then I would never see my boys, forever jumping between Earth and Purgatory to escort souls—not for me. I was happy to share the burden. "But thanks for your vote of confidence."

His arms tightened around me when I tried to squirm free, so I ducked under them rather than struggle to break through them, slipping around his narrow hips and skirting into the bedroom behind his back.

The sight always took my breath away: Knox actually *sleeping* in his bed, not just standing guard next to the hearth. In fact, until recently I hadn't ever seen Knox sleep, but his body needed it to heal from the monumental trauma of that night. Shirtless, the alpha reclined into a mountain of pillows, half sitting up, like he had fought to stay conscious until he just *couldn't* a second longer. His head lolled onto his shoulder, the stubborn creature, all those pillows Gunnar and I had fluffed for him totally wasted. Still, he looked peaceful enough, his eyelids smooth, his handsome scarred features relaxed.

Might wake up to a kink in his neck, but that was a small price to pay for recovery, surely.

At the end of the bed, Declan occupied his usual place, stretched lengthwise, snoring softly on top of the covers with an arm crooked under his head, his back to me. Long red stripes replaced what had once been shredded flesh; I still wasn't used to that either. Charon's brutal whip had left eight neat slices down Declan's back, and while they had been the easiest to heal on the day, my magic and his natural healing ability working together to close his gaping wounds, there was still the risk that they would eventually just scar over.

Leave him branded.

It didn't sit well with me.

But he was alive, same as Knox, and at the end of the day, that was all that mattered.

Moving quietly, mindful of the few floorboards that were

extra creaky, I crept deeper into the room and climbed onto the enormous king-sized bed. It dipped beneath me, the blankets slightly askew under my knees. He looked so peaceful, my noble alpha—the hellhound who had been willing to die for *all* of us.

On that awful day, once we had stabilized Declan, Gunnar and I whisked them both back to the house. Knox's wounds would have been fatal had the angel I'd summoned from the reaping department not arrived in time. At first, Angelus—do *not* get me started on the name—had refused to treat my dying alpha. After all, he had touched a reaper's scythe: he *should* die, or at the very least lose his hands. But then he saw the marks on my neck, my shoulder, my wrist. And then, patiently, he had listened to my story, really absorbed every detail. Knox and I were fated mates, same as Declan and Gunnar and me, and with his alpha blood, Knox had been permitted to return my scythe to its rightful place—though not without cost.

Slowly, the angel and I had fixed him up, me sealing bone and sinew, Angelus growing flesh from nothing. From there, he had returned to the Silver City and summoned a tribunal council to assess the incident. We had been called to testify— Knox gave his deposition from this very bed—and Alexander had disappeared. The trials were then postponed. No penalty had been placed on my beloved hellhound for taking my scythe into his own hands, but he was cautioned from doing it again.

"If I have to choose between my hands and her life, I'll do it again in a *second*," Knox had snarled from beneath his blankets, all those pillows stacked high around him, his hands red and sore and healing.

Today the flesh was pink and soft, like stretching out his fingers risked tearing it along the faded lifelines on his palm. Gently, silently, I lifted Knox's huge hand to examine the new skin, pleased with its progress. Angelus had estimated he would need another week before his full strength returned and suggested Knox not shift in the meantime. My poor alpha had been miserable sitting around in bed these last few days, even with the TV we had set up for him, all the books, the steady onslaught of healthy meals I made him eat, but the only real thing that seemed to make him happy was our company.

I was just about through examining his other hand when Knox exhaled curtly and nudged me away.

"Stop fussing, woman," he muttered, voice rough with sleep, eyes still shut. At the end of the bed, Declan roused with a deep breath of his own, and I shook my head, grinning.

"Hush and let me fuss."

I snatched up his hand and gave the fingertips a hard look; they had been a little too pale that first day, leaving Gunnar and me fretting about circulation through his new skin. Knox shuffled about beneath the covers, then snapped his hand around mine and shot up with more vigor than I'd seen in days, tackling and pinning me to my back with a growl. Months ago, that sound would have terrified me. Tonight, I went down in a fit of squealy giggles, curtained by his black mane, tickled by the ends of his beard.

"Knox, stop," I ordered halfheartedly, squirming when he secured my wrists on either side of my head. "Your hands—"

"They're fine, *mate*." His mouth seized mine midprotest, swallowing my indignant noises with a kiss that made my toes curl. Not only did it thrill me to see his energy up, his movements less stilted, but I'd really missed his rough caress in the short time he had been bedridden. I wriggled beneath him, my effort to escape more for show than anything, my heels digging at the bed, my hips writhing, my back arching. The dip in the mattress told me Declan was up, and the faint tread of bare feet across the hardwood confirmed that the little display had caught Gunnar's eye too.

I sucked in a gasp when Knox dragged an openmouthed kiss along my jaw, my lashes fluttering in the dim lamplight. Outside, another crash of thunder announced that the storm wasn't dying down anytime soon.

"Did you all miss me today?" I asked—moaned, more like, the sound bound to entice the hellhounds closing in on every side. Reaper business had occupied me since this morning, which had left the pack to fend for themselves in my absence. They were good at it now, taking care of each other, fixing meals that didn't just consist of raw meat, but after the Charon debacle, the four of us all preferred to be within an arm's reach.

Because frankly, the memories of that day cut deeper, scarred harder, than any physical injury.

Declan's ragged screams, his back split beneath Charon's whip.

Gunnar's body jittering and contorting, his spine nearly breaking, the awful dance accompanied by that warlock's cruel laughter.

Knox's hands, bony and bloody, the resolve in his eyes as he croaked what *he* thought—what I feared—were his final words.

If I had it my way, I would never be apart from these three hellhounds again. *Never*. But the world we found ourselves in didn't work that way, and for now I'd suffer the nightmares of those images on my own, just as I savored whatever time we had together with a smile on my lips and in my heart.

Really though. *Nightmares*. For the first time in my afterlife, I was afraid to fall asleep—terrified of memories so vivid that it was like we were all back there reliving it.

They would pass in time, as all things did; I kept them to myself, preferring to live in a bubble of sex and love and relief that we were all together again. Each one of us a little broken, sure, but together, we were whole.

A second pair of lips found my skin, and where Knox had been all teeth and force, Declan was subtle and soft, confident in the lazy way his mouth dragged along my flesh, tickled my sides, nibbled at my belly.

"Always and forever, sweet," he murmured against my thighs. Knox leaned back on his elbows, watching the scene unfold before him like a king on his throne, his eyes a brilliant obsidian that I locked onto, even as I threaded my hand into Declan's hair. The hellhound at my thighs flicked his tongue over my clit, the caress featherlight, a sinful tease, and I looked down at him with a hapless moan. He grinned up at me, slowly parting my legs and settling between them, one over each of his shoulders. "For as long as we love you, Hazel, we'll always miss you."

The notion brought tears to my eyes, just as it had the first time we whispered sweet nothings to one another in the aftermath. As soon as Knox and Declan regained consciousness, I'd told them—fervently—that I loved them with every fiber of my being. Gunnar's had been a quiet declaration, the two of us entangled on Knox's armchair after Angelus left, watching our pack sleep away the trauma. He had whispered it against my neck; I had murmured it against his lips.

Declan's tongue swept the full length of my sex, delving between my slick folds, not stopping at the first swirl around my clit. Pleasure bloomed behind my eyelids, and I arched up with a moan, my hand twisting in his hair. Just one touch and he could melt me.

"O-oh," I stammered, undulating against his mouth, my thighs trembling over his shoulders. "My loves—"

Gunnar's snort cut me off. "So sappy, all of you."

A sharp slap had me giggling, though I wasn't sure who

had swatted at who, but when I stole a peek, I found Gunnar shedding his sweatpants. His cock jutted out at a perfect right angle, eager for some attention.

"Even if we *didn't* miss you, per se," Gunnar carried on as he climbed onto the bed, crawling past Declan and up my body. His strong hand cupped my breast, plucking at my nipple even with our gazes locked. "How else are we supposed to act when you strut in here stark naked?"

"How do you think *I* feel all the time? You lot are always naked," I snapped, trailing off with a sharp breath that Gunnar muffled the moment he slammed his mouth to mine. When Declan eased a finger into me and stroked my inner walls, a delicious shiver sleuthed down my spine, languid as the lightest rain droplet parachuting down the windowpane.

You'd think I would be accustomed to the touch of multiple lovers, but the thrill hadn't dimmed even a little. Declan lapping expertly at my sex, his fingertips bruising my hips; Gunnar kissing me like he wanted to consume me, his hand tangled in my hair; Knox watching it all unfold with such keen interest, waiting patiently, biding his time until he could really *take* me...

It would never get old, never lose its thrill. How could it when my body responded like it was *made* for the passions of more than one?

I came apart at the seams under their undivided attention, and Declan kissed me just as deeply as Gunnar when I reached my breaking point, fucking me with his tongue. He groaned, gripping my hips hard, thrusting as deep as he could while pleasure erupted from my core and radiated out like a nuclear shock wave. I cried out into Gunnar's mouth, one hand clutching at his wiry bicep, the other fisted into Declan's hair. Their movements quickened, mouths working me from both ends, threatening to swallow me whole as I writhed through my first climax of the night.

But not the last. Experience had taught me that. Was it fate that made them capable of playing my body like a finely tuned instrument? Because they were just so fucking *good* at it, their fingers, tongues, cocks skilled to a fault.

Stars still danced across my eyes when Declan withdrew, a rush of cool air brushing over my wetness, arousal smeared over my thighs, across his mouth. Without speaking, the pair of hellhounds found a rhythm in their manipulation of my body, Declan rolling me onto my belly and lifting me onto my knees just as Gunnar settled in front of me, the head of his cock teasing my lips. Flushed from head to toe, I found my steps in this complex little dance, arching my hips and my back for Declan, offering myself freely, and sweeping my tongue across my lower lip with a coquettish flutter of my eyelashes for Gunnar.

The hellhound before me swallowed hard, the bulge in his throat bobbing. He was always so talkative, but I was learning how to silence him with subtle movements, with the promise of my surrender.

It was electrifying to somehow be submissive to three ravenous hellhounds, but also completely in control, one word from me capable of bringing this all to a crashing halt—or taking us to spectacular heights.

I'd only just gripped the base of Gunnar's shaft when Declan plunged into me from behind, filling me with a single powerful stroke. Moaning, I fumbled forward, burying my face in the blankets for a moment as I adjusted to the sizeable intrusion. Only I wasn't allowed a moment to myself: Declan's hand wove into my hair, and without any real force, he guided me back up and positioned me over Gunnar's cock. There was beauty in softness, and Declan was a master at it.

An incoherent flood of nonsense spilled from Gunnar's mouth as soon as I wrapped my lips around his silky tip, sucking it with enough force to make his hips buck. My grin had the hellhound at my mercy scowling—had Knox chuckling—and at a pace that was perhaps painfully slow for him, I took him inch by inch into my mouth. Declan, meanwhile, ground against my backside, one hand at the nape of my neck, the other at my hip.

They were good at sharing, Gunnar and Declan. In fact, they almost *always* shared me, taking turns to occupy whatever part of me called to them in the heat of the moment. Knox, meanwhile, usually seemed content to watch, to sit back and allow his pack to ravish me before his eyes, his cock straining when the others finally handed me over.

I flicked my eyes in his direction; a voyeur, my alpha love. Had he always been keen to watch before, or was it a pleasure reserved just for me, for *us*?

We three found our rhythm in time: Gunnar sprawled back on his elbows, his cheeks hollow like he was biting down on them as I pumped half his length with my fist and teased the other half with my tongue. The up-and-down motion of my head set the pace for Declan, thrusting in and out of me at the same pace, his breath strained—like it killed him to go so slow and steady.

That thrilled me too.

As did the knowledge that they could all only hold back for so long. Eventually, the chord would stretch too taut—and snap.

The breakdown of their carefully orchestrated control was a guilty pleasure of mine. As soon as Gunnar started bucking his hips, driving himself into my mouth, Declan faltered too, his thrusts harder, faster, more poignant in the delicious little spots he hit. His hand around the back of my neck tightened, gripping for balance as he pounded into me. We devolved into chaos, into frenzied rutting, both hellhounds setting their own pace, seeking out pleasure that dragged mine right alongside it. Every muscle stiffened inside me, pleasure burning in my core, my eyes watering as Gunnar fucked my face and Declan ravaged my sex.

We came undone together, a symphony of ragged cries filling the room. Gunnar spilled himself down my throat just as Declan stuttered to a halt, buried deep inside me, his hips jerking through a climax that made him hiss my name. I was helpless, trapped between them, forced to ride out the pleasure in whatever position they had me in.

With anyone else, this would have been the end of it.

But as Declan eased out of me and collapsed on the bed, I looked to Knox. Wiping my lips, I left a weak-kneed Gunnar behind to crawl up his alpha's legs. Knox helped a little, yanking the blankets aside to reveal tree trunk thighs and a rigid cock. We needed no foreplay, no tentative touches, no kisses to reacquaint ourselves. I scaled him greedily, licking his cock along the way, flicking my tongue over the tip, wiggling my hips and ass for the others.

Before I could grind down onto him, bury his huge length inside me, Knox snatched my hips and lifted me. Turned me around with his damaged hands so that my back collided roughly with his chest. I let out a shocked breath, legs spread, and my head tilted back onto his shoulder with a drawn-out moan as he steered himself inside me.

Unlike Declan, Knox took his time—a tease, just like I had been with Gunnar, burying his cock into me an inch at a time. Torturous, his pace. I tried to just slam my hips down, but he held firm, setting the tempo for us.

Reminding me who was alpha here.

And I let him.

God, how I let him.

I threaded one hand up and into his hair, using it as an anchor more than anything, my heart skipping a beat at the thought of Knox's usual rough thrusts. Fire raged inside me, a great inferno that required more than the average woman to extinguish. More lovers. More soul mates. More cocks and hands and tongues—*more*. Was I insatiable, or was this just my path?

Perhaps I'd never know, and when Knox's thumb flicked over my swollen clit, I certainly didn't *care*. From this position, I could watch Gunnar and Declan watching me, hunger in their eyes and ecstasy in their smiles. Knox shuffled about for a better angle, something that allowed him to thrust up at his leisure, to take me however he saw fit. Once again, there was nothing I could do but hold on for the ride.

And kiss him. I flicked my tongue at his cheek when he started to rock, then dragged my parted lips over his scruff, the coarse black and newly grey-tinted scuff along his jaw. I arched back to nibble at his ear, but as his pace quickened, I just gave in to the unfolding bliss—to his fingers expertly playing my clit, his curt breaths against my temple, his arm locked around my waist.

My third climax came quickly this time, long before him, the pleasure hot and luxe, like liquid gold seeping through my veins. Knox showed no sign of stopping anytime soon, not even when I mewled at the overstimulation, my sounds stirring the others. Gunnar and Declan crept closer, Gunnar toying with my nipples and Declan taking over for Knox at the crest of my sex. Together, the trio milked—maybe even forced—another orgasm out of me before the alpha splintered, before he too snapped and lost himself inside of me.

One thing I had learned over the last week and a half was that group sex was *messy*. Normally I wasn't one to skimp on a gratuitously steamy shower in the aftermath, maybe even a bath in the huge soaker tub attached to my private lavatory, but tonight, I didn't want to get out of bed—didn't want to leave this hellhound heap unless absolutely necessary. So, with a snap of my fingers, any evidence of our lovemaking vanished.

"Handy little spell, that one," Gunnar muttered, stretching his long body out vertically, feet at the pillows, head at the end of the bed.

"It kind of takes the fun out of it," I said as I climbed off Knox and snuggled into his chest. He pressed a soft kiss to my forehead, stroking my hair, his eyes heavy and his heart pounding beneath my palm. Declan's head quickly settled in the dip of my waist, his arms circling my legs, my butt to his chest.

"Well, I don't want to leave this bed until morning," he insisted softly, his preferences echoing my own.

"Maybe for a midnight snack," Knox rumbled, to which Gunnar chuckled, reaching across his alpha to walk his fingers up my calf.

"I already know what I want."

"A healthy slice of reaper?" Declan said, his voice tinged with exhaustion again. "Make mine a double."

"Shut up and go to sleep," I ordered, eyes closed, lips quirked. "You all need it."

Sex took a lot out of anyone, supernatural or otherwise, but Knox and Declan were low on energy already—and any extra cardiovascular activities risked putting a strain on their healing injuries.

Not that either of them seemed to mind.

Still, they were out in a matter of minutes, dead to the world, both of them snoring softly. My eyes flickered open to find Gunnar watching all of us from the end of the bed, his head pillowed on his folded arms. When our gazes met, we exchanged little smiles, just for the two of us, and he eventually closed his eyes first with a long, contented sigh.

Lightning streaked across the bay window, the flash

illuminating the steady stream of rain. Thunder answered its mate with a roaring *crack-boom*, the storm ongoing, stamping this Halloween night in misery.

Unless you were inside, surrounded by the hellhounds you loved, no longer alone, never to be alone again, listening to raindrops hammer the windows. Then...

Then, tonight was absolute perfection.

October crashed into November in a flurry of wild storms and sleet, but when it finally settled, the second last month of the year turned mild—as if to apologize for drowning the West Coast in misery for days on end.

Today, sunrise was a beautiful affair, the sky dotted with light grey stretches of overcast. As the sun crept over the horizon, rosy hues tinted the underbelly of the clouds. A gorgeous landscape painting, possibility and promise warming all around me—and Lunadell's tallest skyscraper beneath me. I stood with my toes kissing the sharp corner building, the stonework cool to the touch. My black robes billowed in the gentle morning winds, my hair wild and free, my scythe's blade catching the first sunbeams spilling over the city.

My city.

In the week of biting storms, every day grey and miserable, my pack had passed the trials. Through the foulest weather, they had tracked their souls, rounded them up, found my scythe in a city of snaking roads, in a test laden with angel trickery. Knox had been able to shift and lead. Declan's back bore the scars of Charon's cruelty, but faintly now, allowing him full mobility. And Gunnar—Gunnar did as he was told, unflinchingly, obedient and anticipatory of my slightest command.

My pack had impressed the angel responsible for administering their trials, but their story had made the rounds upstairs already: the hellhound pack willing to sacrifice themselves for their reaper.

And then, of course, *I* was the reaper who had killed Charon—but that was neither here nor there. The god's death had been a necessity; I had just been carrying out my duty to protect the souls of this realm and nothing more.

Never mind that it brought me *immense* joy to cleave that fucker in half, to slice his awful head clean off his shoulders—

No matter. Enemy vanquished, trials conquered, my boys and I could finally move forward.

Now the real work began.

Death had started whispering in my ear last night, his sweet voice relaying the names of impending deaths, souls for me to reap. Ages. Occupations. Addresses and locations. Crimes. Punishment. Illnesses and family sorrows. It was ongoing and ever-present, relentless—and would stay that way until a suitable second reaper was located to take on Alexander's former pack and reap Lunadell alongside me. Until then, it was all mine, from the downtown core shaking off the night at my feet to the sleepy suburbs on the perimeter, right on out to the scattered farmsteads to the east. Mine.

Alexander's former pack—

No.

Julian's pack. That was the alpha's name—Julian. He and his had been reaping with stand-in reapers until last night, one day after my pack's success was formalized, when all the substitutes went back to their posts and I returned, officially, to my sacred duty. The seven hounds had worked flawlessly with me through the night, following orders, corralling souls. None were as sweet as Declan, nor as swift as Gunnar, and I preferred Knox's quiet confidence to Julian's barking. But they had done the job, and that was that. We had escorted twelve to purgatory during their shift, mostly from a cluster of retirement homes, and I'd ordered them to spend the day resting, dismissing them just before sunrise.

They would meet me back here at sunset, and it would start all over again.

Hidden along the celestial plane, I closed my eyes and listened, Death's seductive song tickling my ear. More to reap today, more tomorrow, more forever.

The whisper faded into the depths at the sound of claws on stone. I glanced over my shoulder—and there were my hellhounds, my boys, my pack. Red-eyed and focused, shifted and ready for work. Right on time. They strolled across the rooftop, enormous black hounds in all their glory. There were no more wards around our territory, no more talks of leaving this life; each one saw the merit in it, the responsibility and necessity of shepherding departed souls into the beyond. They were *ready*, at long last, to reap.

After three months away, I was out of shape, a full night of reaping weighing heavily on me—until now. The sight of my pack refueled me, rejuvenated me, breathed life back into me. I stood a little taller as they approached, smiled wider, loved harder.

"Only nine souls today," I said, ruffling Declan's ears when he hopped up on the skyscraper's ledge alongside me. "An easy start."

Knox nosed at my hand, my leg, as he fell in line to my right, Gunnar next to him. Facing the city once more, I squinted against the sunrise, then bit back a knowing smile when I caught three black noses wriggling. They smelled the promise of orchids in the air, the scent of souls. Knox lifted his head, ears stiff, eyes scanning the cityscape, while Gunnar's lean figure trembled with energy. Declan,

435

meanwhile, peered up at me with his tongue lolling out of his mouth, his tail wagging.

I had missed this—the anticipation before a reap. Training the pack had been life-changing in so many ways, but I craved the work again. For ten long years, reaping had been my life, my obsession, my purpose. Today, I returned to it just as fervent, but it was no longer my obsession, my life, or my heart. These three hellhounds possessed both my life and my heart, but I loved that I could finally share my passion with my mates.

"Prepare yourselves... Ten seconds out, Dennis Roger Pinkerton, fifty-two, heart attack," I told them. "In the shower, the poor thing."

The pack stiffened, counting down the moments until release. We all looked north to the clustered upscale condos, an explosion of orchids in the air, the celestial plane humming with a new soul.

"Okay, boys..." I tapped my scythe on the rooftop, my heart full to bursting. "Let's get to work."

THE END

ACKNOWLEDGMENTS

Thank you to Amanda, my editorial QUEEN, who is always ready to read my latest concoction. You make my first draft worries go away, and that's a valuable skill. Shout out to Sandra, my phenomenal proofreader at One Love Editing. You may specialize in contemporary, but I'll bring you over to the dark side yet.

Thank you to all my many Liz Meldon readers who followed me on this reverse harem adventure. I'm so grateful for your continued support and excitement about all my new projects. You make this easy. You make this fun. Here's to many, many more books in the future.

Much love to my friends, my family, and my sun and stars for always supporting my author dream.

And finally, thank *you*, dear reader, for taking this journey with me. *Reaper's Pack* was an emotional book for me to write. Each of the main characters has facets of me in them, and I took a lot of the loneliness and isolation I've felt since becoming someone with chronic health issues and channeled it into Hazel and her harem. Writing their happy ending has been cathartic and uplifting, and I hope it felt that way for you, too.

Don't forget to leave a little review, either on Amazon, Goodreads, or your social media. As an indie author, I rely on reader squees to help spread the word about my work, and I appreciate every word you write!

See you in **September 2020** for my next reverse harem standalone novel, *Caged Kitten*, which is currently available for preorder on Amazon!!

xoxoxo
   Rhea

ABOUT THE AUTHOR

Rhea Watson is a Canadian reverse harem author who loves a good paranormal romance. She writes layered alpha heroes with rough exteriors who melt for their strong, independent soulmates.

In her spare time, Rhea babies her herb garden, bows to her cat's every whim, and flies through Netflix shows like it's her day job.

HANG OUT WITH RHEA IN HER FACEBOOK READERS GROUP!

Printed in Great Britain
by Amazon

26238592R00260